STAR WARS

LOST STARS

Original Story:
Claudia Gray

Art and Adaptation:
Yusaku Komiyama

3

CHARACTERS

STAR WARS: LOST STARS

On the day the Galactic Empire assumes control over the remote, rocky planet of Jelucan, where two distinct social classes (first-wavers and second-wavers) wage a fierce rivalry, second-waver Thane and first-waver Ciena have a fateful encounter that changes their lives forever. They dream of joining the Imperial Academy.

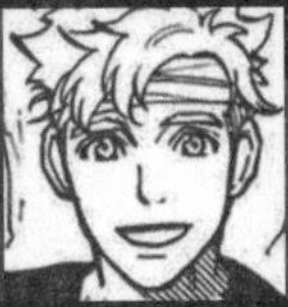

Thane Kyrell

Fled the Galactic Empire and joined the Rebel Alliance on Wedge's invitation. He tries to recruit Ciena to the cause, but she refuses.

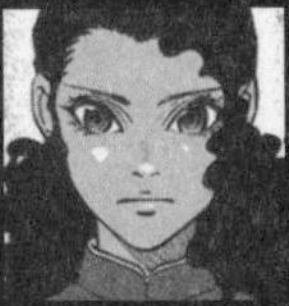

Ciena Ree

A lieutenant in the Imperial fleet. She rejects Thane's request and dedicates herself to the Empire to make up for Thane's crime of deserting the fleet.

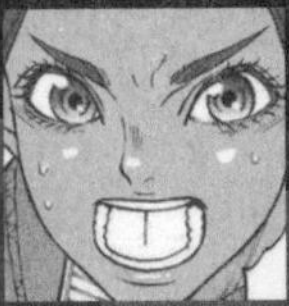

Kendy Idele

Ciena's former roommate. Joined the Rebel Alliance.

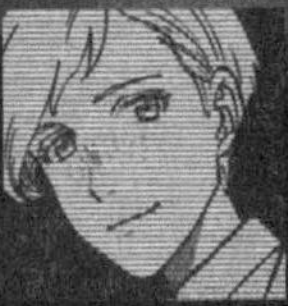

Jude Edivon

Ciena's close friend. Died on the Death Star.

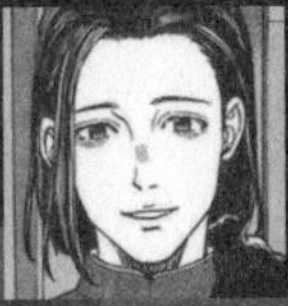

Nash Windrider

Thane's former roommate. Always worried about Ciena.

STORY

STAR WARS: LOST STARS

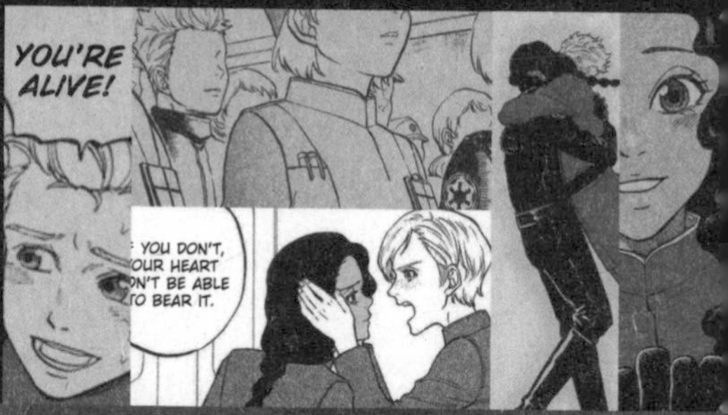
F YOU DON'T, OUR HEART N'T BE ABLE TO BEAR IT.
YOU'RE ALIVE!

Not long after the Empire destroys the planet Alderaan, the Rebel Alliance strikes back by blowing up the Death Star.

Jude was on the Death Star at the time of its destruction. As Ciena mourns the loss of her friend, even more bad news arrives—Thane has abandoned his post and deserted the Imperial army. Ciena tracks him down but ultimately accepts his rejection of the Empire. She delivers a false report: "Lieutenant Kyrell committed suicide."

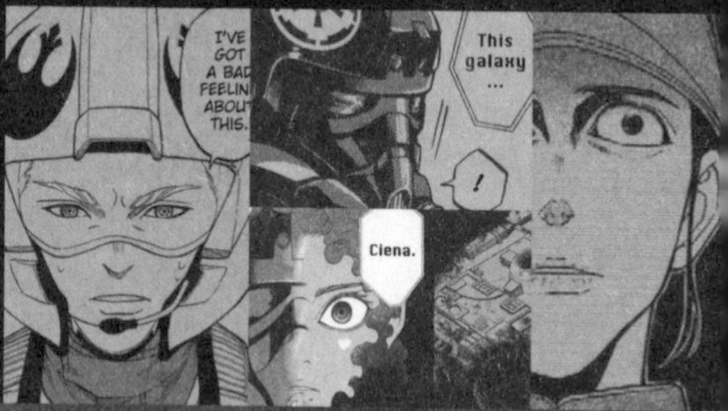
This galaxy ...
!
I'VE GOT A BAD FEELIN ABOUT THIS.
Ciena.

Years later, Ciena's mother is arrested on false charges of embezzling funds. If Ciena protests the Empire's decision, she will lose her rank and ensure that her entire family has no future. Thane appears and urges her to run away too, but Ciena is trapped by the Empire's curse, unable to fight against the army that nurtured her or run away with her lover. She feels compelled to reject his urgent plea.

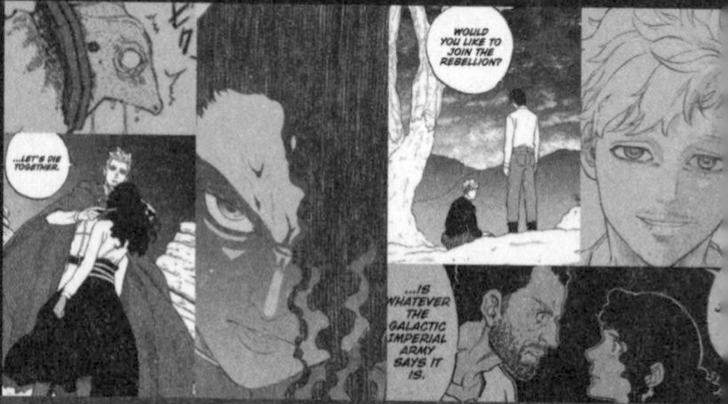
WOULD YOU LIKE TO JOIN THE REBELLION?
...IS WHATEVER THE GALACTIC IMPERIAL ARMY SAYS IT IS.
...LET'S DIE TOGETHER.

Some time later, Thane joins the Rebel Alliance. He and Ciena meet again under the worst possible circumstances—in the midst of battle...

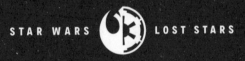

STAR WARS LOST STARS

VOLUME 3 CONTENTS

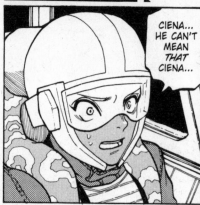

Chapter. 13

CIENA... HE CAN'T MEAN *THAT* CIENA...

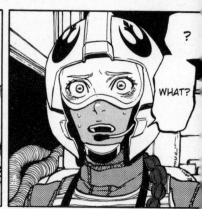

?

WHAT?

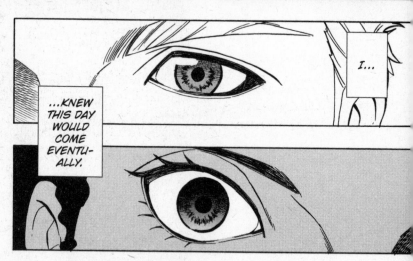

I...

...KNEW THIS DAY WOULD COME EVENTUALLY.

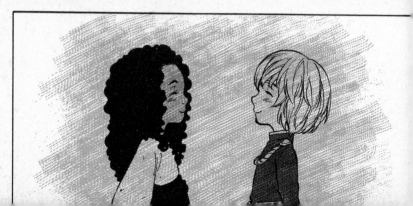

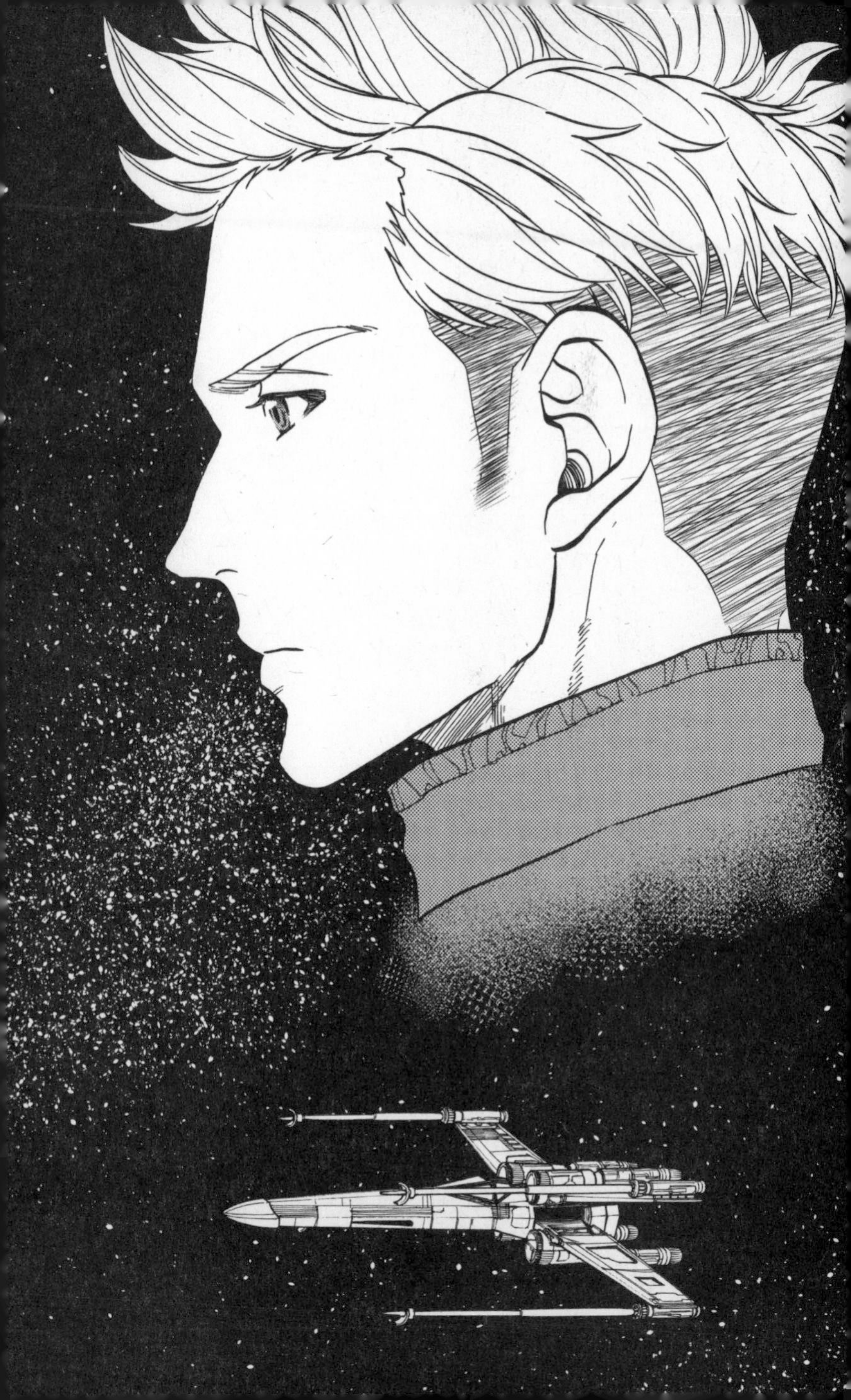

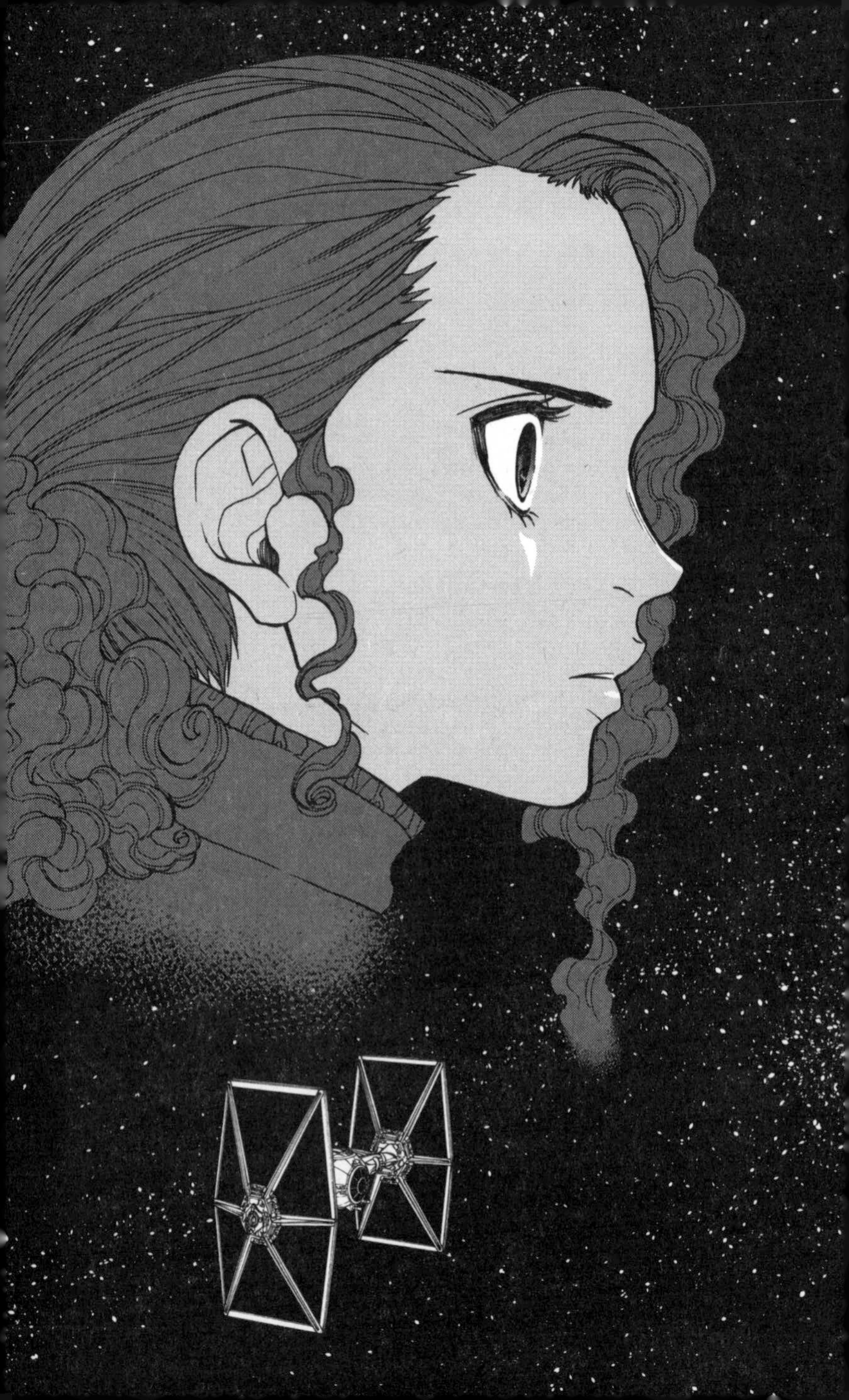

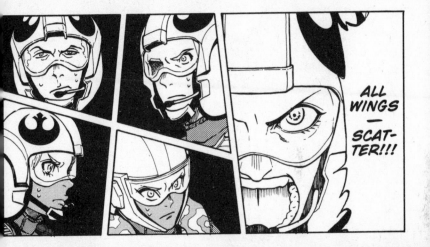

ALL WINGS — SCAT- TER!!!

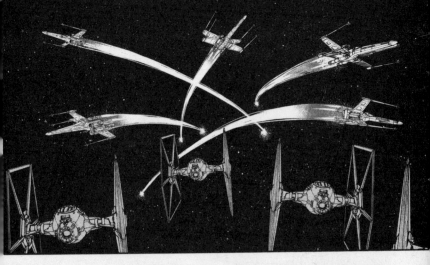

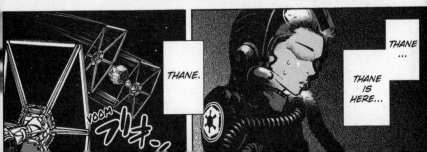

THANE.

THANE ...

THANE IS HERE...

VOOM フリオ〜

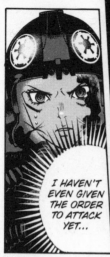

!!!

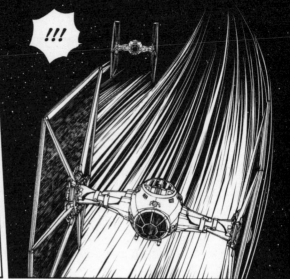

I HAVEN'T EVEN GIVEN THE ORDER TO ATTACK YET...

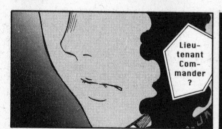

Lieu-tenant Com-mander?

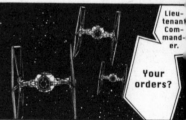

Lieu-tenant Com-mand-er.

Your orders?

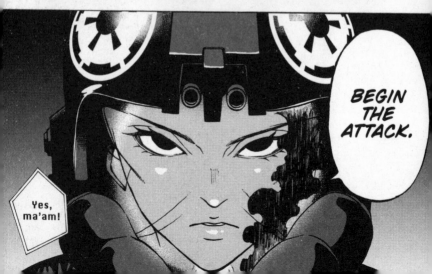

BEGIN THE ATTACK.

Yes, ma'am!

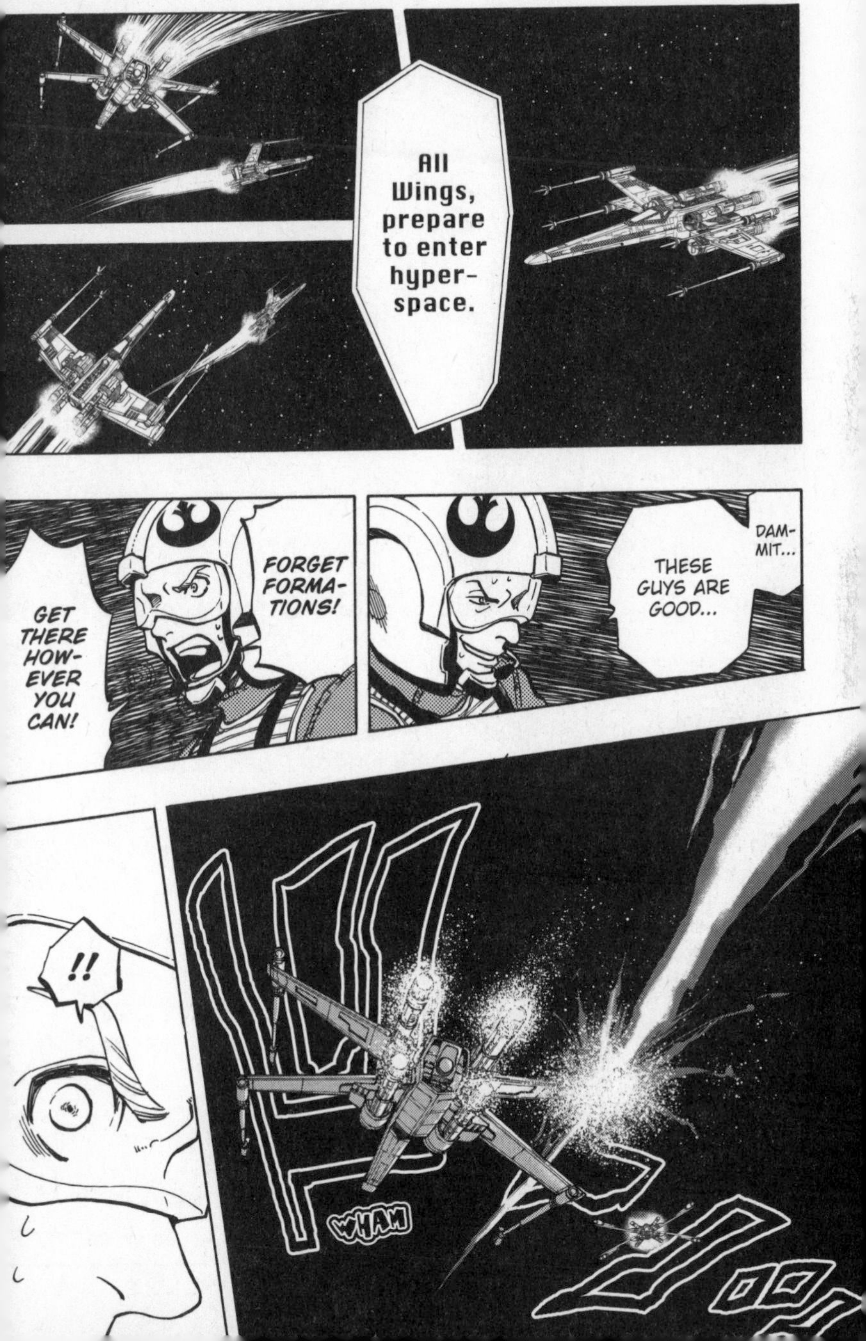
All Wings, prepare to enter hyper-space.
DAM-MIT...
THESE GUYS ARE GOOD...
FORGET FORMA-TIONS!
GET THERE HOW-EVER YOU CAN!
WHAM
!!

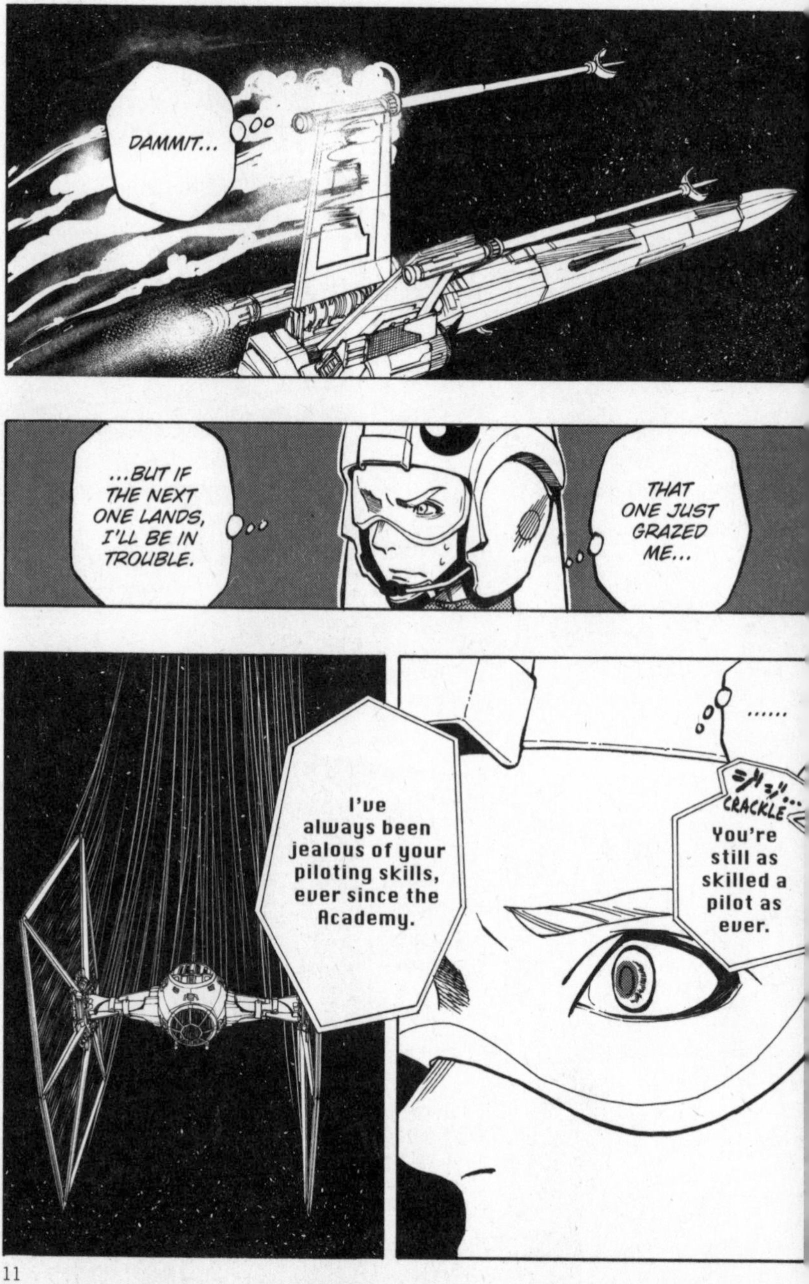
DAMMIT...
THAT ONE JUST GRAZED ME...
...BUT IF THE NEXT ONE LANDS, I'LL BE IN TROUBLE.
......
CRACKLE
You're still as skilled a pilot as ever.
I've always been jealous of your piloting skills, ever since the Academy.

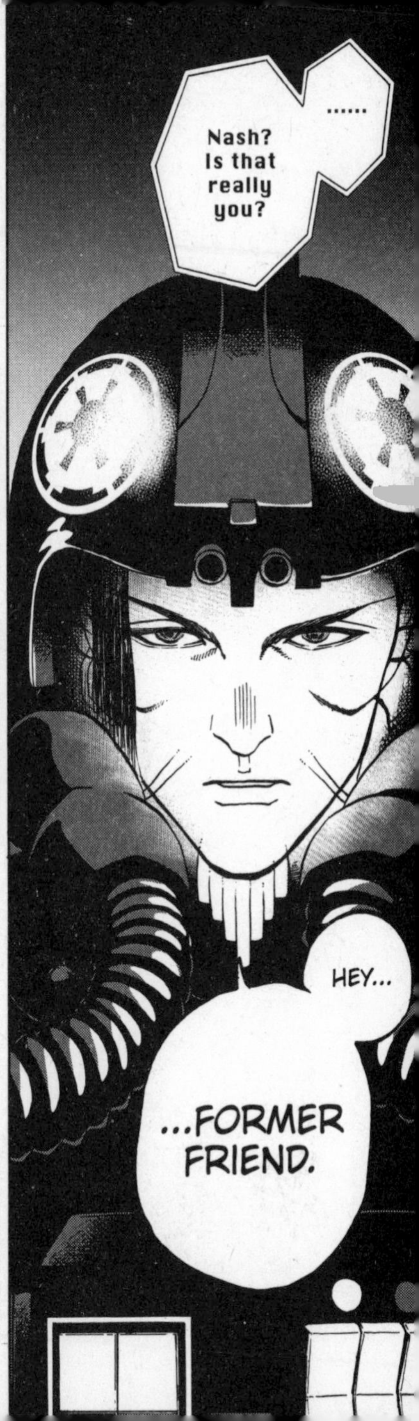
......
Nash? Is that really you?
HEY...
...FORMER FRIEND.

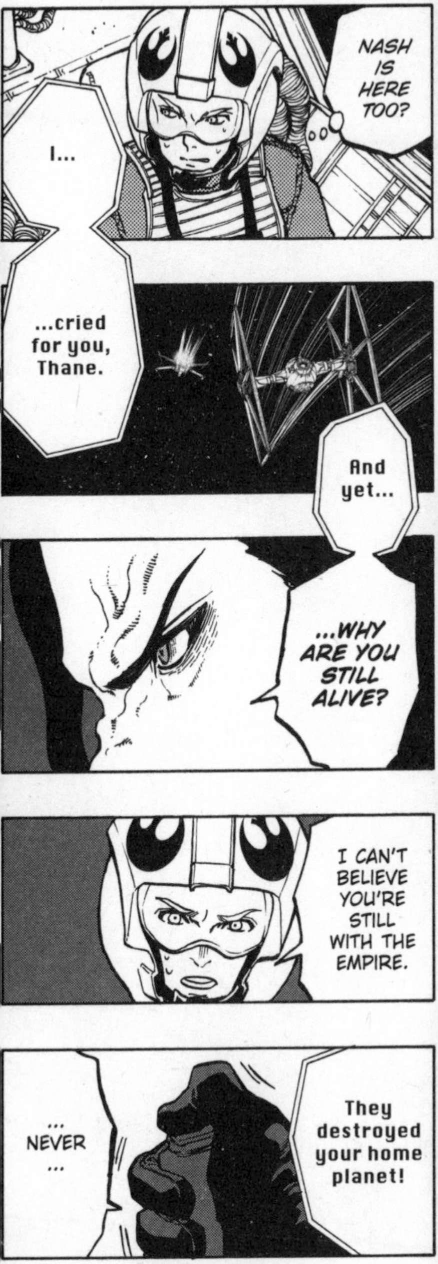
NASH IS HERE TOO?
I...
...cried for you, Thane.
And yet...
...WHY ARE YOU STILL ALIVE?
I CAN'T BELIEVE YOU'RE STILL WITH THE EMPIRE.
They destroyed your home planet!
... NEVER ...

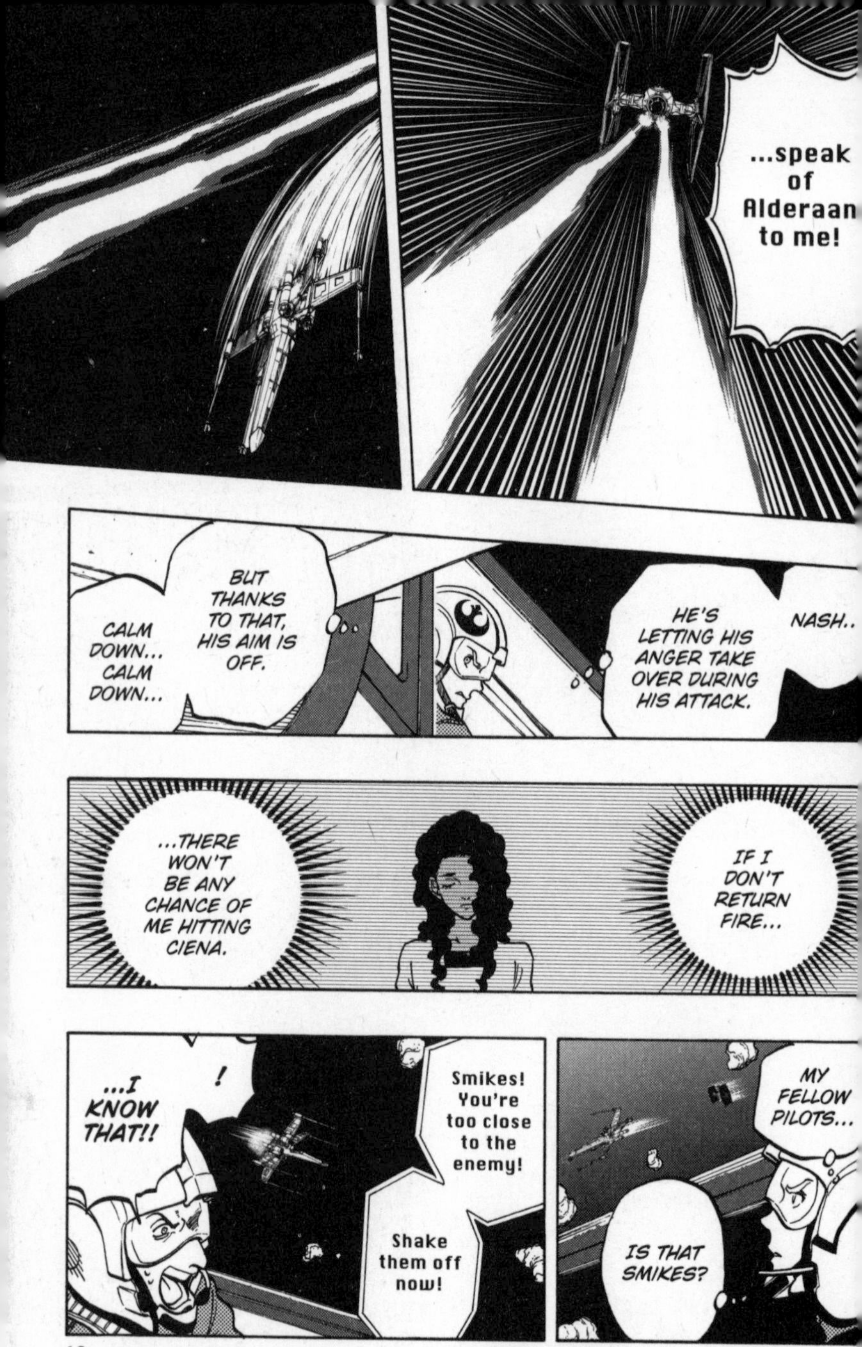
...speak of Alderaan to me!
NASH..
HE'S LETTING HIS ANGER TAKE OVER DURING HIS ATTACK.
BUT THANKS TO THAT, HIS AIM IS OFF.
CALM DOWN... CALM DOWN...
IF I DON'T RETURN FIRE...
...THERE WON'T BE ANY CHANCE OF ME HITTING CIENA.
MY FELLOW PILOTS...
IS THAT SMIKES?
Smikes! You're too close to the enemy!
Shake them off now!
!
...I KNOW THAT!!

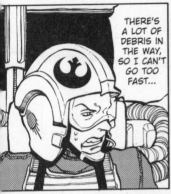

DAM-MIT!
THERE'S A LOT OF DEBRIS IN THE WAY, SO I CAN'T GO TOO FAST...
THIS IS BAD...
HE'S GRADUALLY BEING PUSHED BACK INTO AN ASTEROID FIELD.
HE NEEDS COVER...
CRACKLE
Looks like your skills have gone downhill...
...since you became rebel scum!
!

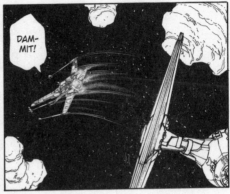

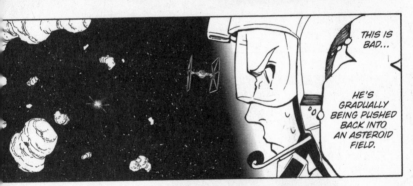

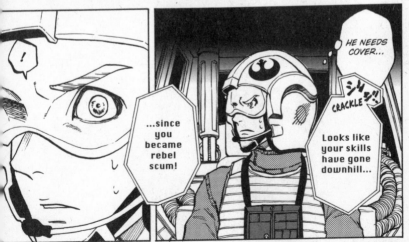

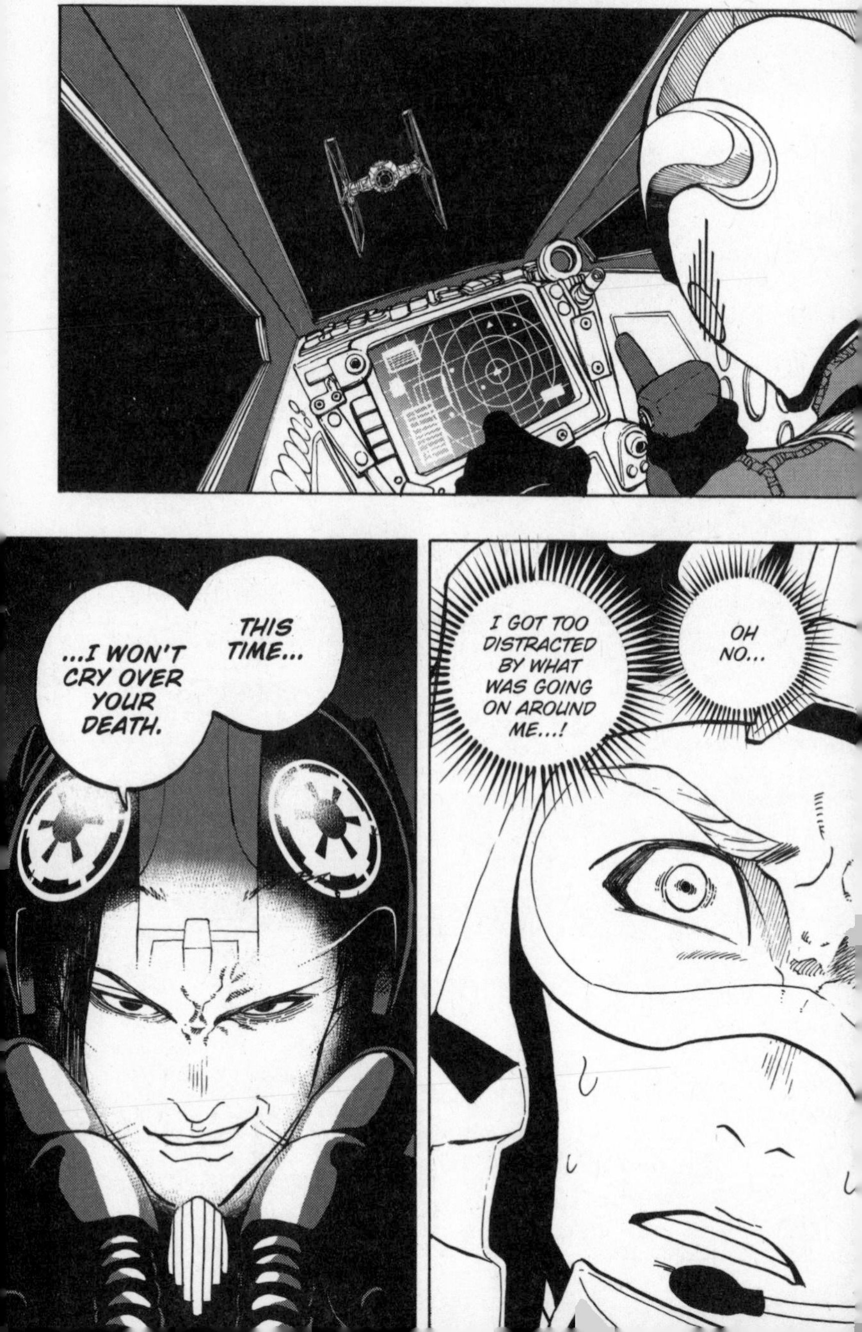
OH NO...
I GOT TOO DISTRACTED BY WHAT WAS GOING ON AROUND ME...!
THIS TIME...
...I WON'T CRY OVER YOUR DEATH.

!?
THAT TIE FIGHTER...
IS IT COVERING ME...?
WAAAAAH!!!

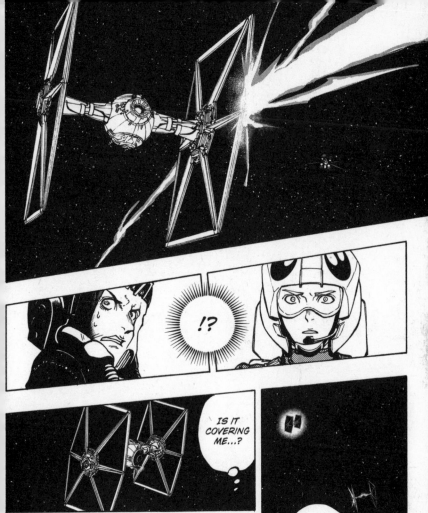

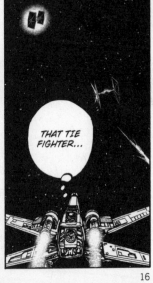

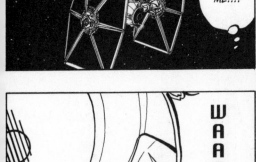

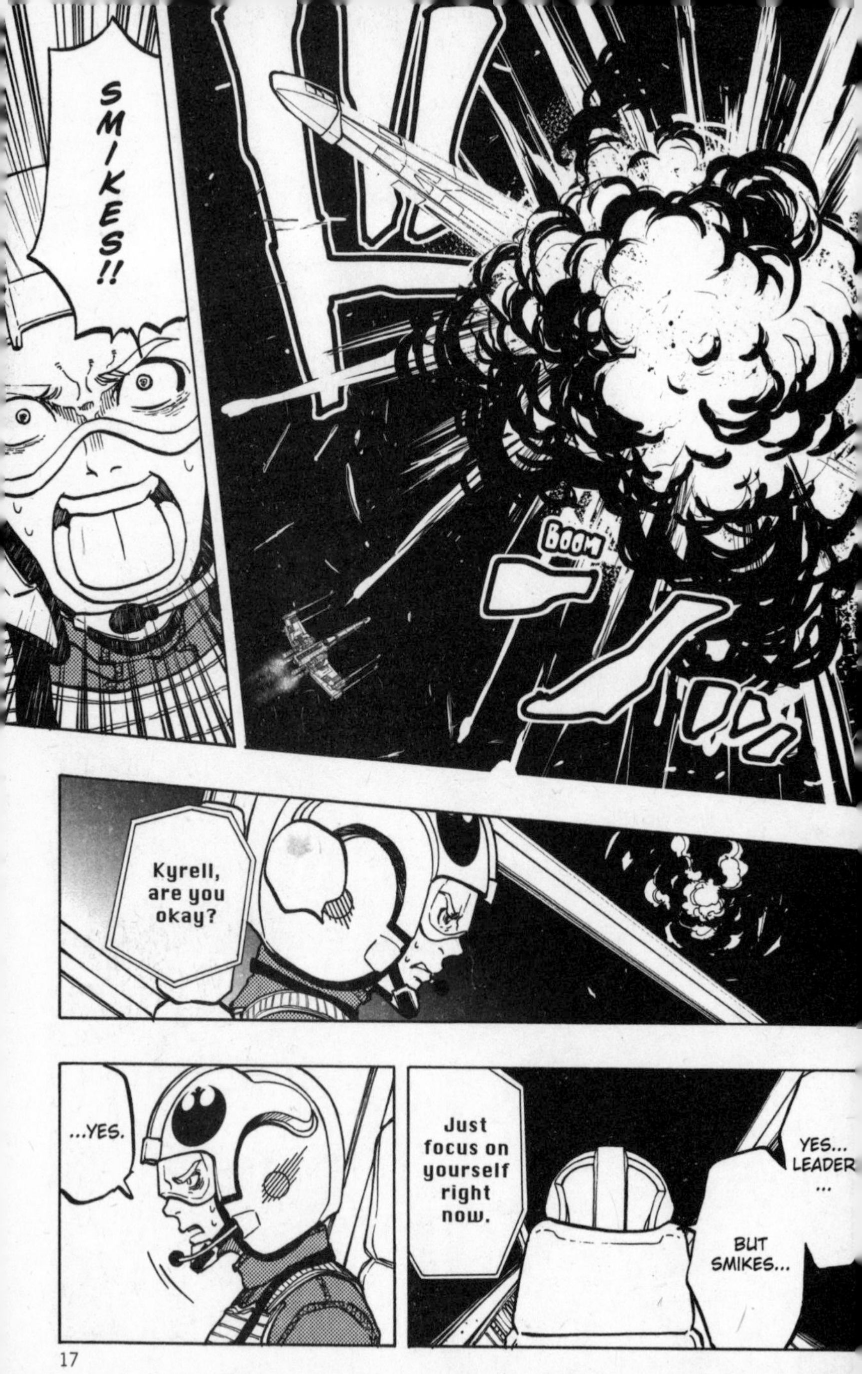
Boom
SMIKES!!
Kyrell, are you okay?
YES... LEADER ...
Just focus on yourself right now.
BUT SMIKES...
...YES.

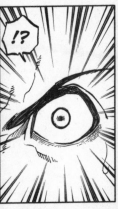

!?

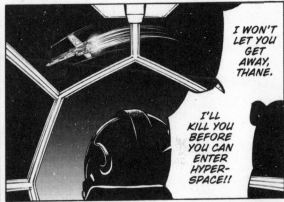

I WON'T LET YOU GET AWAY, THANE.

I'LL KILL YOU BEFORE YOU CAN ENTER HYPER-SPACE!!

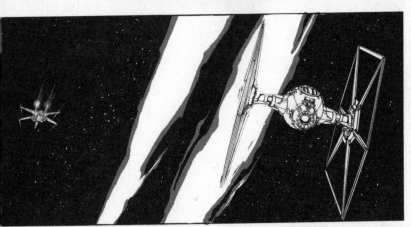

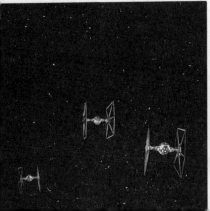

DAMMIT...

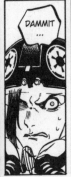

WHY...

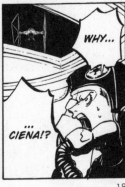

...CIENA!?

18

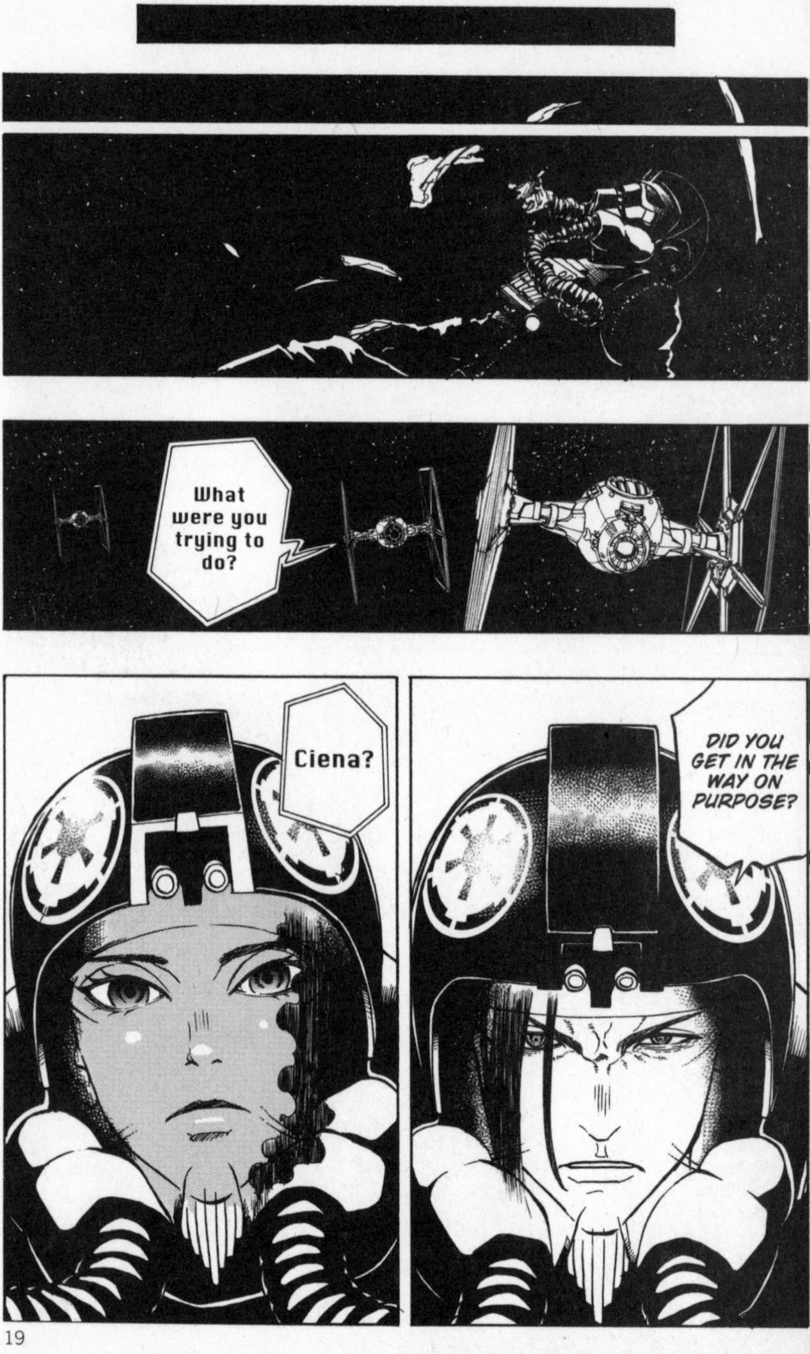
What were you trying to do?
DID YOU GET IN THE WAY ON PURPOSE?
Ciena?

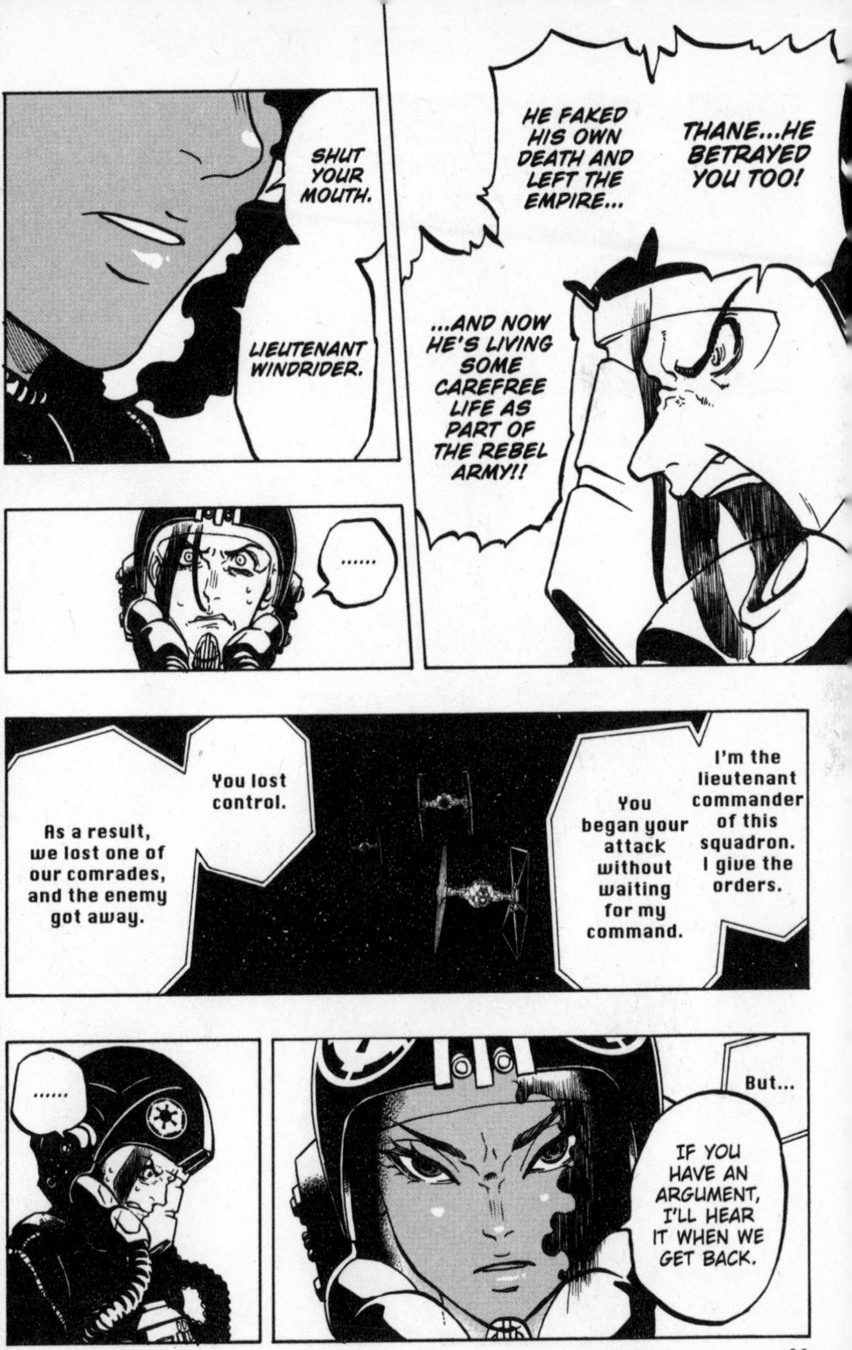
THANE...HE BETRAYED YOU TOO!
HE FAKED HIS OWN DEATH AND LEFT THE EMPIRE...
...AND NOW HE'S LIVING SOME CAREFREE LIFE AS PART OF THE REBEL ARMY!!
SHUT YOUR MOUTH.
LIEUTENANT WINDRIDER.
......
I'm the lieutenant commander of this squadron. I give the orders.
You began your attack without waiting for my command.
You lost control.
As a result, we lost one of our comrades, and the enemy got away.
But...
IF YOU HAVE AN ARGUMENT, I'LL HEAR IT WHEN WE GET BACK.
......

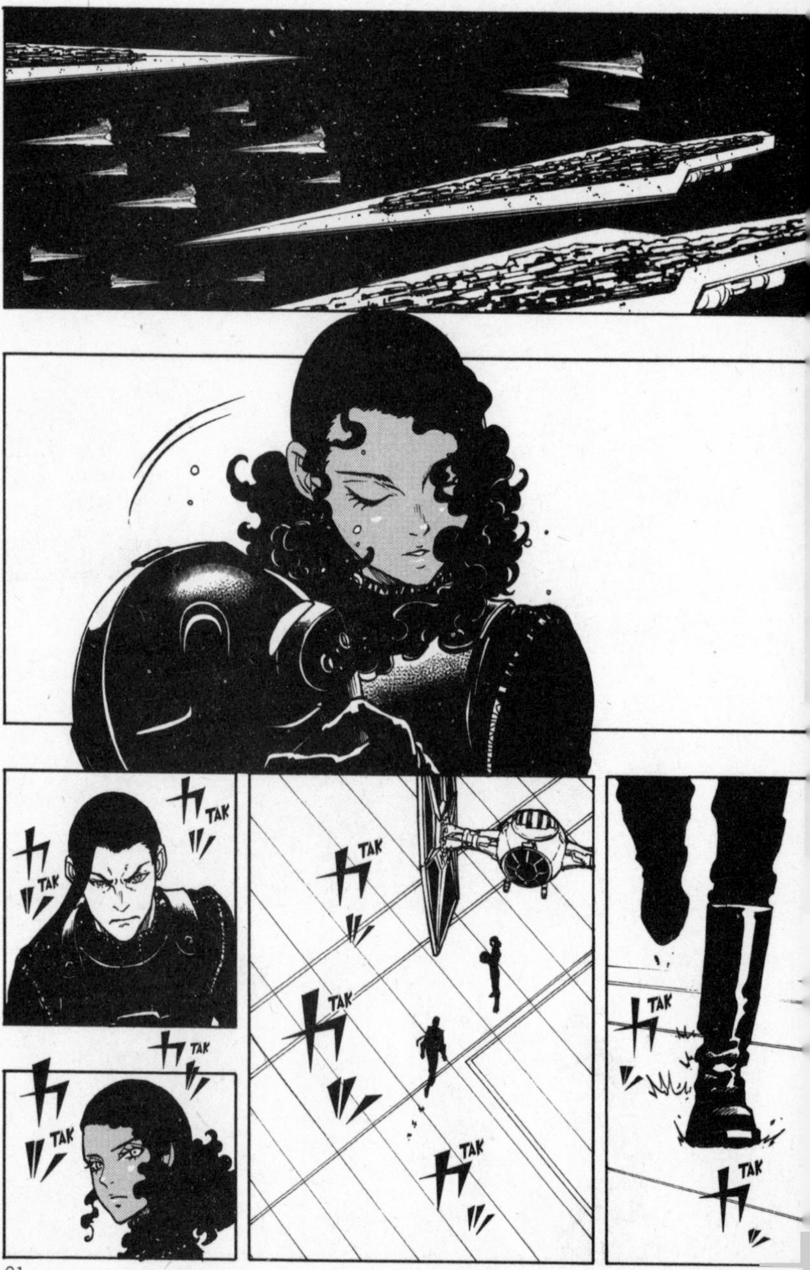
カ TAK
カ TAK
カ TAK
カ TAK
カ TAK
カ TAK
カ TAK
カ TAK
カ TAK

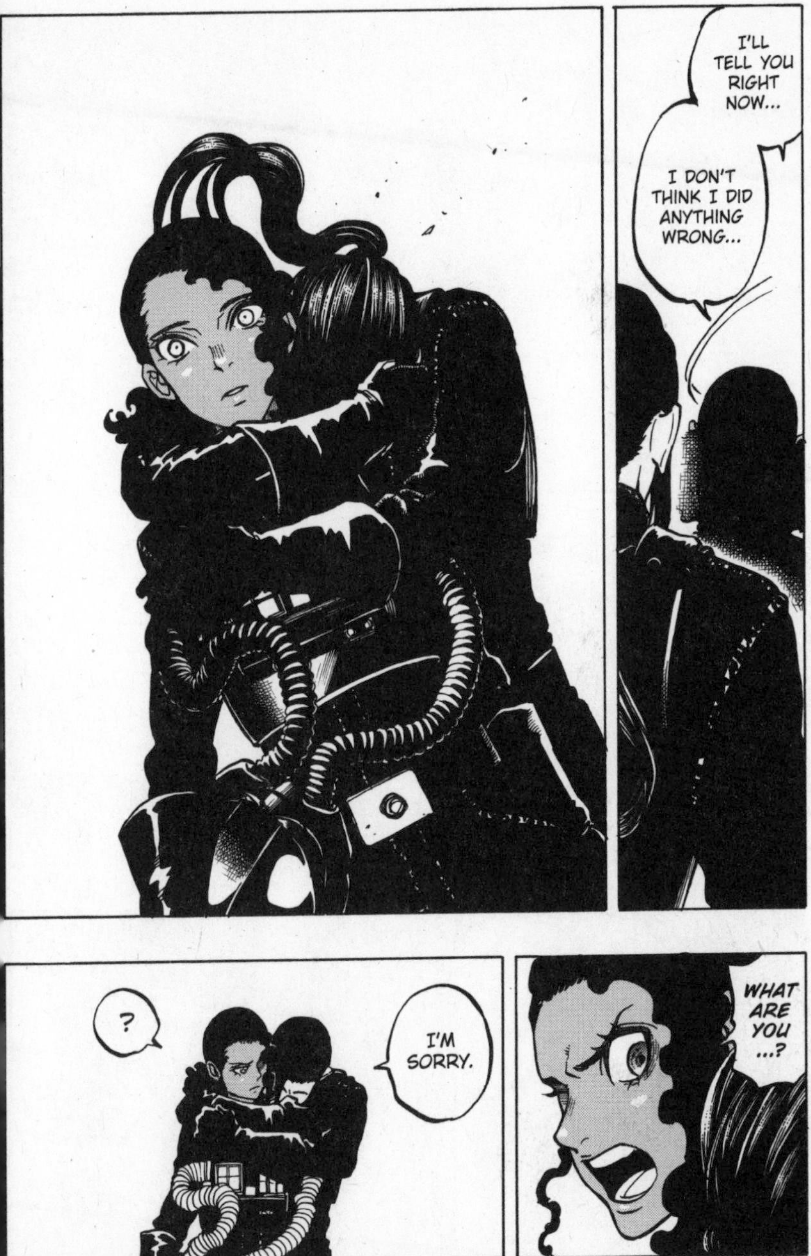
I'LL TELL YOU RIGHT NOW...
I DON'T THINK I DID ANYTHING WRONG...
WHAT ARE YOU ...?
I'M SORRY.
?

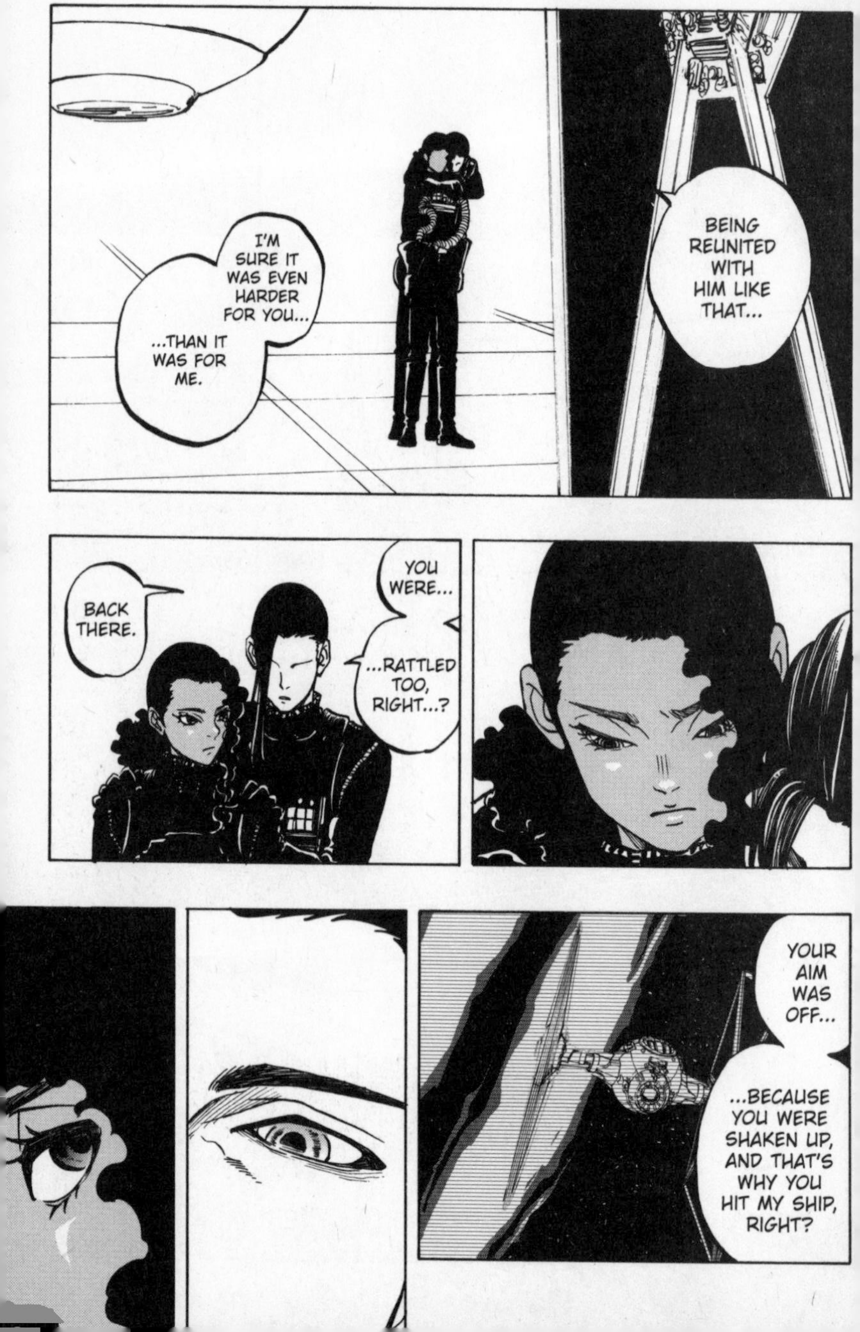
BEING REUNITED WITH HIM LIKE THAT...
I'M SURE IT WAS EVEN HARDER FOR YOU...
...THAN IT WAS FOR ME.
YOU WERE...
...RATTLED TOO, RIGHT...?
BACK THERE.
YOUR AIM WAS OFF...
...BECAUSE YOU WERE SHAKEN UP, AND THAT'S WHY YOU HIT MY SHIP, RIGHT?

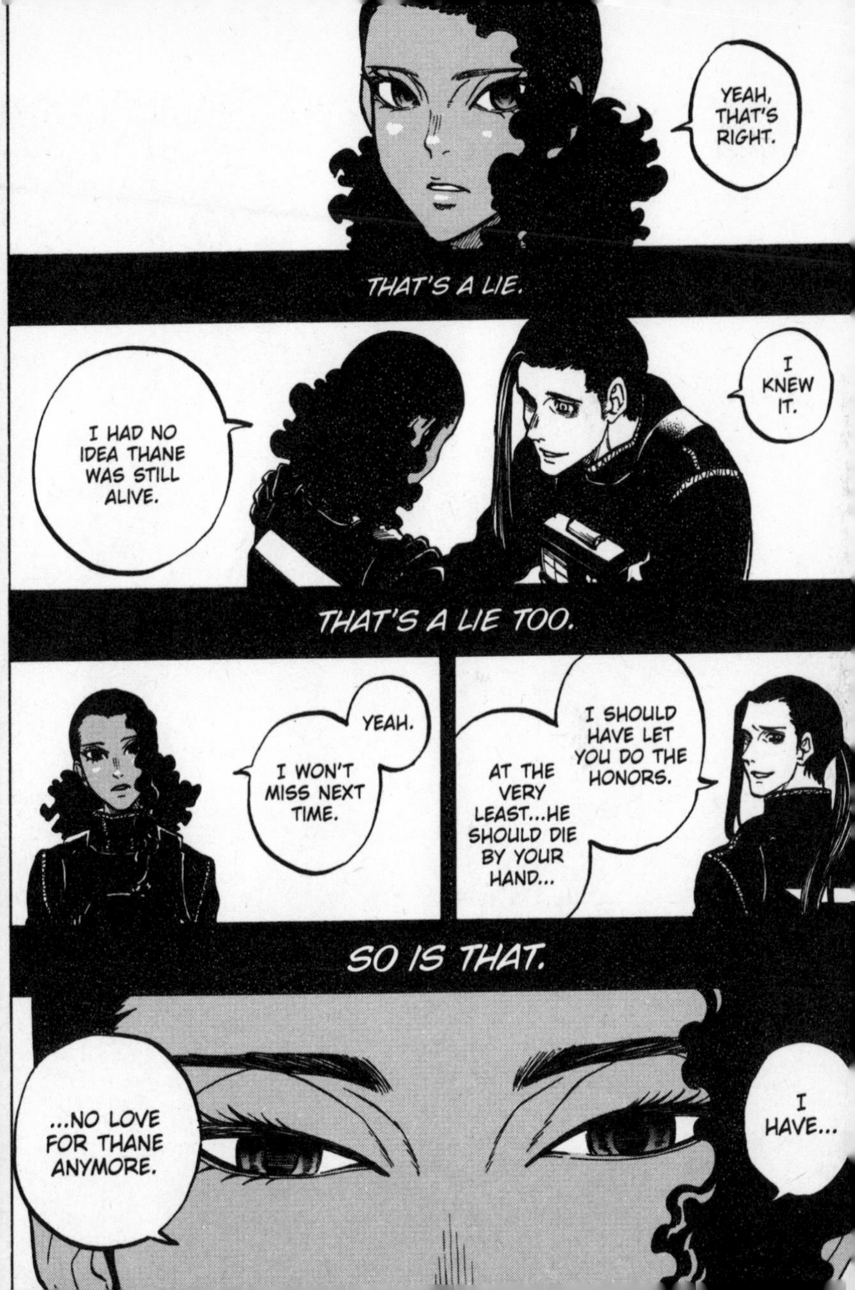
YEAH, THAT'S RIGHT.
THAT'S A LIE.
I KNEW IT.
I HAD NO IDEA THANE WAS STILL ALIVE.
THAT'S A LIE TOO.
I SHOULD HAVE LET YOU DO THE HONORS.
AT THE VERY LEAST...HE SHOULD DIE BY YOUR HAND...
YEAH.
I WON'T MISS NEXT TIME.
SO IS THAT.
I HAVE...
...NO LOVE FOR THANE ANYMORE.

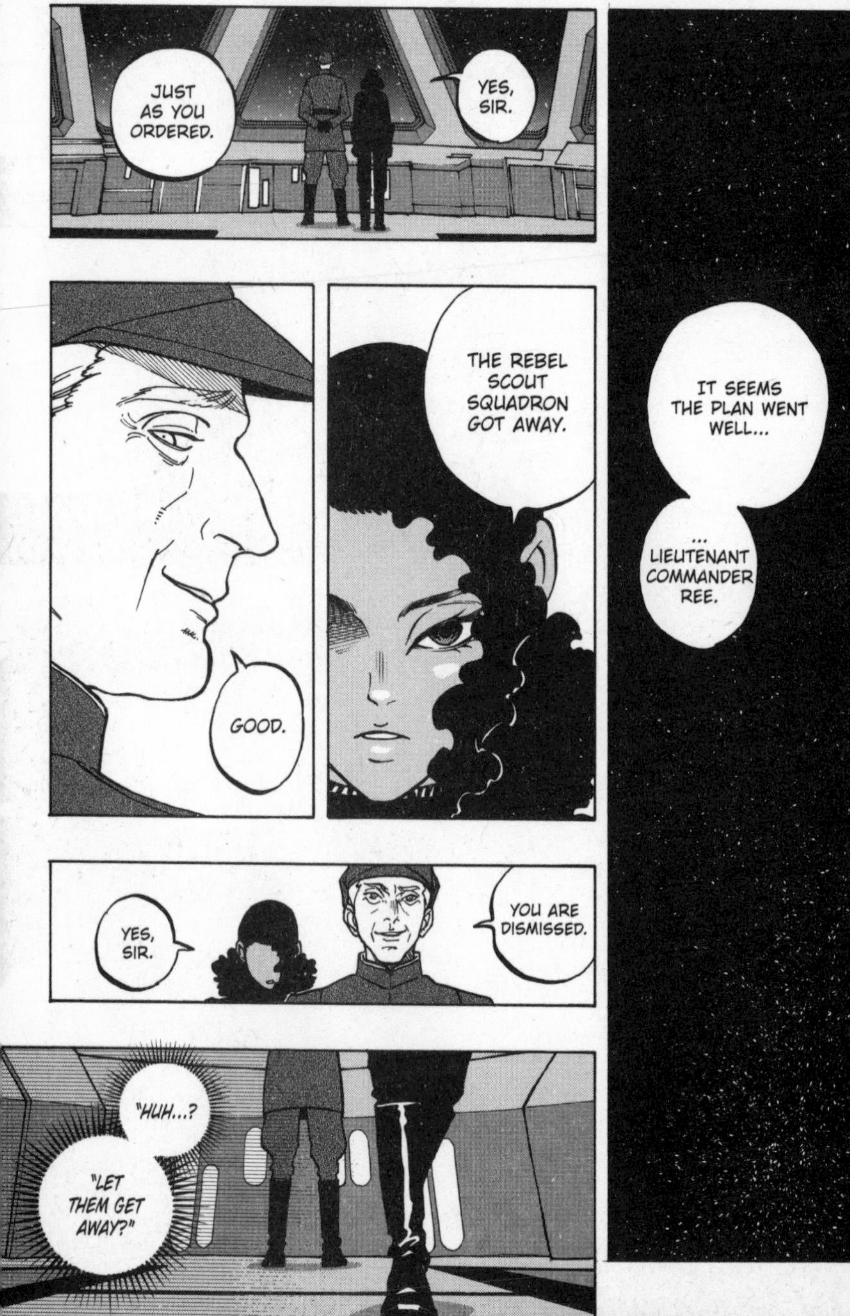
IT SEEMS THE PLAN WENT WELL...
...LIEUTENANT COMMANDER REE.
YES, SIR.
JUST AS YOU ORDERED.
THE REBEL SCOUT SQUADRON GOT AWAY.
GOOD.
YOU ARE DISMISSED.
YES, SIR.
"HUH...?
"LET THEM GET AWAY?"

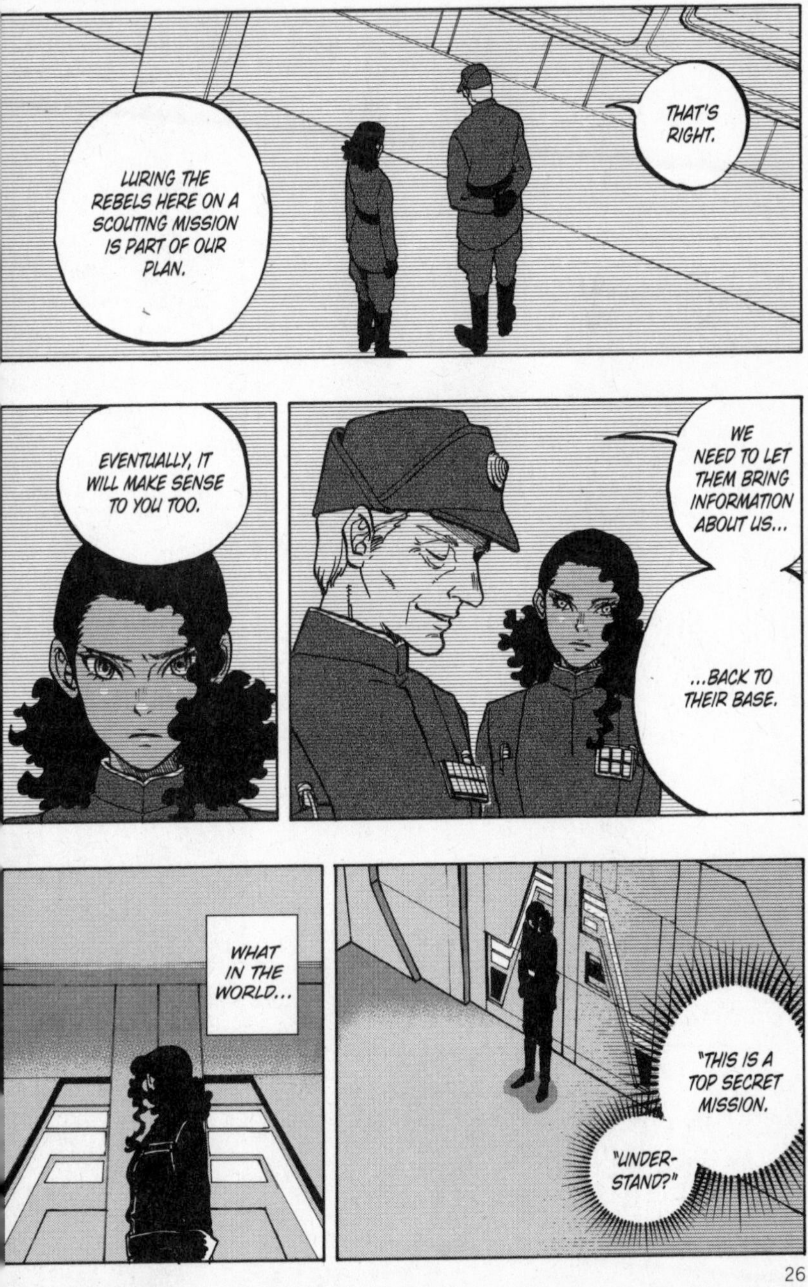
THAT'S RIGHT.
LURING THE REBELS HERE ON A SCOUTING MISSION IS PART OF OUR PLAN.
WE NEED TO LET THEM BRING INFORMATION ABOUT US...
...BACK TO THEIR BASE.
EVENTUALLY, IT WILL MAKE SENSE TO YOU TOO.
"THIS IS A TOP SECRET MISSION.
"UNDER-STAND?"
WHAT IN THE WORLD...

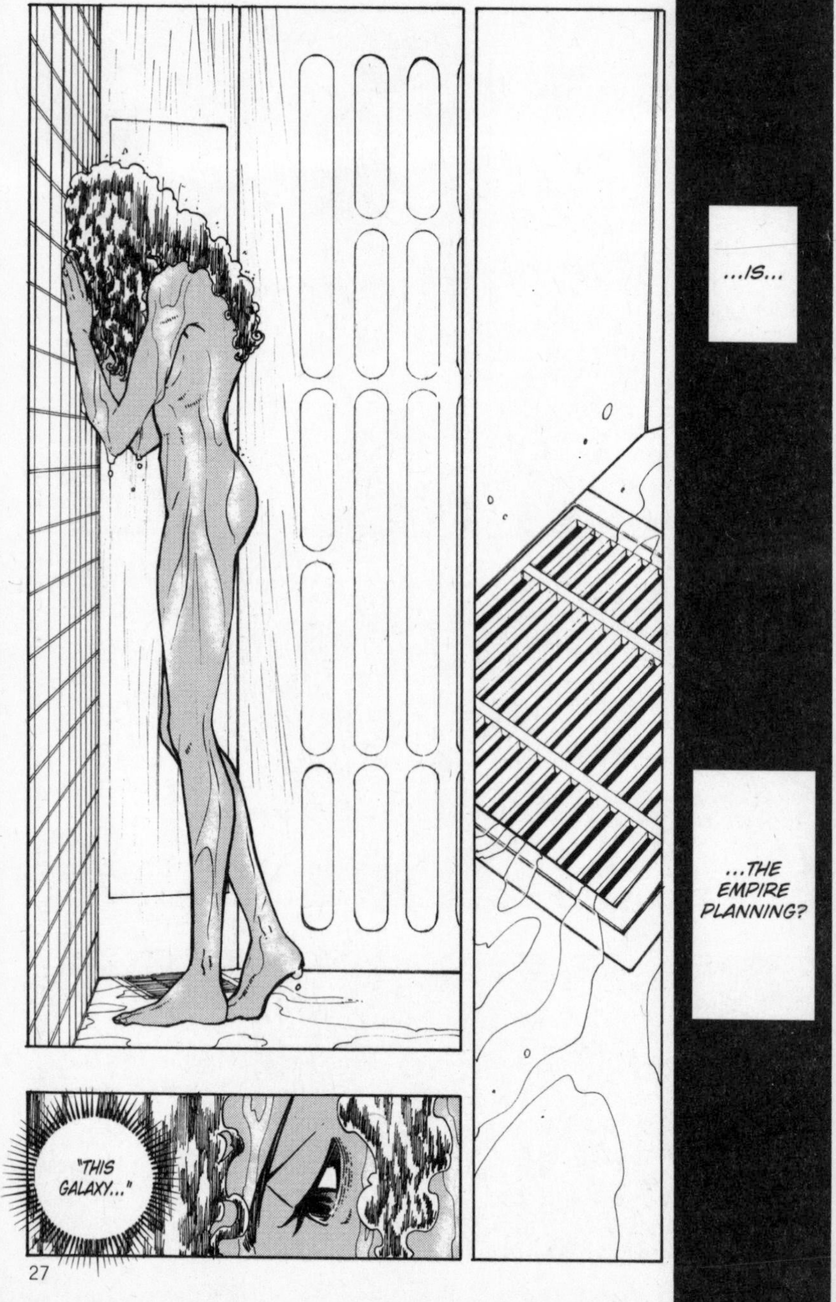
...IS...
...THE EMPIRE PLANNING?
"THIS GALAXY..."

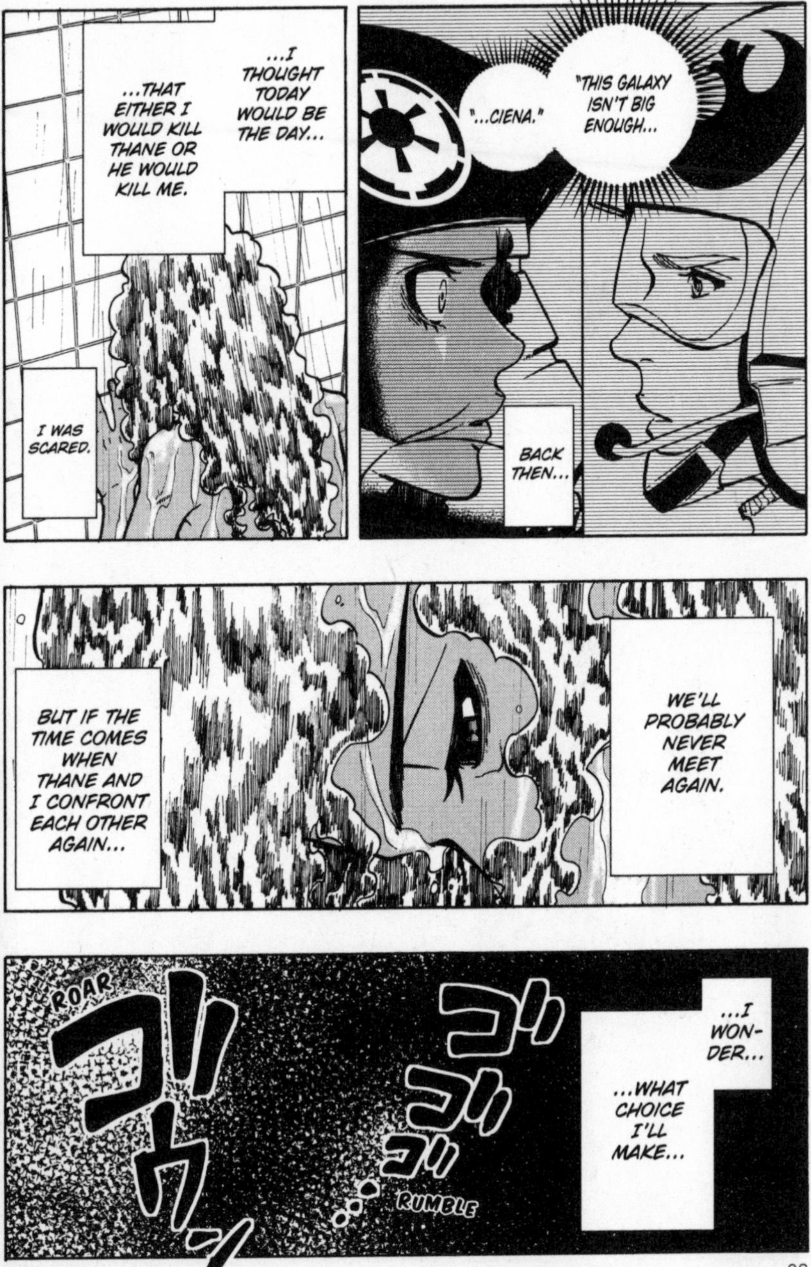
"THIS GALAXY ISN'T BIG ENOUGH...
"...CIENA."
BACK THEN...
...I THOUGHT TODAY WOULD BE THE DAY...
...THAT EITHER I WOULD KILL THANE OR HE WOULD KILL ME.
I WAS SCARED.
WE'LL PROBABLY NEVER MEET AGAIN.
BUT IF THE TIME COMES WHEN THANE AND I CONFRONT EACH OTHER AGAIN...
...I WONDER...
...WHAT CHOICE I'LL MAKE...
ゴゴゴ
RUMBLE
ゴウ
ROAR

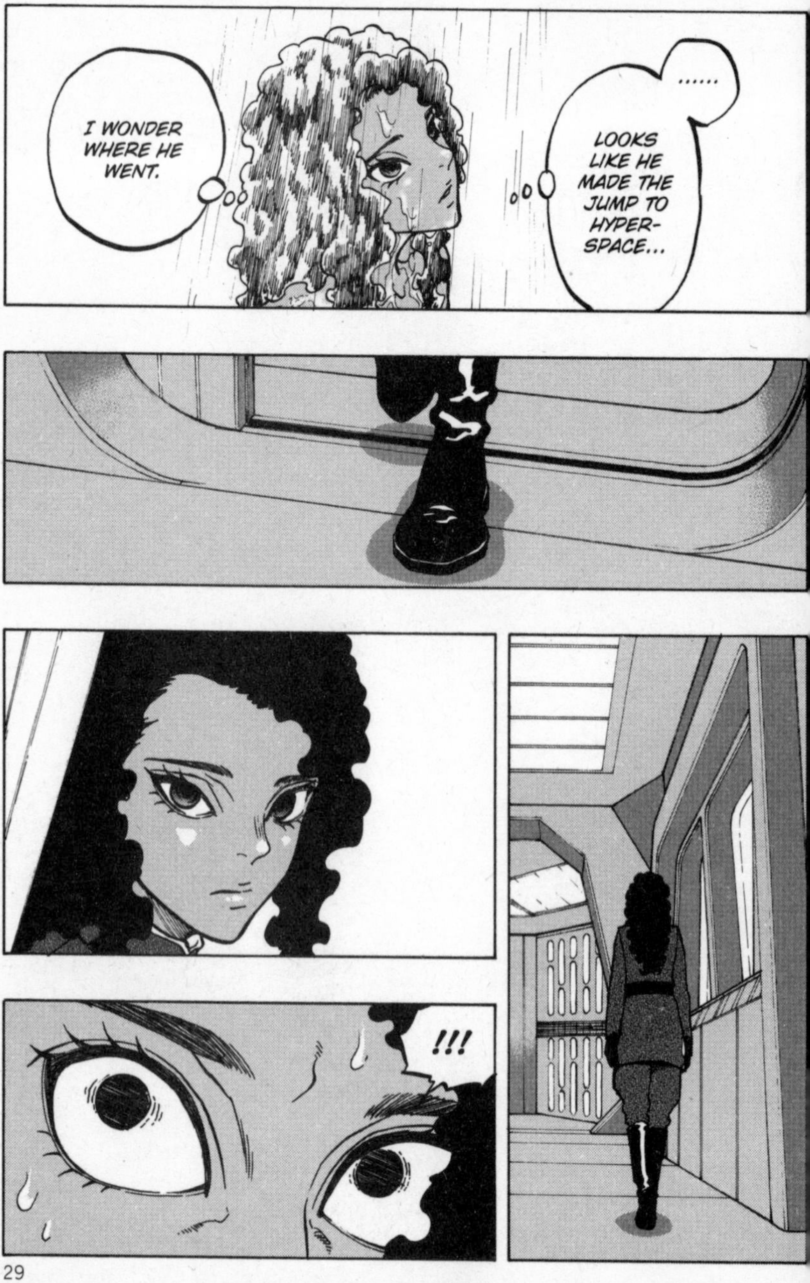
......
LOOKS LIKE HE MADE THE JUMP TO HYPER-SPACE...
I WONDER WHERE HE WENT.
!!!

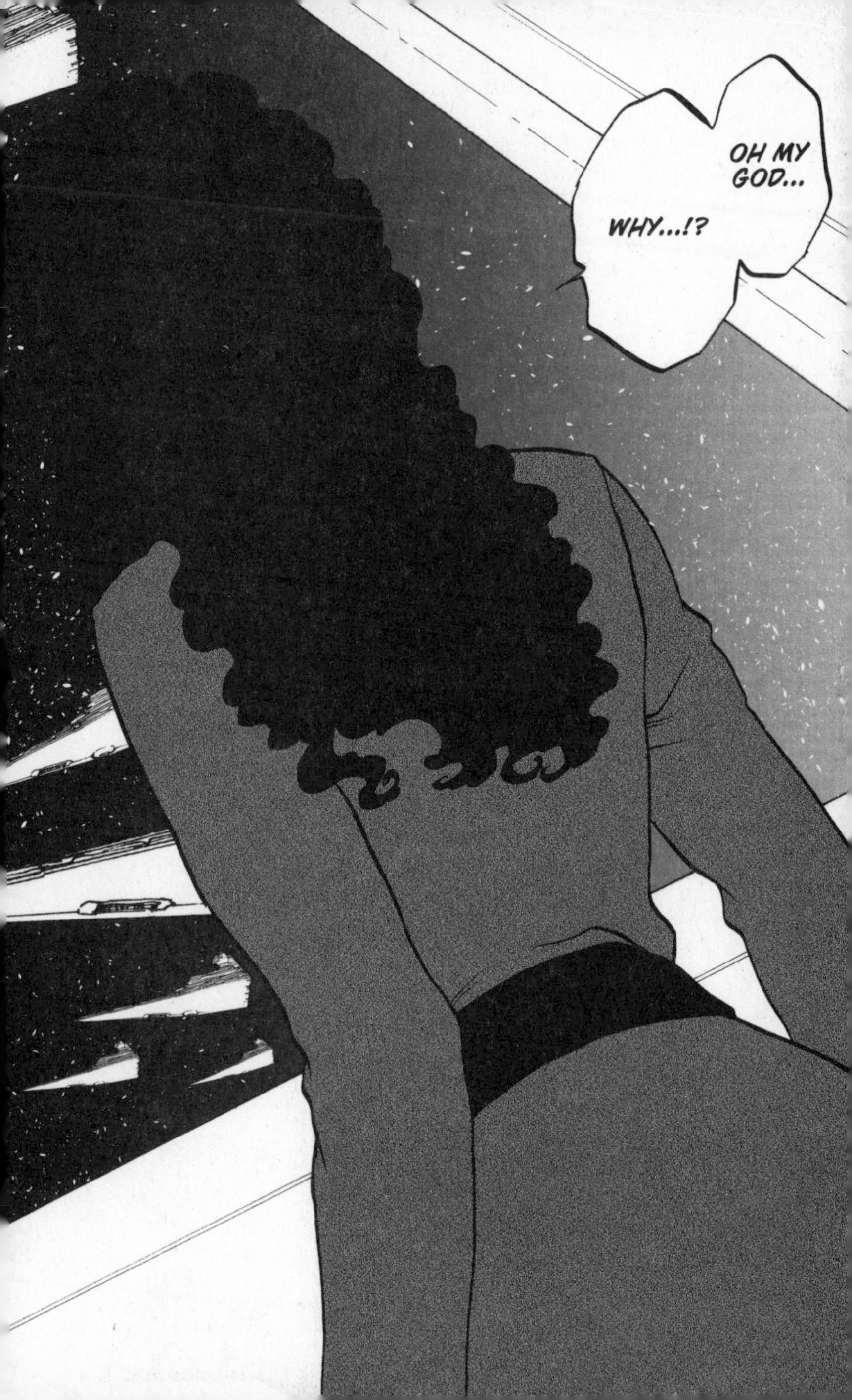
OH MY GOD...
WHY...!?

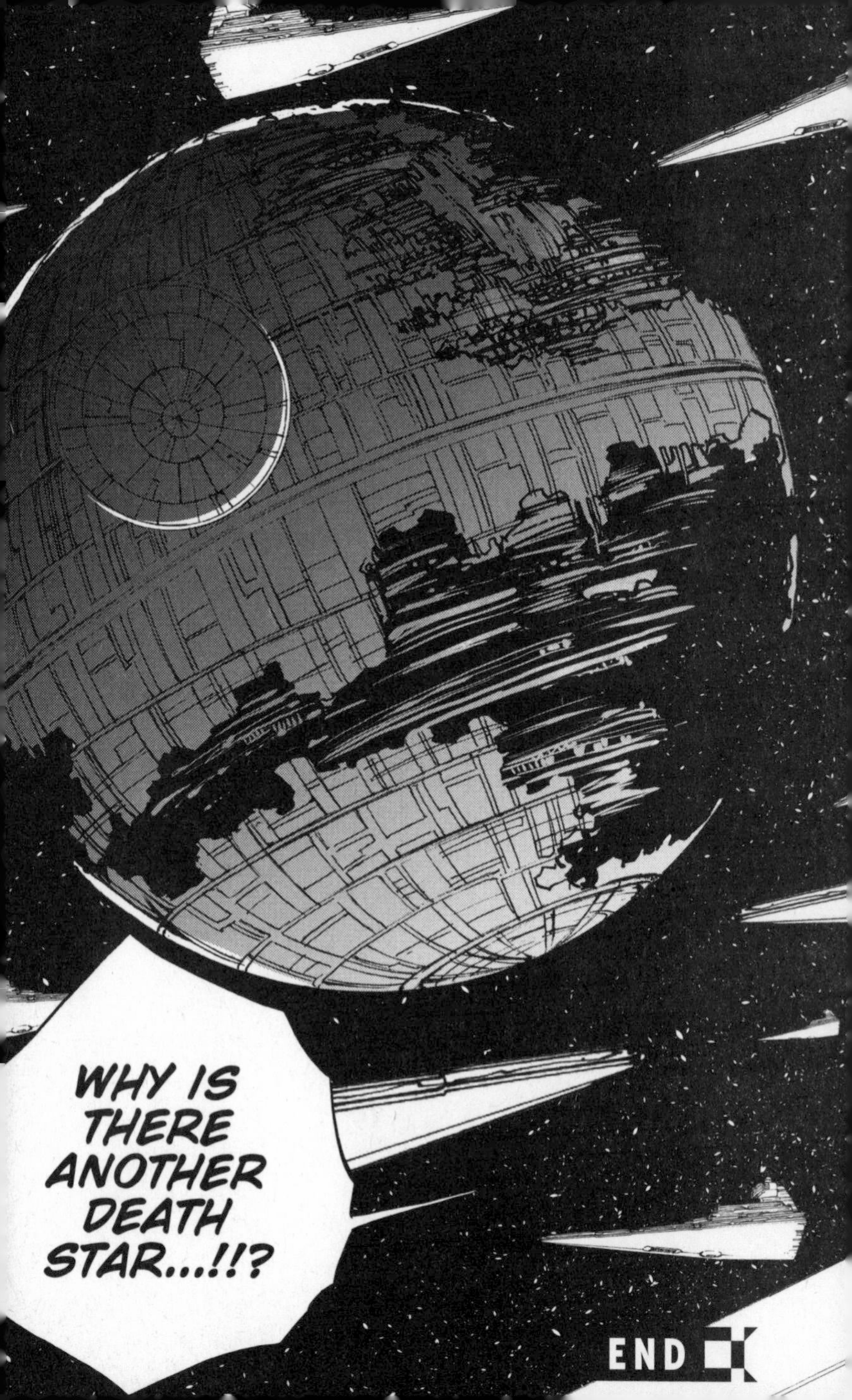
WHY IS THERE ANOTHER DEATH STAR...!!?
END

STAR WARS
LOST STARS
ロスト・スターズ

Chapter. 14

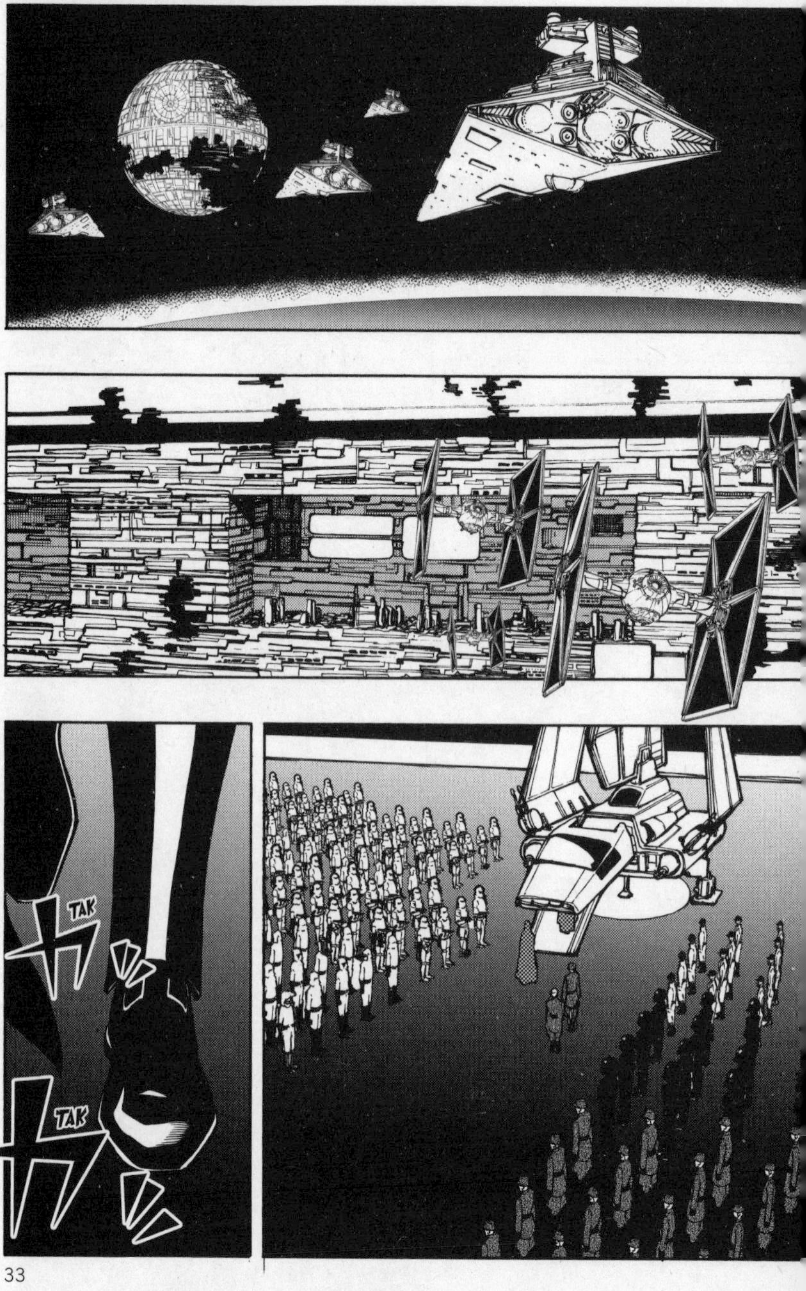
TAK
TAK

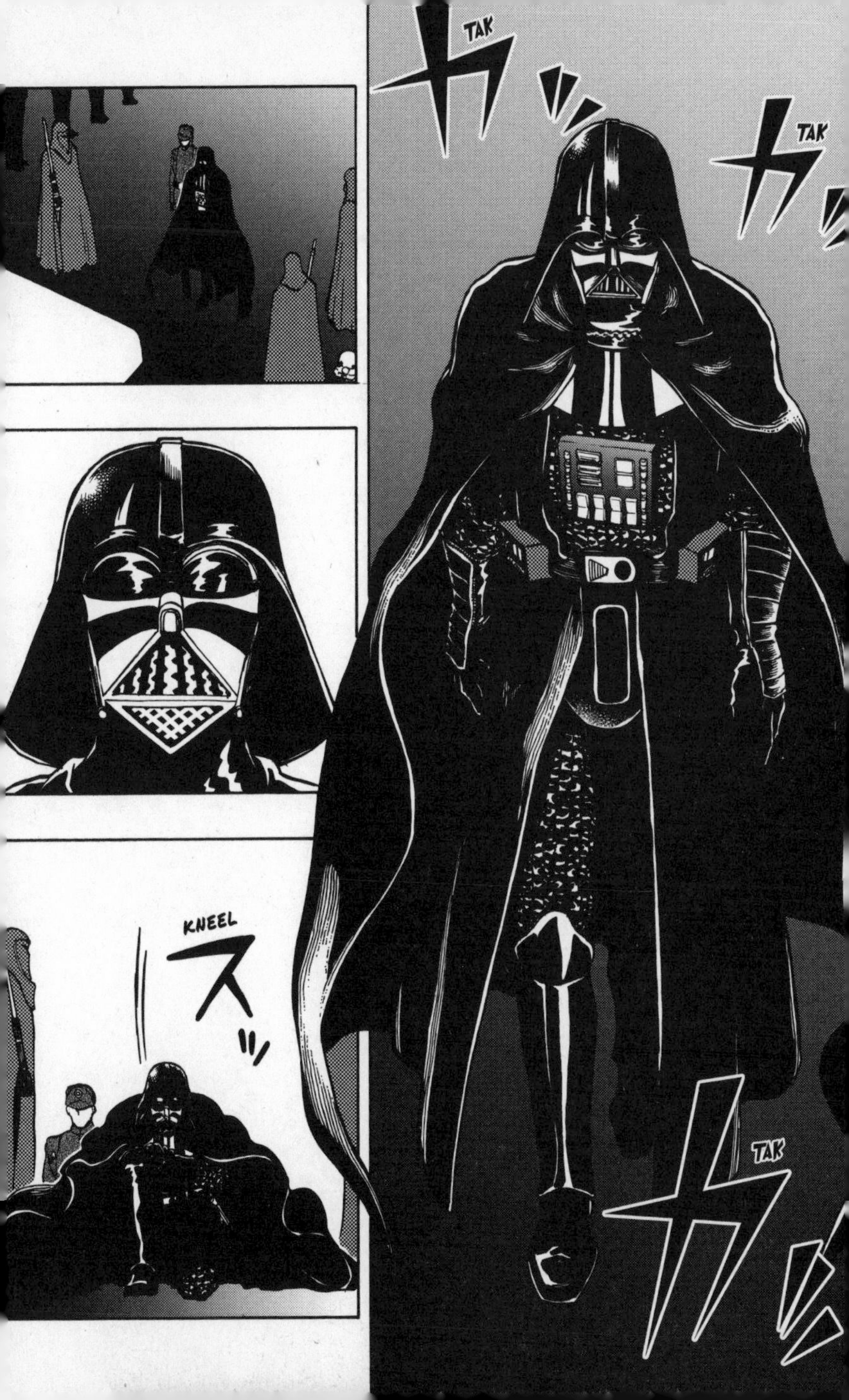
TAK
カッ
TAK
カッ
TAK
カッ
KNEEL
スッ

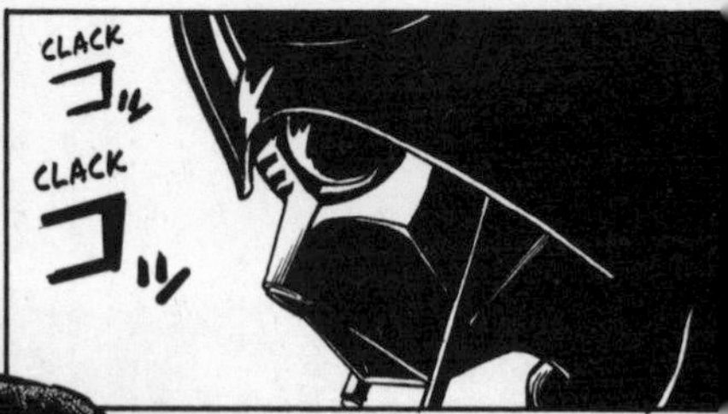
CLACK
コッ
CLACK
コッ
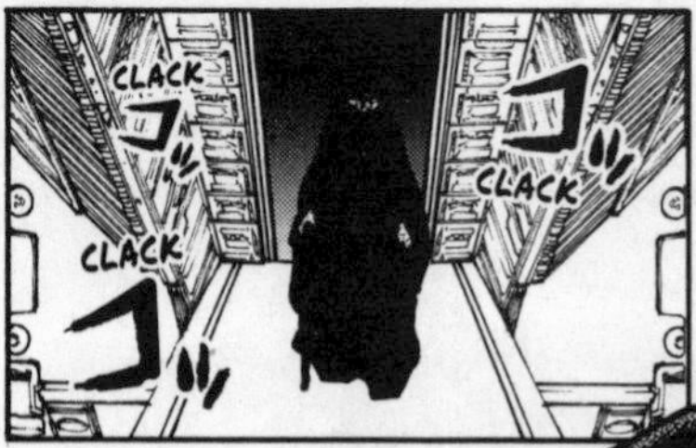
CLACK
コッ
CLACK
コッ
CLACK
コッ
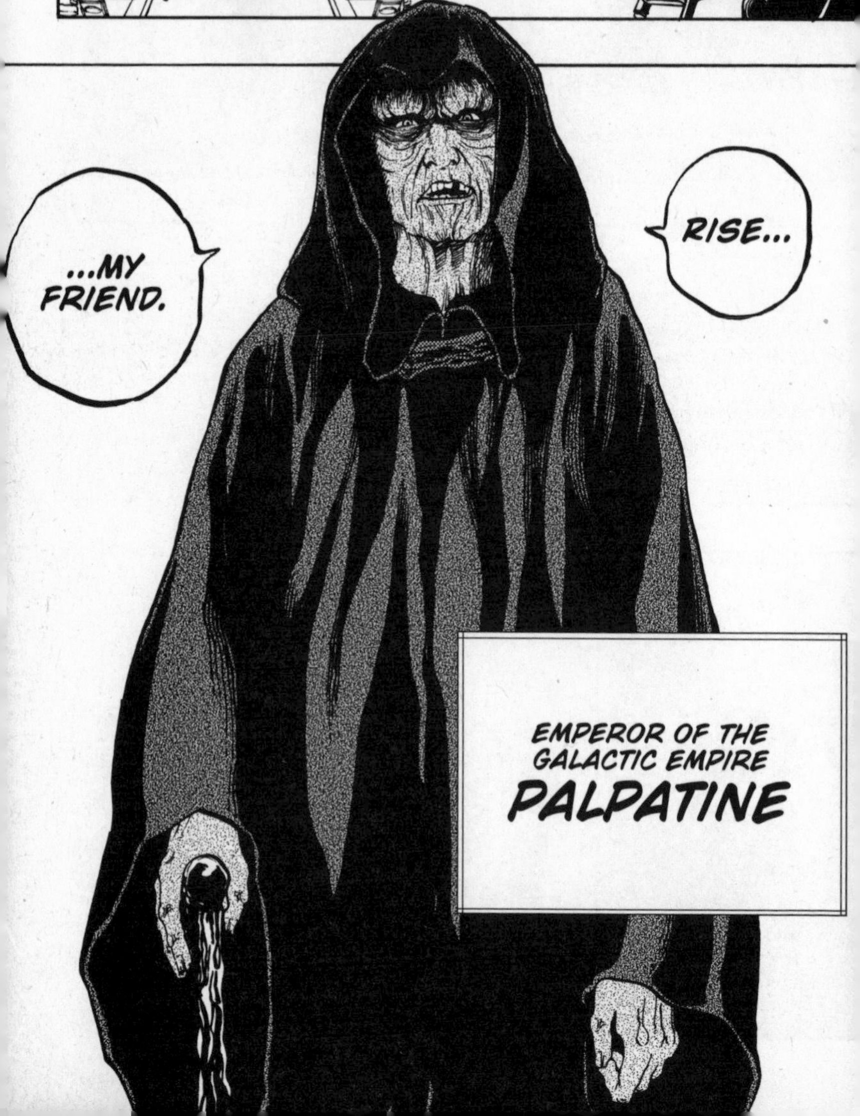
RISE...
...MY FRIEND.
EMPEROR OF THE GALACTIC EMPIRE
PALPATINE

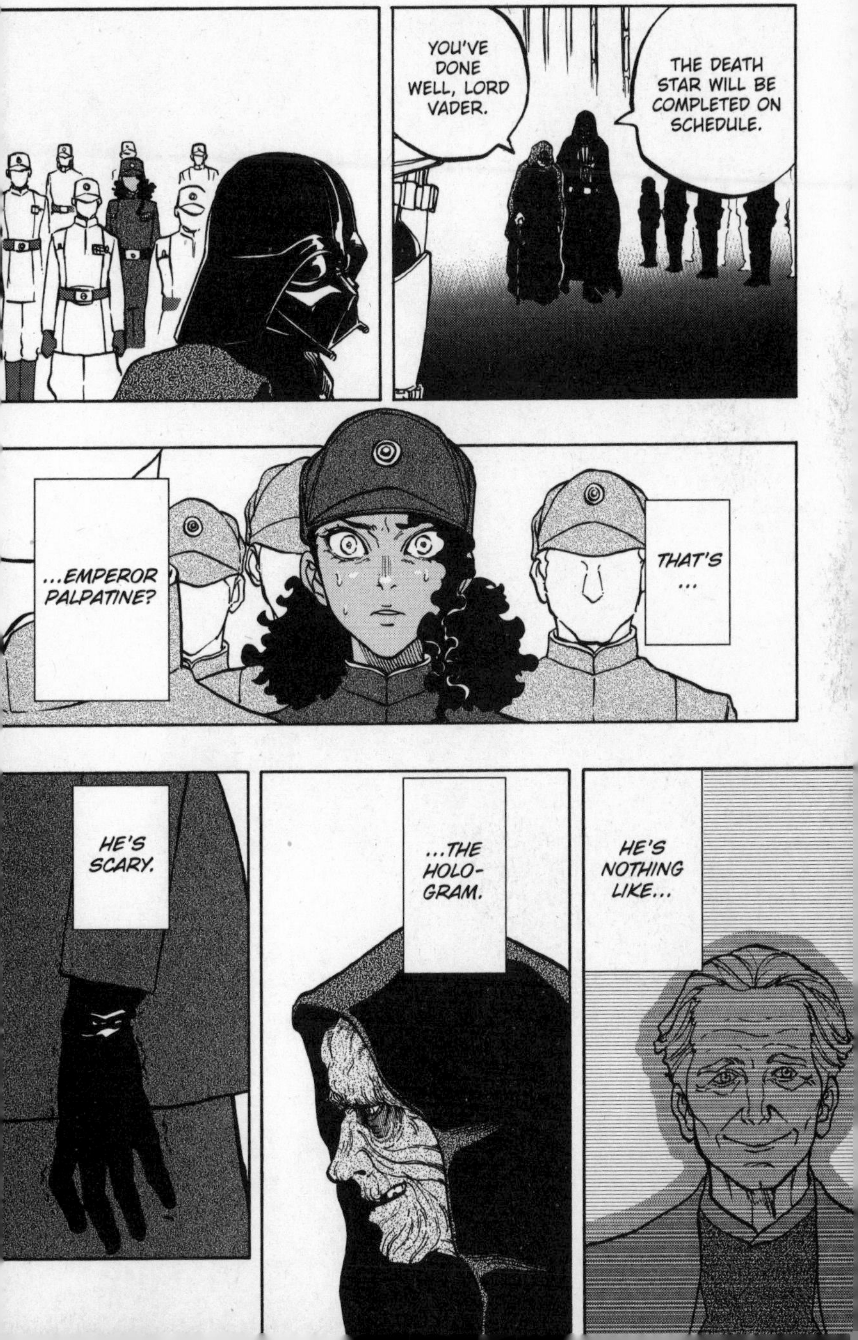
THE DEATH STAR WILL BE COMPLETED ON SCHEDULE.
YOU'VE DONE WELL, LORD VADER.
THAT'S...
...EMPEROR PALPATINE?
HE'S NOTHING LIKE...
...THE HOLO-GRAM.
HE'S SCARY.

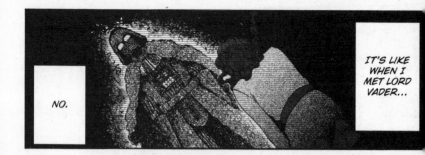

IT'S LIKE WHEN I MET LORD VADER...
NO.
THE EMPEROR IS SURROUNDED BY AN AURA...
...ALMOST UNIMAGINABLY DARK.
MALI-CIOUS...
...AND THREAT-ENING.

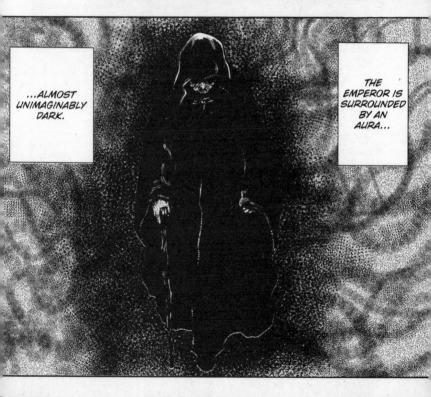

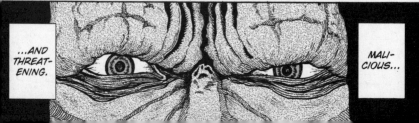

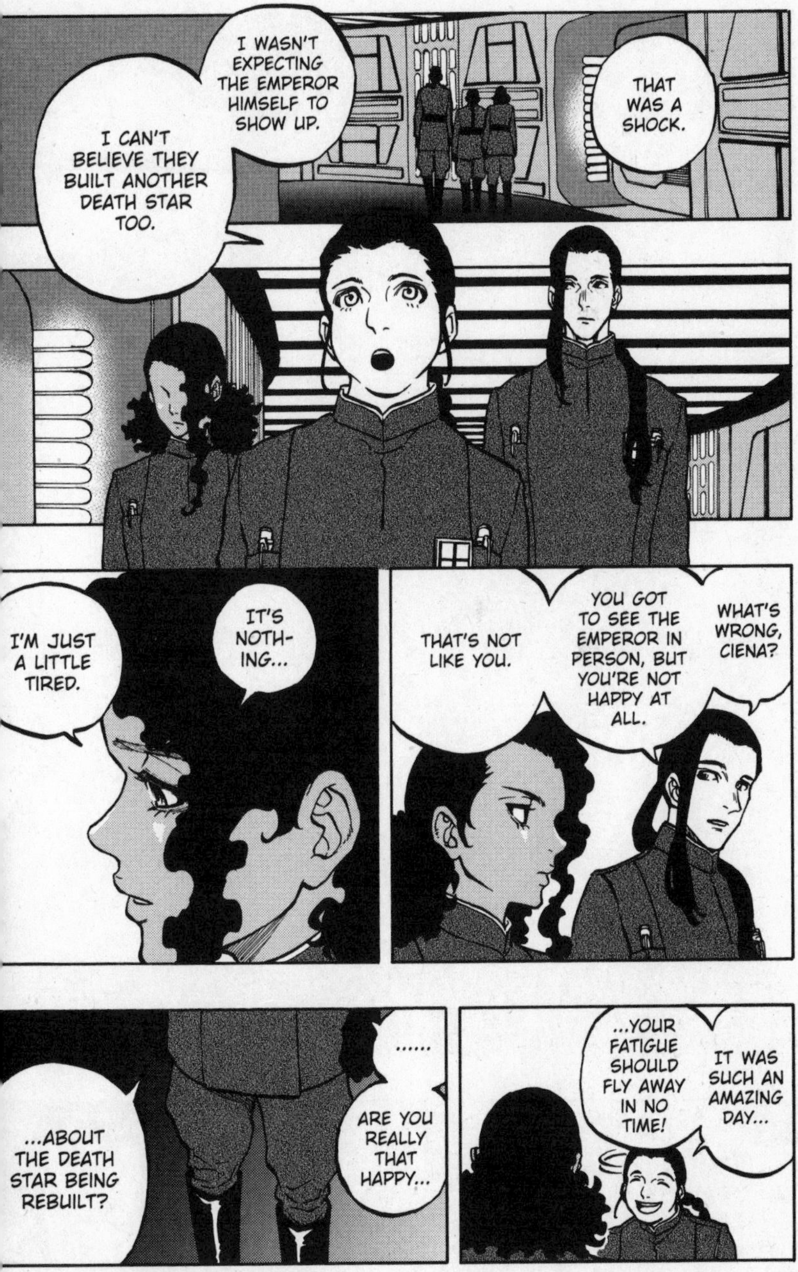
THAT WAS A SHOCK.
I WASN'T EXPECTING THE EMPEROR HIMSELF TO SHOW UP.
I CAN'T BELIEVE THEY BUILT ANOTHER DEATH STAR TOO.
WHAT'S WRONG, CIENA?
YOU GOT TO SEE THE EMPEROR IN PERSON, BUT YOU'RE NOT HAPPY AT ALL.
THAT'S NOT LIKE YOU.
IT'S NOTH-ING...
I'M JUST A LITTLE TIRED.
IT WAS SUCH AN AMAZING DAY...
...YOUR FATIGUE SHOULD FLY AWAY IN NO TIME!
......
ARE YOU REALLY THAT HAPPY...
...ABOUT THE DEATH STAR BEING REBUILT?

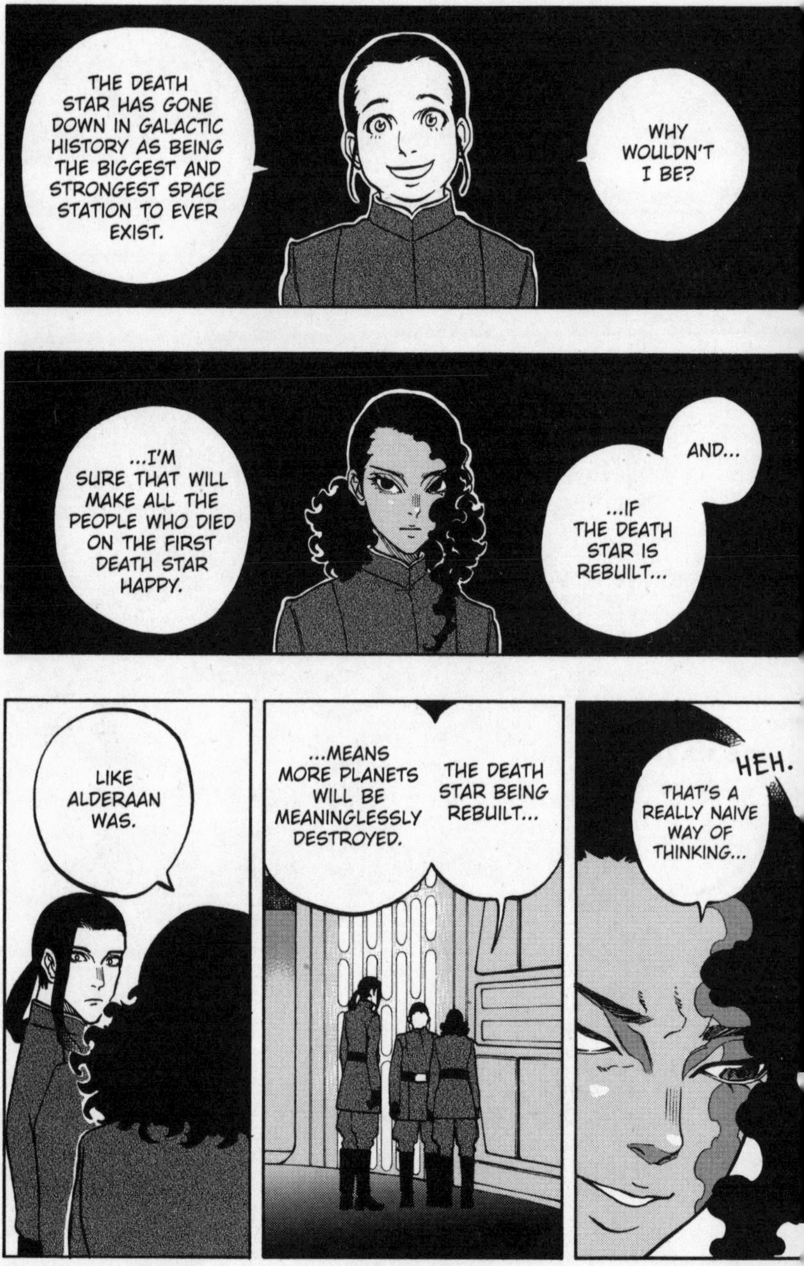
WHY WOULDN'T I BE?
THE DEATH STAR HAS GONE DOWN IN GALACTIC HISTORY AS BEING THE BIGGEST AND STRONGEST SPACE STATION TO EVER EXIST.
AND...
...IF THE DEATH STAR IS REBUILT...
...I'M SURE THAT WILL MAKE ALL THE PEOPLE WHO DIED ON THE FIRST DEATH STAR HAPPY.
HEH.
THAT'S A REALLY NAIVE WAY OF THINKING...
THE DEATH STAR BEING REBUILT...
...MEANS MORE PLANETS WILL BE MEANINGLESSLY DESTROYED.
LIKE ALDERAAN WAS.

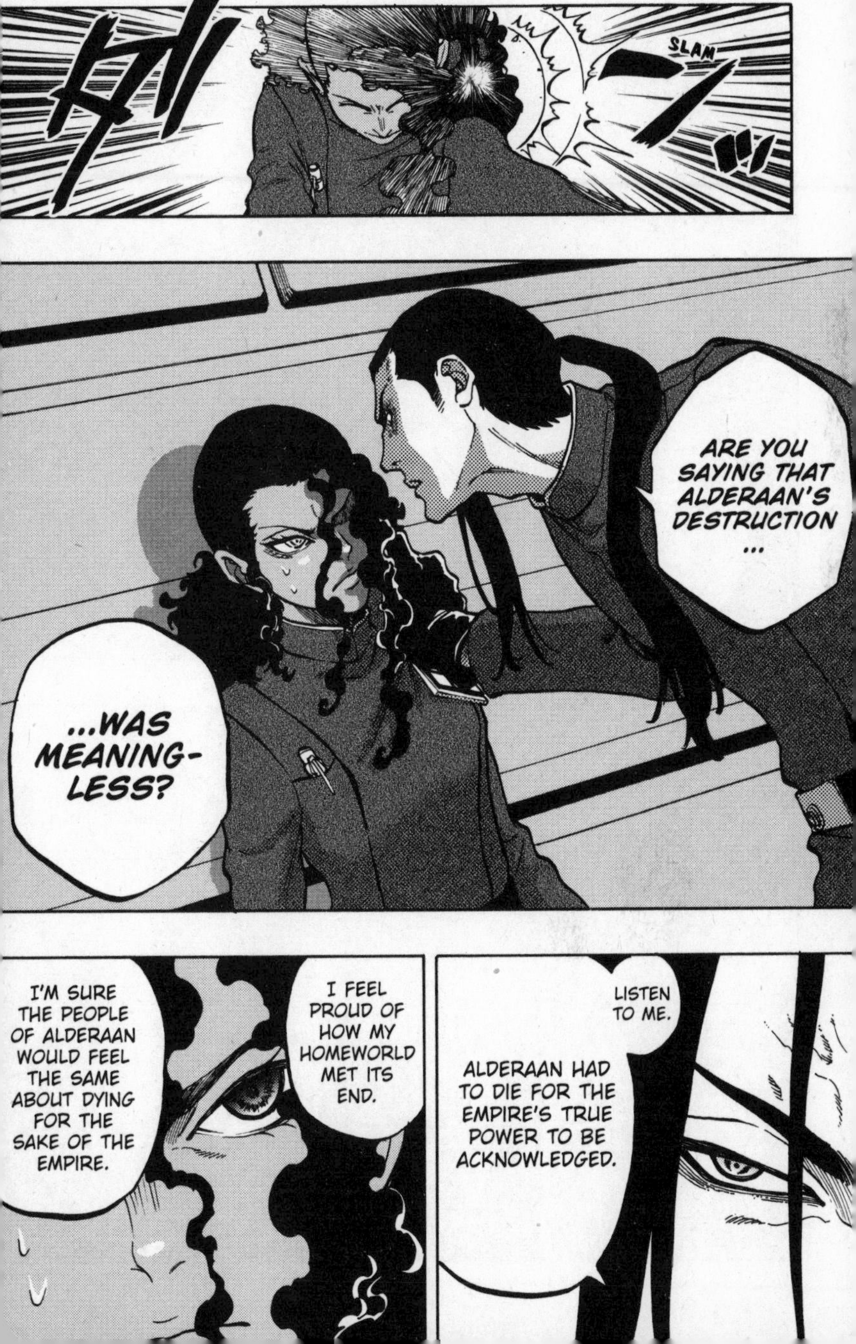
SLAM
ARE YOU SAYING THAT ALDERAAN'S DESTRUCTION ...
...WAS MEANING-LESS?
LISTEN TO ME.
ALDERAAN HAD TO DIE FOR THE EMPIRE'S TRUE POWER TO BE ACKNOWLEDGED.
I FEEL PROUD OF HOW MY HOMEWORLD MET ITS END.
I'M SURE THE PEOPLE OF ALDERAAN WOULD FEEL THE SAME ABOUT DYING FOR THE SAKE OF THE EMPIRE.

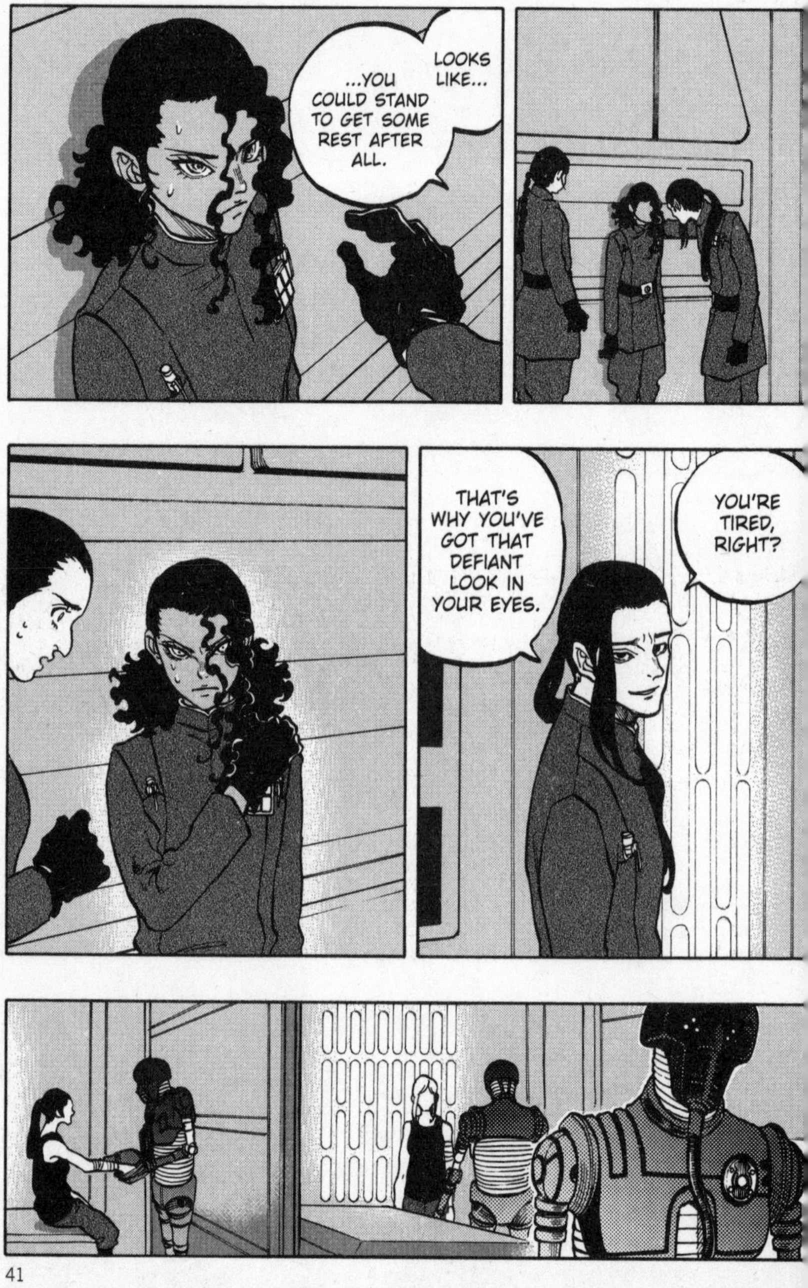
LOOKS LIKE... ...YOU COULD STAND TO GET SOME REST AFTER ALL.
YOU'RE TIRED, RIGHT?
THAT'S WHY YOU'VE GOT THAT DEFIANT LOOK IN YOUR EYES.

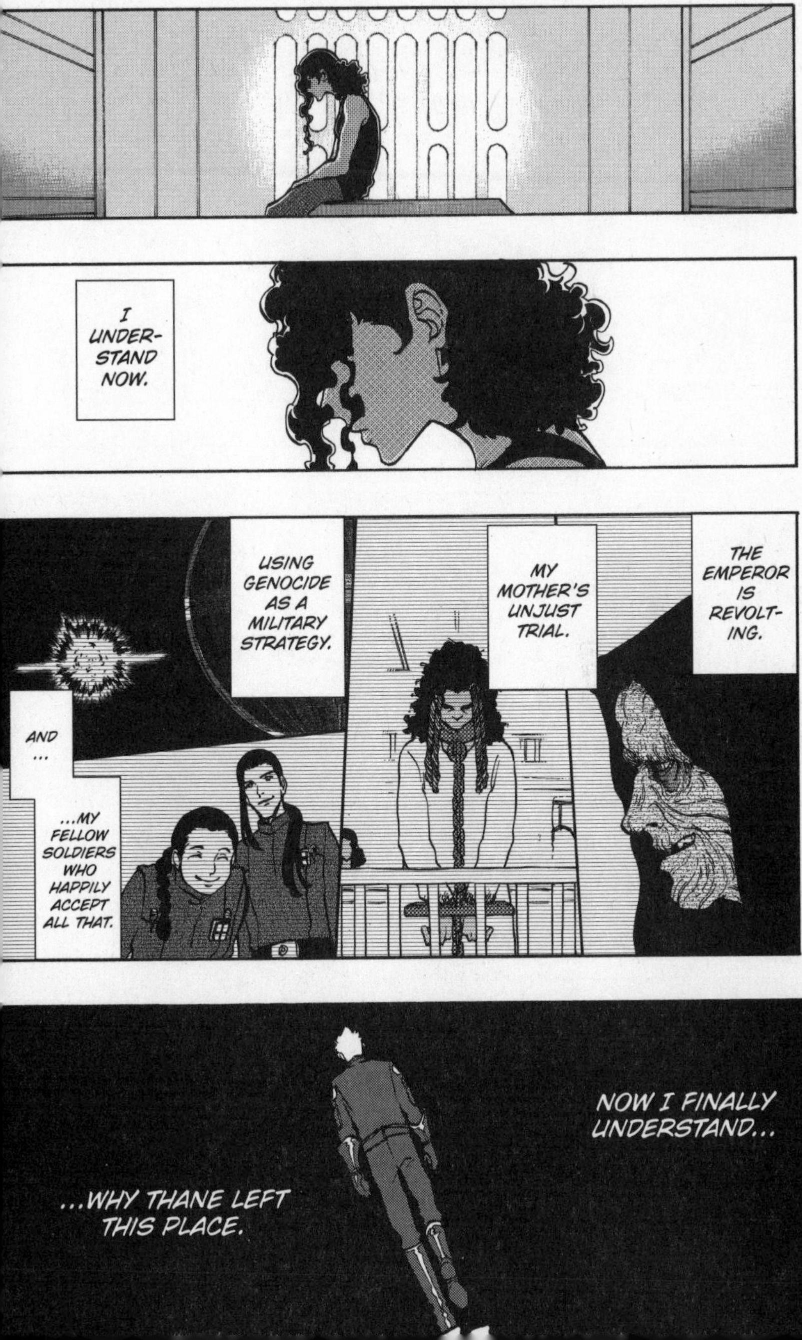
I UNDER-STAND NOW.
THE EMPEROR IS REVOLT-ING.
MY MOTHER'S UNJUST TRIAL.
USING GENOCIDE AS A MILITARY STRATEGY.
AND ...
...MY FELLOW SOLDIERS WHO HAPPILY ACCEPT ALL THAT.
NOW I FINALLY UNDERSTAND...
...WHY THANE LEFT THIS PLACE.

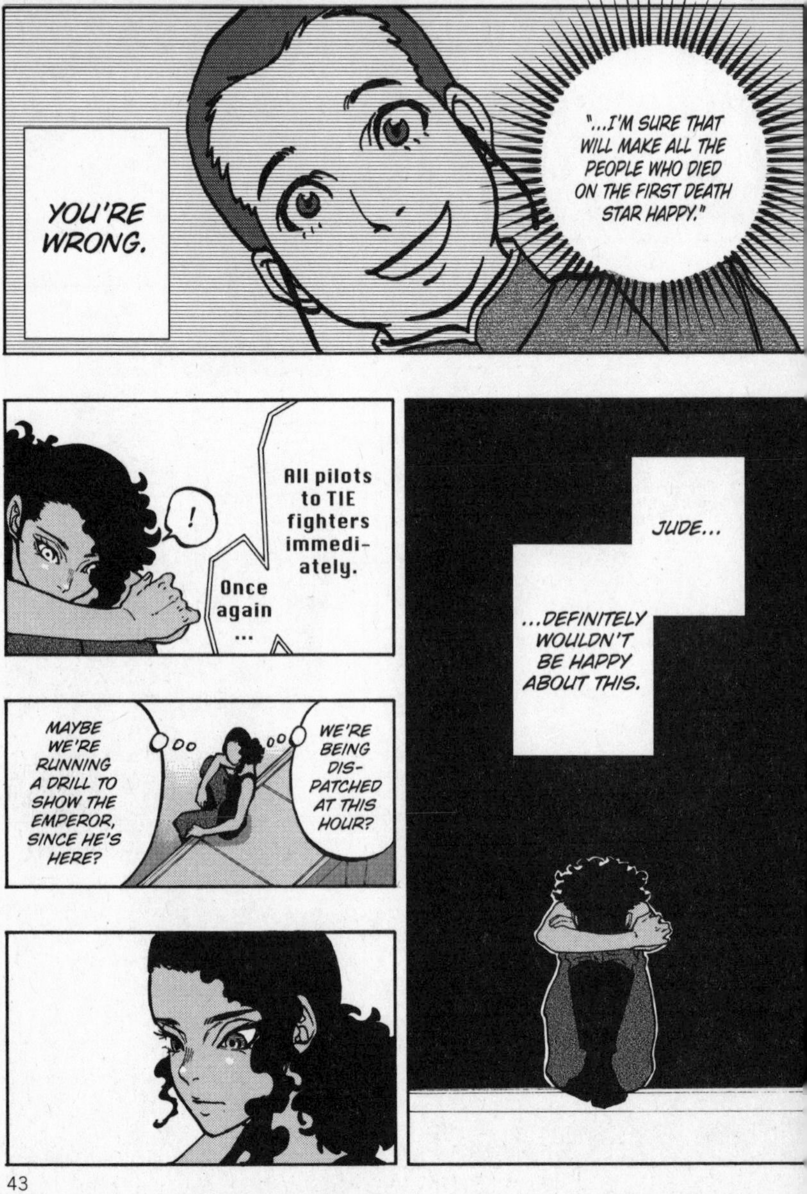
"...I'M SURE THAT WILL MAKE ALL THE PEOPLE WHO DIED ON THE FIRST DEATH STAR HAPPY."
YOU'RE WRONG.
JUDE...
...DEFINITELY WOULDN'T BE HAPPY ABOUT THIS.
All pilots to TIE fighters immediately.
Once again ...
!
WE'RE BEING DIS-PATCHED AT THIS HOUR?
MAYBE WE'RE RUNNING A DRILL TO SHOW THE EMPEROR, SINCE HE'S HERE?

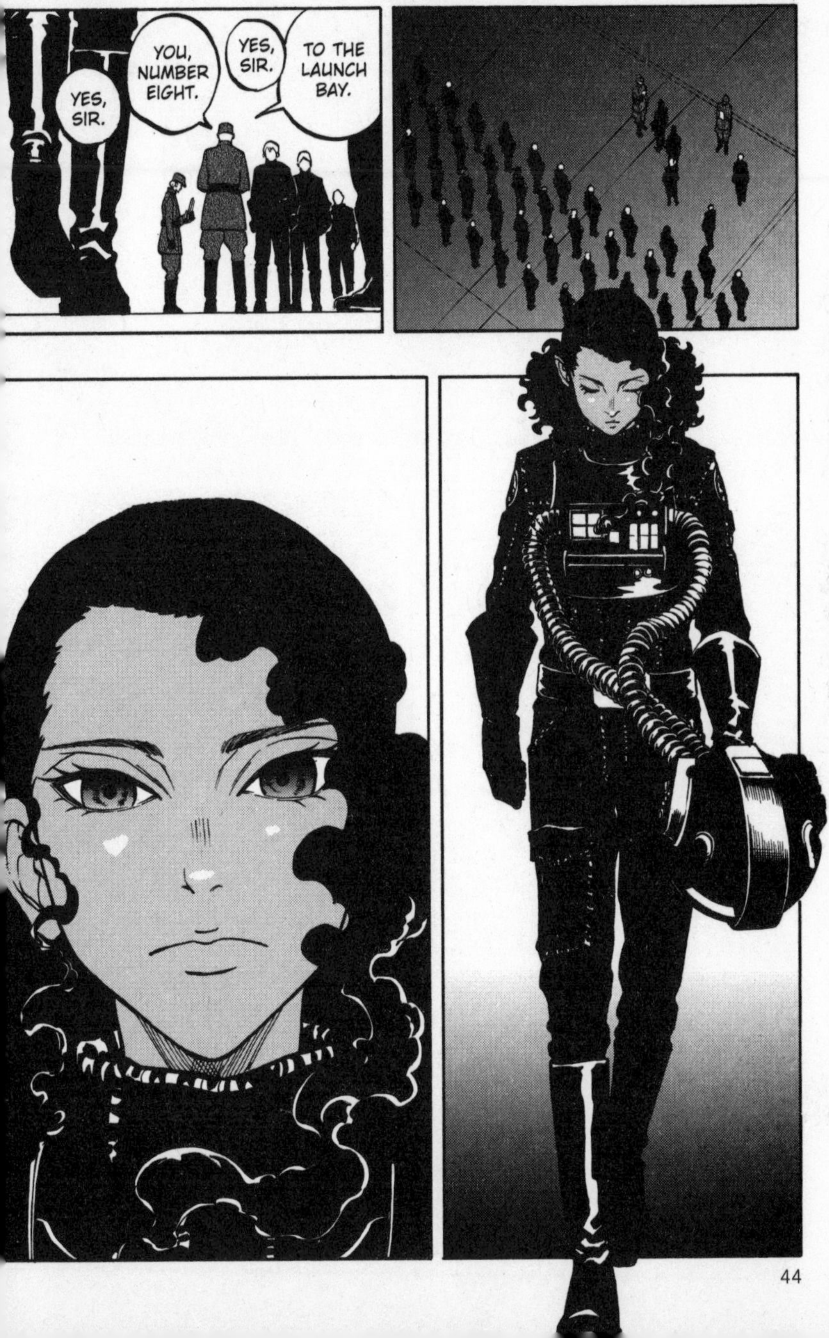
TO THE LAUNCH BAY.
YES, SIR.
YOU, NUMBER EIGHT.
YES, SIR.

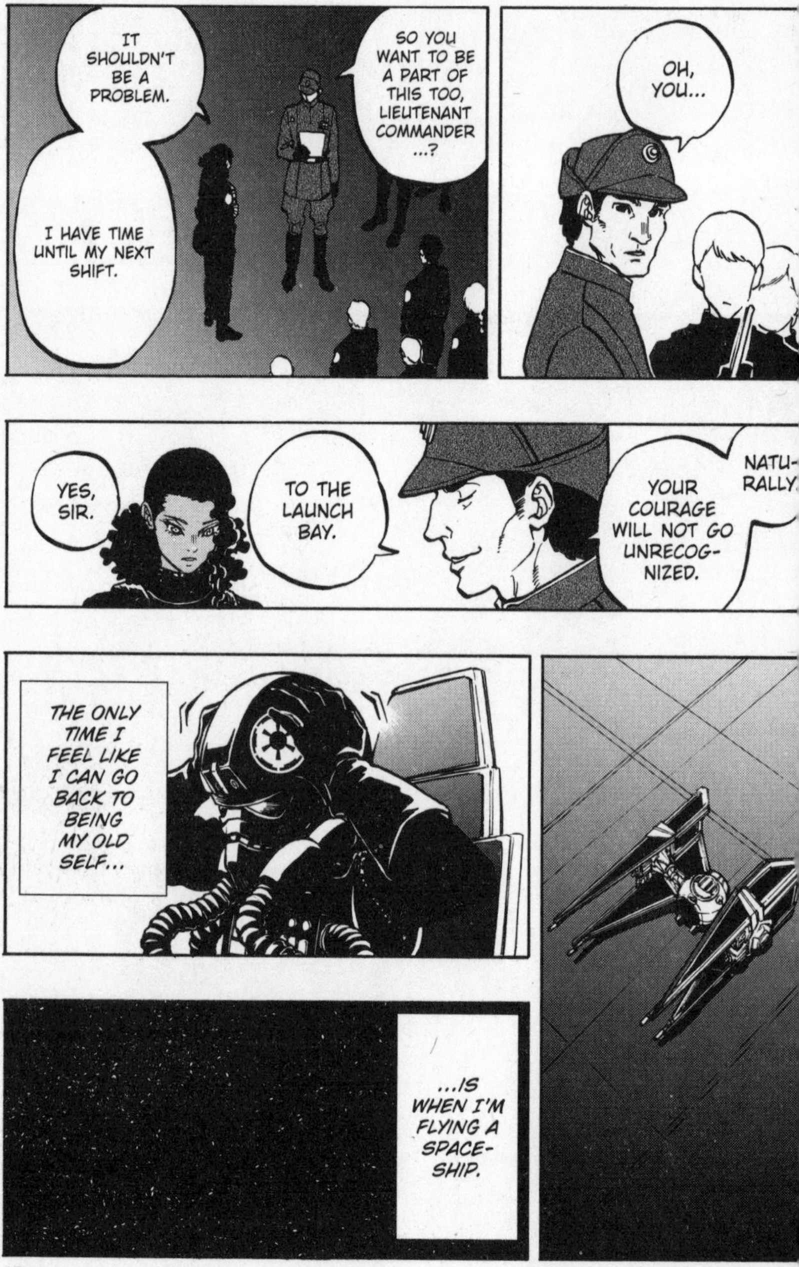
OH, YOU...
SO YOU WANT TO BE A PART OF THIS TOO, LIEUTENANT COMMANDER ...?
IT SHOULDN'T BE A PROBLEM.
I HAVE TIME UNTIL MY NEXT SHIFT.
NATU-RALLY.
YOUR COURAGE WILL NOT GO UNRECOG-NIZED.
TO THE LAUNCH BAY.
YES, SIR.
THE ONLY TIME I FEEL LIKE I CAN GO BACK TO BEING MY OLD SELF...
...IS WHEN I'M FLYING A SPACE-SHIP.

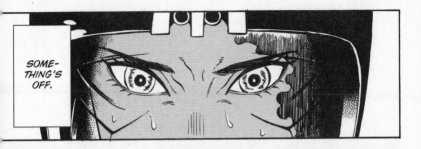

SOME-
THING'S
OFF.

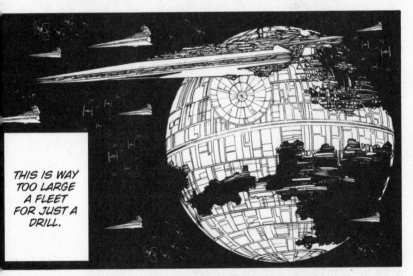

THIS IS WAY
TOO LARGE
A FLEET
FOR JUST A
DRILL.

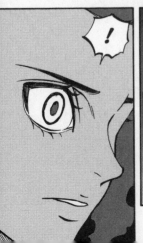

!

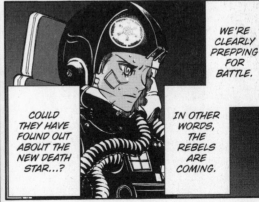

WE'RE
CLEARLY
PREPPING
FOR
BATTLE.

IN OTHER
WORDS,
THE
REBELS
ARE
COMING.

COULD
THEY HAVE
FOUND OUT
ABOUT THE
NEW DEATH
STAR...?

46

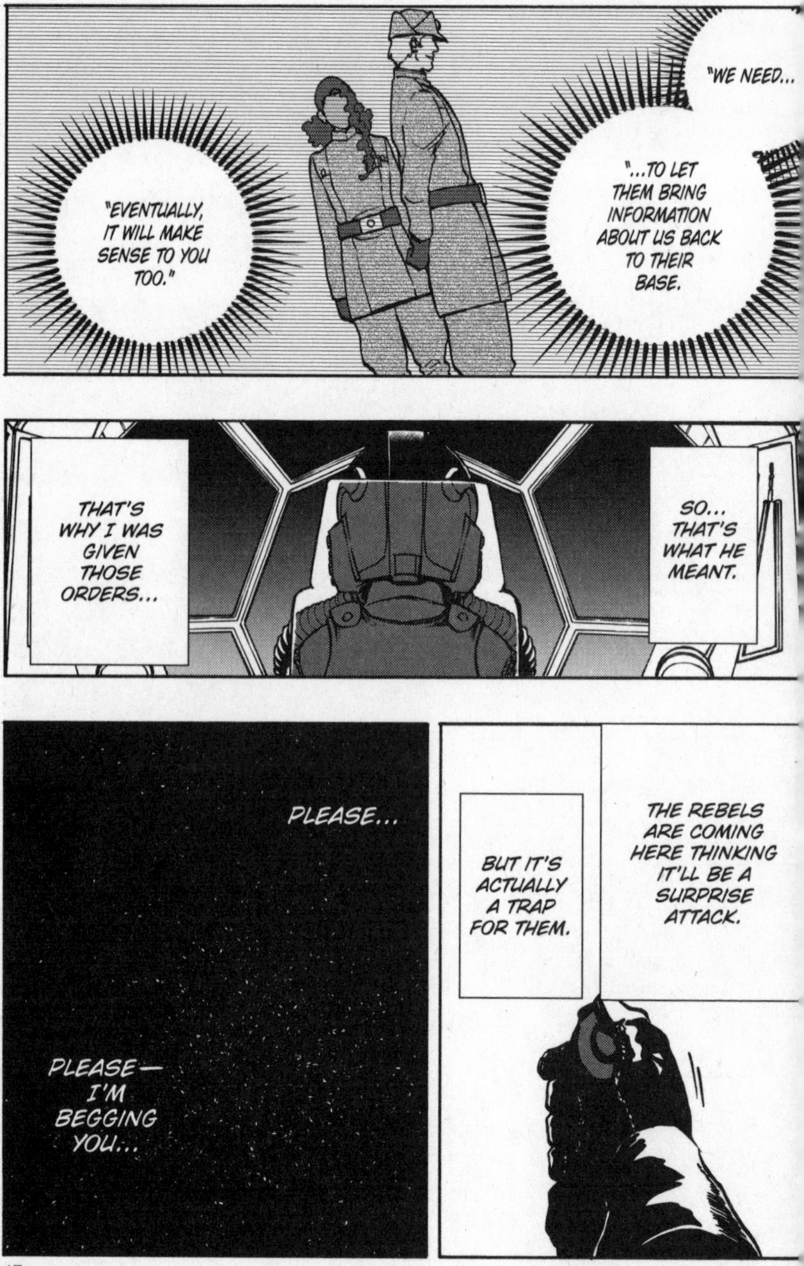
"WE NEED...
"...TO LET THEM BRING INFORMATION ABOUT US BACK TO THEIR BASE.
"EVENTUALLY, IT WILL MAKE SENSE TO YOU TOO."
SO... THAT'S WHAT HE MEANT.
THAT'S WHY I WAS GIVEN THOSE ORDERS...
THE REBELS ARE COMING HERE THINKING IT'LL BE A SURPRISE ATTACK.
BUT IT'S ACTUALLY A TRAP FOR THEM.
PLEASE...
PLEASE— I'M BEGGING YOU...

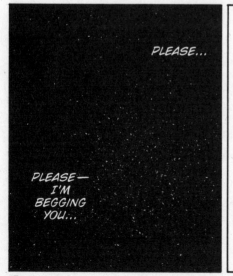

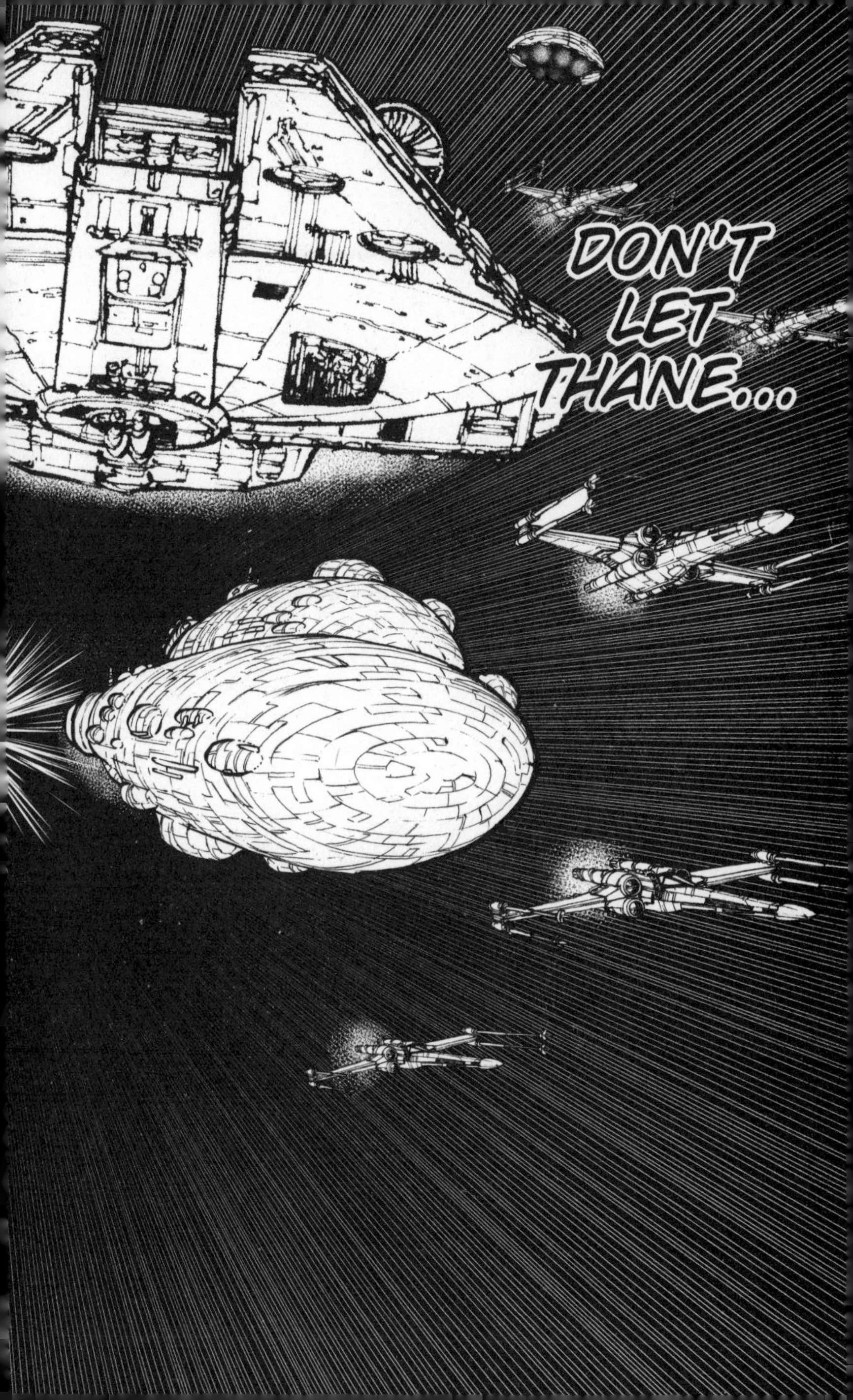
DON'T LET THANE...

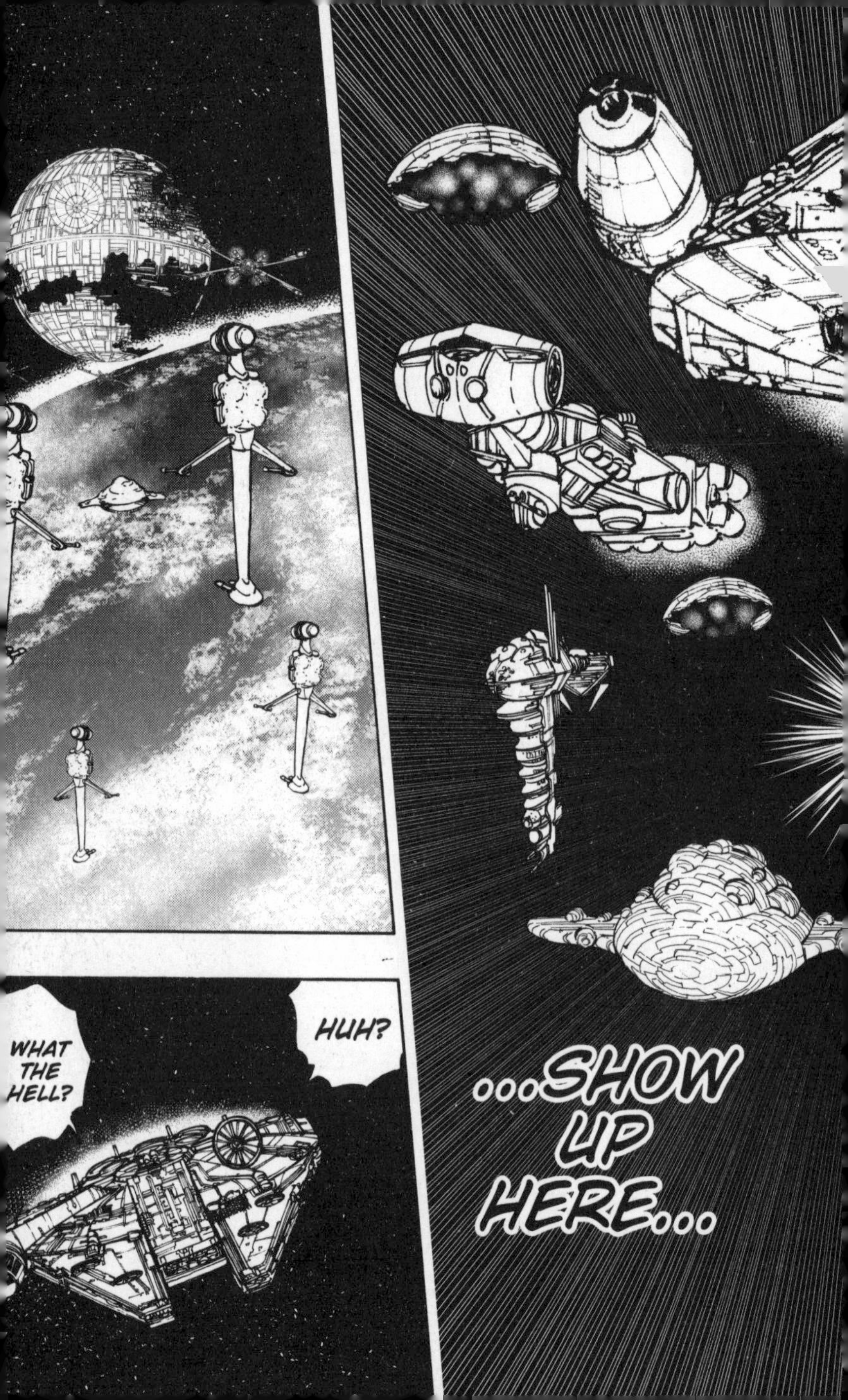
...SHOW UP HERE...
HUH?
WHAT THE HELL?

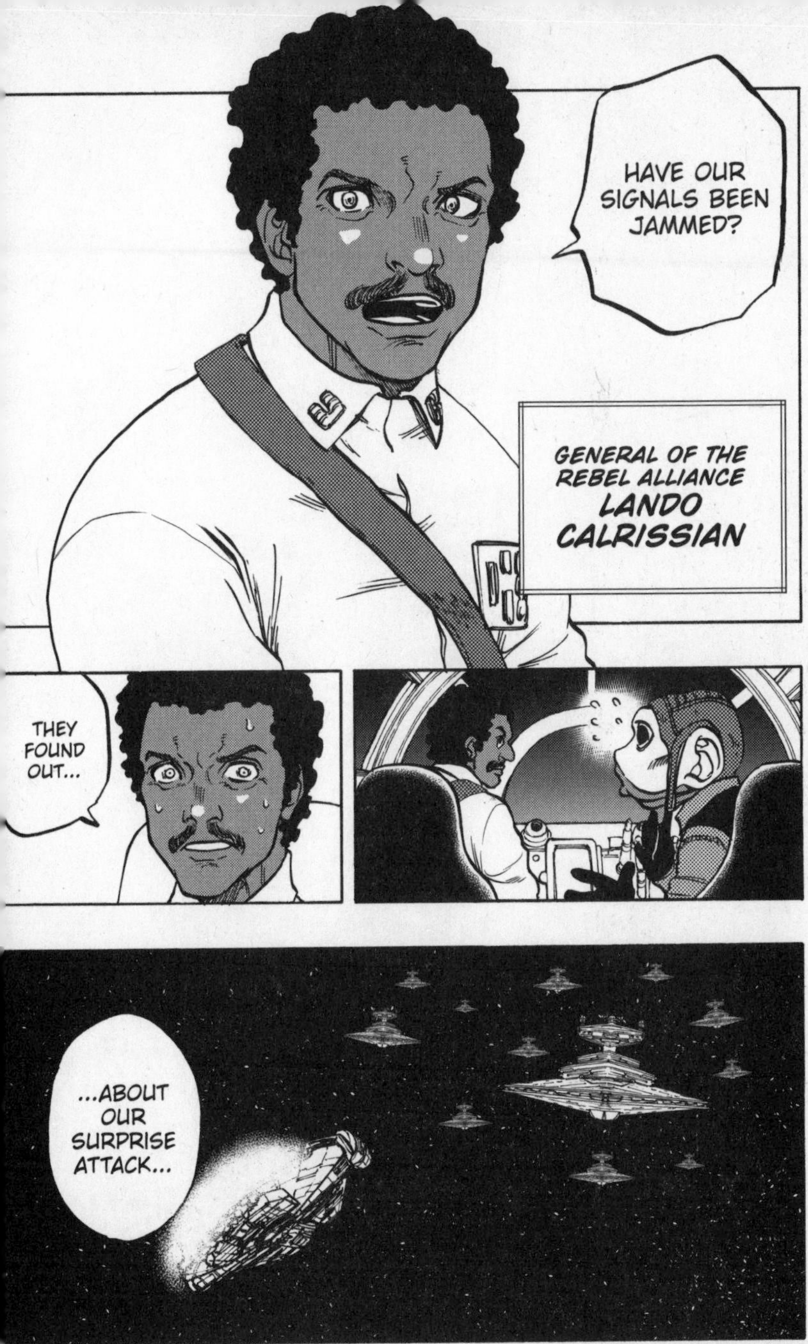
HAVE OUR SIGNALS BEEN JAMMED?
GENERAL OF THE REBEL ALLIANCE LANDO CALRISSIAN
THEY FOUND OUT...
...ABOUT OUR SURPRISE ATTACK...

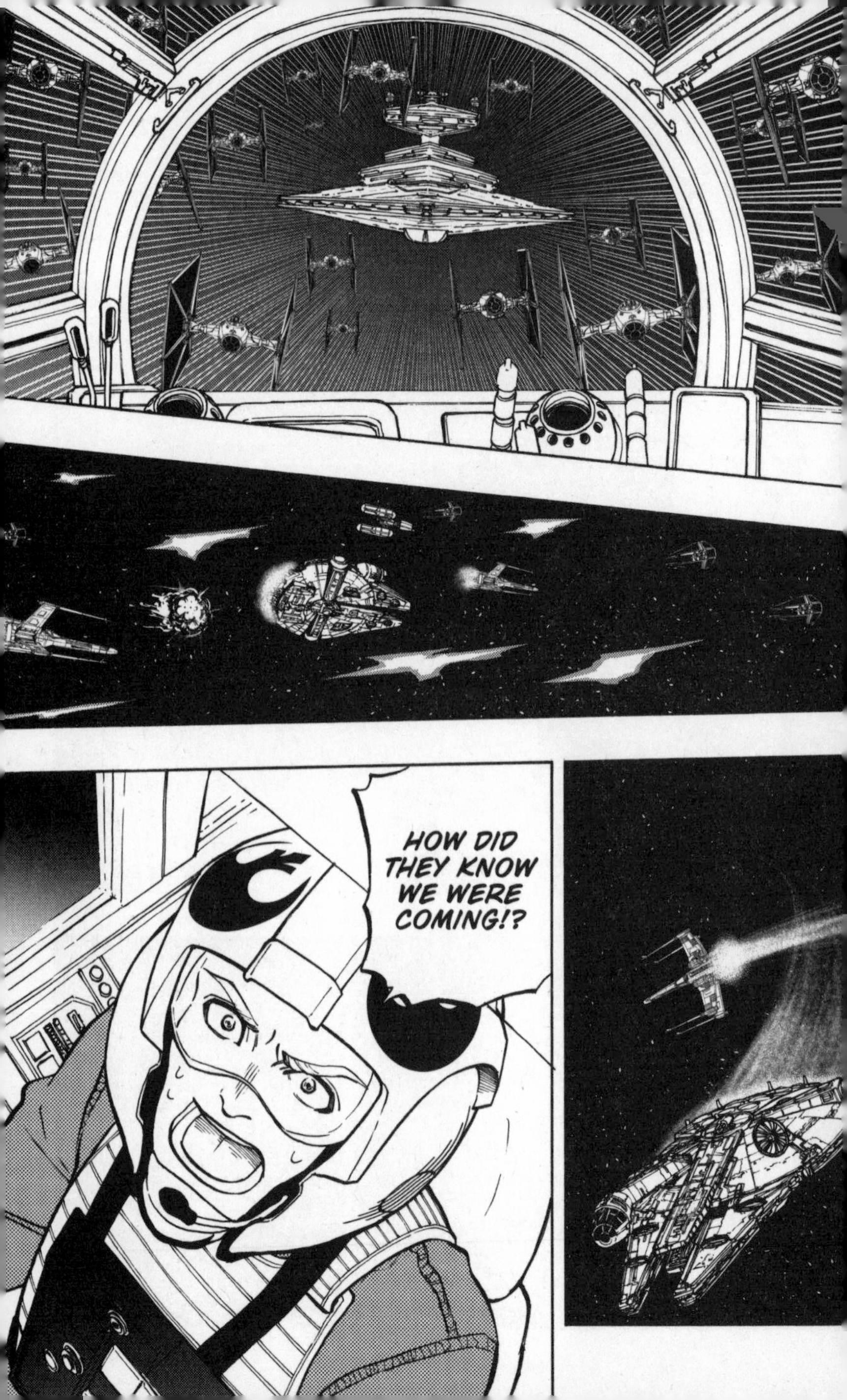
HOW DID THEY KNOW WE WERE COMING!?

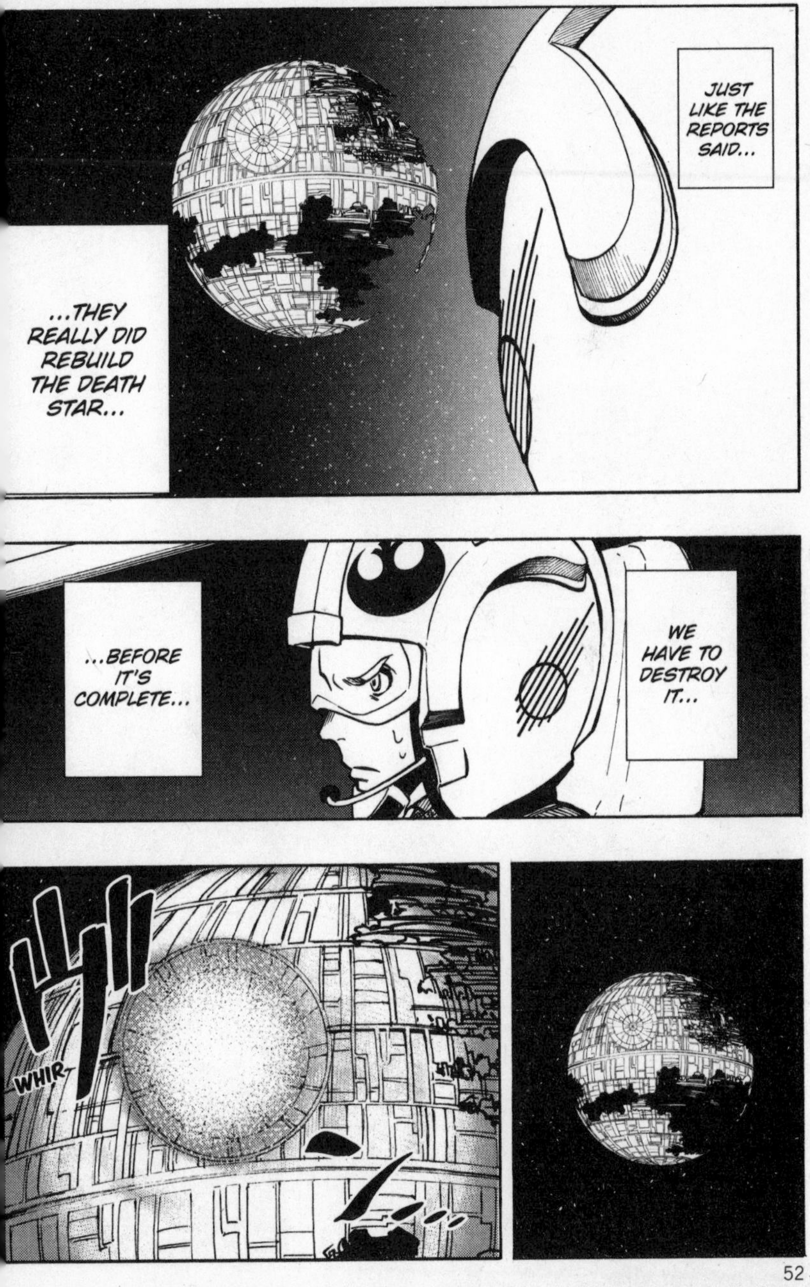
JUST LIKE THE REPORTS SAID...
...THEY REALLY DID REBUILD THE DEATH STAR...
WE HAVE TO DESTROY IT...
...BEFORE IT'S COMPLETE...
WHIR

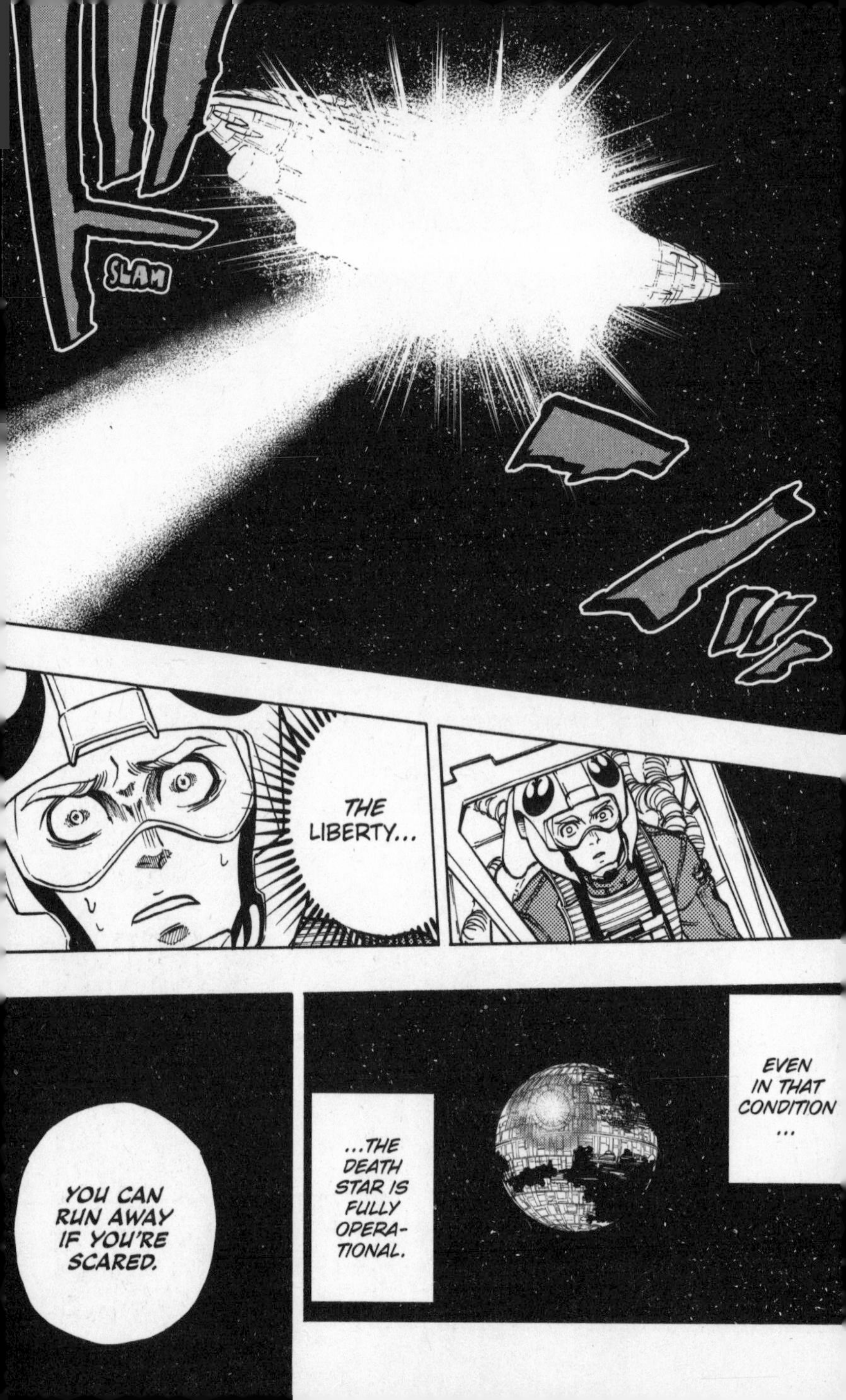
SLAM
THE LIBERTY...
EVEN IN THAT CONDITION ...
...THE DEATH STAR IS FULLY OPERA-TIONAL.
YOU CAN RUN AWAY IF YOU'RE SCARED.

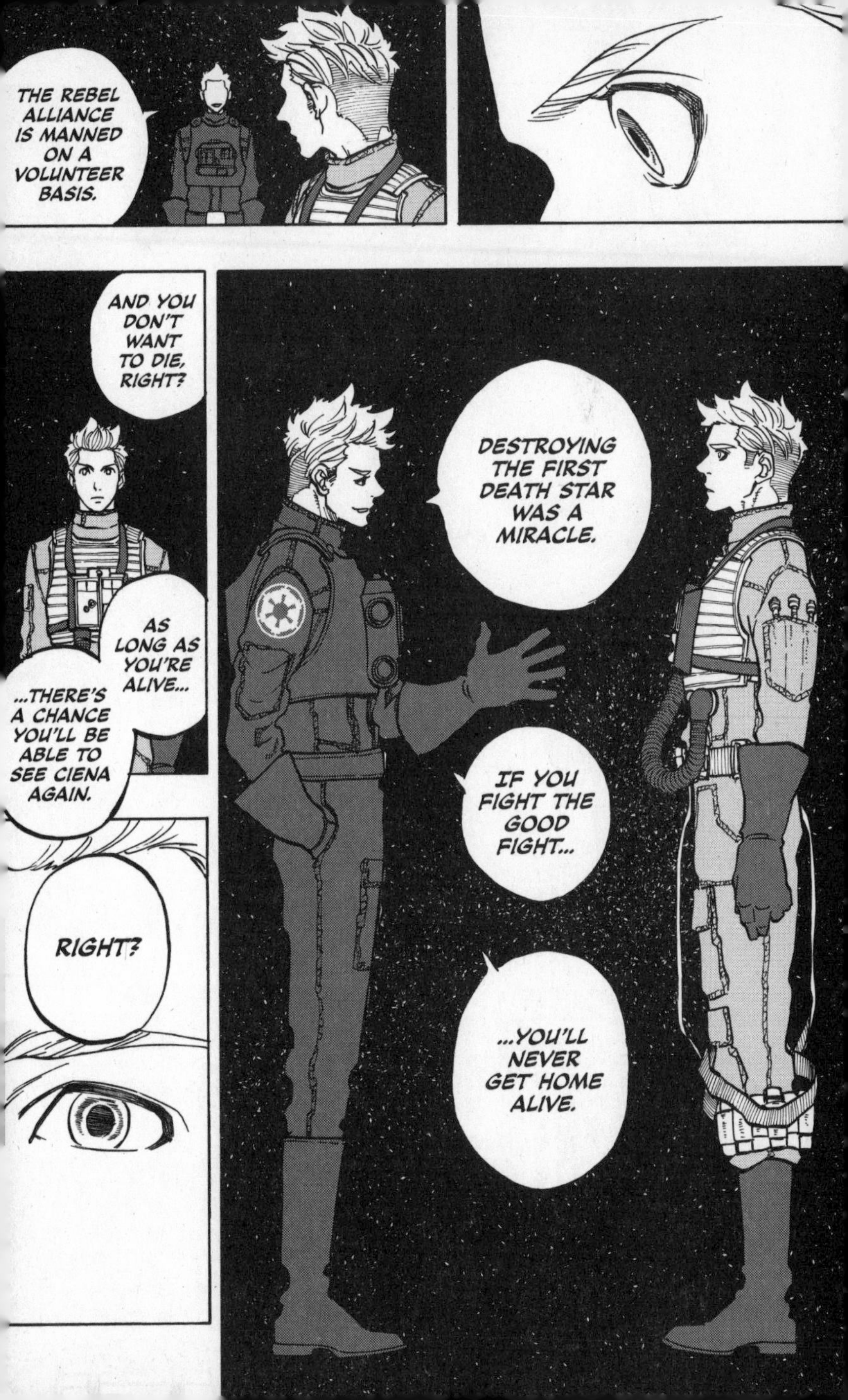
THE REBEL ALLIANCE IS MANNED ON A VOLUNTEER BASIS.
DESTROYING THE FIRST DEATH STAR WAS A MIRACLE.
IF YOU FIGHT THE GOOD FIGHT...
...YOU'LL NEVER GET HOME ALIVE.
AND YOU DON'T WANT TO DIE, RIGHT?
AS LONG AS YOU'RE ALIVE...
...THERE'S A CHANCE YOU'LL BE ABLE TO SEE CIENA AGAIN.
RIGHT?

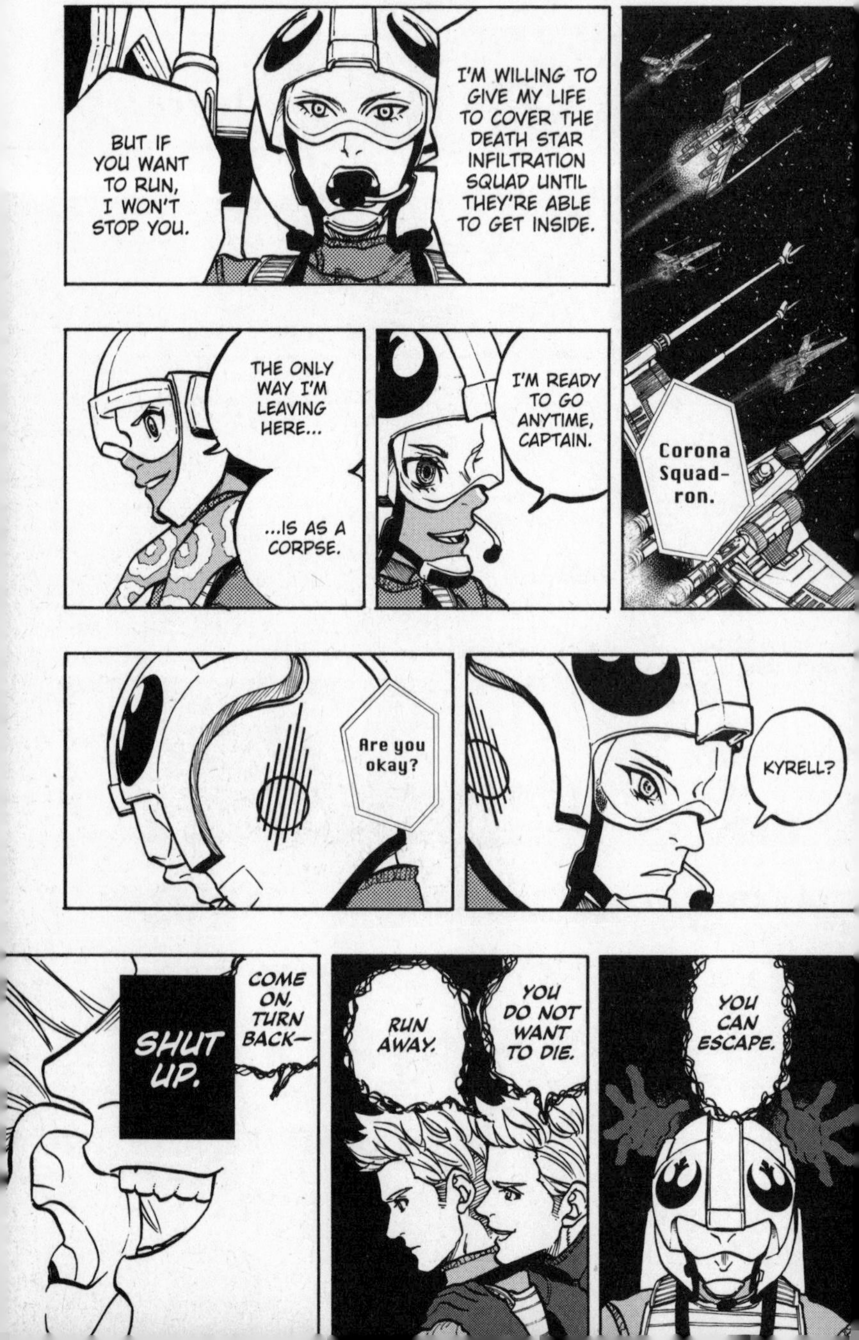
Corona Squadron.
I'M WILLING TO GIVE MY LIFE TO COVER THE DEATH STAR INFILTRATION SQUAD UNTIL THEY'RE ABLE TO GET INSIDE.
BUT IF YOU WANT TO RUN, I WON'T STOP YOU.
I'M READY TO GO ANYTIME, CAPTAIN.
THE ONLY WAY I'M LEAVING HERE...
...IS AS A CORPSE.
KYRELL?
Are you okay?
YOU CAN ESCAPE.
YOU DO NOT WANT TO DIE.
RUN AWAY.
COME ON, TURN BACK—
SHUT UP.

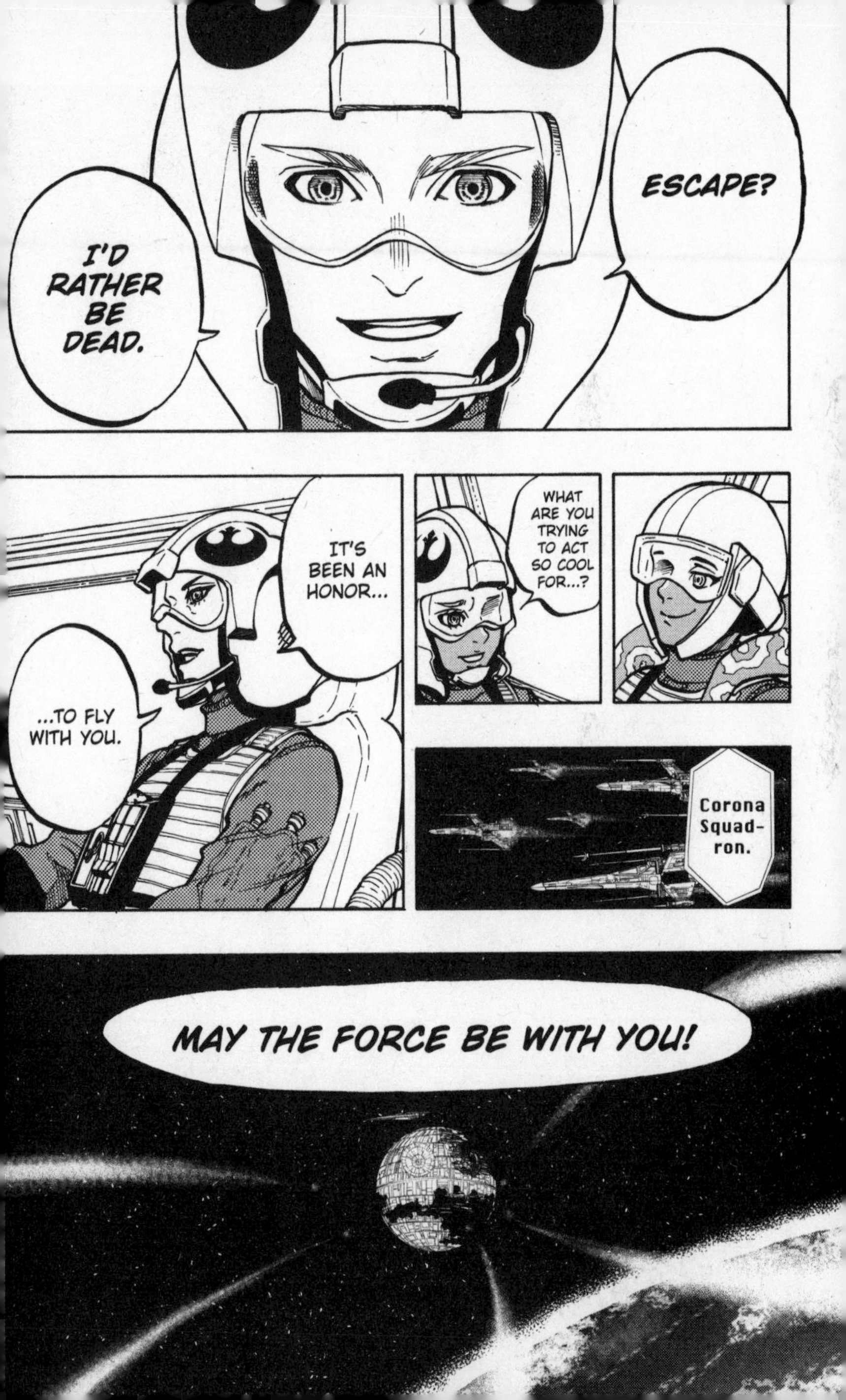
ESCAPE?
I'D RATHER BE DEAD.
WHAT ARE YOU TRYING TO ACT SO COOL FOR...?
Corona Squad-ron.
IT'S BEEN AN HONOR...
...TO FLY WITH YOU.
MAY THE FORCE BE WITH YOU!

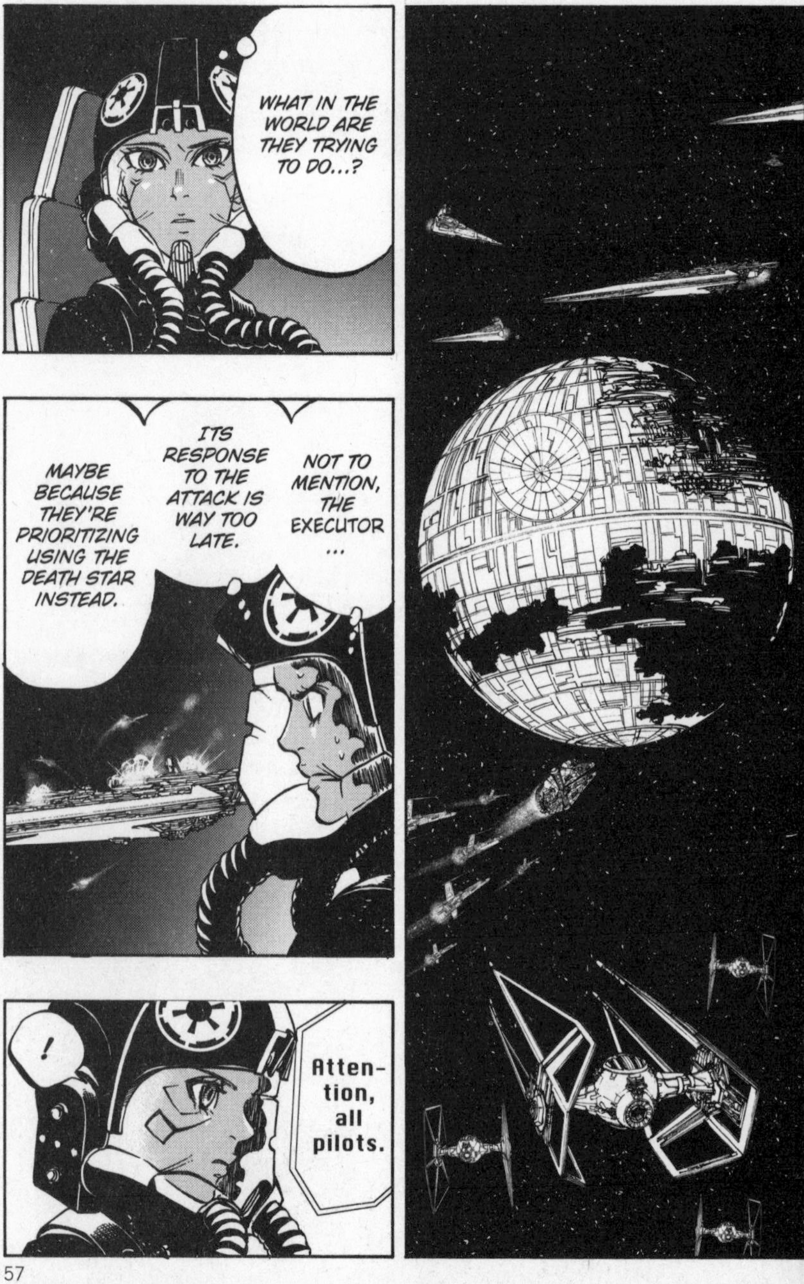
WHAT IN THE WORLD ARE THEY TRYING TO DO...?
NOT TO MENTION, THE EXECUTOR...
ITS RESPONSE TO THE ATTACK IS WAY TOO LATE.
MAYBE BECAUSE THEY'RE PRIORITIZING USING THE DEATH STAR INSTEAD.
Atten-tion, all pilots.
!

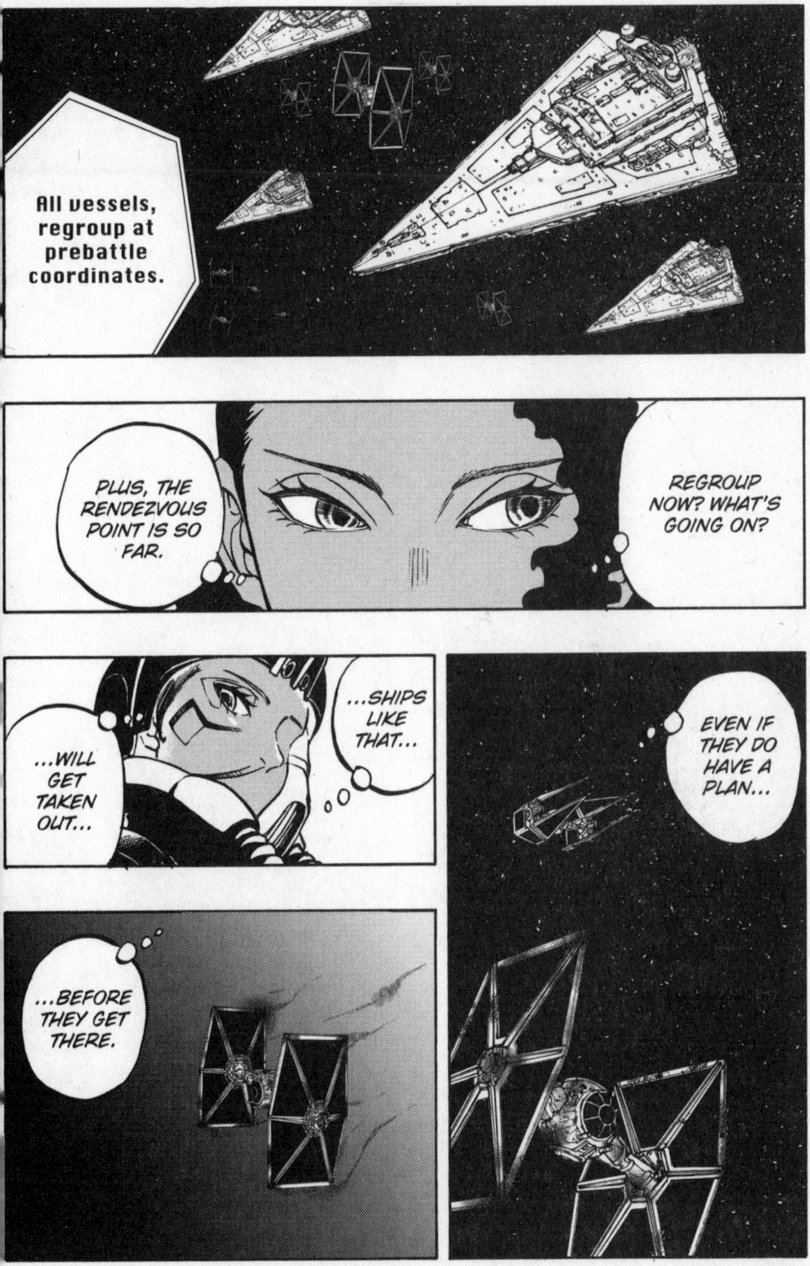
All vessels, regroup at prebattle coordinates.
REGROUP NOW? WHAT'S GOING ON?
PLUS, THE RENDEZVOUS POINT IS SO FAR.
EVEN IF THEY DO HAVE A PLAN...
...SHIPS LIKE THAT...
...WILL GET TAKEN OUT...
...BEFORE THEY GET THERE.

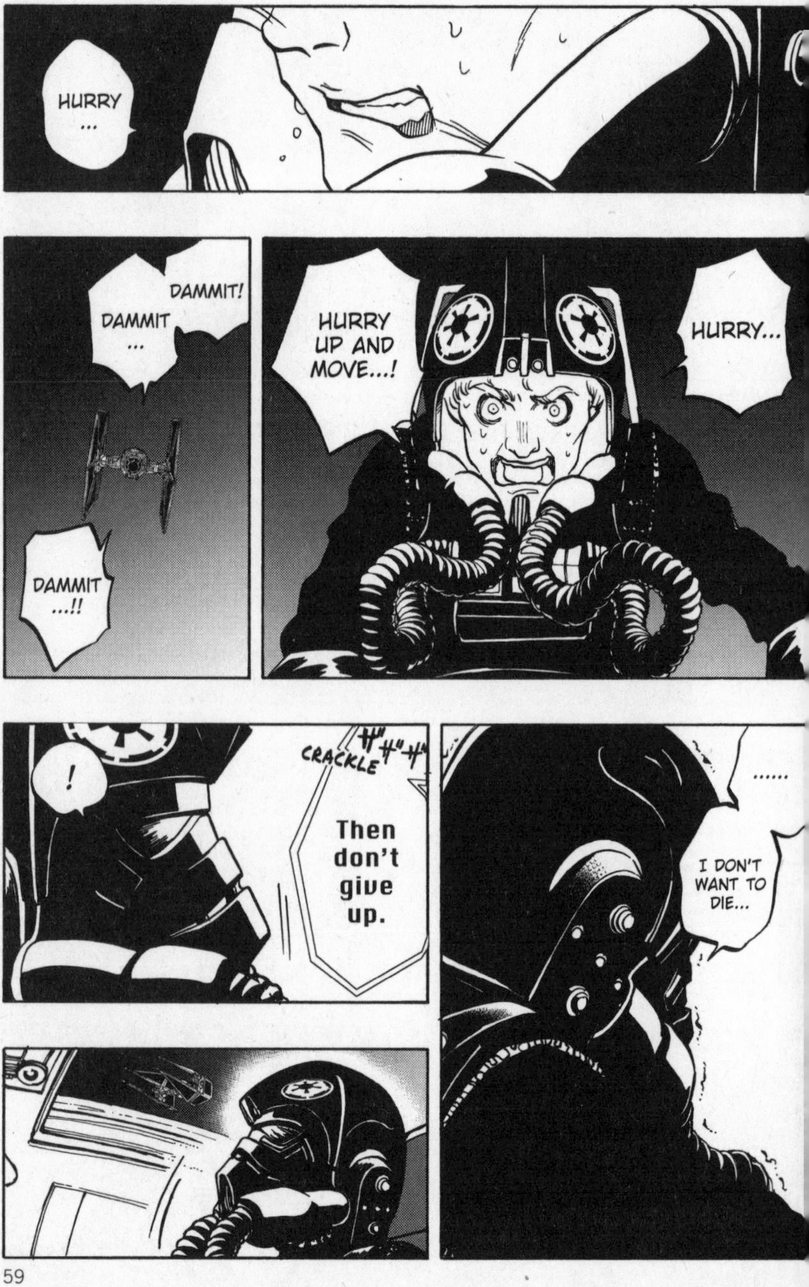
HURRY ...
HURRY...
HURRY UP AND MOVE...!
DAMMIT! DAMMIT ...
DAMMIT ...!!
......
I DON'T WANT TO DIE...
CRACKLE
Then don't give up.
!

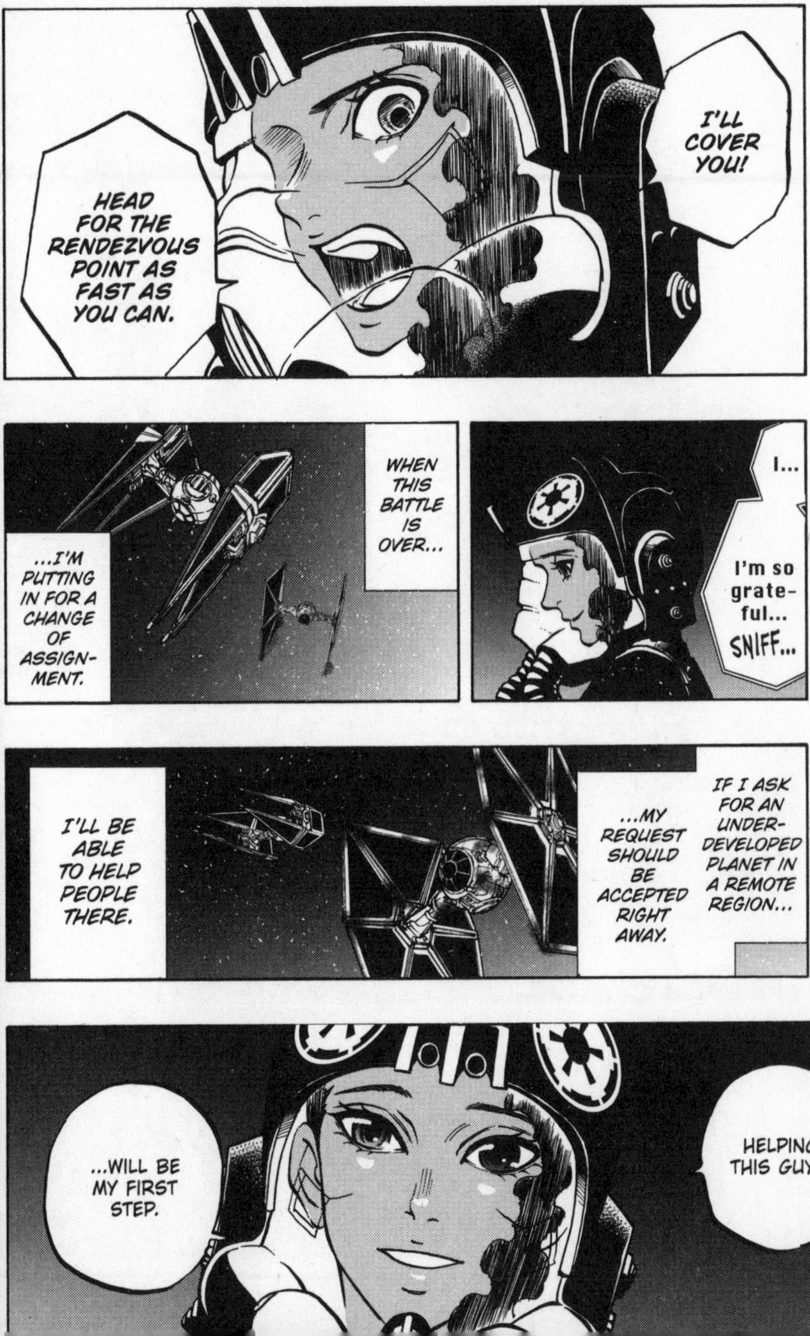
I'LL COVER YOU!
HEAD FOR THE RENDEZVOUS POINT AS FAST AS YOU CAN.
I...
I'm so grateful...
SNIFF...
WHEN THIS BATTLE IS OVER...
...I'M PUTTING IN FOR A CHANGE OF ASSIGNMENT.
IF I ASK FOR AN UNDERDEVELOPED PLANET IN A REMOTE REGION...
...MY REQUEST SHOULD BE ACCEPTED RIGHT AWAY.
I'LL BE ABLE TO HELP PEOPLE THERE.
HELPING THIS GUY...
...WILL BE MY FIRST STEP.

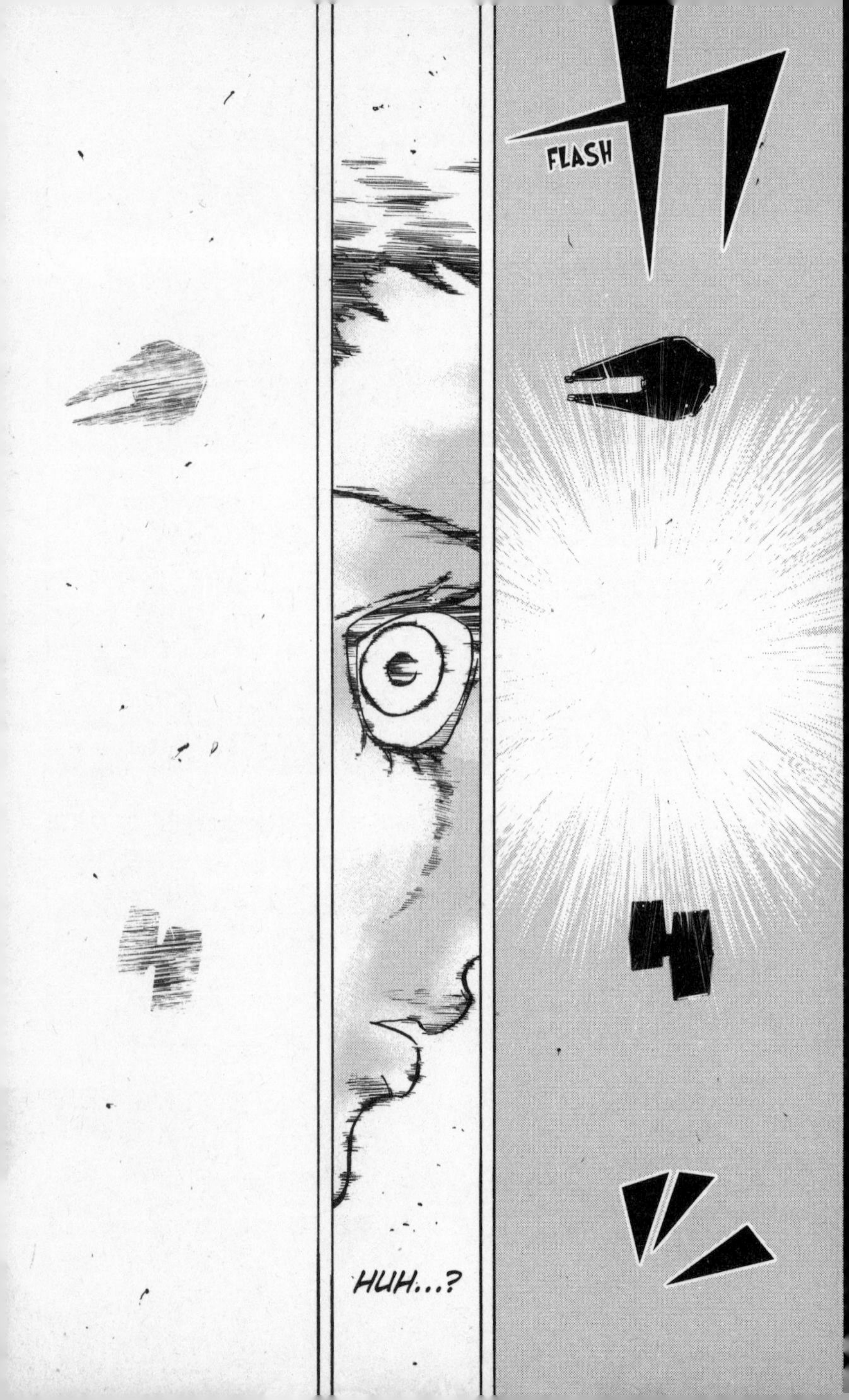
FLASH
HUH...?

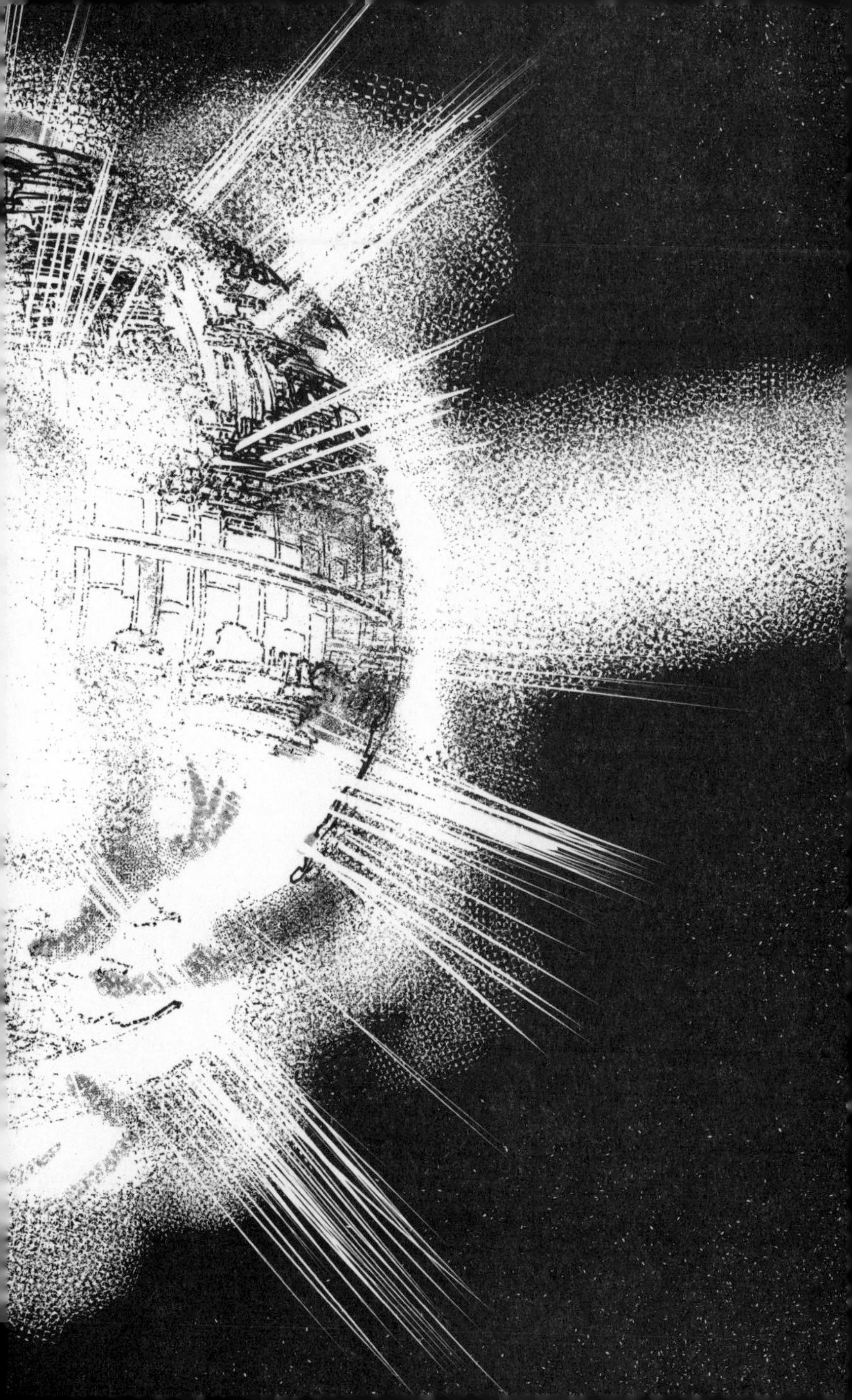

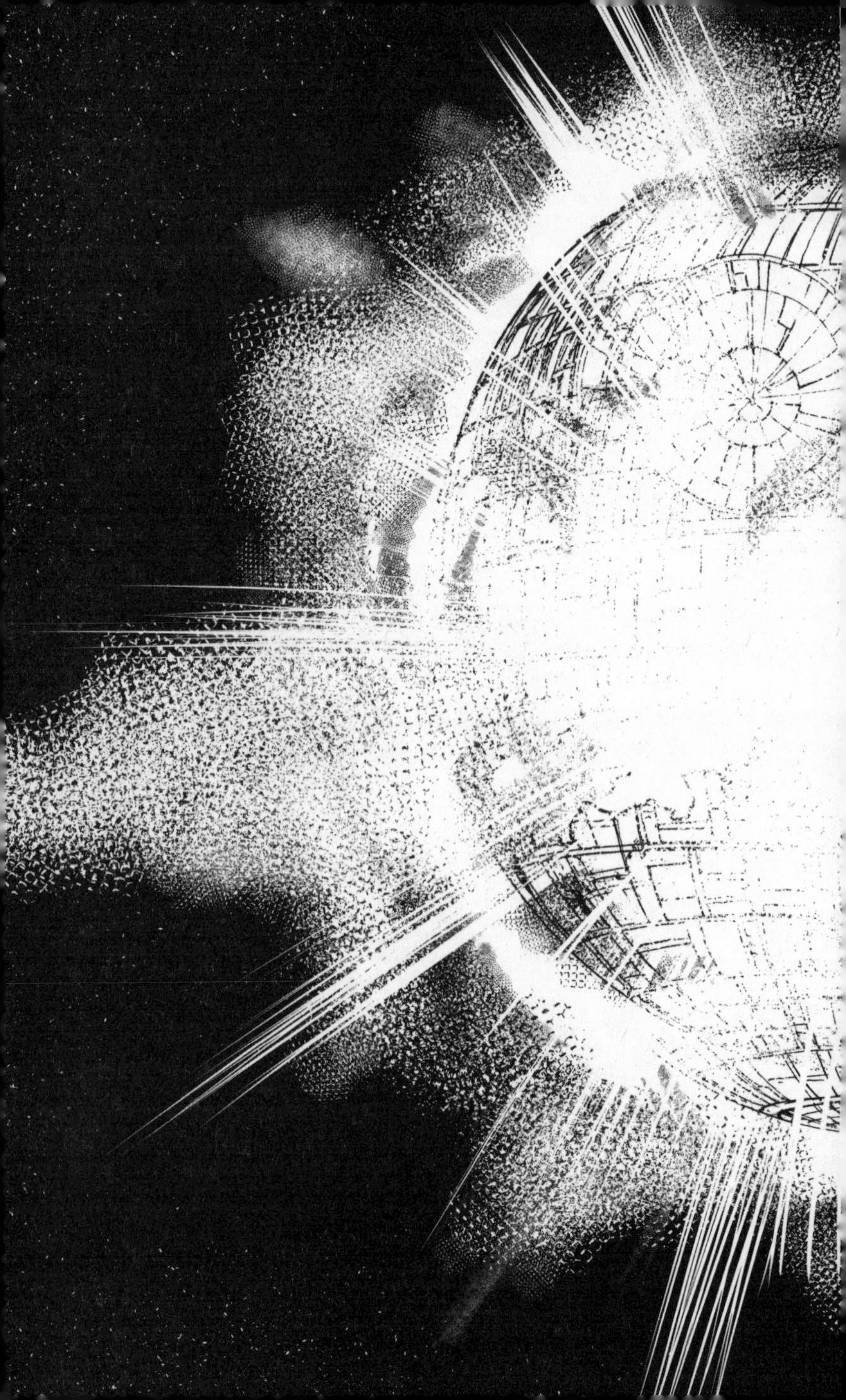

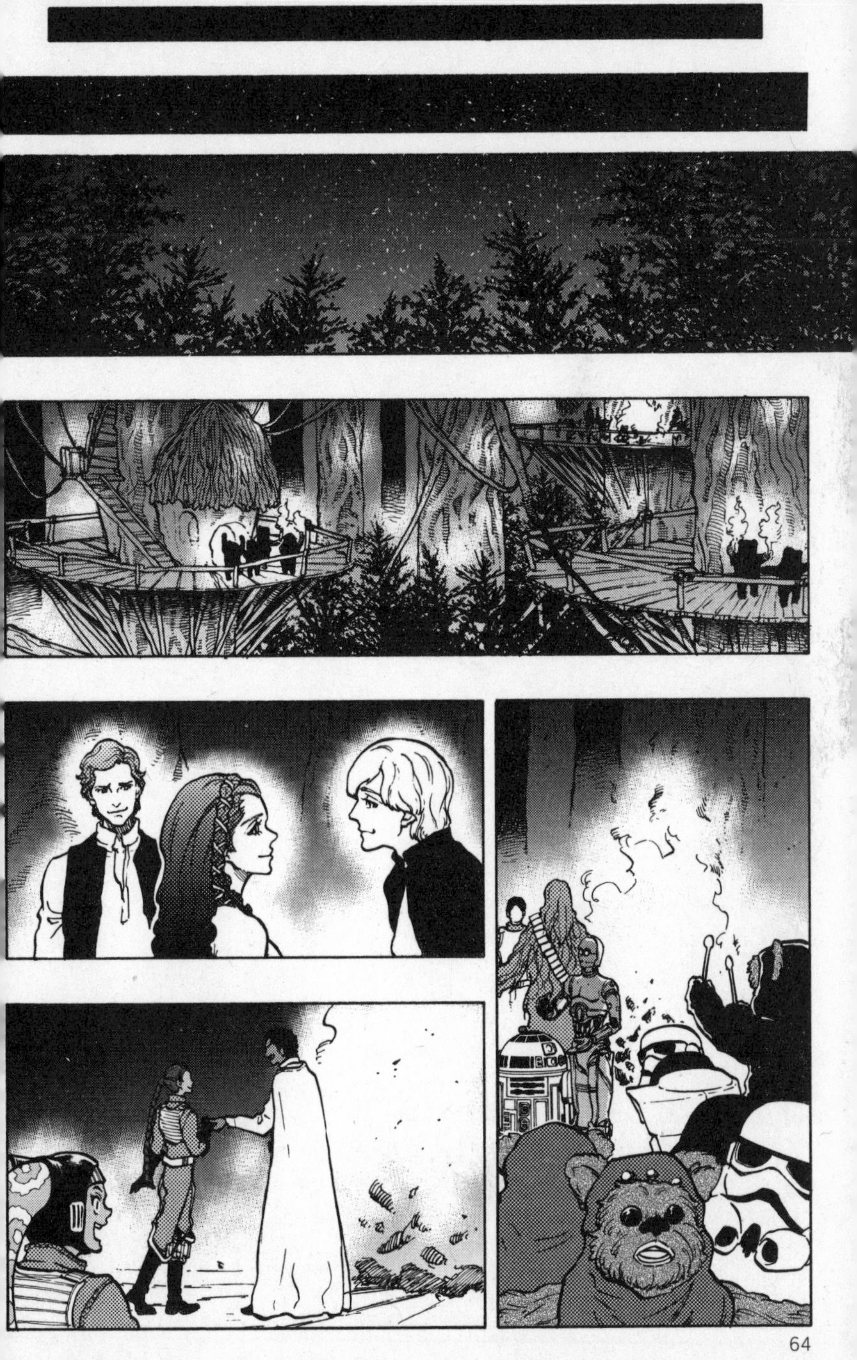

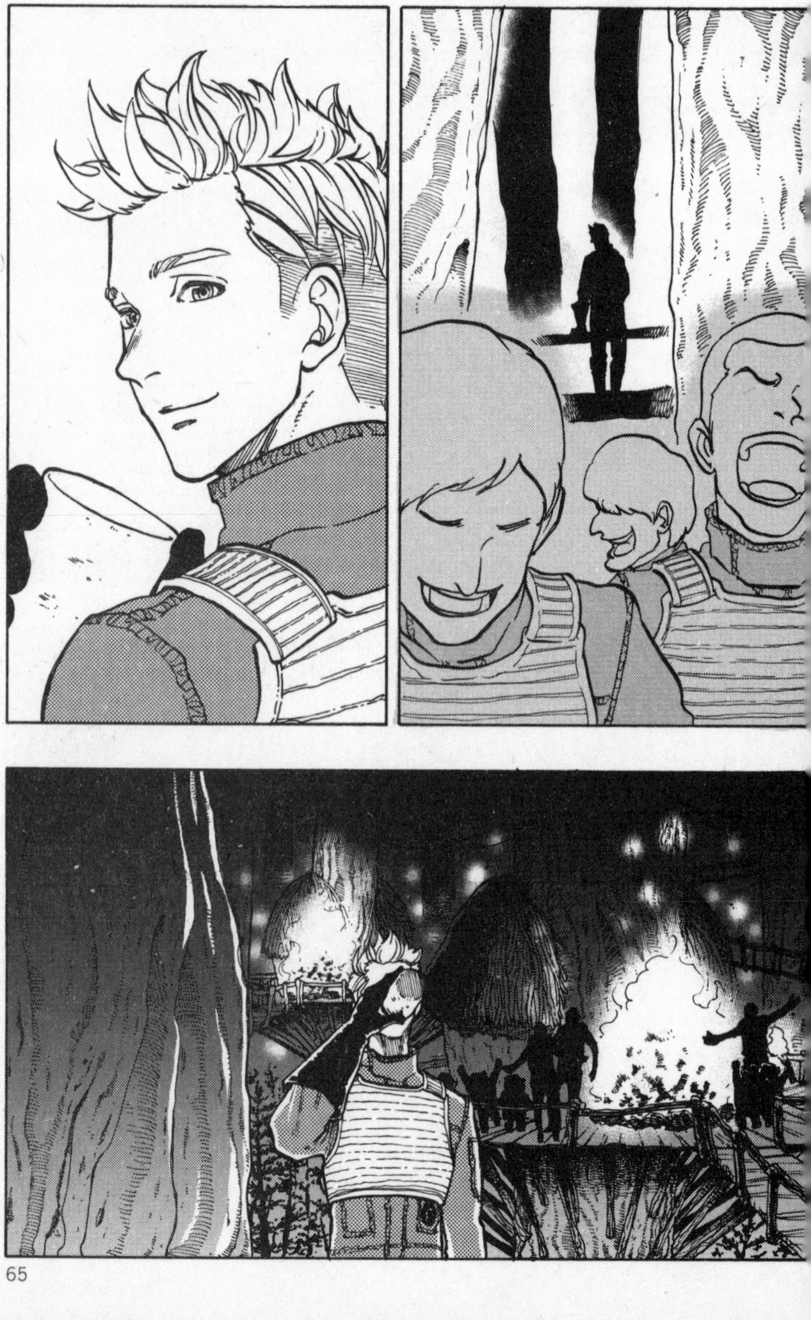

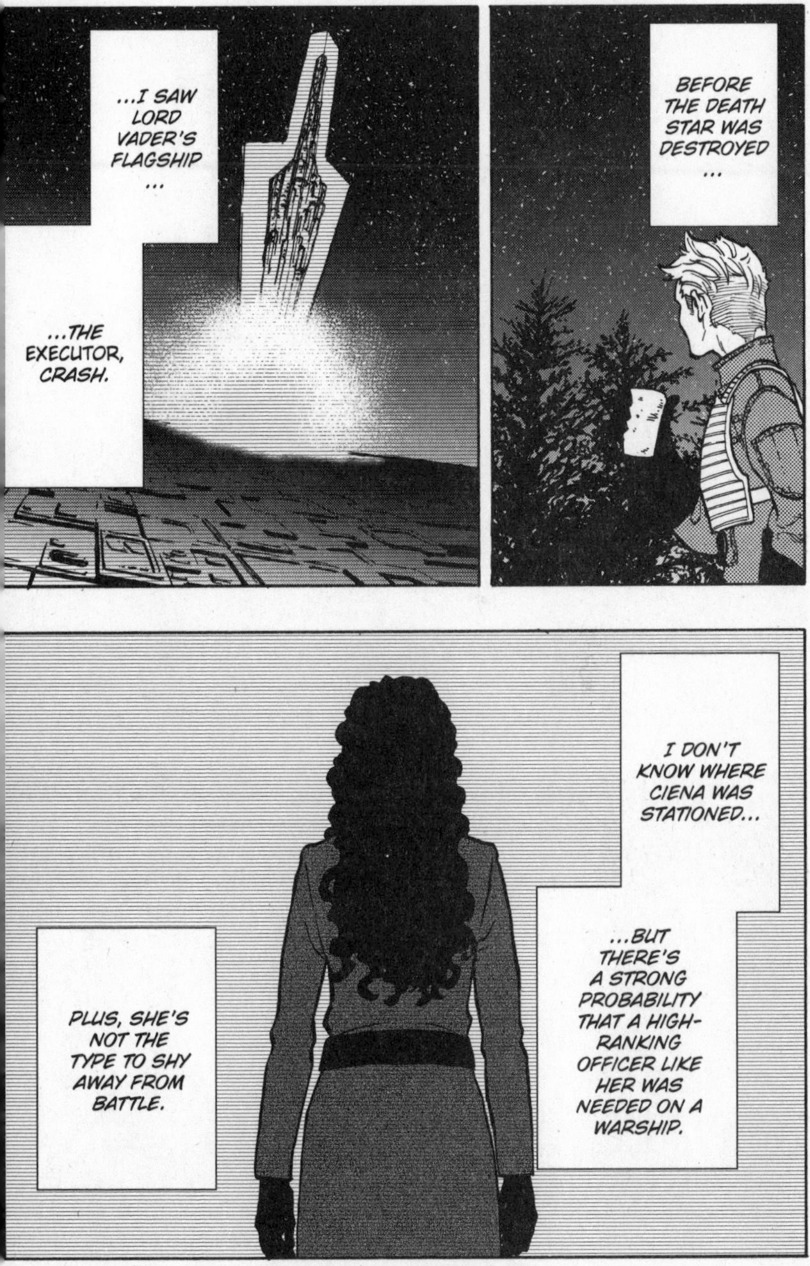
BEFORE THE DEATH STAR WAS DESTROYED ...
...I SAW LORD VADER'S FLAGSHIP ...
...THE EXECUTOR, CRASH.
I DON'T KNOW WHERE CIENA WAS STATIONED...
...BUT THERE'S A STRONG PROBABILITY THAT A HIGH-RANKING OFFICER LIKE HER WAS NEEDED ON A WARSHIP.
PLUS, SHE'S NOT THE TYPE TO SHY AWAY FROM BATTLE.

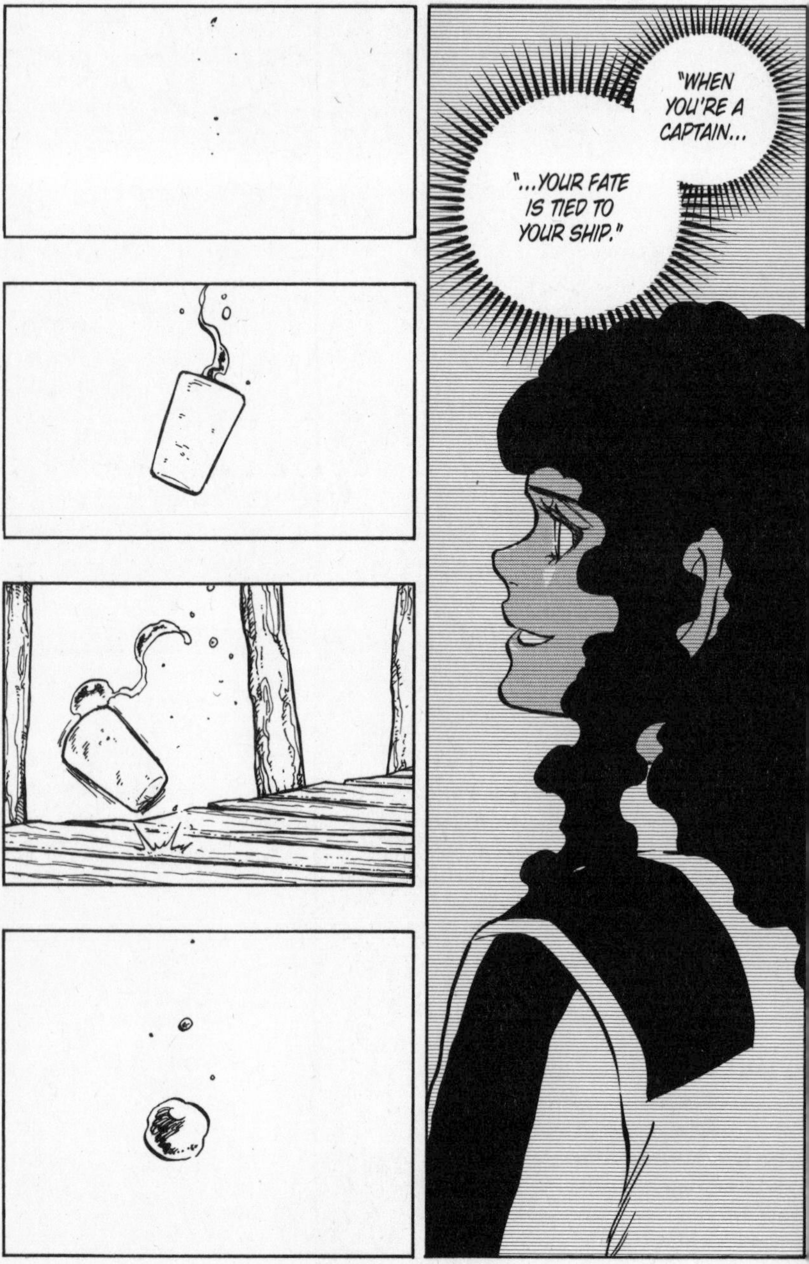
"WHEN YOU'RE A CAPTAIN...
"...YOUR FATE IS TIED TO YOUR SHIP."

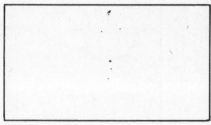

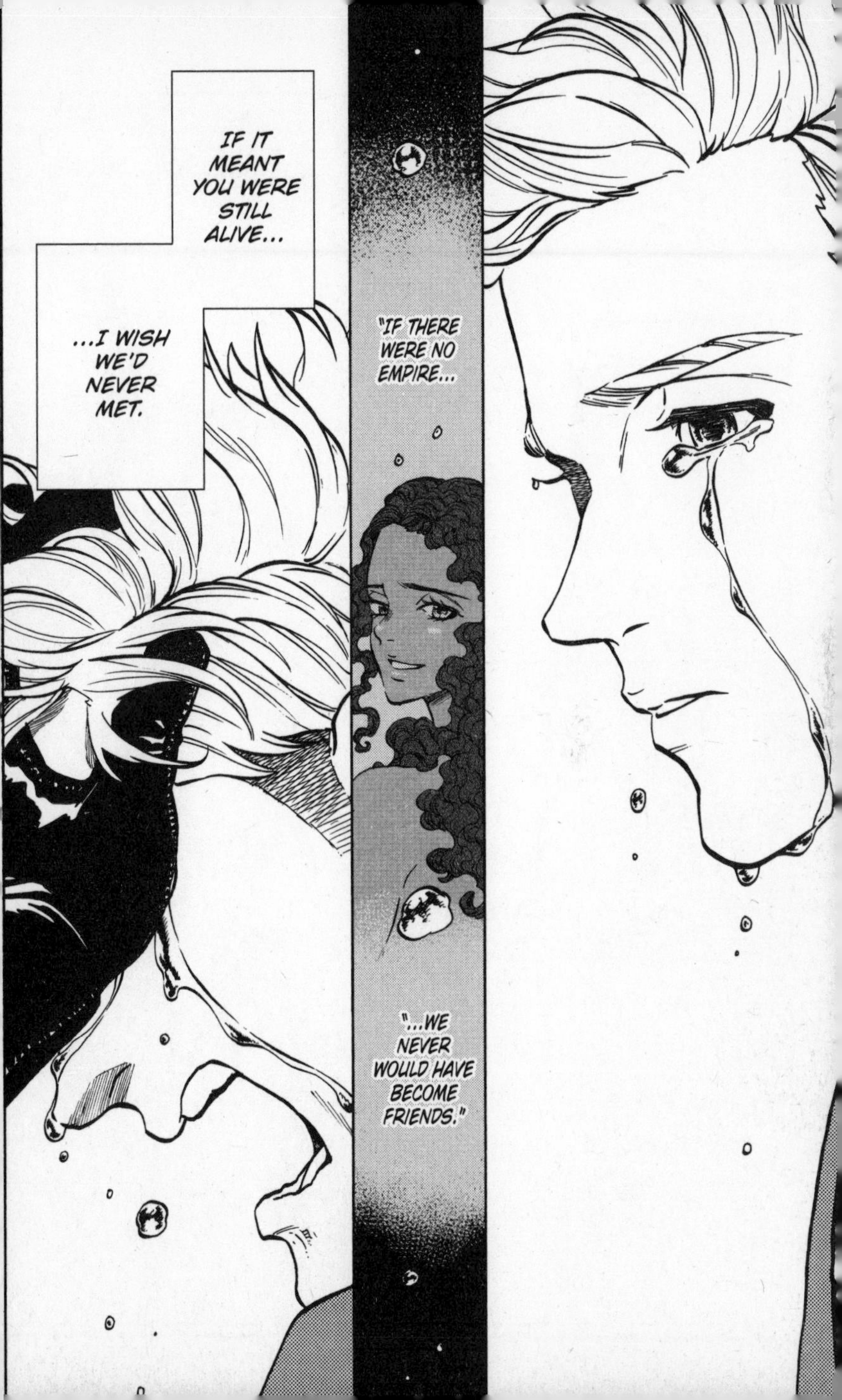
"IF THERE WERE NO EMPIRE...
"...WE NEVER WOULD HAVE BECOME FRIENDS."
IF IT MEANT YOU WERE STILL ALIVE...
...I WISH WE'D NEVER MET.

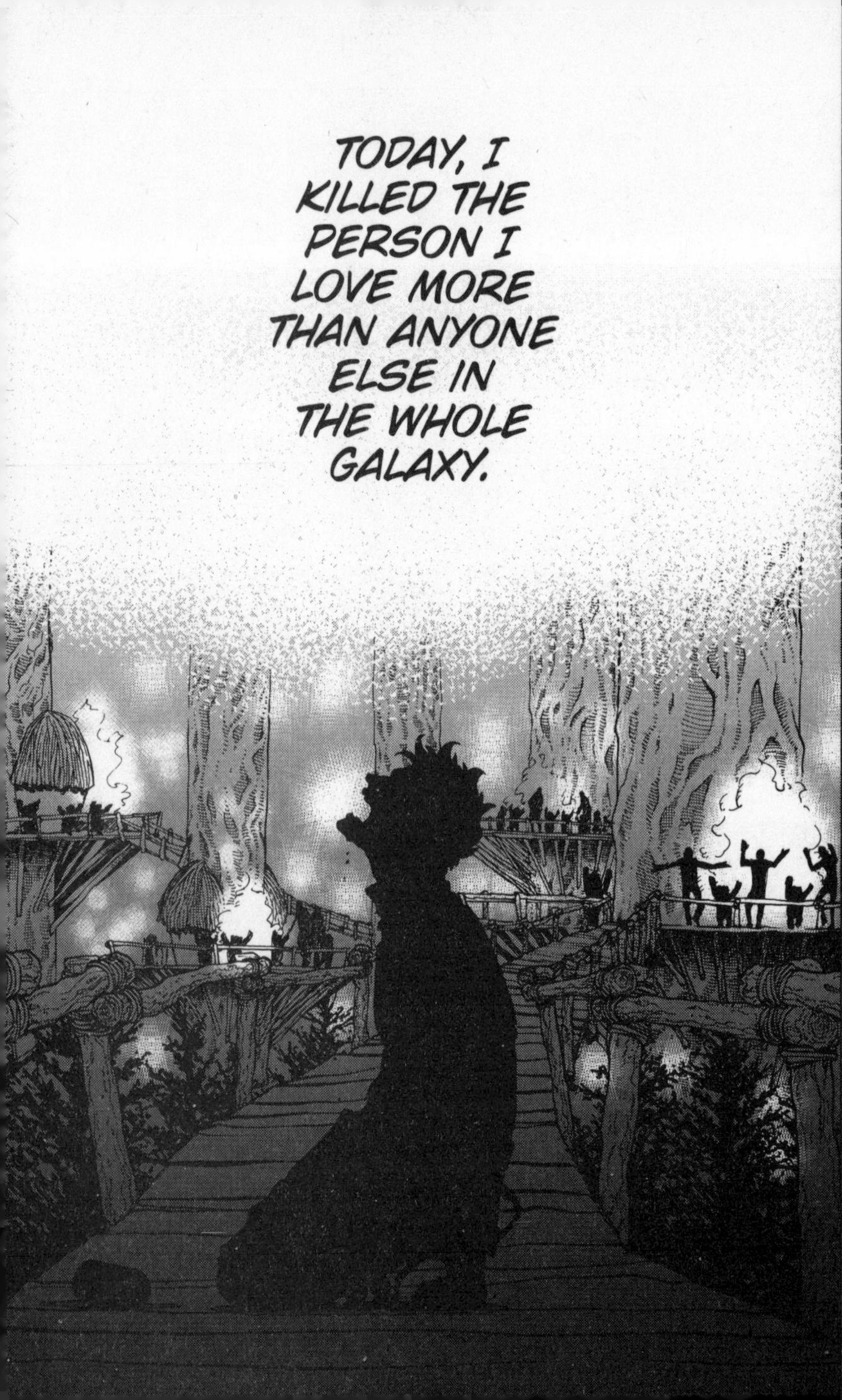
TODAY, I KILLED THE PERSON I LOVE MORE THAN ANYONE ELSE IN THE WHOLE GALAXY.

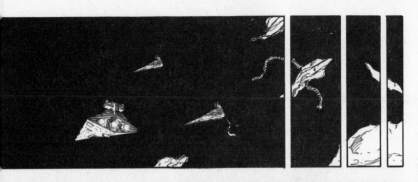

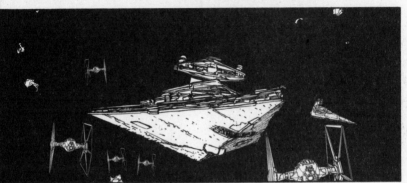

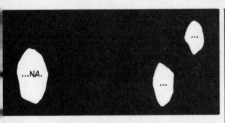

...NA.

...

...

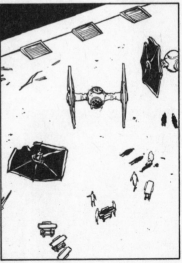

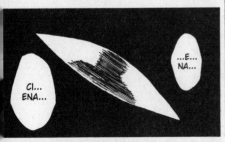

...E...
NA...

CI...
ENA...

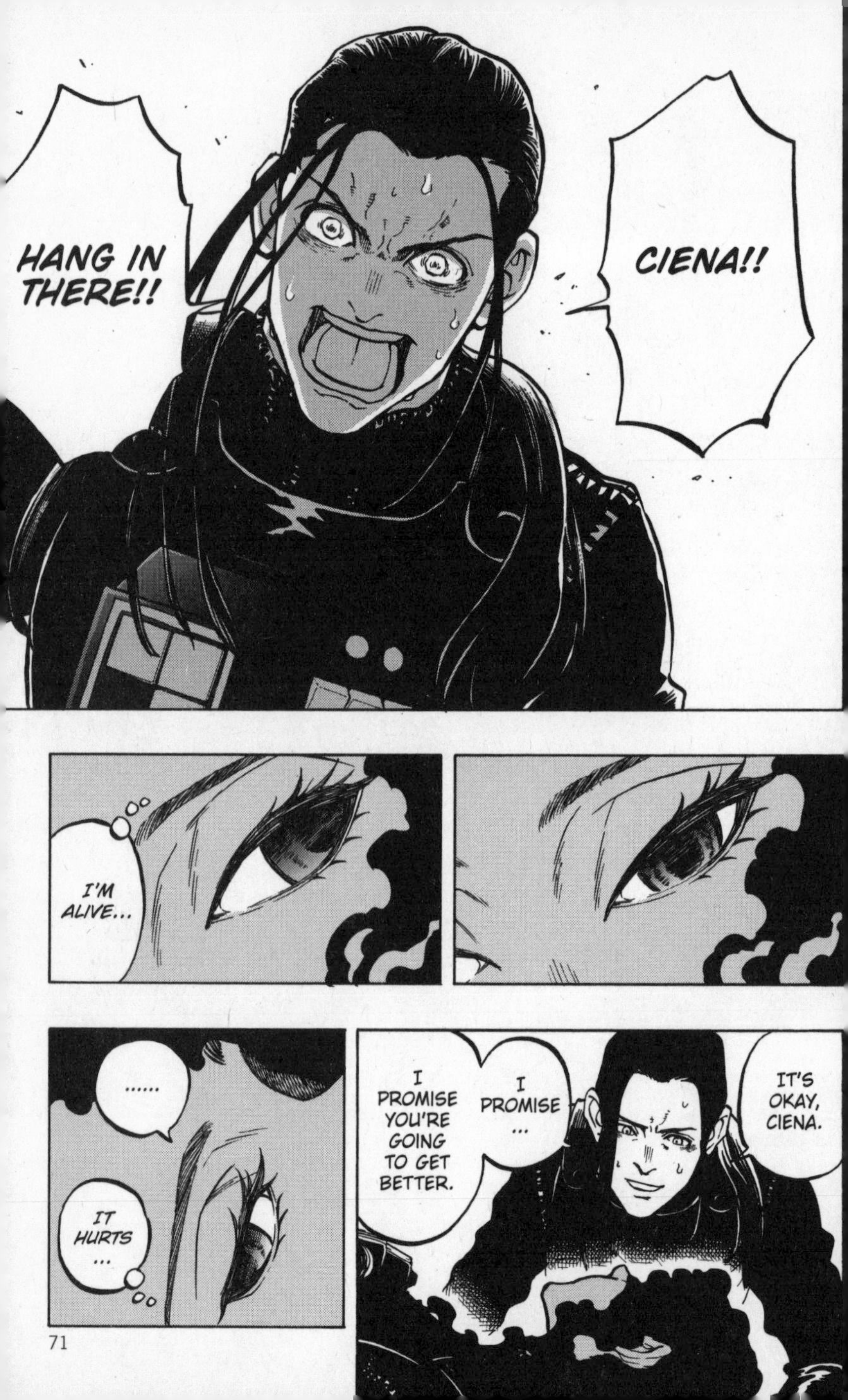
CIENA!!
HANG IN THERE!!
I'M ALIVE...
IT'S OKAY, CIENA.
I PROMISE...
I PROMISE YOU'RE GOING TO GET BETTER.
......
IT HURTS...

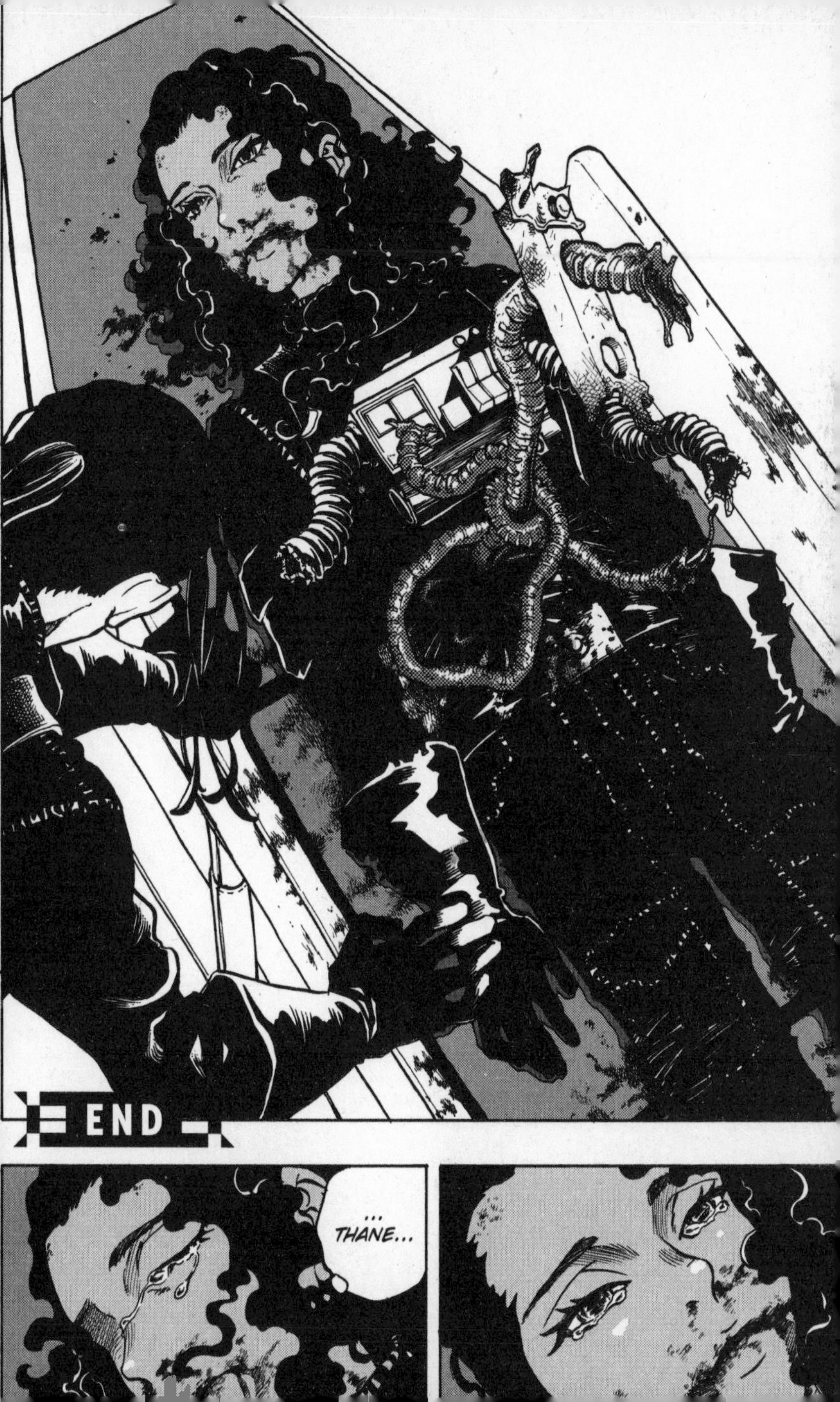
END
... THANE...

STAR WARS
LOST STARS
ロスト・スターズ

Chapter. 15

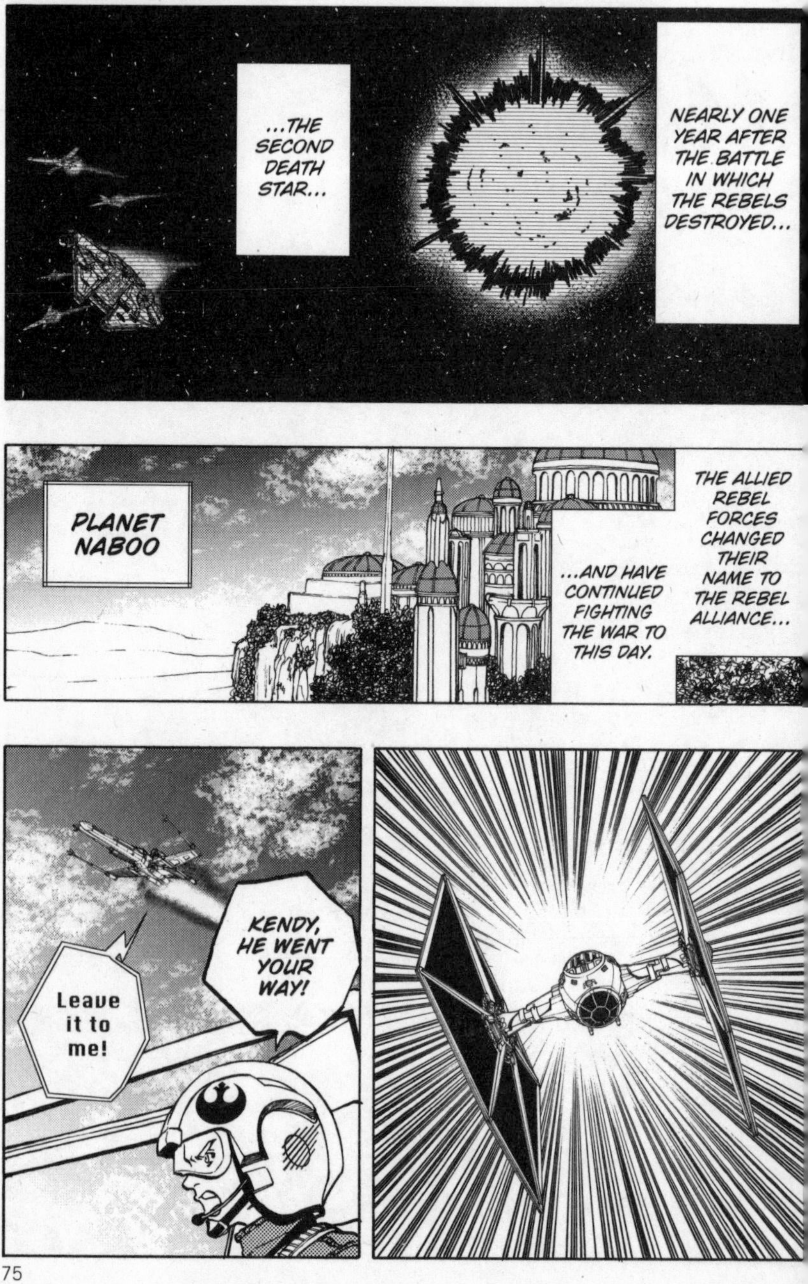
NEARLY ONE YEAR AFTER THE BATTLE IN WHICH THE REBELS DESTROYED...
...THE SECOND DEATH STAR...
THE ALLIED REBEL FORCES CHANGED THEIR NAME TO THE REBEL ALLIANCE...
...AND HAVE CONTINUED FIGHTING THE WAR TO THIS DAY.
PLANET NABOO
KENDY, HE WENT YOUR WAY!
Leave it to me!

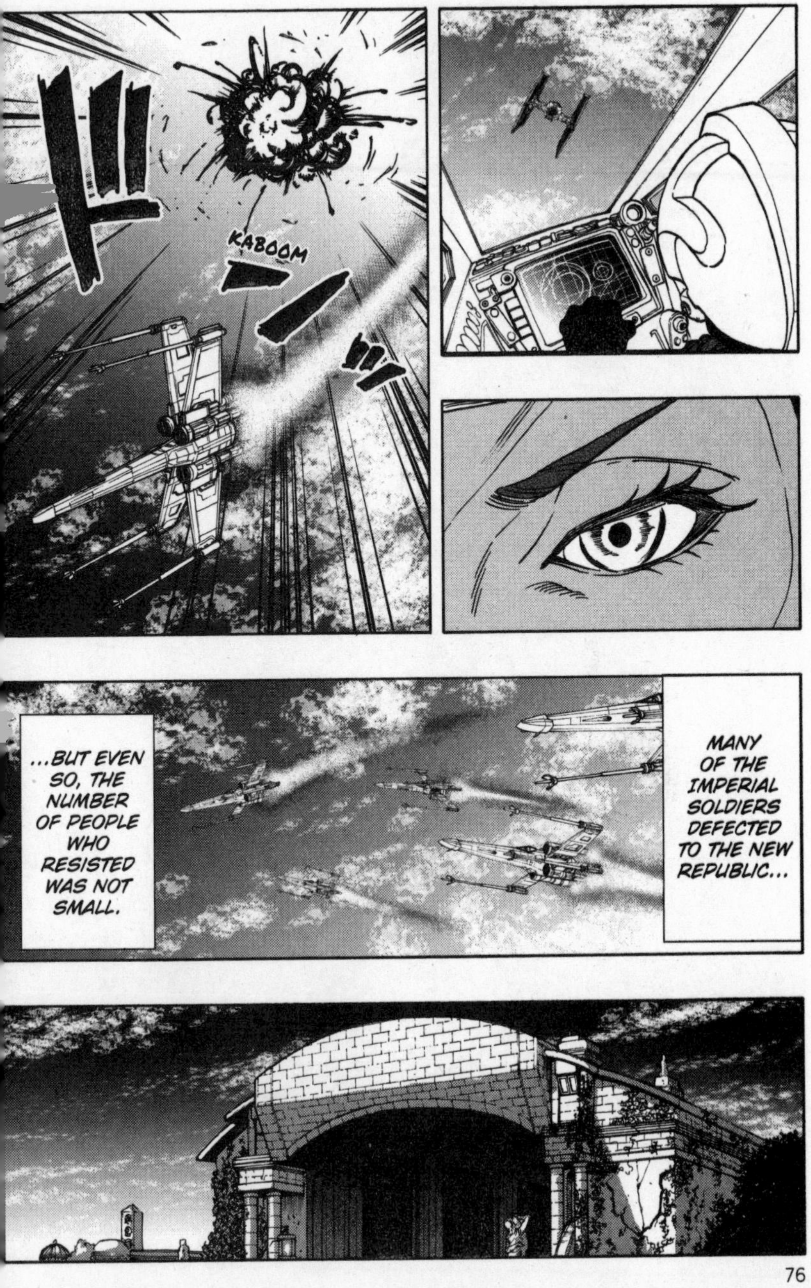
KABOOM
MANY OF THE IMPERIAL SOLDIERS DEFECTED TO THE NEW REPUBLIC...
...BUT EVEN SO, THE NUMBER OF PEOPLE WHO RESISTED WAS NOT SMALL.

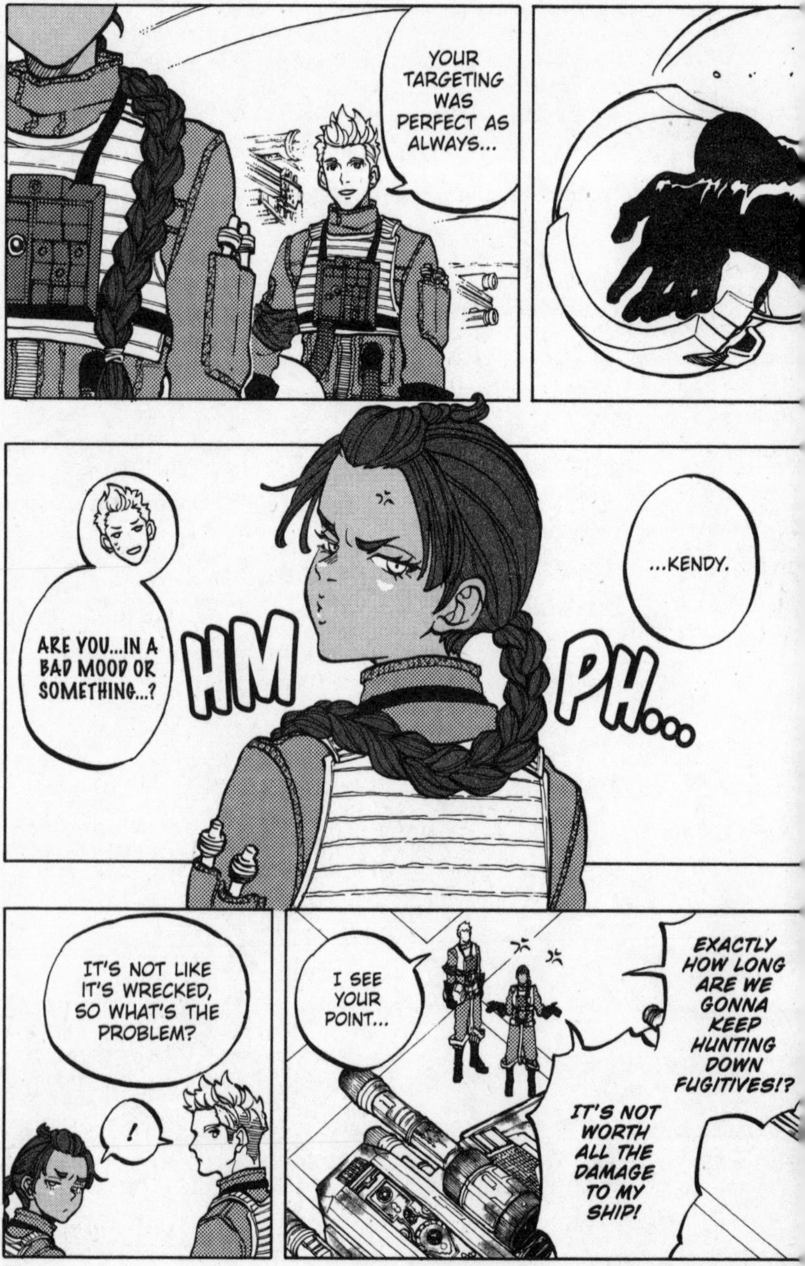
YOUR TARGETING WAS PERFECT AS ALWAYS...
...KENDY.
HMPH...
ARE YOU...IN A BAD MOOD OR SOMETHING...?
EXACTLY HOW LONG ARE WE GONNA KEEP HUNTING DOWN FUGITIVES!?
IT'S NOT WORTH ALL THE DAMAGE TO MY SHIP!
I SEE YOUR POINT...
IT'S NOT LIKE IT'S WRECKED, SO WHAT'S THE PROBLEM?
!

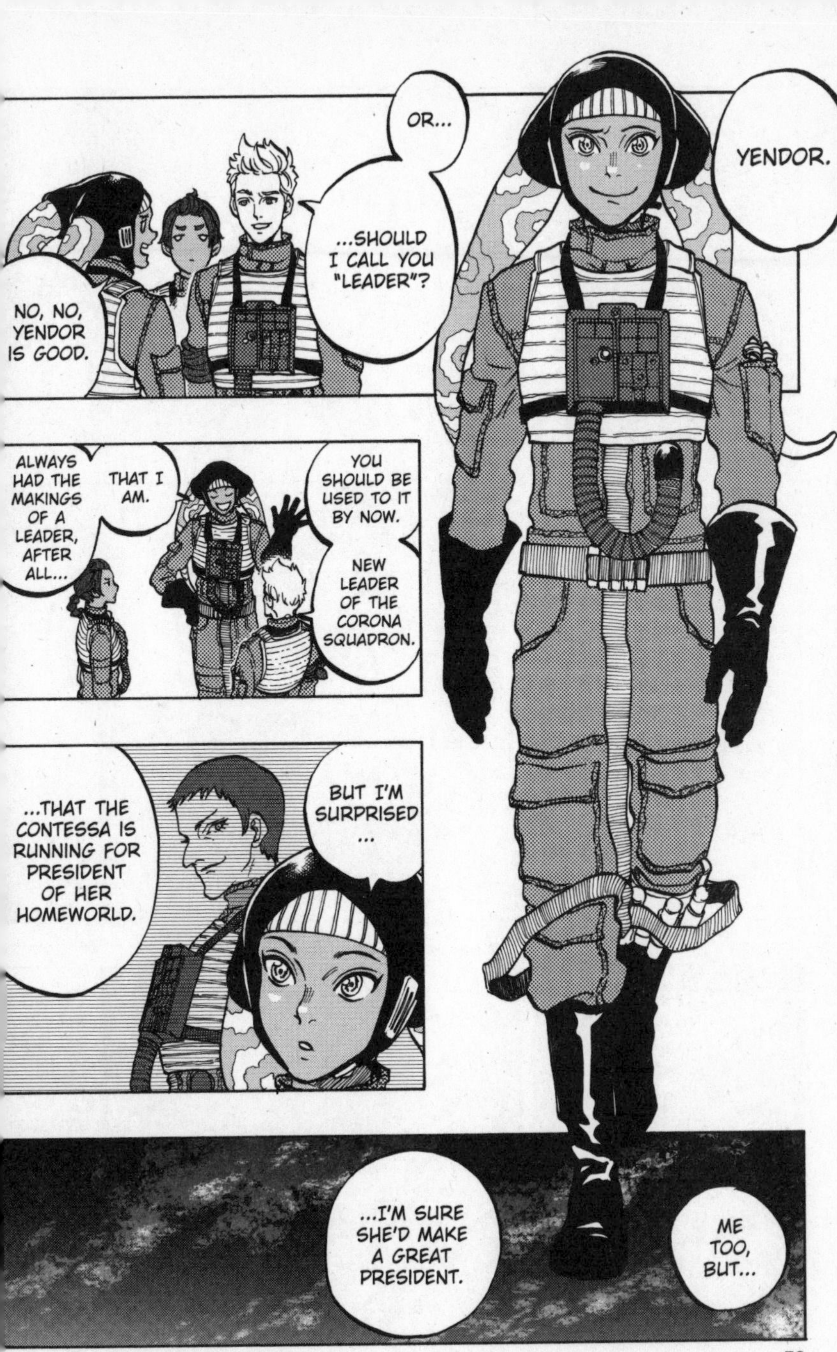
YENDOR.
OR...
...SHOULD I CALL YOU "LEADER"?
NO, NO, YENDOR IS GOOD.
YOU SHOULD BE USED TO IT BY NOW.
NEW LEADER OF THE CORONA SQUADRON.
THAT I AM.
ALWAYS HAD THE MAKINGS OF A LEADER, AFTER ALL...
BUT I'M SURPRISED...
...THAT THE CONTESSA IS RUNNING FOR PRESIDENT OF HER HOMEWORLD.
ME TOO, BUT...
...I'M SURE SHE'D MAKE A GREAT PRESIDENT.

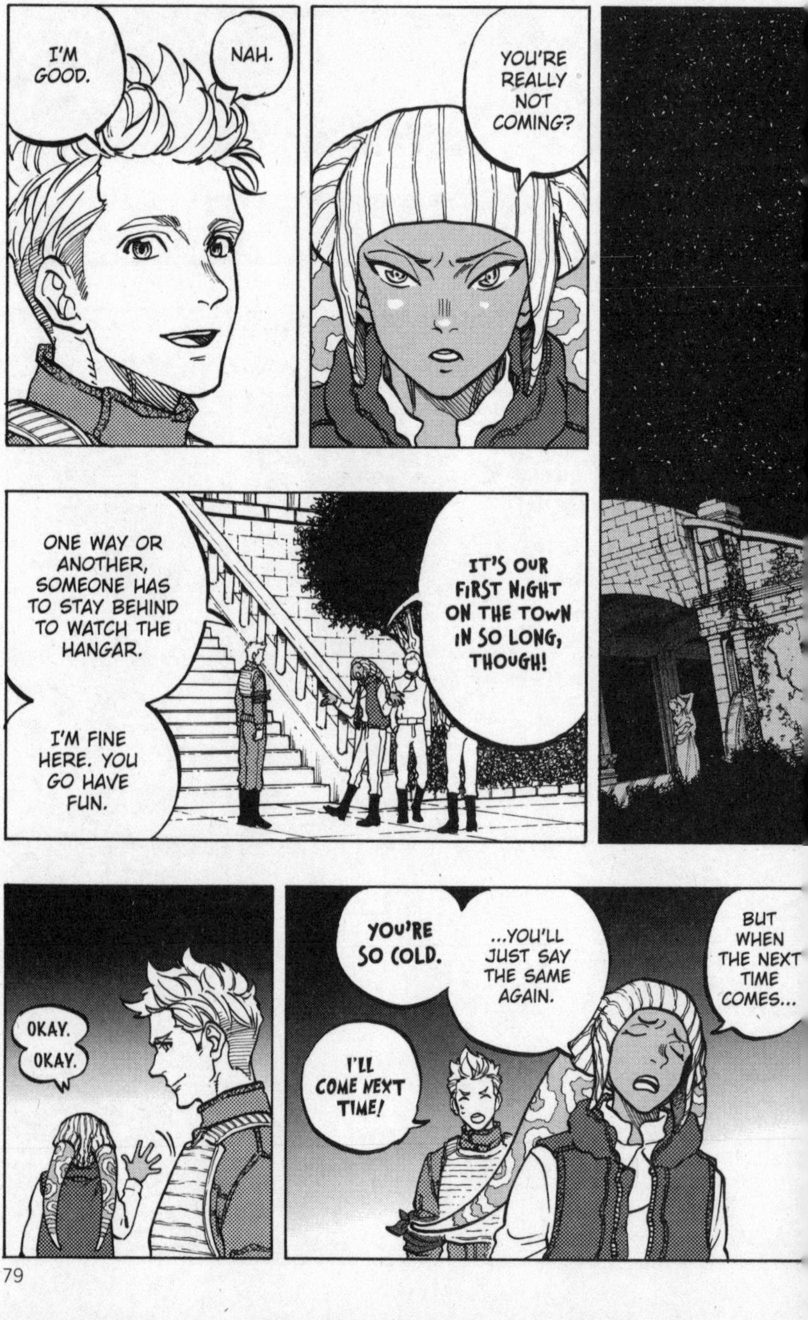
YOU'RE REALLY NOT COMING?
NAH.
I'M GOOD.
IT'S OUR FIRST NIGHT ON THE TOWN IN SO LONG, THOUGH!
ONE WAY OR ANOTHER, SOMEONE HAS TO STAY BEHIND TO WATCH THE HANGAR.
I'M FINE HERE. YOU GO HAVE FUN.
BUT WHEN THE NEXT TIME COMES...
...YOU'LL JUST SAY THE SAME AGAIN.
YOU'RE SO COLD.
I'LL COME NEXT TIME!
OKAY. OKAY.

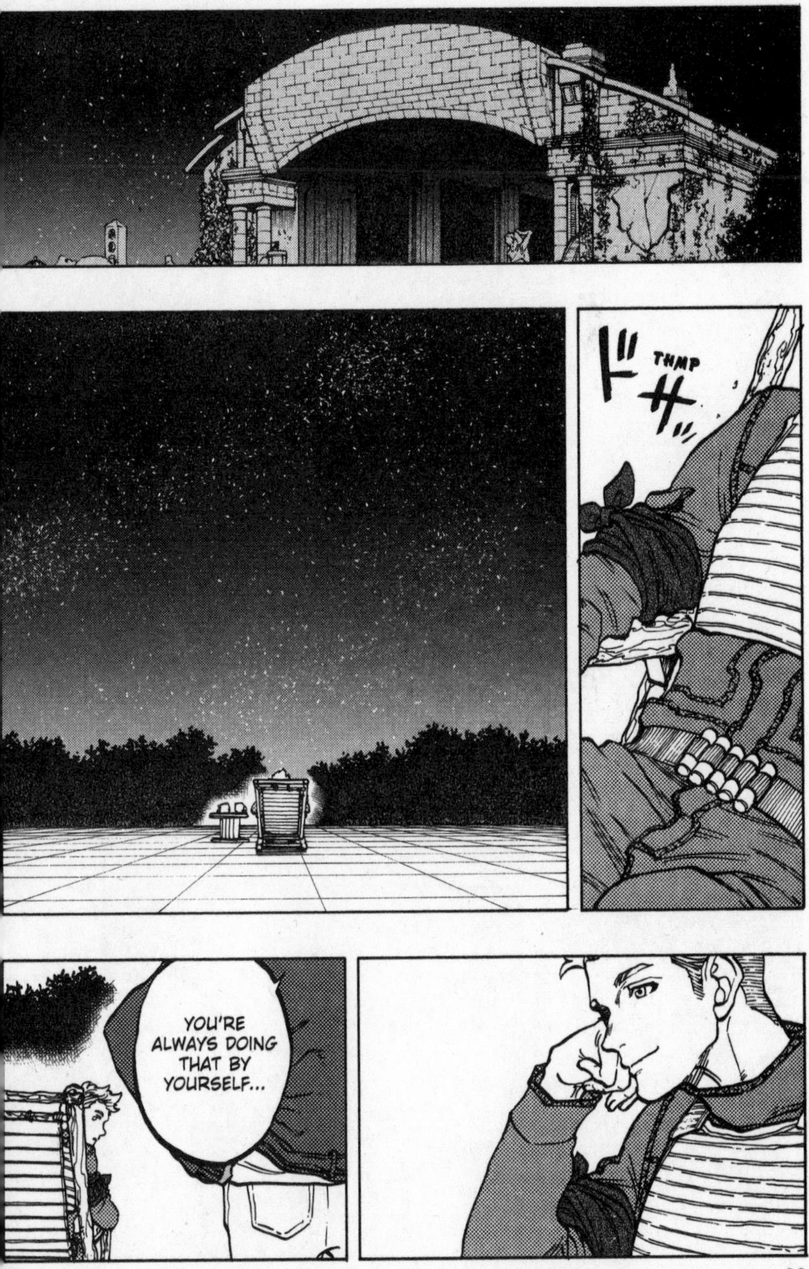
ドサ
THMP
YOU'RE ALWAYS DOING THAT BY YOURSELF...

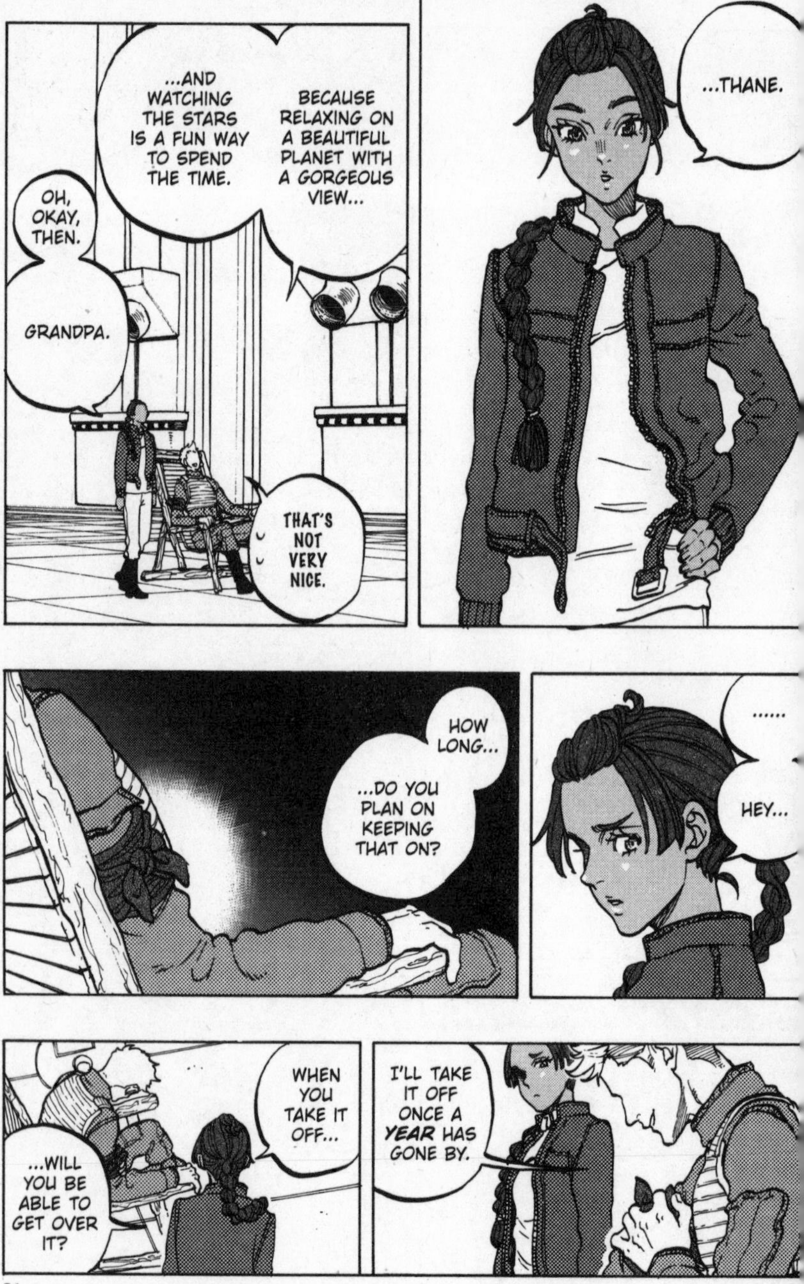

...THANE.
BECAUSE RELAXING ON A BEAUTIFUL PLANET WITH A GORGEOUS VIEW...
...AND WATCHING THE STARS IS A FUN WAY TO SPEND THE TIME.
OH, OKAY, THEN.
GRANDPA.
THAT'S NOT VERY NICE.
......
HEY...
HOW LONG...
...DO YOU PLAN ON KEEPING THAT ON?
I'LL TAKE IT OFF ONCE A *YEAR* HAS GONE BY.
WHEN YOU TAKE IT OFF...
...WILL YOU BE ABLE TO GET OVER IT?

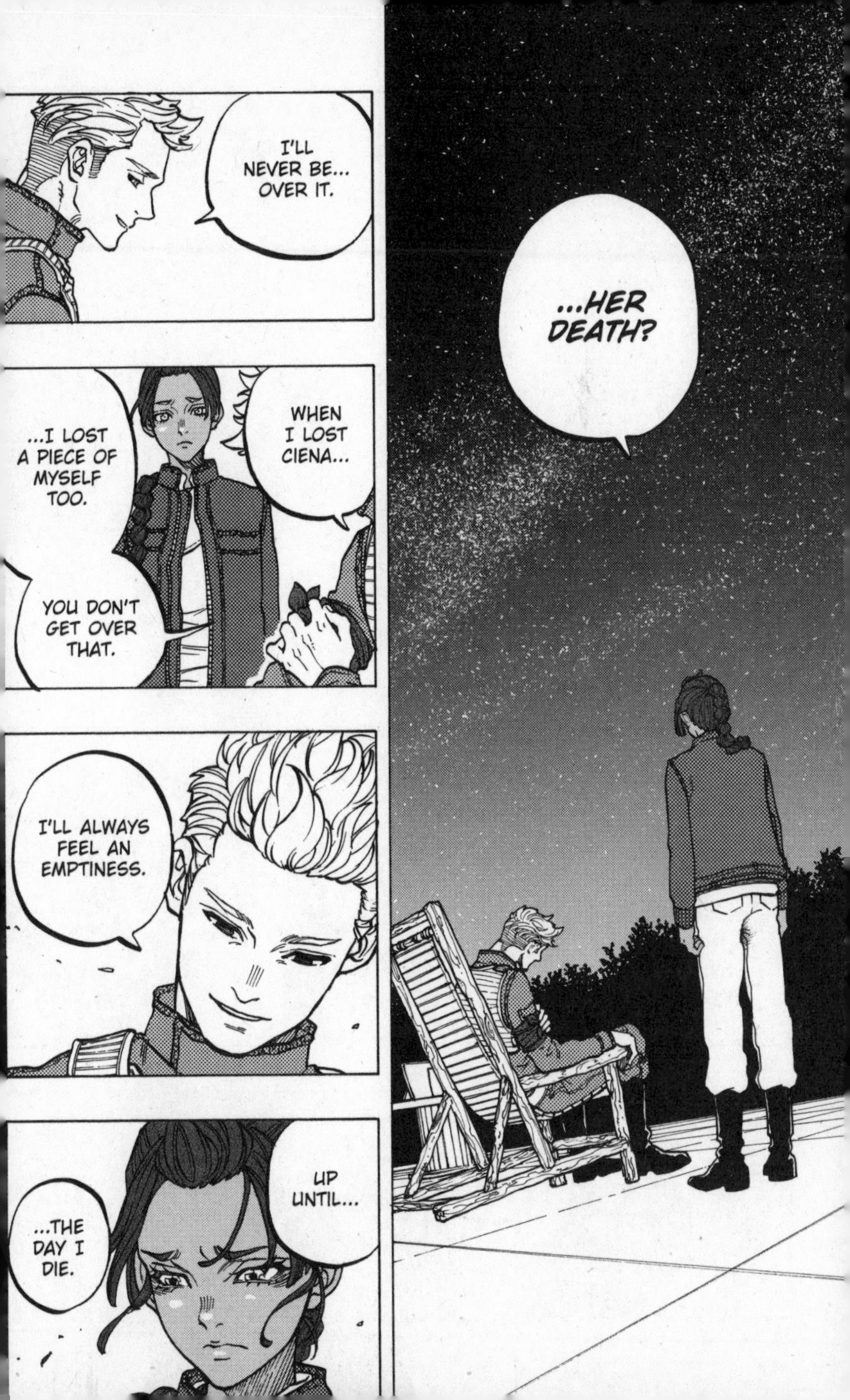
...HER DEATH?
I'LL NEVER BE... OVER IT.
WHEN I LOST CIENA...
...I LOST A PIECE OF MYSELF TOO.
YOU DON'T GET OVER THAT.
I'LL ALWAYS FEEL AN EMPTINESS.
UP UNTIL...
...THE DAY I DIE.

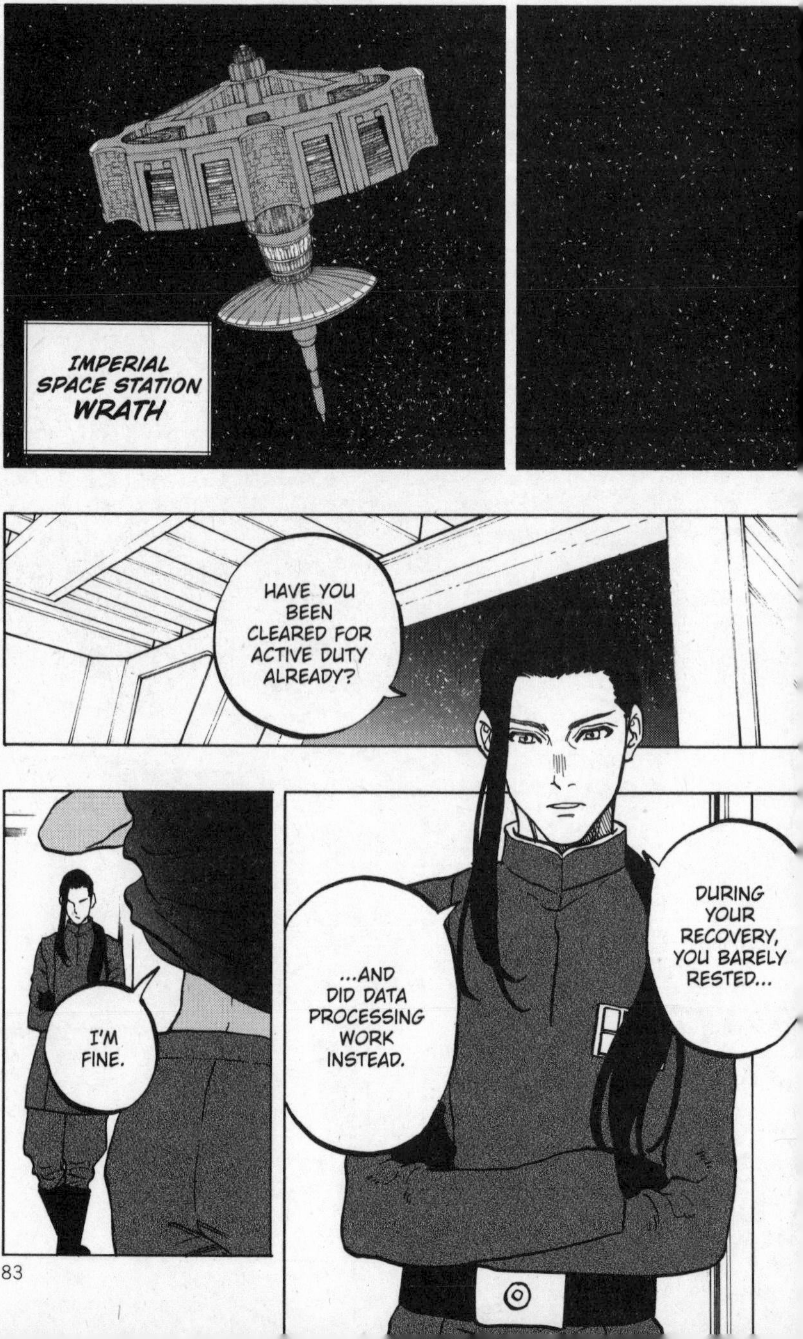
IMPERIAL SPACE STATION WRATH
HAVE YOU BEEN CLEARED FOR ACTIVE DUTY ALREADY?
DURING YOUR RECOVERY, YOU BARELY RESTED...
...AND DID DATA PROCESSING WORK INSTEAD.
I'M FINE.

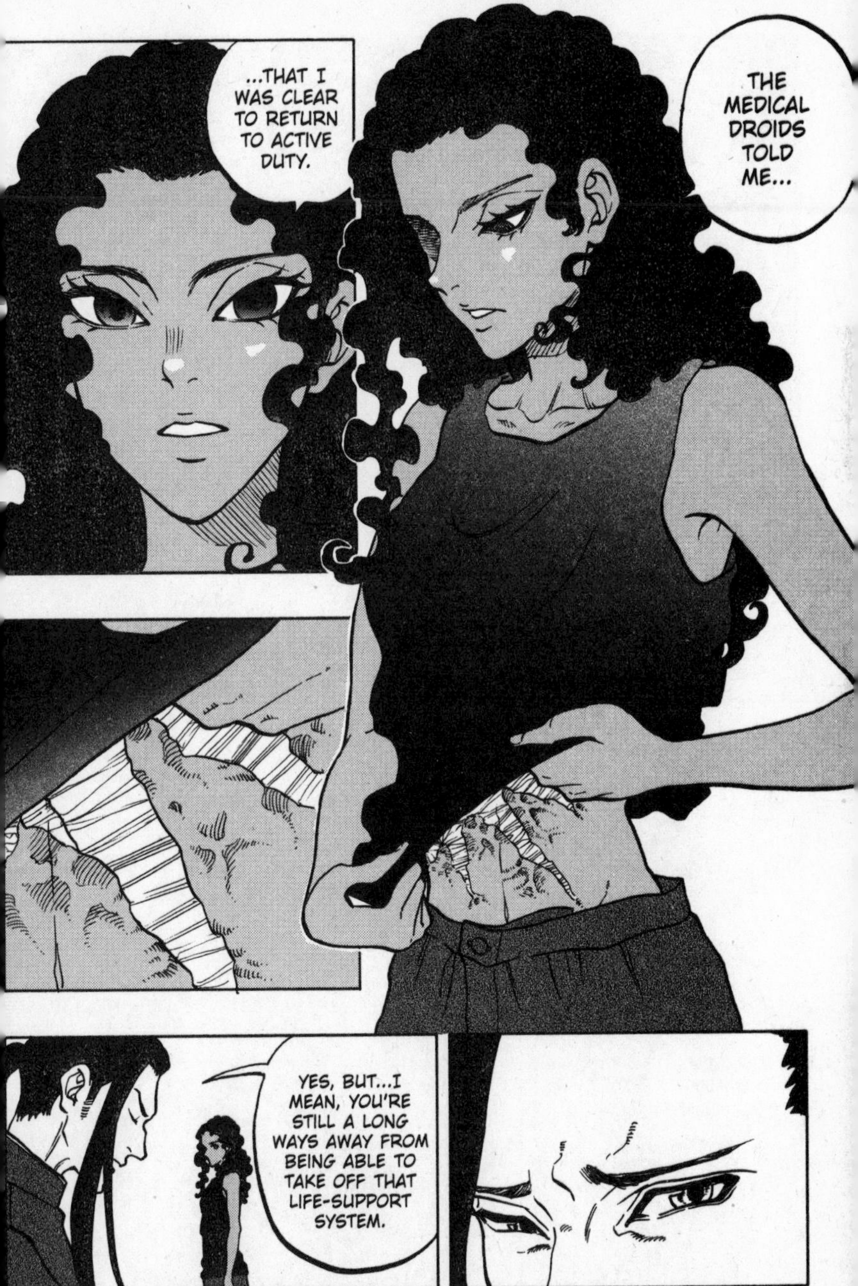
THE MEDICAL DROIDS TOLD ME...
...THAT I WAS CLEAR TO RETURN TO ACTIVE DUTY.
YES, BUT...I MEAN, YOU'RE STILL A LONG WAYS AWAY FROM BEING ABLE TO TAKE OFF THAT LIFE-SUPPORT SYSTEM.

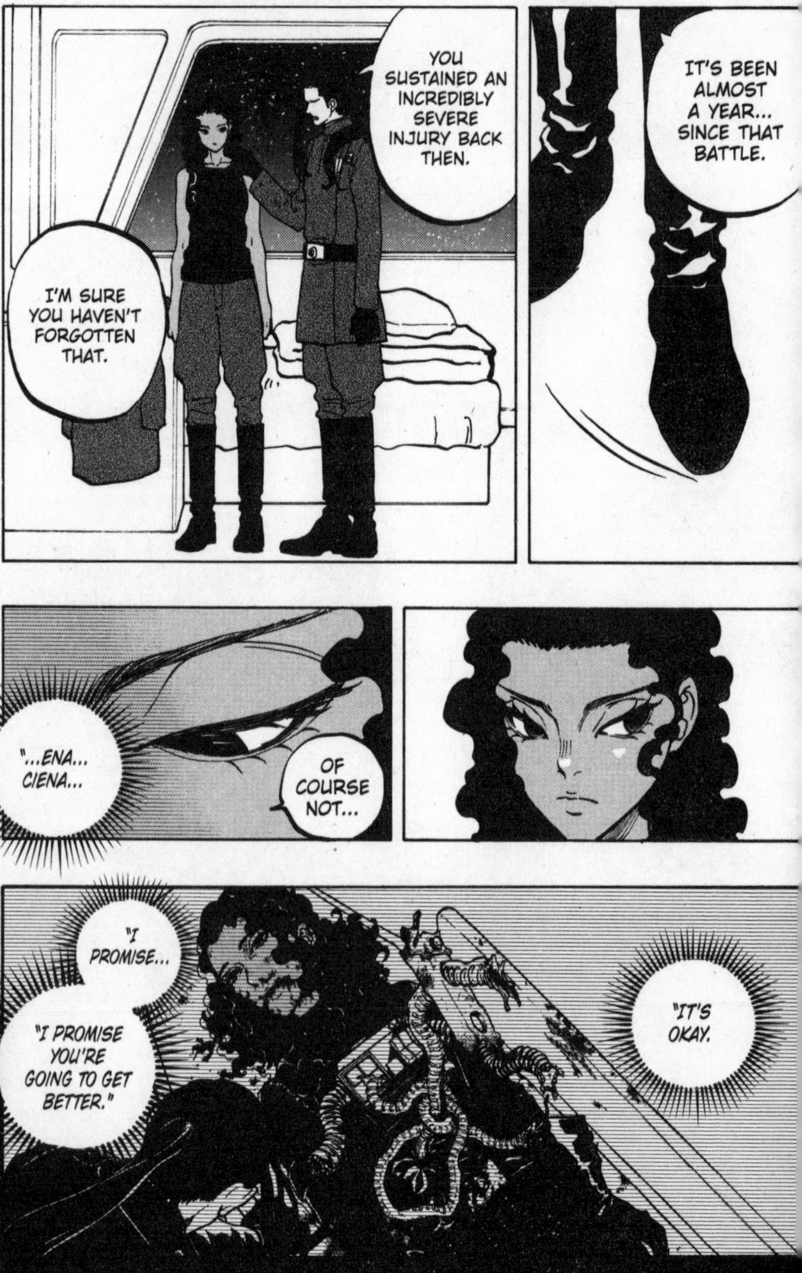
IT'S BEEN ALMOST A YEAR... SINCE THAT BATTLE.
YOU SUSTAINED AN INCREDIBLY SEVERE INJURY BACK THEN.
I'M SURE YOU HAVEN'T FORGOTTEN THAT.
OF COURSE NOT...
"...ENA... CIENA...
"IT'S OKAY.
"I PROMISE...
"I PROMISE YOU'RE GOING TO GET BETTER."

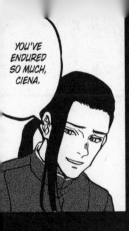

YOU'VE ENDURED SO MUCH, CIENA.

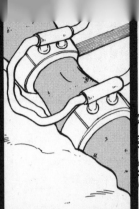

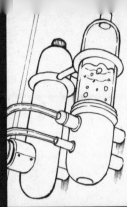

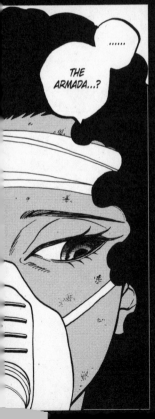

......

THE ARMADA...?

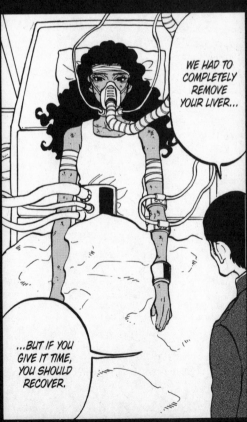

WE HAD TO COMPLETELY REMOVE YOUR LIVER...

...BUT IF YOU GIVE IT TIME, YOU SHOULD RECOVER.

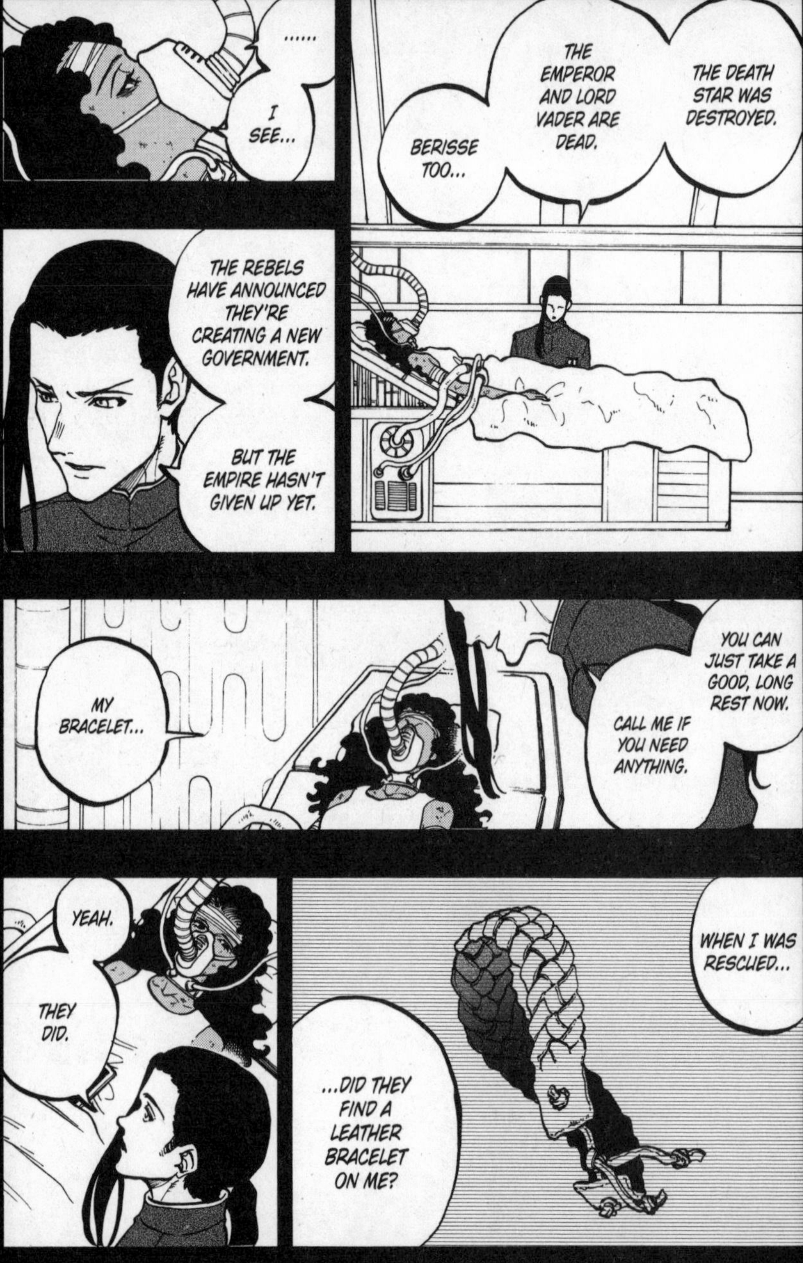
THE DEATH STAR WAS DESTROYED.
THE EMPEROR AND LORD VADER ARE DEAD.
BERISSE TOO...
......
I SEE...
THE REBELS HAVE ANNOUNCED THEY'RE CREATING A NEW GOVERNMENT.
BUT THE EMPIRE HASN'T GIVEN UP YET.
YOU CAN JUST TAKE A GOOD, LONG REST NOW.
CALL ME IF YOU NEED ANYTHING.
MY BRACELET...
WHEN I WAS RESCUED...
...DID THEY FIND A LEATHER BRACELET ON ME?
YEAH.
THEY DID.

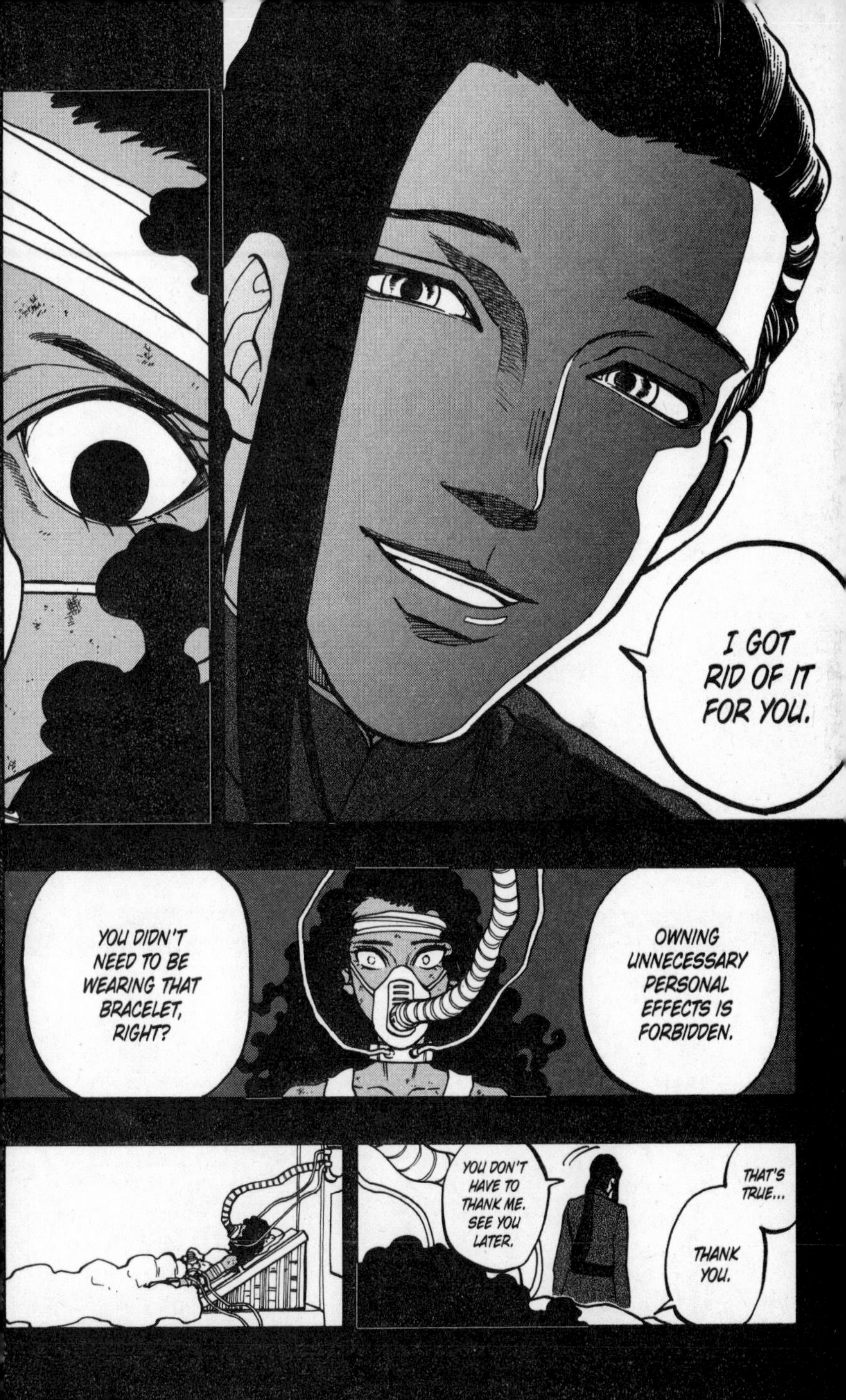
I GOT RID OF IT FOR YOU.
OWNING UNNECESSARY PERSONAL EFFECTS IS FORBIDDEN.
YOU DIDN'T NEED TO BE WEARING THAT BRACELET, RIGHT?
THAT'S TRUE...
THANK YOU.
YOU DON'T HAVE TO THANK ME. SEE YOU LATER.

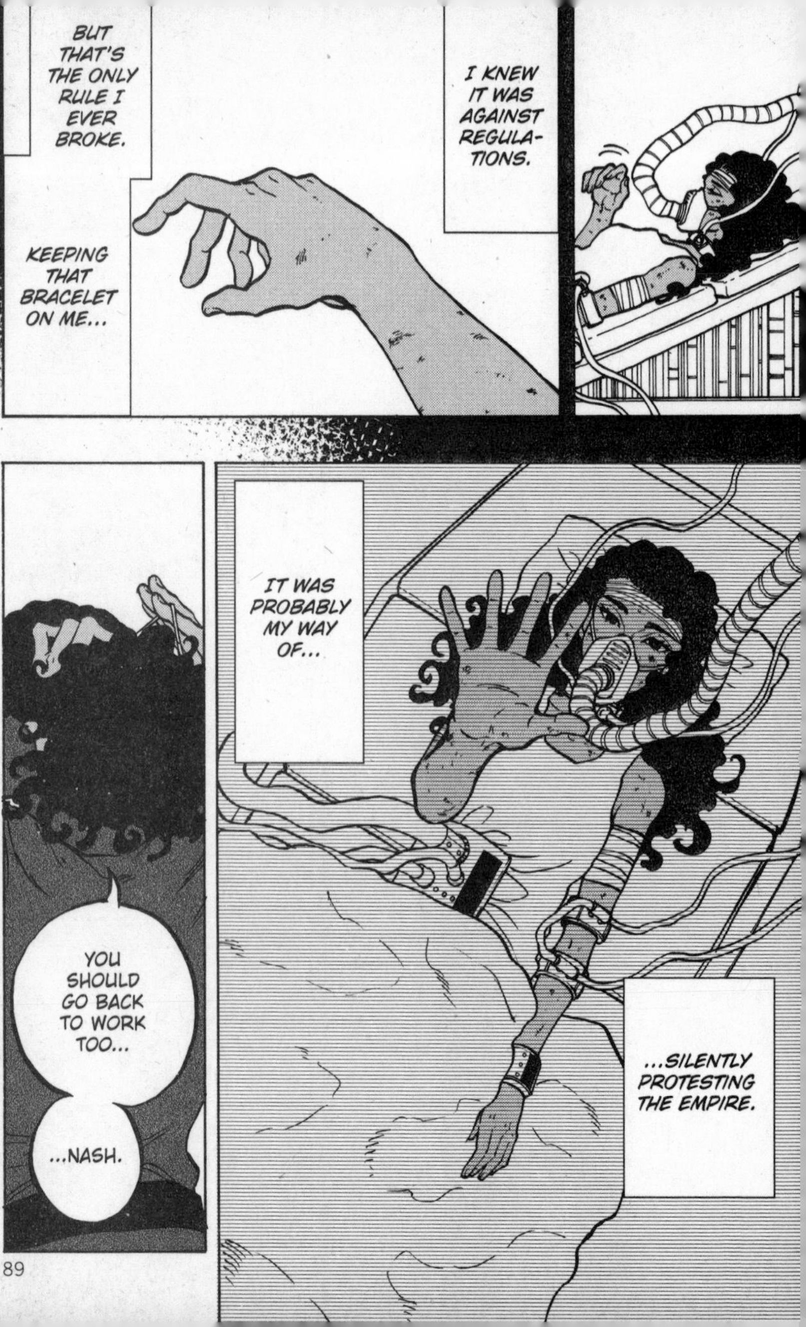
I KNEW IT WAS AGAINST REGULATIONS.
BUT THAT'S THE ONLY RULE I EVER BROKE.
KEEPING THAT BRACELET ON ME...
IT WAS PROBABLY MY WAY OF...
...SILENTLY PROTESTING THE EMPIRE.
YOU SHOULD GO BACK TO WORK TOO...
...NASH.

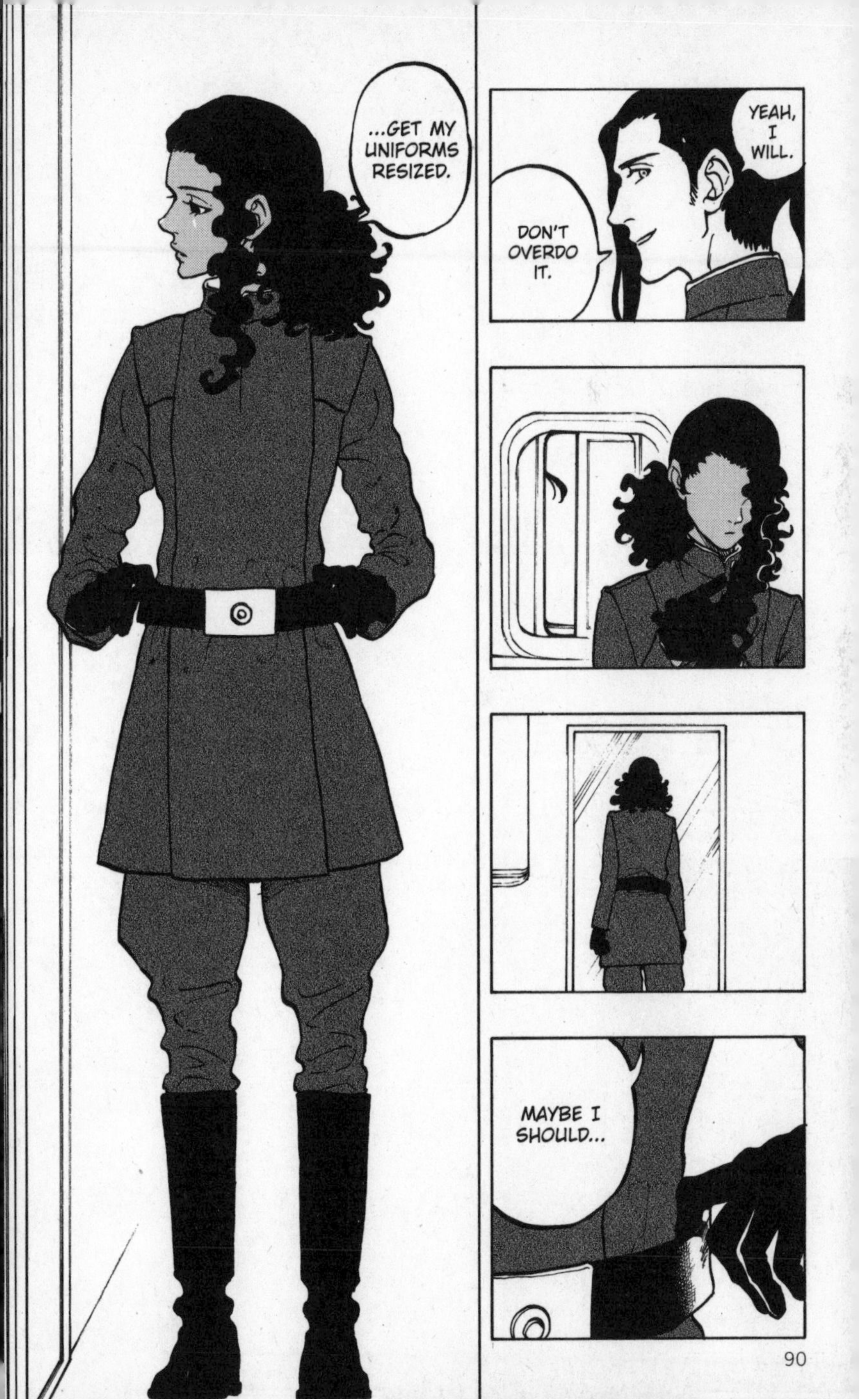
YEAH, I WILL.
DON'T OVERDO IT.
MAYBE I SHOULD...
...GET MY UNIFORMS RESIZED.

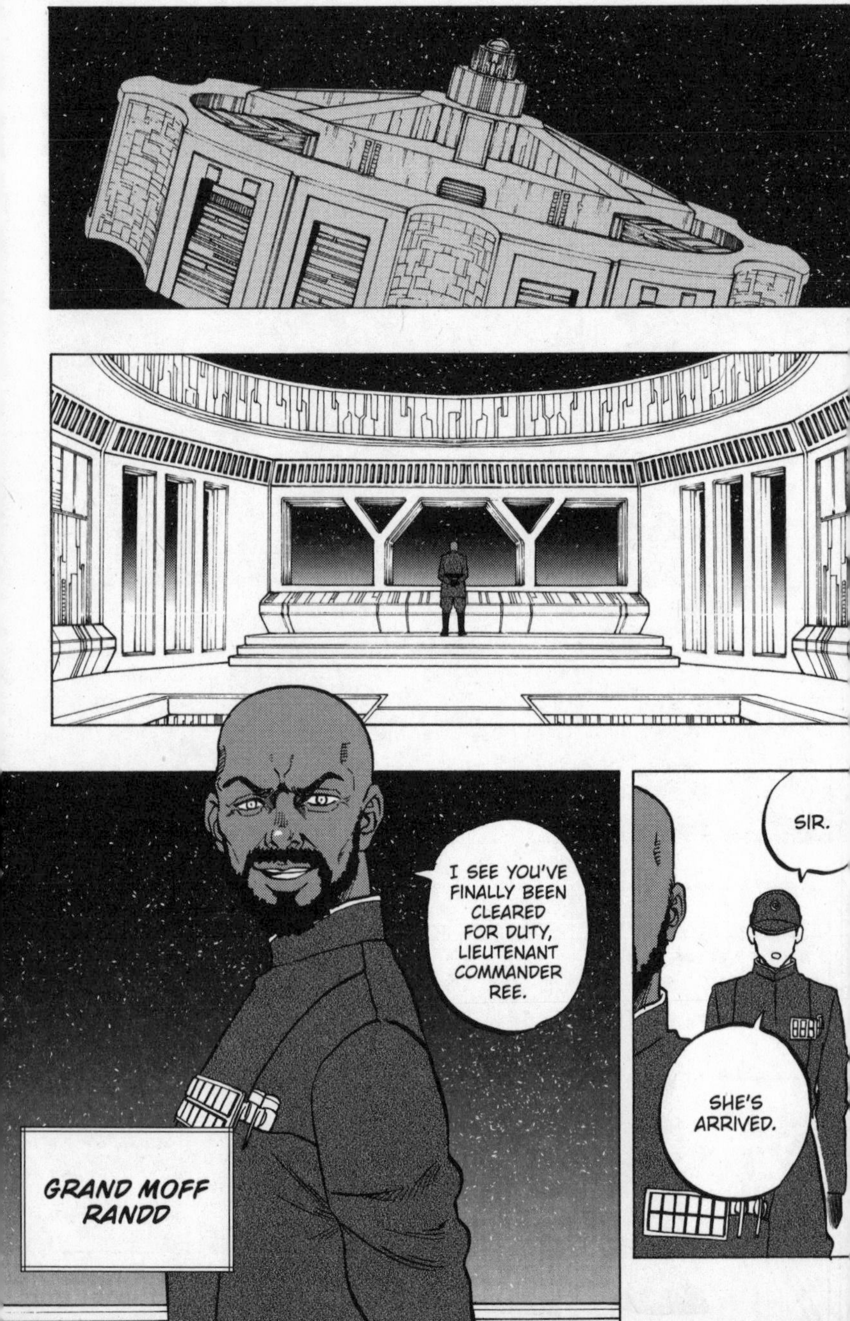
SIR.
SHE'S ARRIVED.
I SEE YOU'VE FINALLY BEEN CLEARED FOR DUTY, LIEUTENANT COMMANDER REE.
GRAND MOFF RANDD

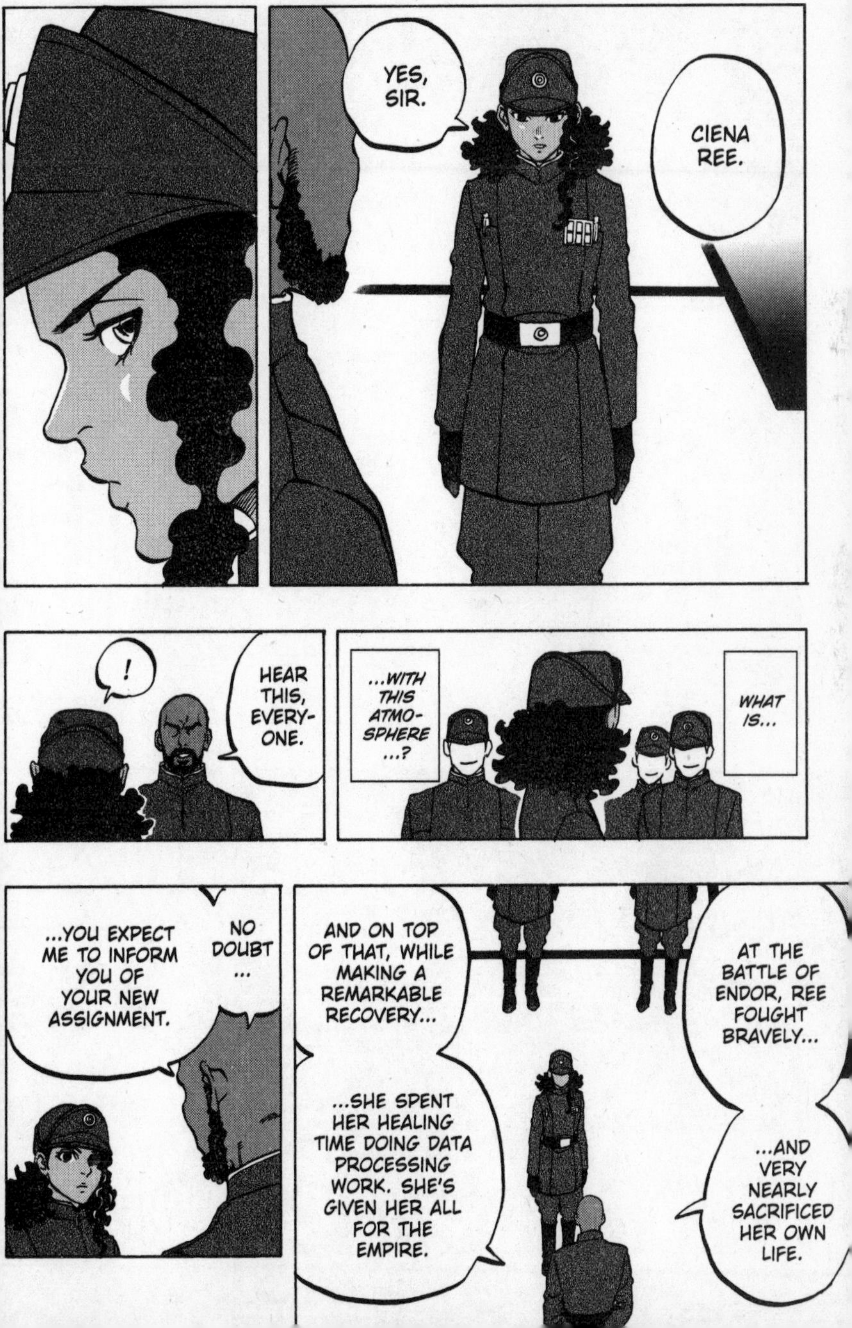
CIENA REE.
YES, SIR.
WHAT IS...
...WITH THIS ATMOSPHERE...?
HEAR THIS, EVERYONE.
!
AT THE BATTLE OF ENDOR, REE FOUGHT BRAVELY...
...AND VERY NEARLY SACRIFICED HER OWN LIFE.
AND ON TOP OF THAT, WHILE MAKING A REMARKABLE RECOVERY...
...SHE SPENT HER HEALING TIME DOING DATA PROCESSING WORK. SHE'S GIVEN HER ALL FOR THE EMPIRE.
NO DOUBT...
...YOU EXPECT ME TO INFORM YOU OF YOUR NEW ASSIGNMENT.

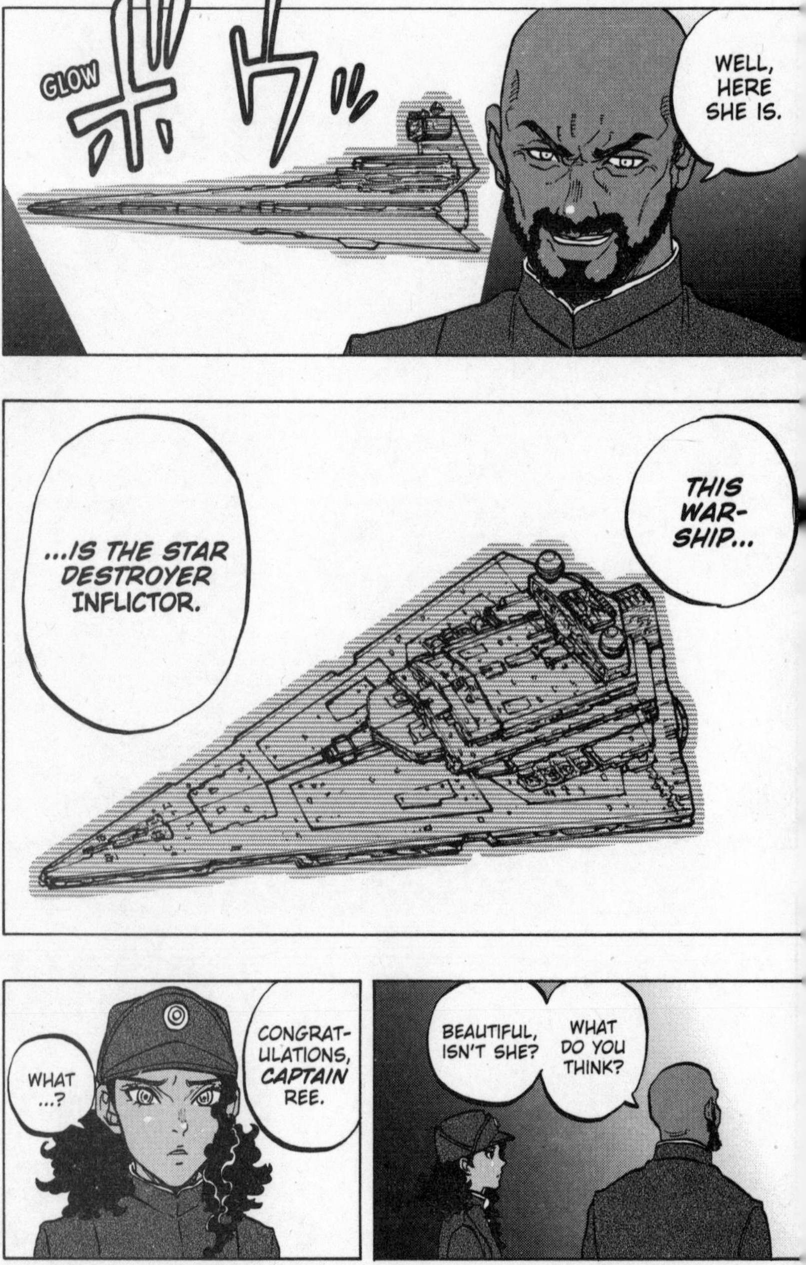
WELL, HERE SHE IS.
GLOW
THIS WARSHIP...
...IS THE STAR DESTROYER INFLICTOR.
WHAT DO YOU THINK?
BEAUTIFUL, ISN'T SHE?
CONGRATULATIONS, CAPTAIN REE.
WHAT ...?

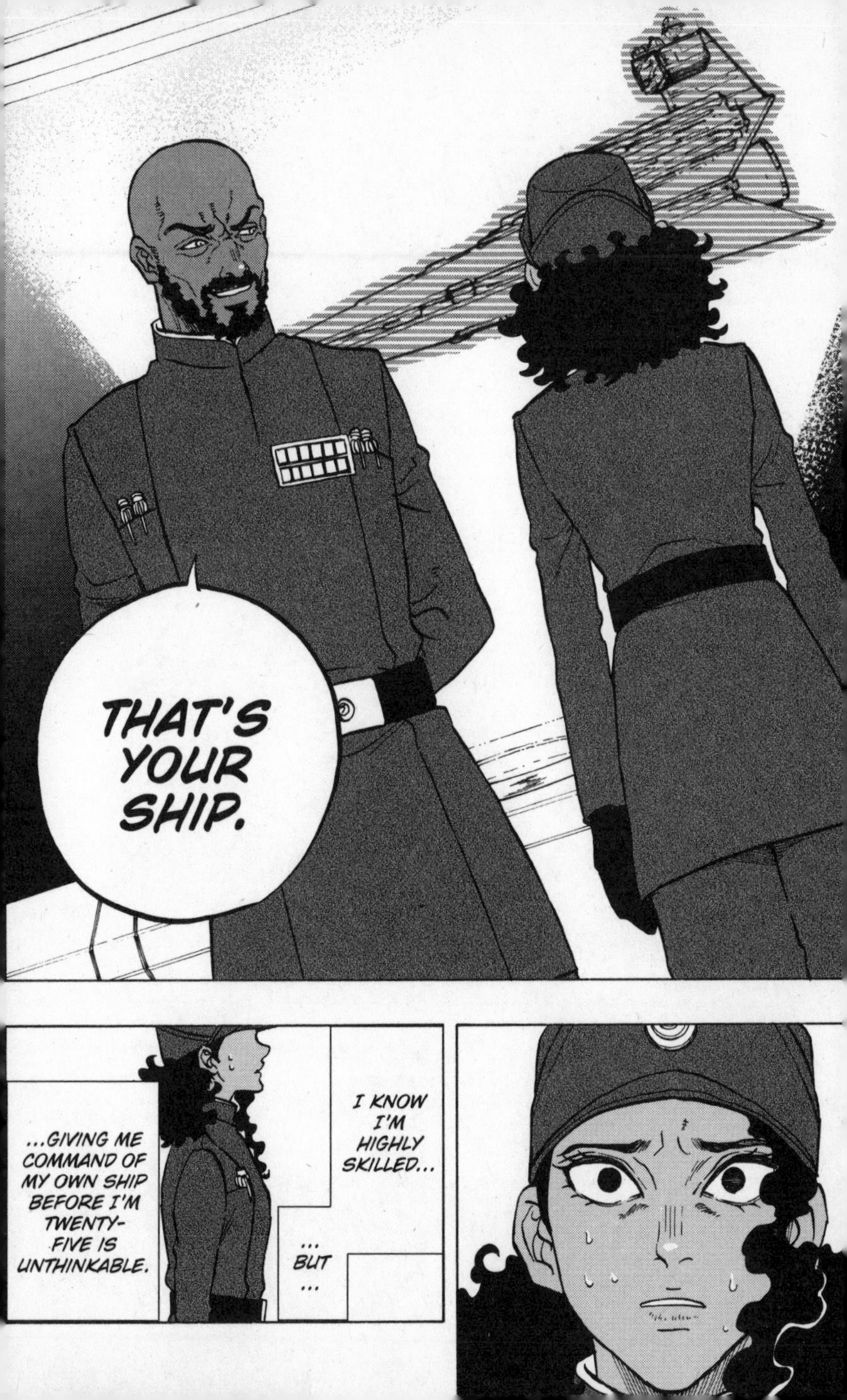
THAT'S YOUR SHIP.
I KNOW I'M HIGHLY SKILLED...
...BUT...
...GIVING ME COMMAND OF MY OWN SHIP BEFORE I'M TWENTY-FIVE IS UNTHINKABLE.

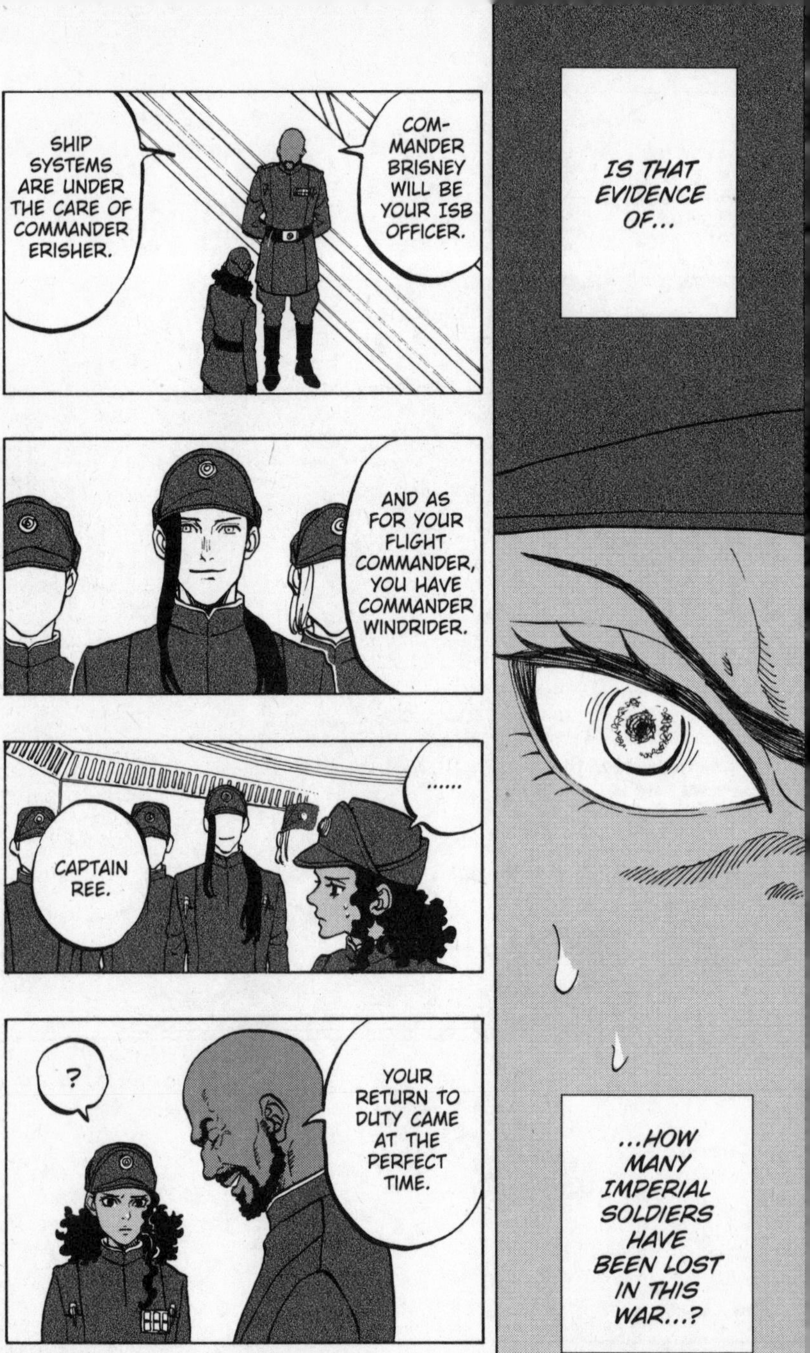
IS THAT EVIDENCE OF...
...HOW MANY IMPERIAL SOLDIERS HAVE BEEN LOST IN THIS WAR...?
COM-MANDER BRISNEY WILL BE YOUR ISB OFFICER.
SHIP SYSTEMS ARE UNDER THE CARE OF COMMANDER ERISHER.
AND AS FOR YOUR FLIGHT COMMANDER, YOU HAVE COMMANDER WINDRIDER.
......
CAPTAIN REE.
YOUR RETURN TO DUTY CAME AT THE PERFECT TIME.
?

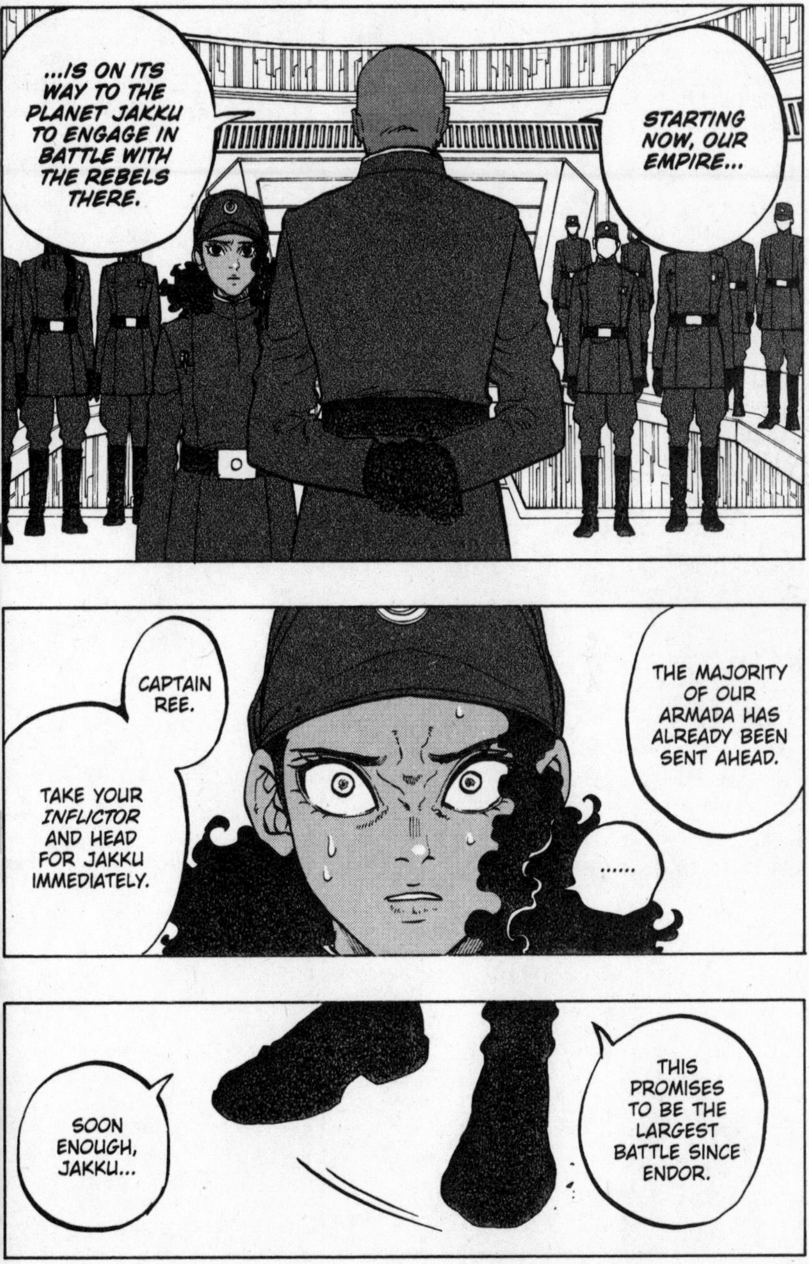
STARTING NOW, OUR EMPIRE...
...IS ON ITS WAY TO THE PLANET JAKKU TO ENGAGE IN BATTLE WITH THE REBELS THERE.
THE MAJORITY OF OUR ARMADA HAS ALREADY BEEN SENT AHEAD.
CAPTAIN REE.
TAKE YOUR INFLICTOR AND HEAD FOR JAKKU IMMEDIATELY.
......
THIS PROMISES TO BE THE LARGEST BATTLE SINCE ENDOR.
SOON ENOUGH, JAKKU...

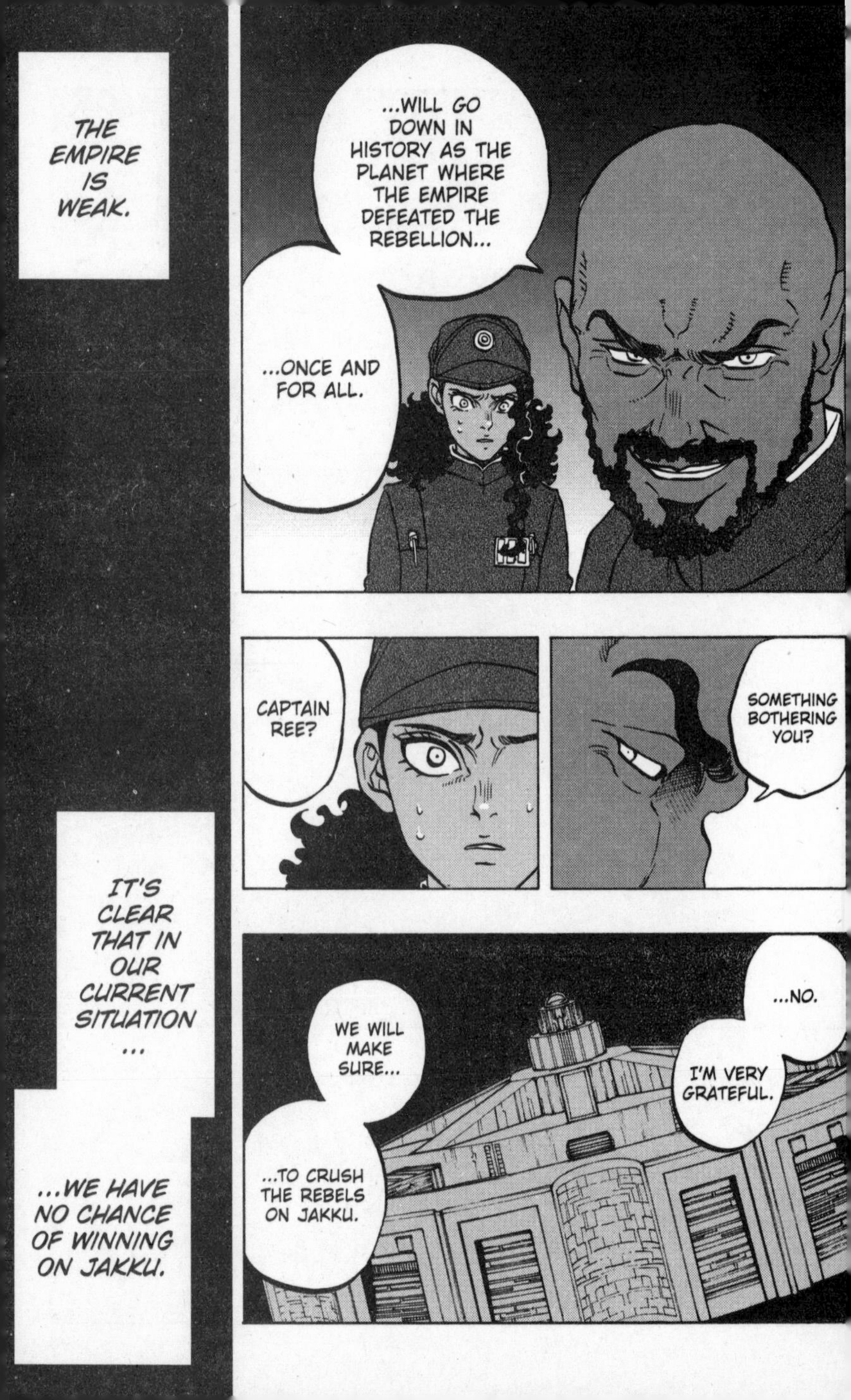
...WILL GO DOWN IN HISTORY AS THE PLANET WHERE THE EMPIRE DEFEATED THE REBELLION...
...ONCE AND FOR ALL.
SOMETHING BOTHERING YOU?
CAPTAIN REE?
...NO.
I'M VERY GRATEFUL.
WE WILL MAKE SURE...
...TO CRUSH THE REBELS ON JAKKU.
THE EMPIRE IS WEAK.
IT'S CLEAR THAT IN OUR CURRENT SITUATION...
...WE HAVE NO CHANCE OF WINNING ON JAKKU.

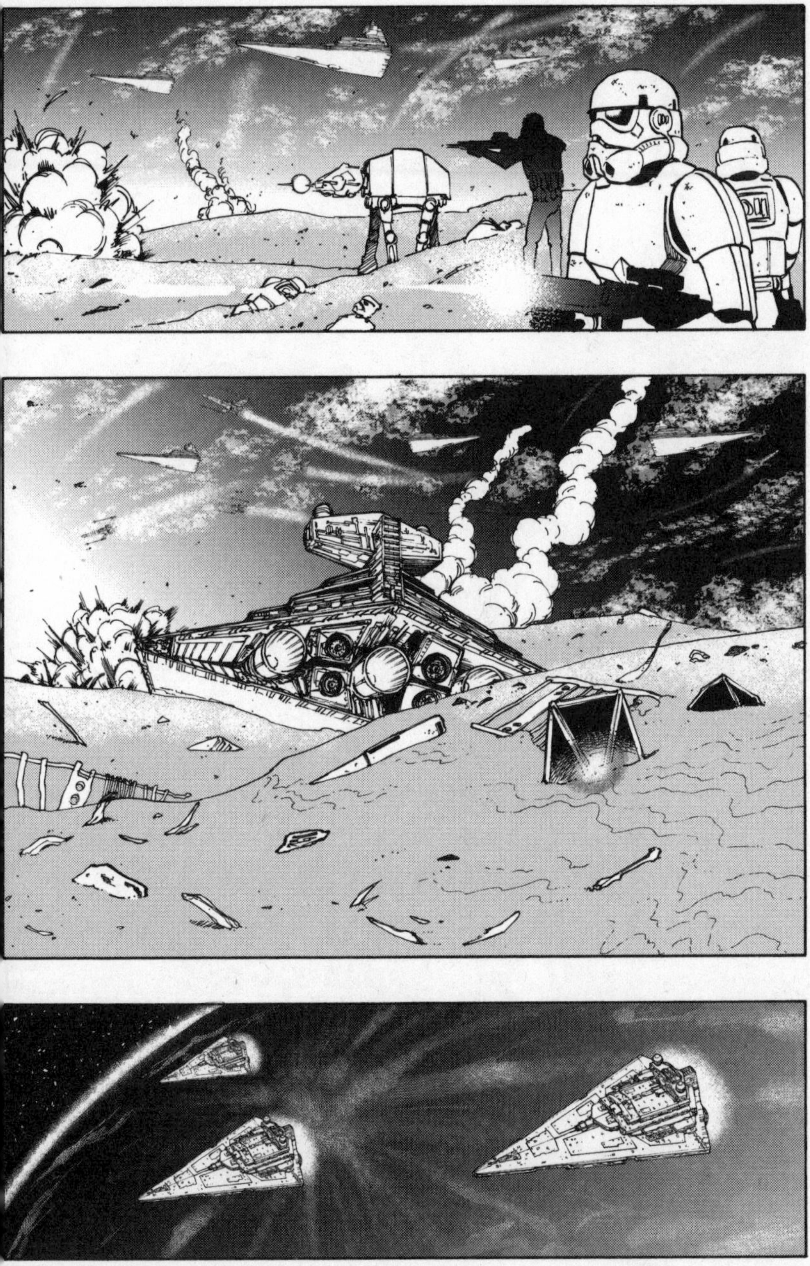

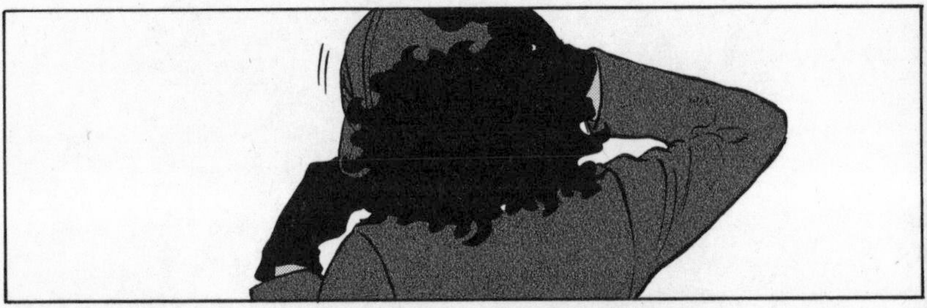

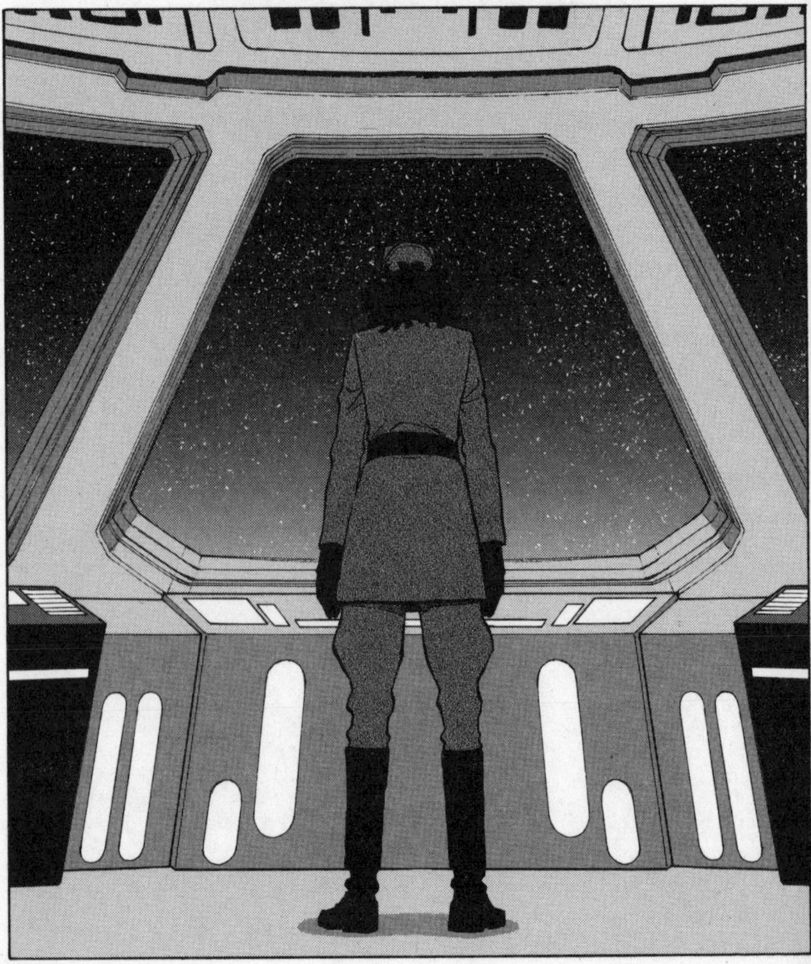

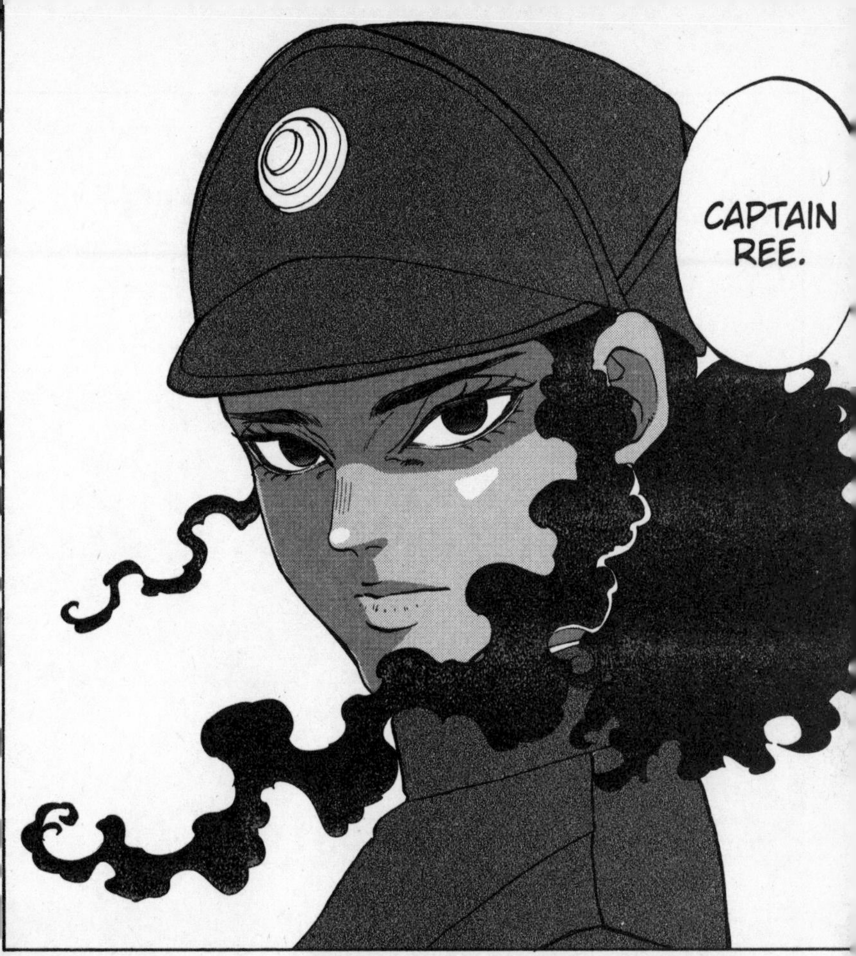
CAPTAIN REE.
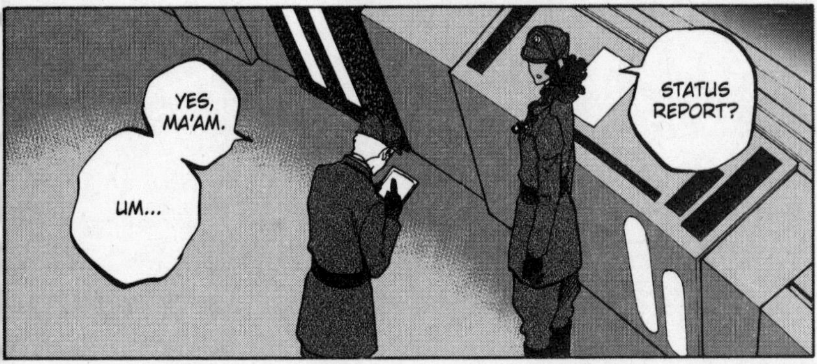
STATUS REPORT?
YES, MA'AM.
UM...

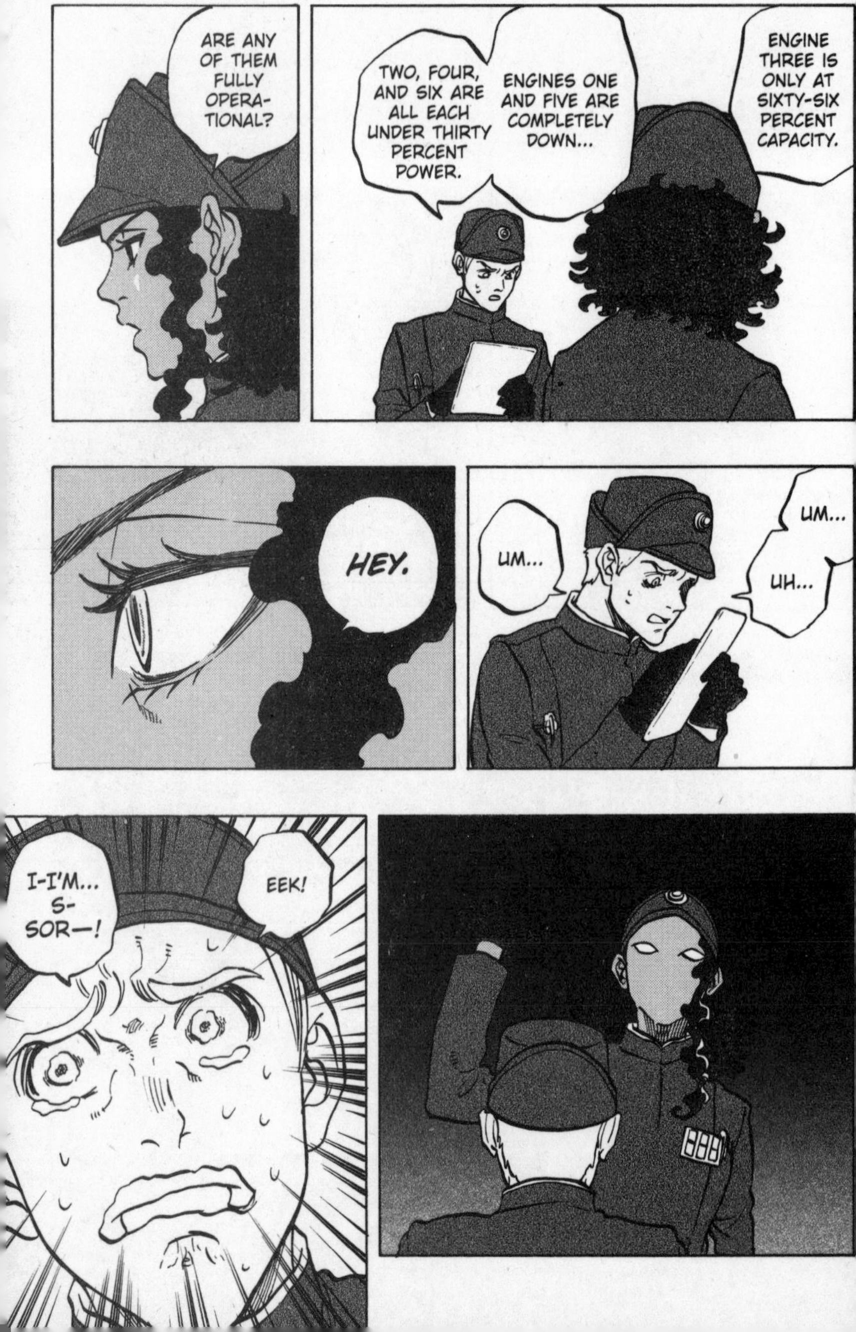
ENGINE THREE IS ONLY AT SIXTY-SIX PERCENT CAPACITY.
ENGINES ONE AND FIVE ARE COMPLETELY DOWN...
TWO, FOUR, AND SIX ARE ALL EACH UNDER THIRTY PERCENT POWER.
ARE ANY OF THEM FULLY OPERA-TIONAL?
UM...
UH...
UM...
HEY.
EEK!
I-I'M... S-SOR—!

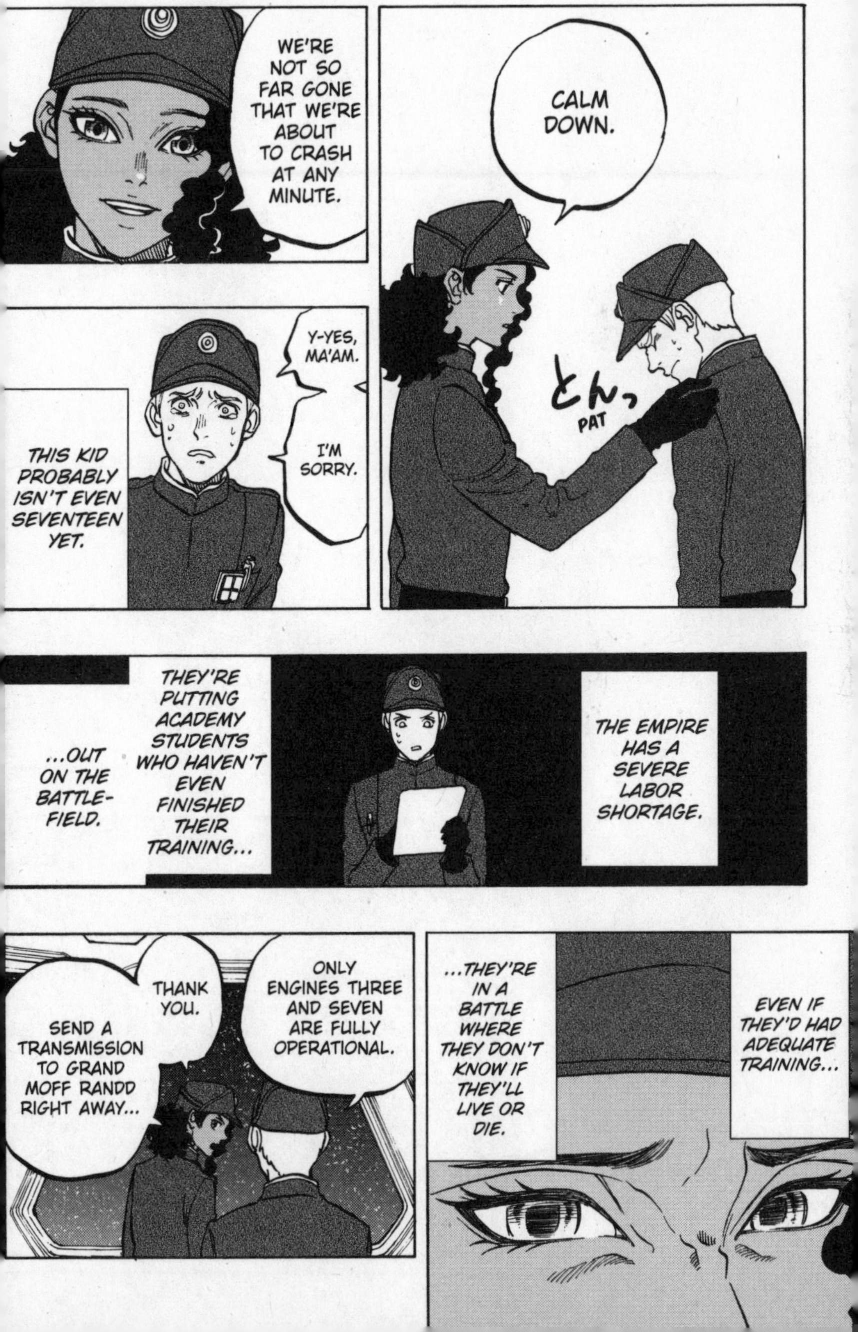
CALM DOWN.
とんっ
PAT
WE'RE NOT SO FAR GONE THAT WE'RE ABOUT TO CRASH AT ANY MINUTE.
Y-YES, MA'AM.
I'M SORRY.
THIS KID PROBABLY ISN'T EVEN SEVENTEEN YET.
THE EMPIRE HAS A SEVERE LABOR SHORTAGE.
THEY'RE PUTTING ACADEMY STUDENTS WHO HAVEN'T EVEN FINISHED THEIR TRAINING...
...OUT ON THE BATTLE-FIELD.
EVEN IF THEY'D HAD ADEQUATE TRAINING...
...THEY'RE IN A BATTLE WHERE THEY DON'T KNOW IF THEY'LL LIVE OR DIE.
ONLY ENGINES THREE AND SEVEN ARE FULLY OPERATIONAL.
THANK YOU.
SEND A TRANSMISSION TO GRAND MOFF RANDD RIGHT AWAY...

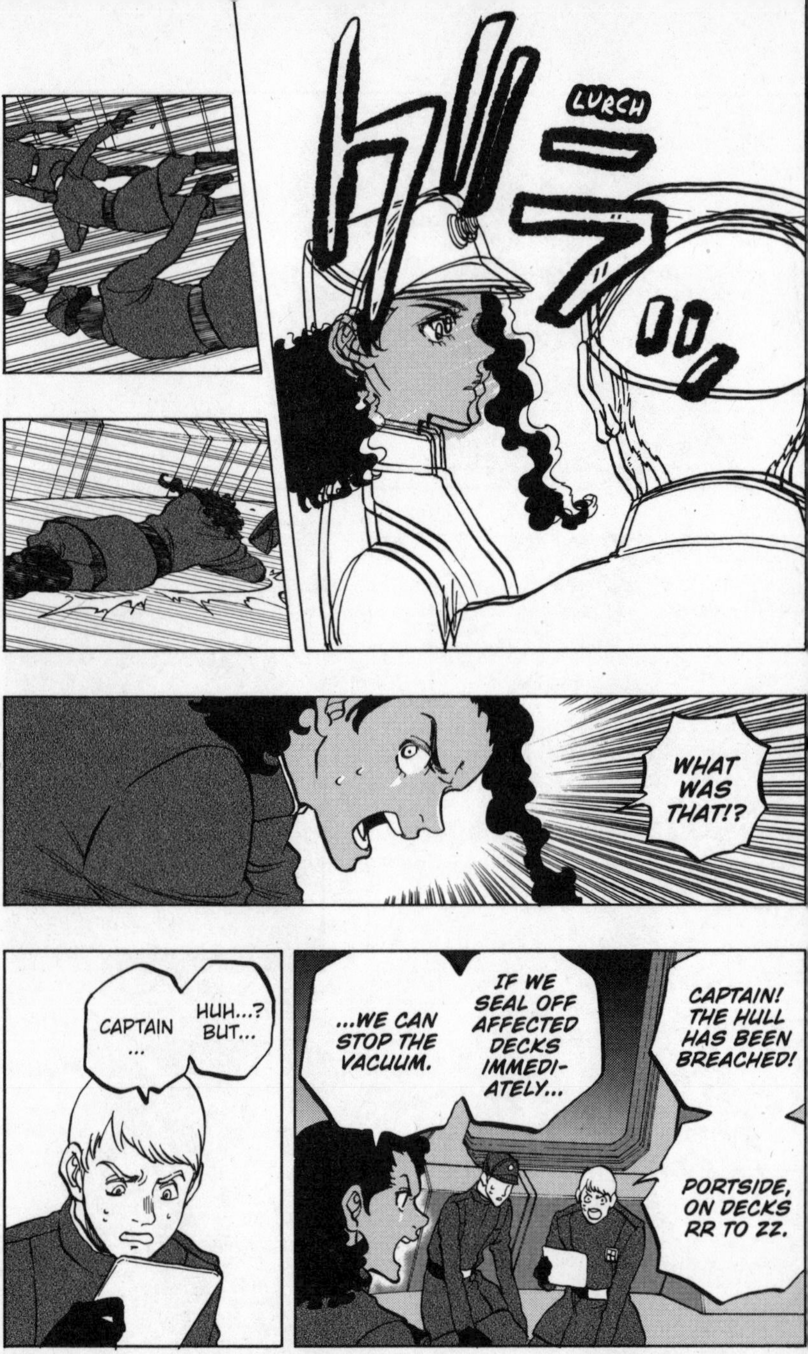
グラッ
LURCH
WHAT WAS THAT!?
CAPTAIN! THE HULL HAS BEEN BREACHED!
PORTSIDE, ON DECKS RR TO ZZ.
IF WE SEAL OFF AFFECTED DECKS IMMEDI-ATELY...
...WE CAN STOP THE VACUUM.
HUH...? BUT...
CAPTAIN ...

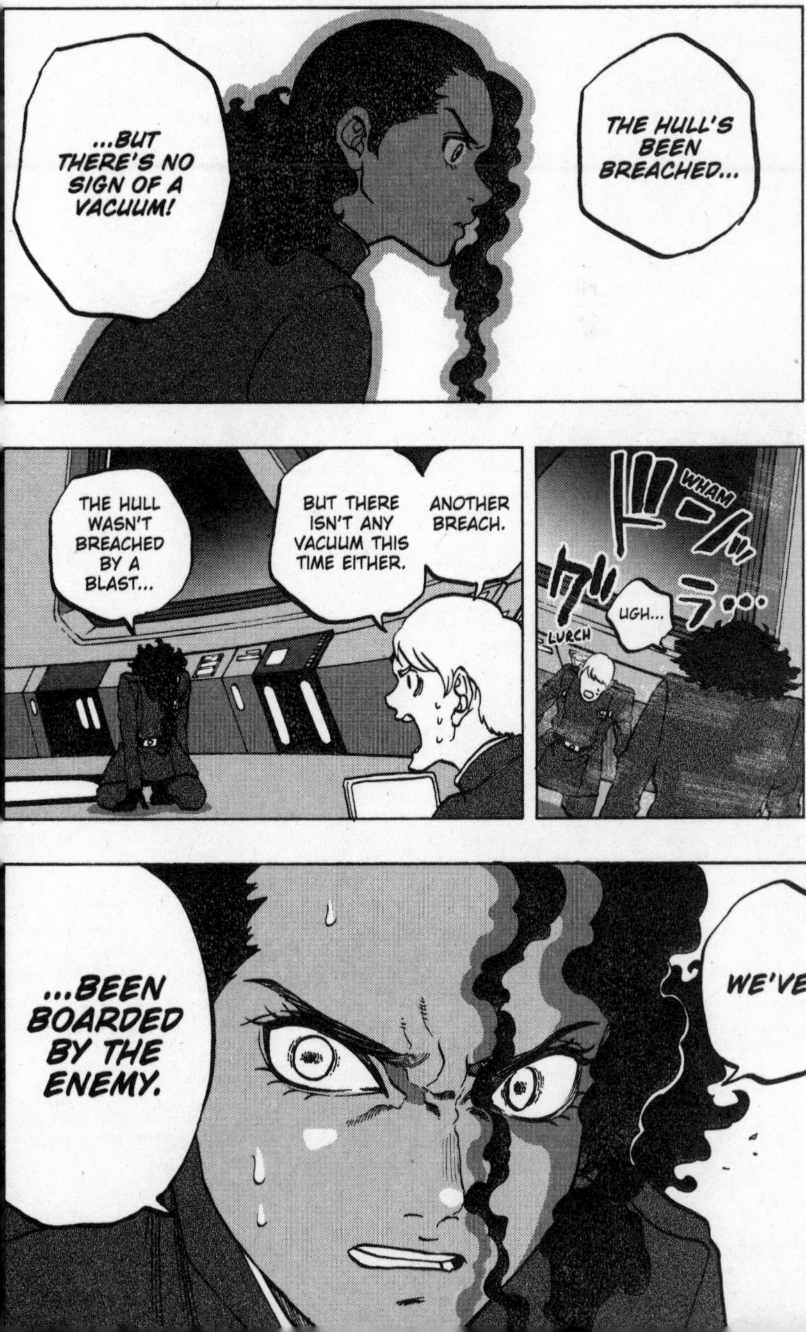
THE HULL'S BEEN BREACHED...
...BUT THERE'S NO SIGN OF A VACUUM!
WHAM
UGH...
LURCH
ANOTHER BREACH.
BUT THERE ISN'T ANY VACUUM THIS TIME EITHER.
THE HULL WASN'T BREACHED BY A BLAST...
WE'VE...
...BEEN BOARDED BY THE ENEMY.

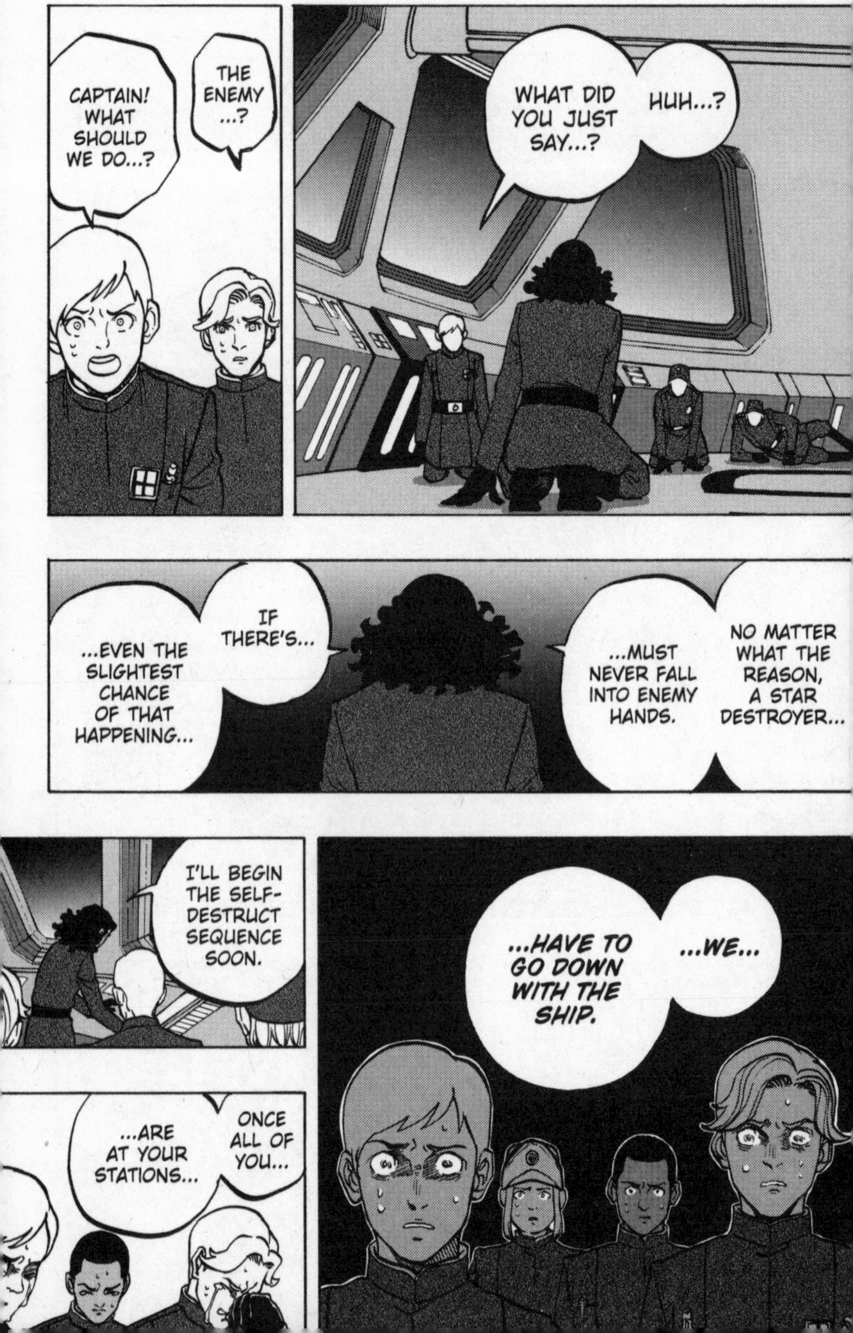
HUH...?
WHAT DID YOU JUST SAY...?
THE ENEMY ...?
CAPTAIN! WHAT SHOULD WE DO...?
NO MATTER WHAT THE REASON, A STAR DESTROYER...
...MUST NEVER FALL INTO ENEMY HANDS.
IF THERE'S...
...EVEN THE SLIGHTEST CHANCE OF THAT HAPPENING...
...WE...
...HAVE TO GO DOWN WITH THE SHIP.
I'LL BEGIN THE SELF-DESTRUCT SEQUENCE SOON.
ONCE ALL OF YOU...
...ARE AT YOUR STATIONS...

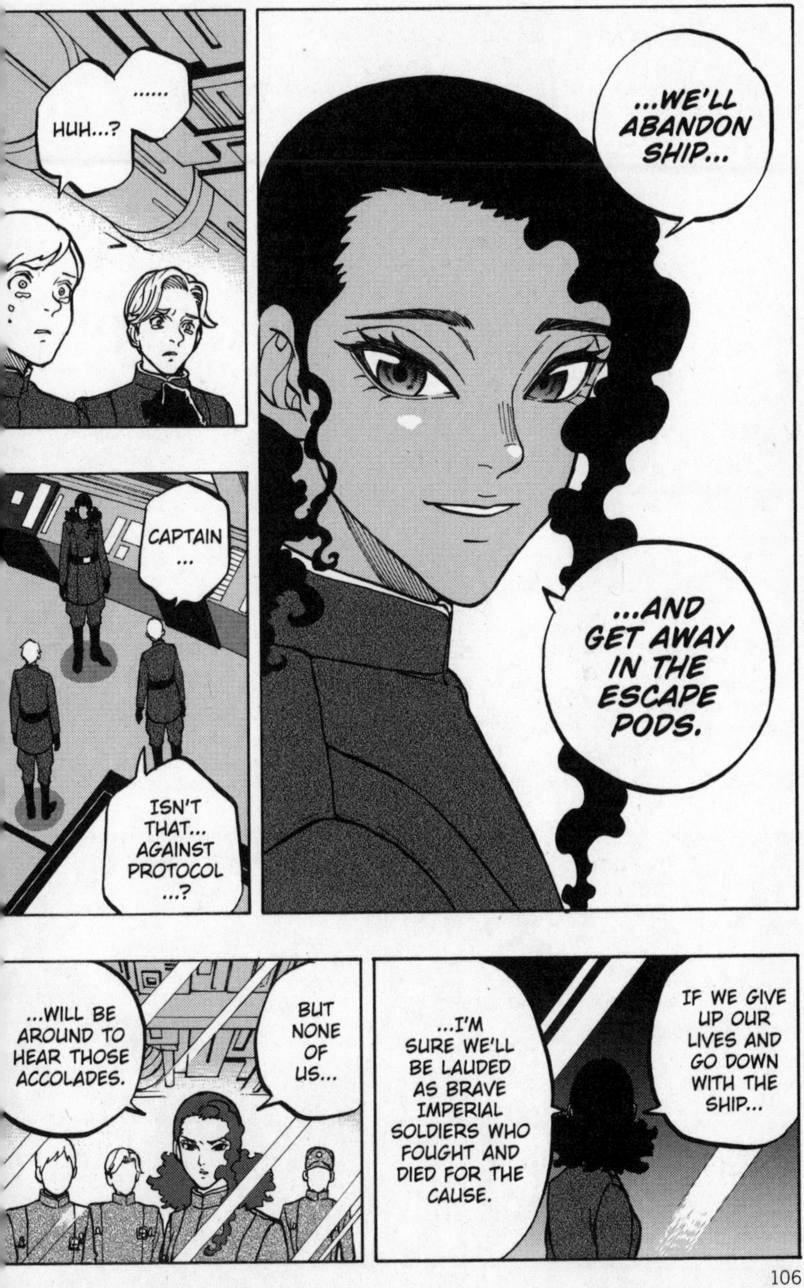
...WE'LL ABANDON SHIP...
...AND GET AWAY IN THE ESCAPE PODS.
......
HUH...?
CAPTAIN ...
ISN'T THAT... AGAINST PROTOCOL ...?
IF WE GIVE UP OUR LIVES AND GO DOWN WITH THE SHIP...
...I'M SURE WE'LL BE LAUDED AS BRAVE IMPERIAL SOLDIERS WHO FOUGHT AND DIED FOR THE CAUSE.
BUT NONE OF US...
...WILL BE AROUND TO HEAR THOSE ACCOLADES.

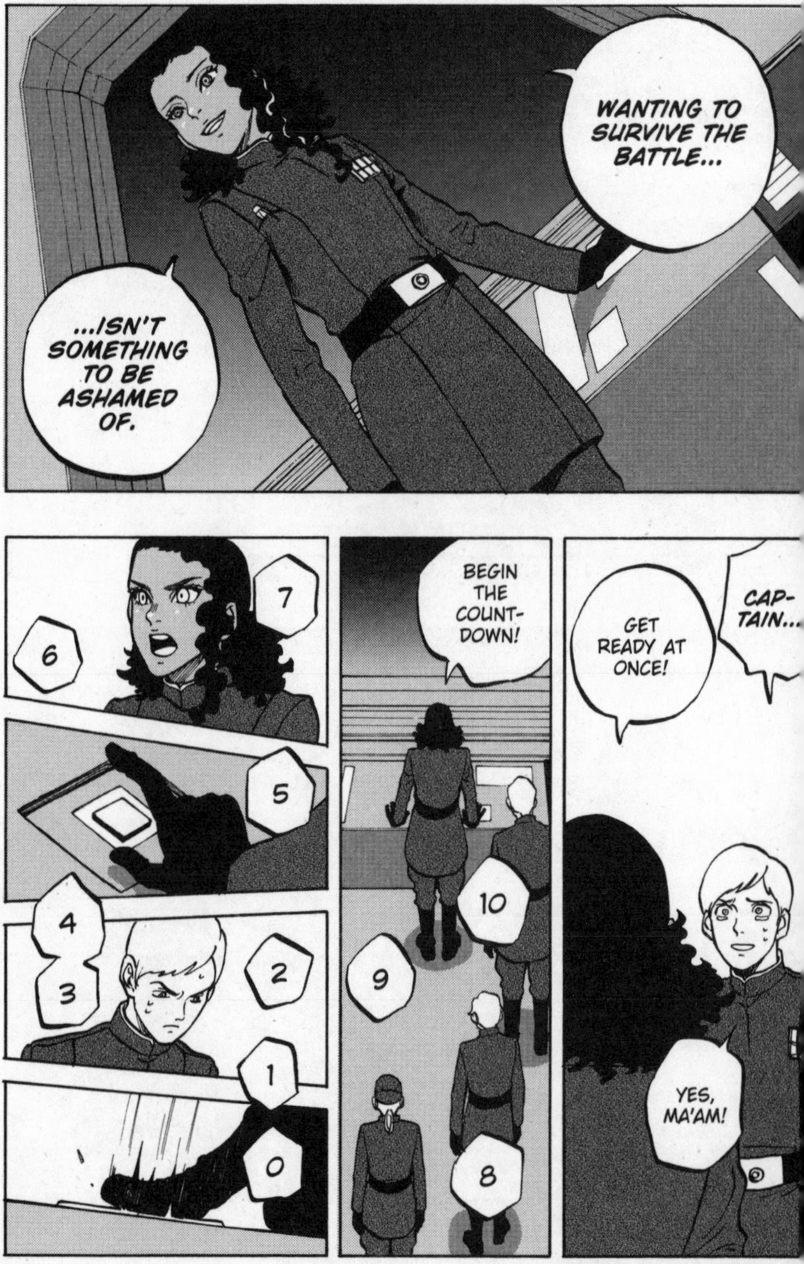
WANTING TO SURVIVE THE BATTLE...
...ISN'T SOMETHING TO BE ASHAMED OF.
CAP-TAIN...
GET READY AT ONCE!
YES, MA'AM!
BEGIN THE COUNT-DOWN!
10
9
8
7
6
5
4
3
2
1
0

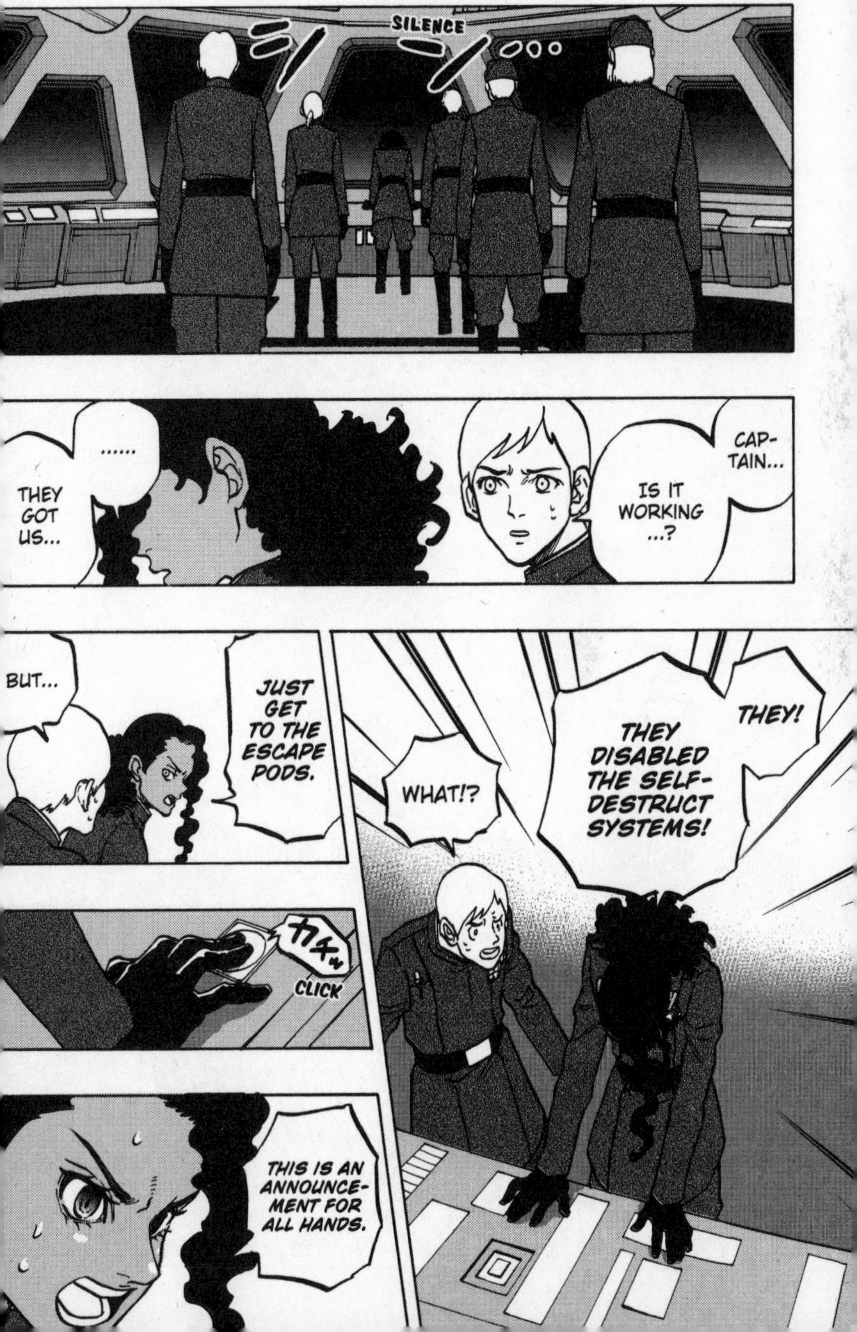
SILENCE
CAP-TAIN... IS IT WORKING ...?
...... THEY GOT US...
THEY! THEY DISABLED THE SELF-DESTRUCT SYSTEMS!
WHAT!?
JUST GET TO THE ESCAPE PODS.
BUT...
カチッ
CLICK
THIS IS AN ANNOUNCE-MENT FOR ALL HANDS.

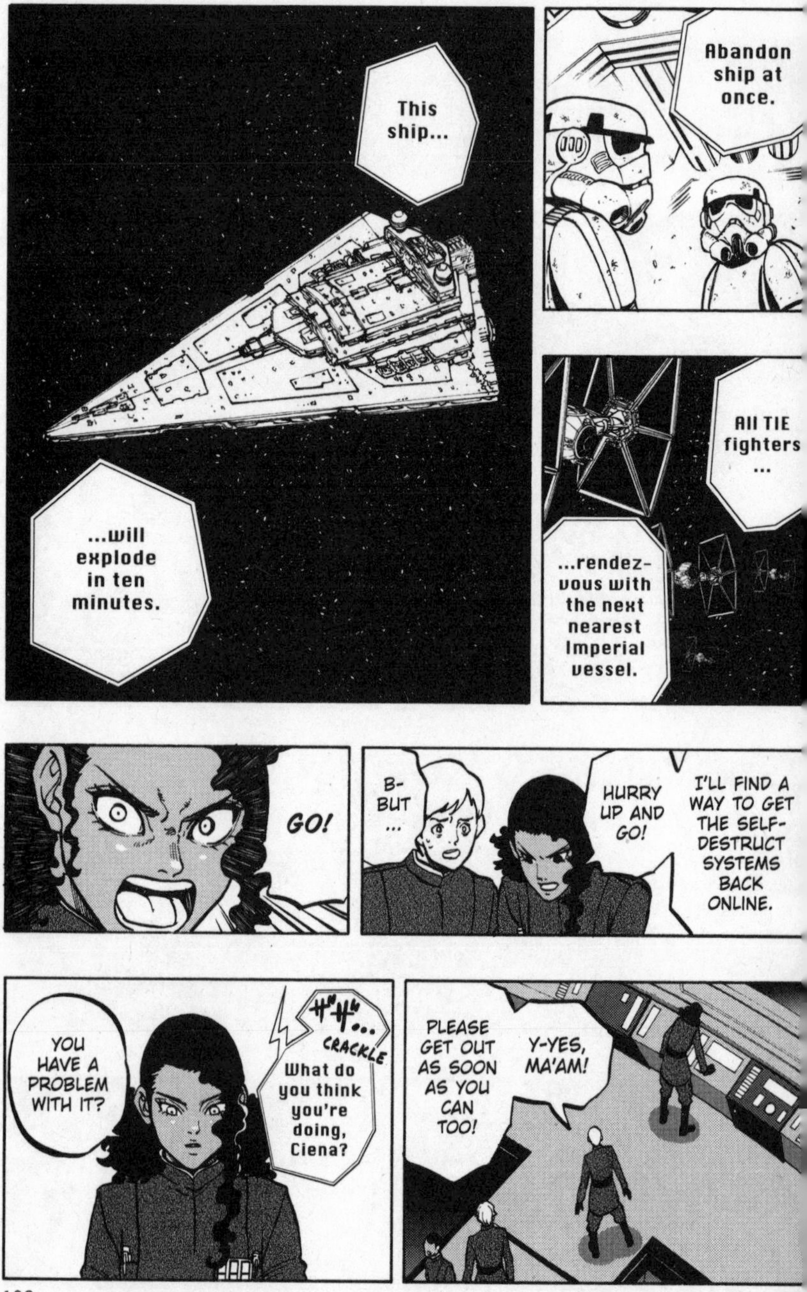
Abandon ship at once.
All TIE fighters...
...rendezvous with the next nearest Imperial vessel.
This ship...
...will explode in ten minutes.
I'LL FIND A WAY TO GET THE SELF-DESTRUCT SYSTEMS BACK ONLINE.
HURRY UP AND GO!
B-BUT...
GO!
Y-YES, MA'AM!
PLEASE GET OUT AS SOON AS YOU CAN TOO!
ザザ...
CRACKLE
What do you think you're doing, Ciena?
YOU HAVE A PROBLEM WITH IT?

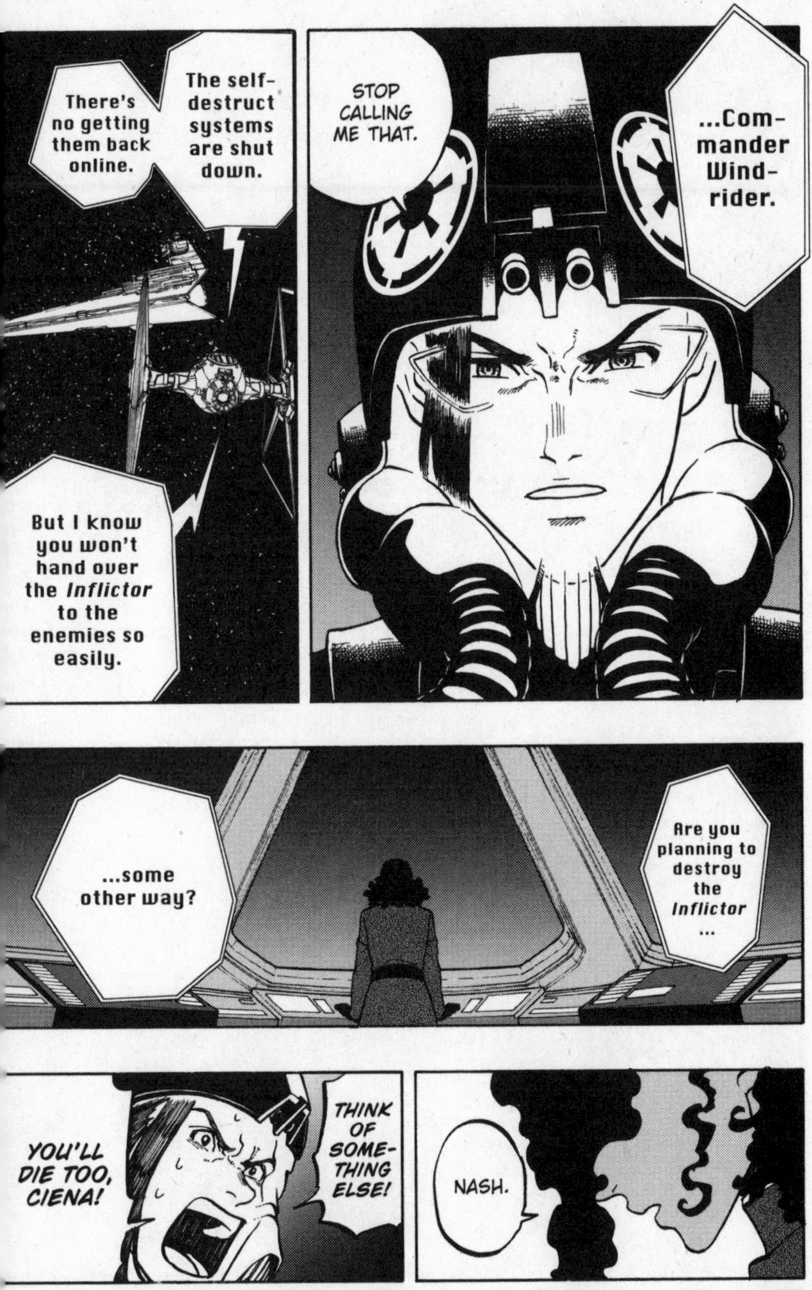
...Commander Windrider.
STOP CALLING ME THAT.
The self-destruct systems are shut down.
There's no getting them back online.
But I know you won't hand over the *Inflictor* to the enemies so easily.
Are you planning to destroy the *Inflictor* ...
...some other way?
NASH.
THINK OF SOMETHING ELSE!
YOU'LL DIE TOO, CIENA!

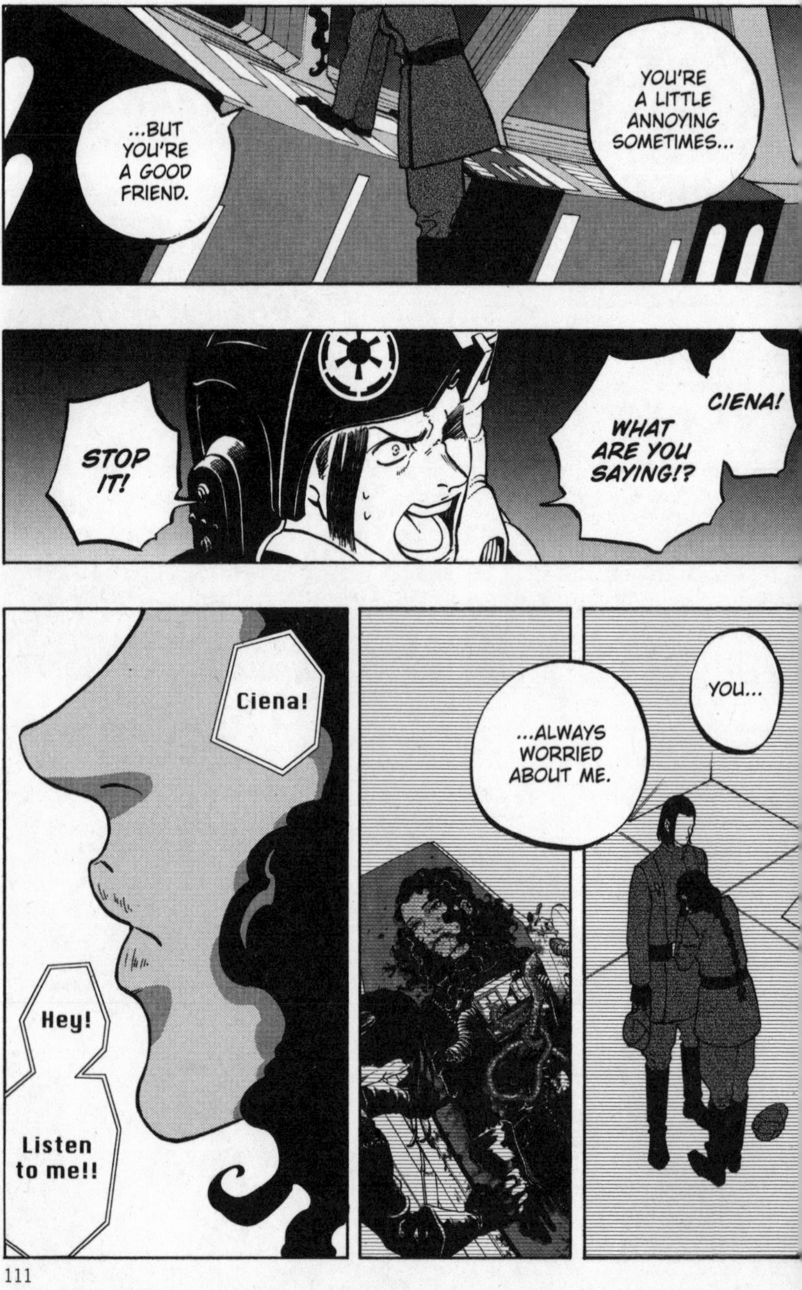
YOU'RE A LITTLE ANNOYING SOMETIMES...
...BUT YOU'RE A GOOD FRIEND.
CIENA!
WHAT ARE YOU SAYING!?
STOP IT!
YOU...
...ALWAYS WORRIED ABOUT ME.
Ciena!
Hey!
Listen to me!!

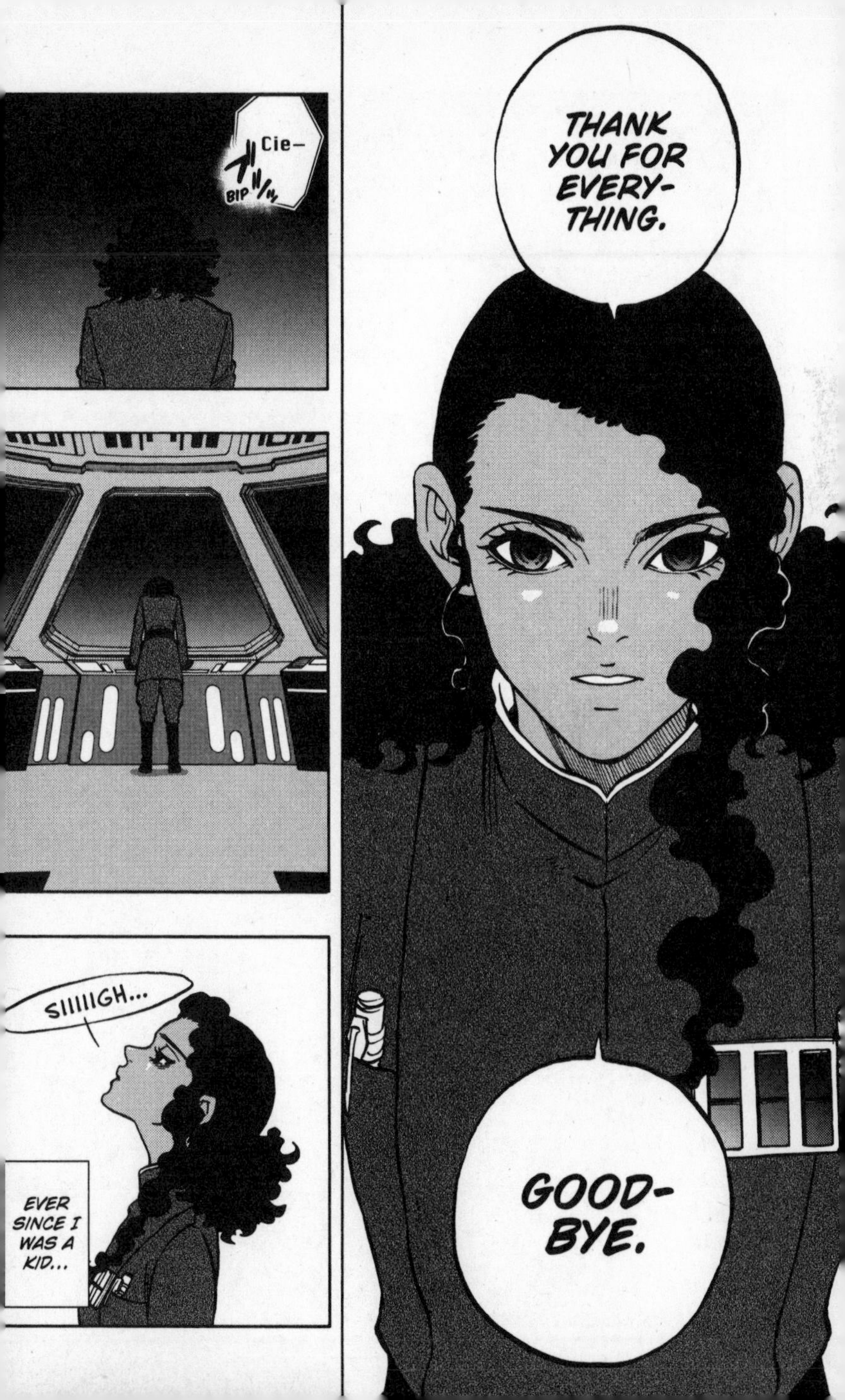
THANK YOU FOR EVERY-THING.
GOOD-BYE.
Cie–
BIP
SIIIIGH...
EVER SINCE I WAS A KID...

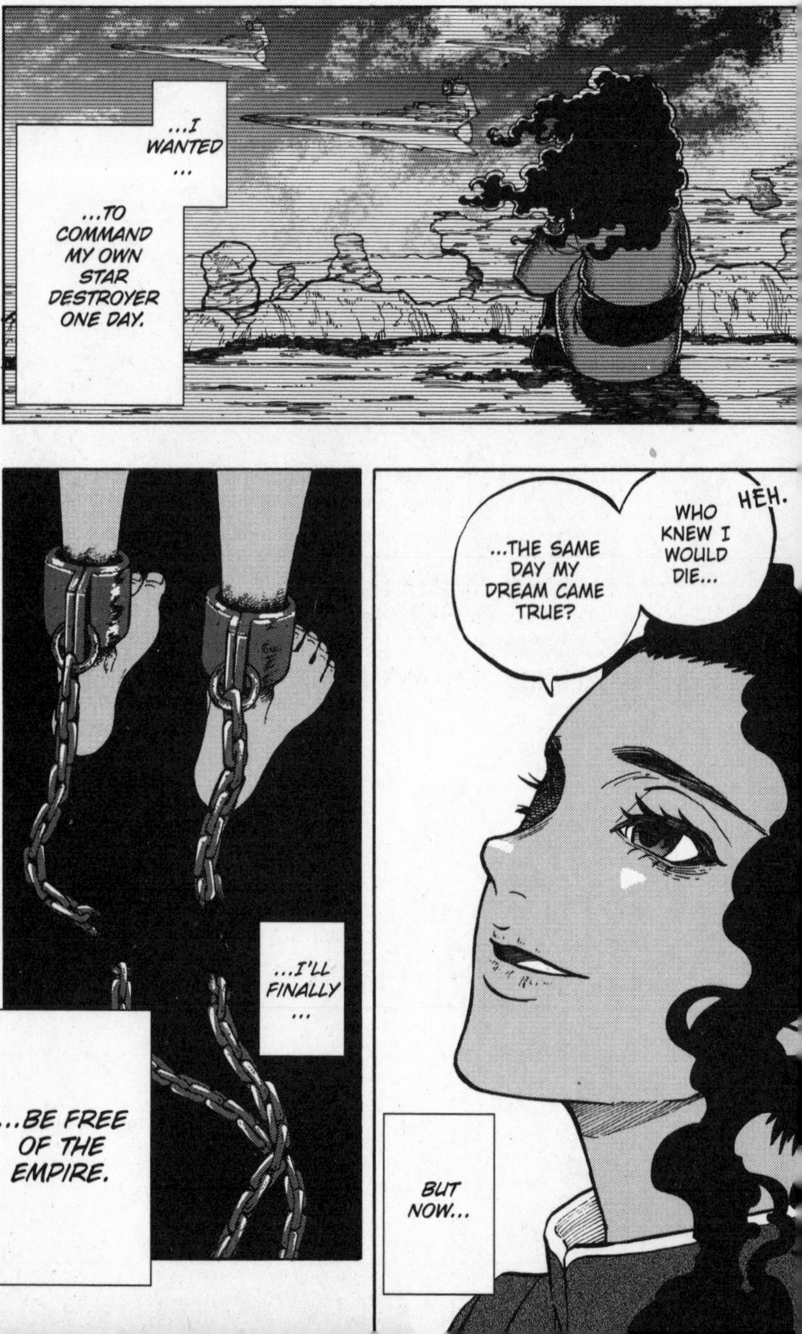
...I WANTED ...
...TO COMMAND MY OWN STAR DESTROYER ONE DAY.
HEH.
WHO KNEW I WOULD DIE...
...THE SAME DAY MY DREAM CAME TRUE?
BUT NOW...
...I'LL FINALLY ...
...BE FREE OF THE EMPIRE.

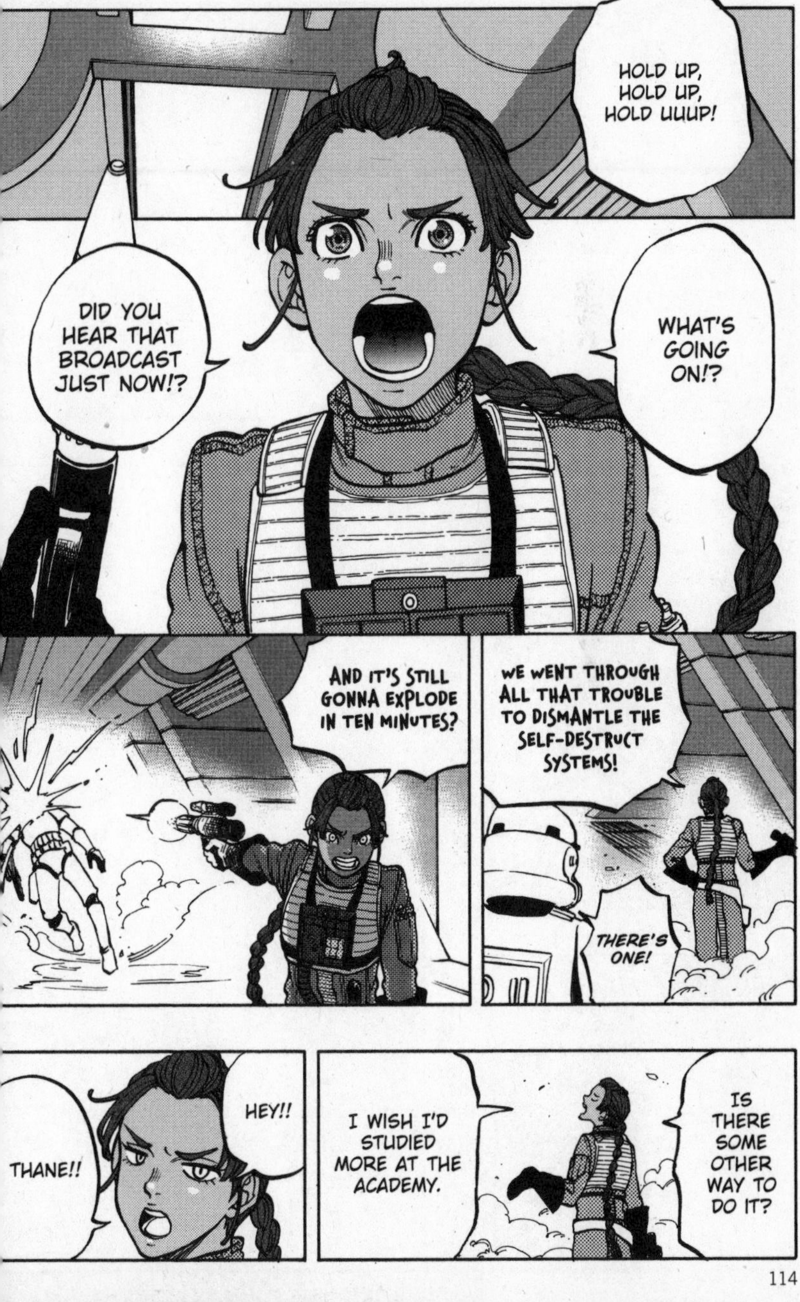
HOLD UP, HOLD UP, HOLD UUUP!
WHAT'S GOING ON!?
DID YOU HEAR THAT BROADCAST JUST NOW!?
WE WENT THROUGH ALL THAT TROUBLE TO DISMANTLE THE SELF-DESTRUCT SYSTEMS!
THERE'S ONE!
AND IT'S STILL GONNA EXPLODE IN TEN MINUTES?
IS THERE SOME OTHER WAY TO DO IT?
I WISH I'D STUDIED MORE AT THE ACADEMY.
HEY!!
THANE!!

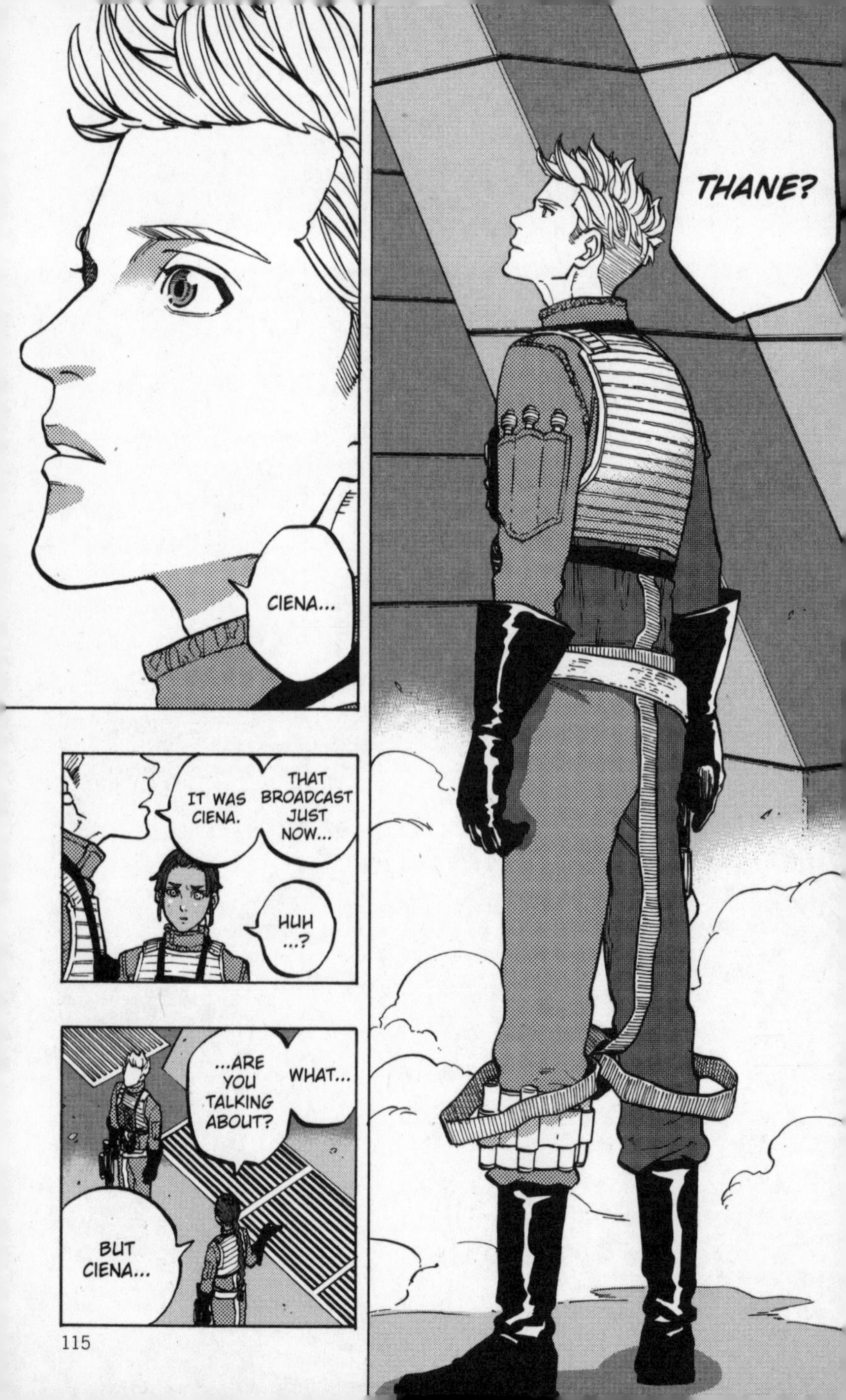
THANE?
CIENA...
THAT BROADCAST JUST NOW...
IT WAS CIENA.
HUH ...?
WHAT...
...ARE YOU TALKING ABOUT?
BUT CIENA...

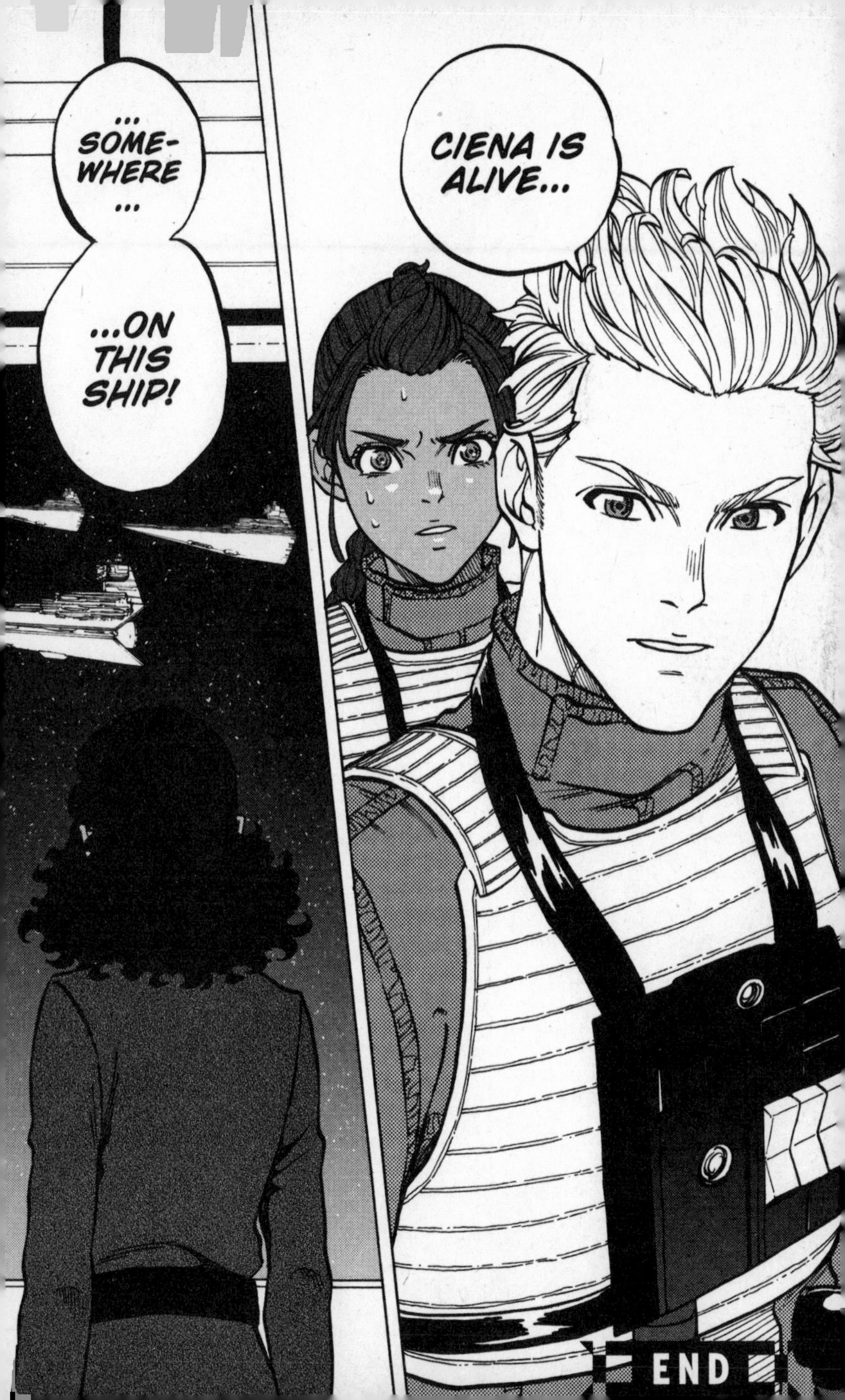
CIENA IS ALIVE...
...SOMEWHERE...
...ON THIS SHIP!
END

STAR WARS
LOST STARS
ロスト・スター

STAR WARS
LOST STARS

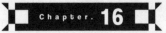

Chapter. 16

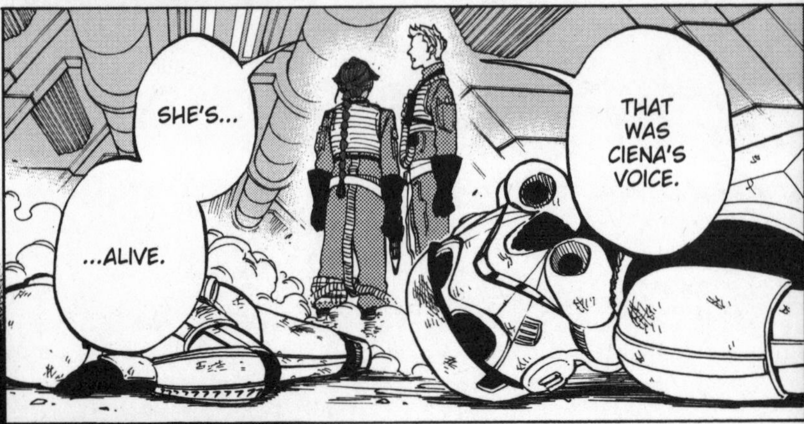
THAT WAS CIENA'S VOICE.
SHE'S...
...ALIVE.

A LITTLE BIT EARLIER

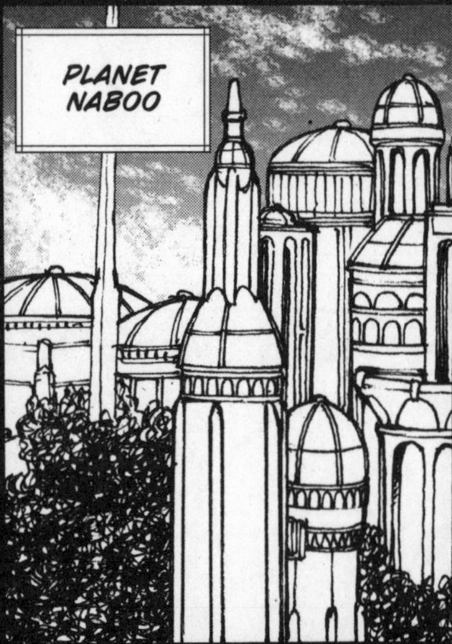
PLANET NABOO

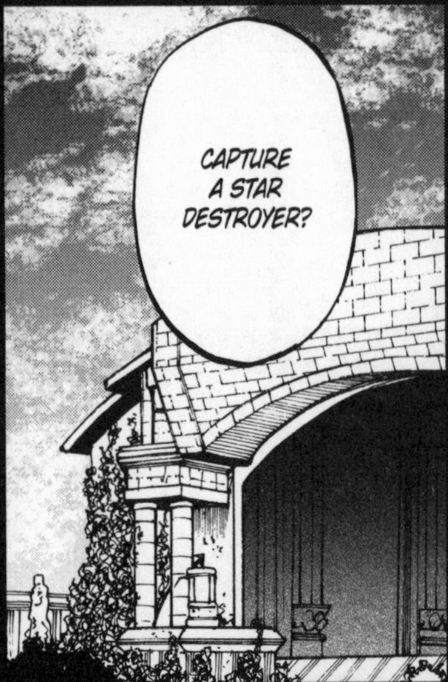
CAPTURE A STAR DESTROYER?

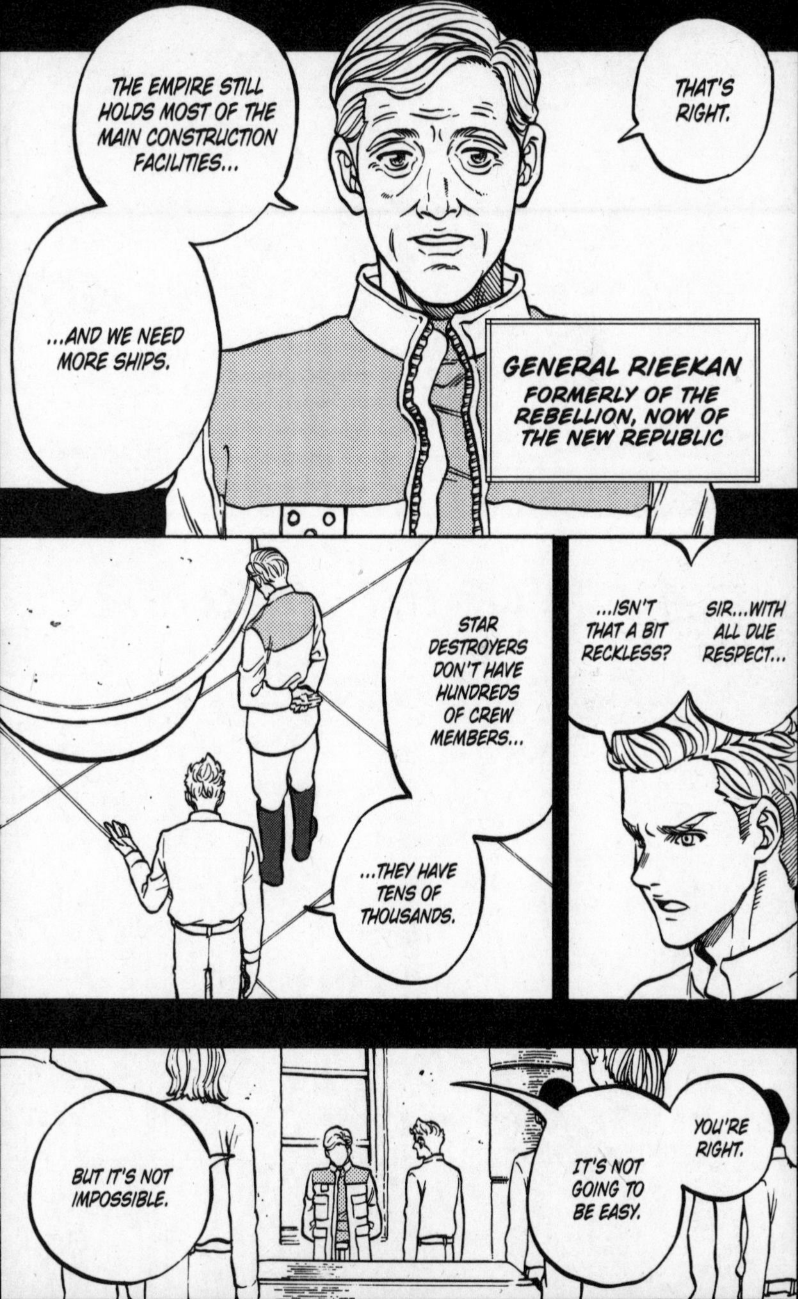
THAT'S RIGHT.
THE EMPIRE STILL HOLDS MOST OF THE MAIN CONSTRUCTION FACILITIES...
GENERAL RIEEKAN
FORMERLY OF THE REBELLION, NOW OF THE NEW REPUBLIC
...AND WE NEED MORE SHIPS.
SIR...WITH ALL DUE RESPECT...
...ISN'T THAT A BIT RECKLESS?
STAR DESTROYERS DON'T HAVE HUNDREDS OF CREW MEMBERS...
...THEY HAVE TENS OF THOUSANDS.
YOU'RE RIGHT.
IT'S NOT GOING TO BE EASY.
BUT IT'S NOT IMPOSSIBLE.

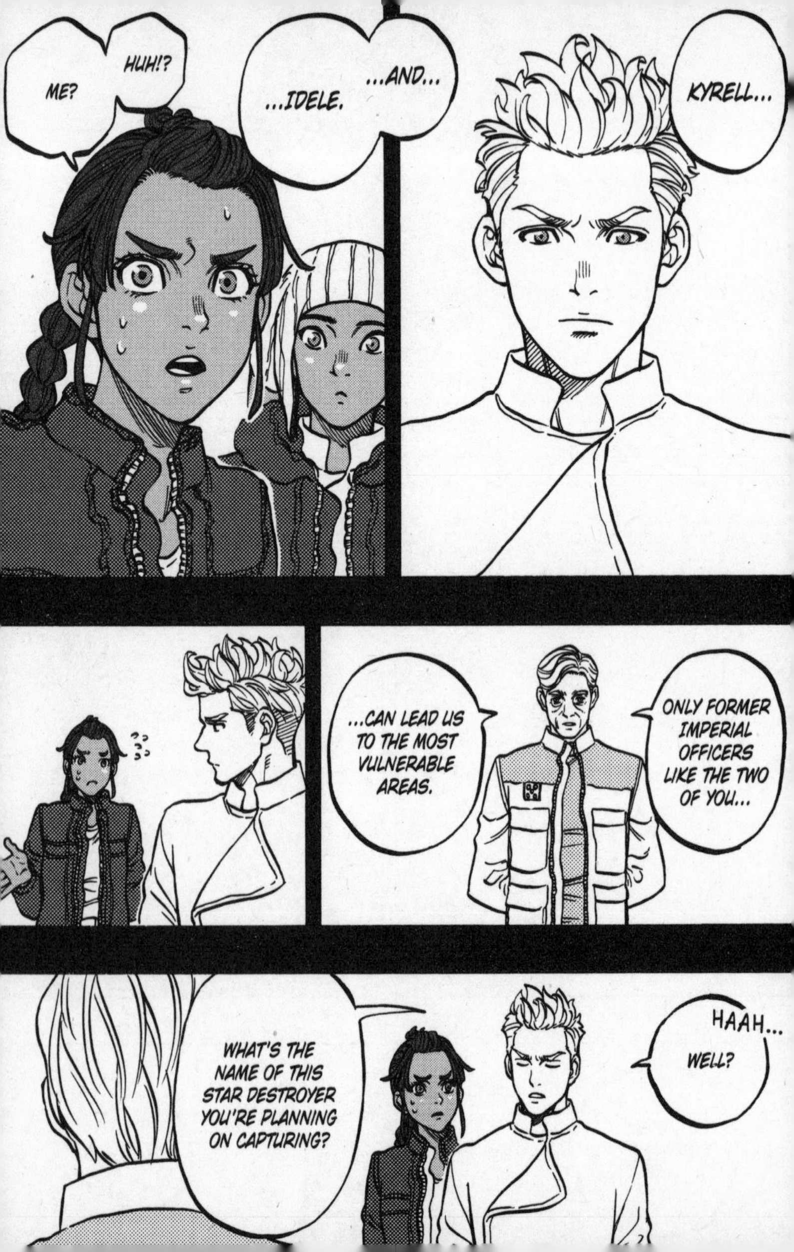
KYRELL...
...AND...
...IDELE.
HUH!?
ME?
ONLY FORMER IMPERIAL OFFICERS LIKE THE TWO OF YOU...
...CAN LEAD US TO THE MOST VULNERABLE AREAS.
HAAH...
WELL?
WHAT'S THE NAME OF THIS STAR DESTROYER YOU'RE PLANNING ON CAPTURING?

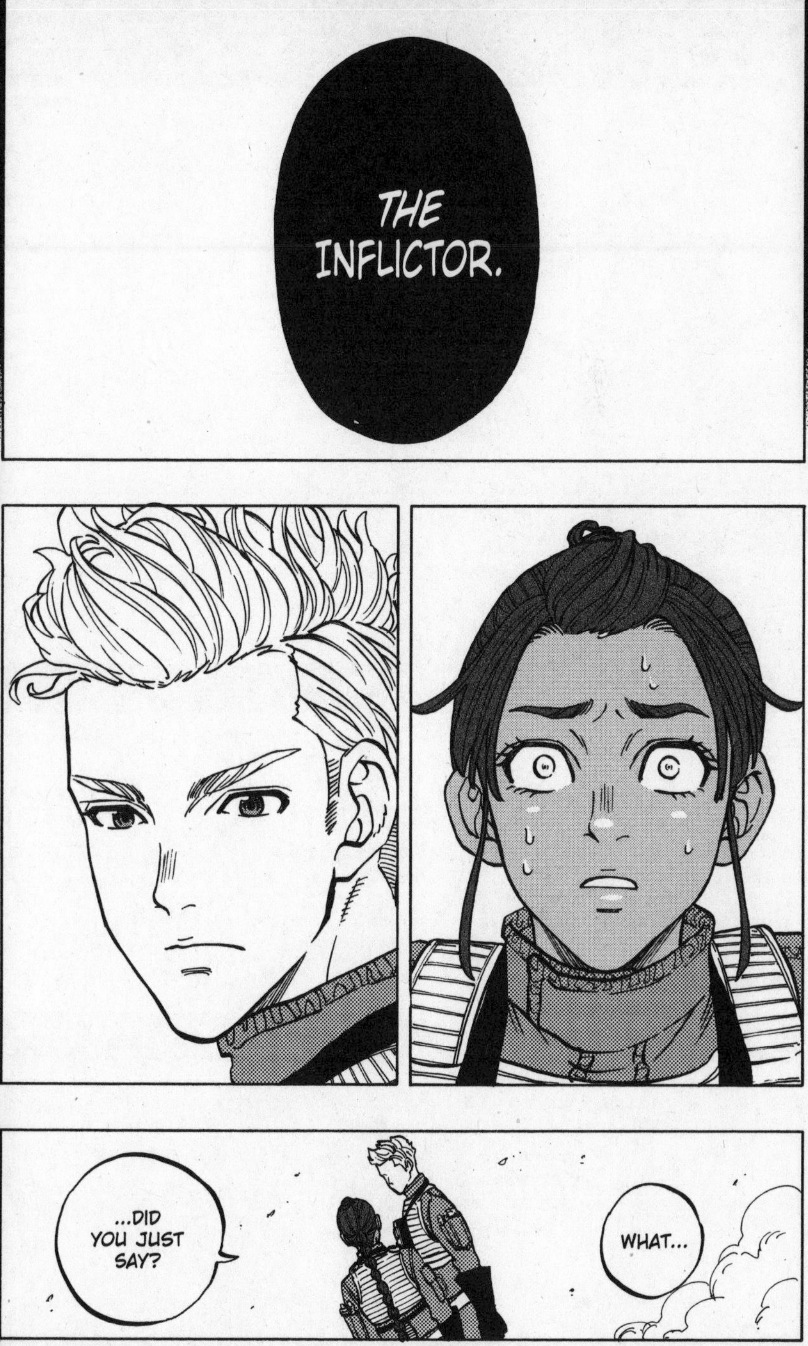
THE INFLICTOR.
WHAT...
...DID YOU JUST SAY?

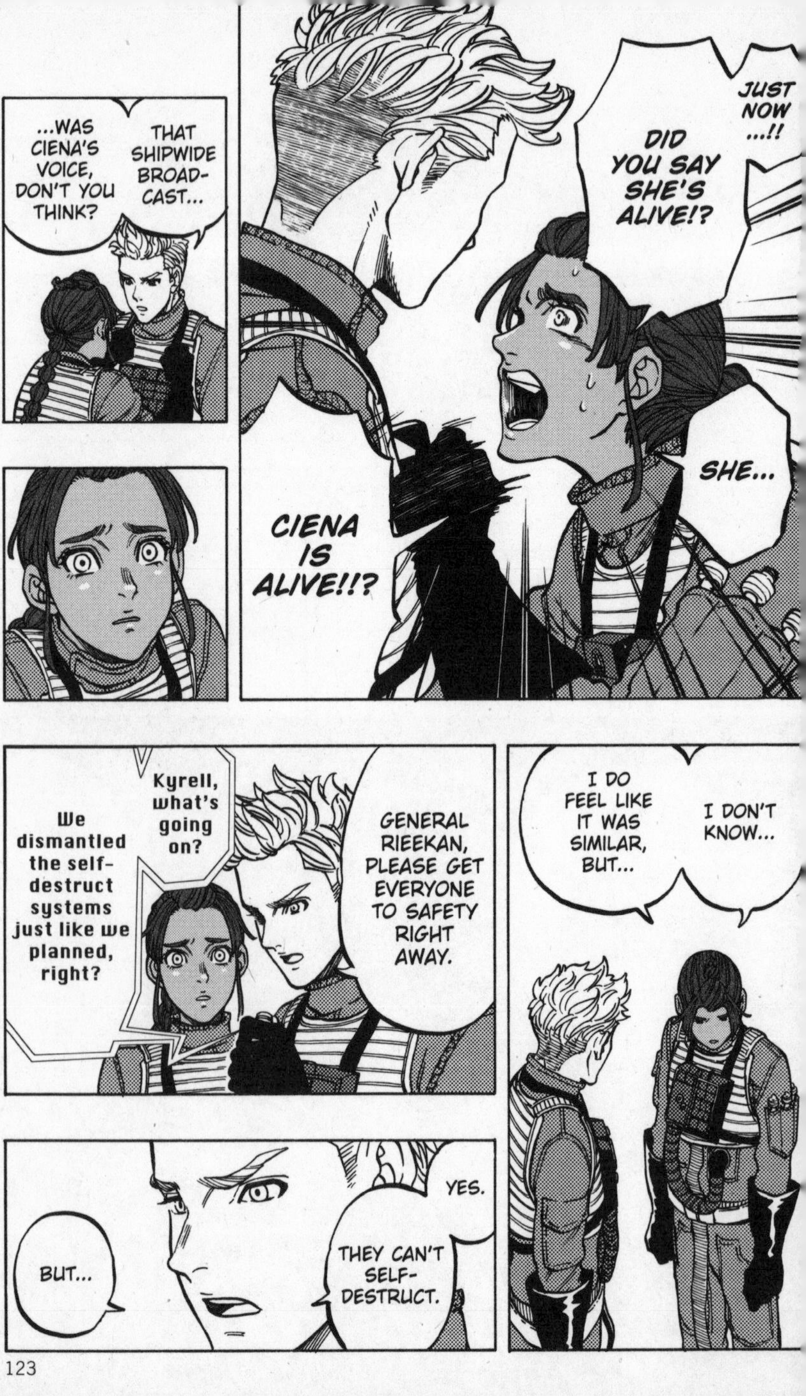
JUST NOW...!!
DID YOU SAY SHE'S ALIVE!?
SHE...
CIENA IS ALIVE!!?
THAT SHIPWIDE BROADCAST...
...WAS CIENA'S VOICE, DON'T YOU THINK?
I DON'T KNOW...
I DO FEEL LIKE IT WAS SIMILAR, BUT...
GENERAL RIEEKAN, PLEASE GET EVERYONE TO SAFETY RIGHT AWAY.
Kyrell, what's going on?
We dismantled the self-destruct systems just like we planned, right?
YES.
THEY CAN'T SELF-DESTRUCT.
BUT...

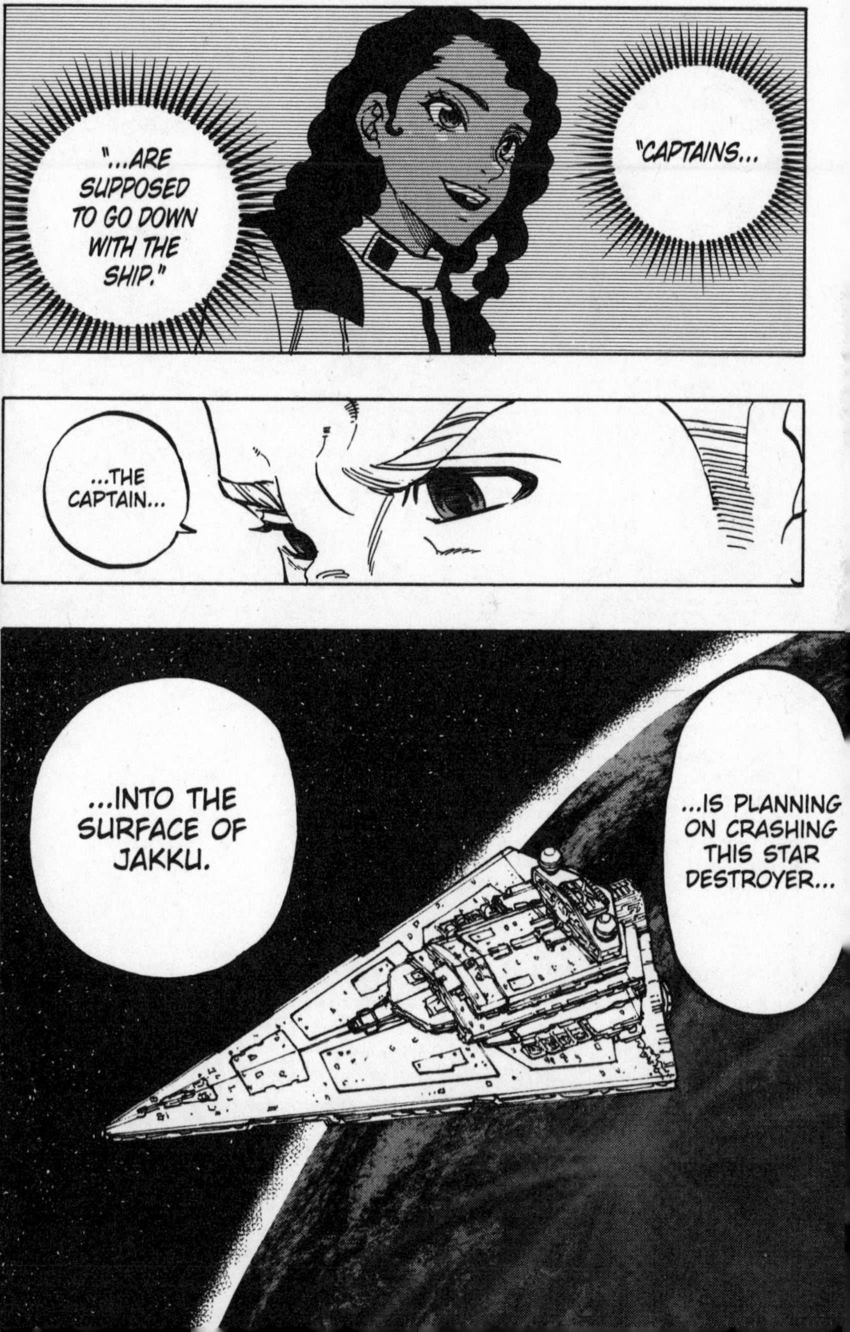
"CAPTAINS...
"...ARE SUPPOSED TO GO DOWN WITH THE SHIP."
...THE CAPTAIN...
...IS PLANNING ON CRASHING THIS STAR DESTROYER...
...INTO THE SURFACE OF JAKKU.

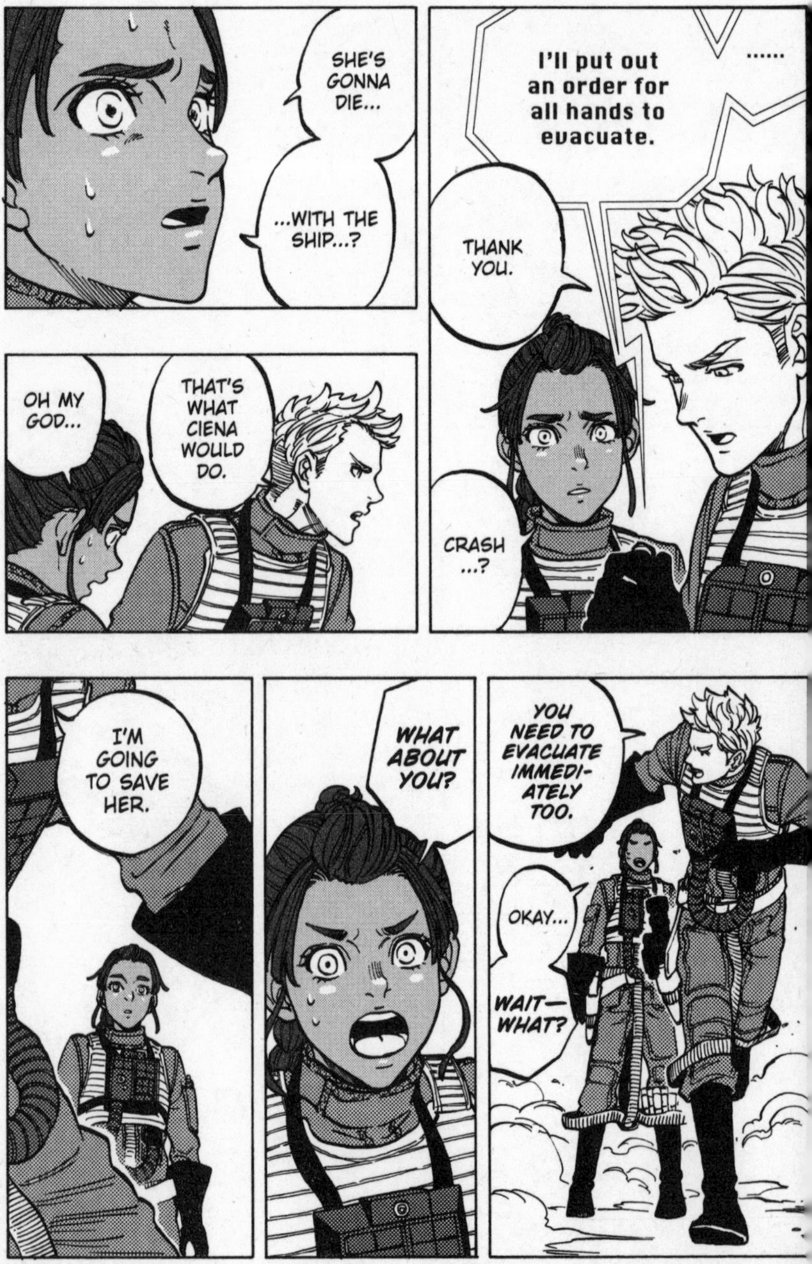
......
I'll put out an order for all hands to evacuate.
THANK YOU.
CRASH ...?
SHE'S GONNA DIE...
...WITH THE SHIP...?
THAT'S WHAT CIENA WOULD DO.
OH MY GOD...
YOU NEED TO EVACUATE IMMEDI-ATELY TOO.
OKAY...
WAIT— WHAT?
WHAT ABOUT YOU?
I'M GOING TO SAVE HER.

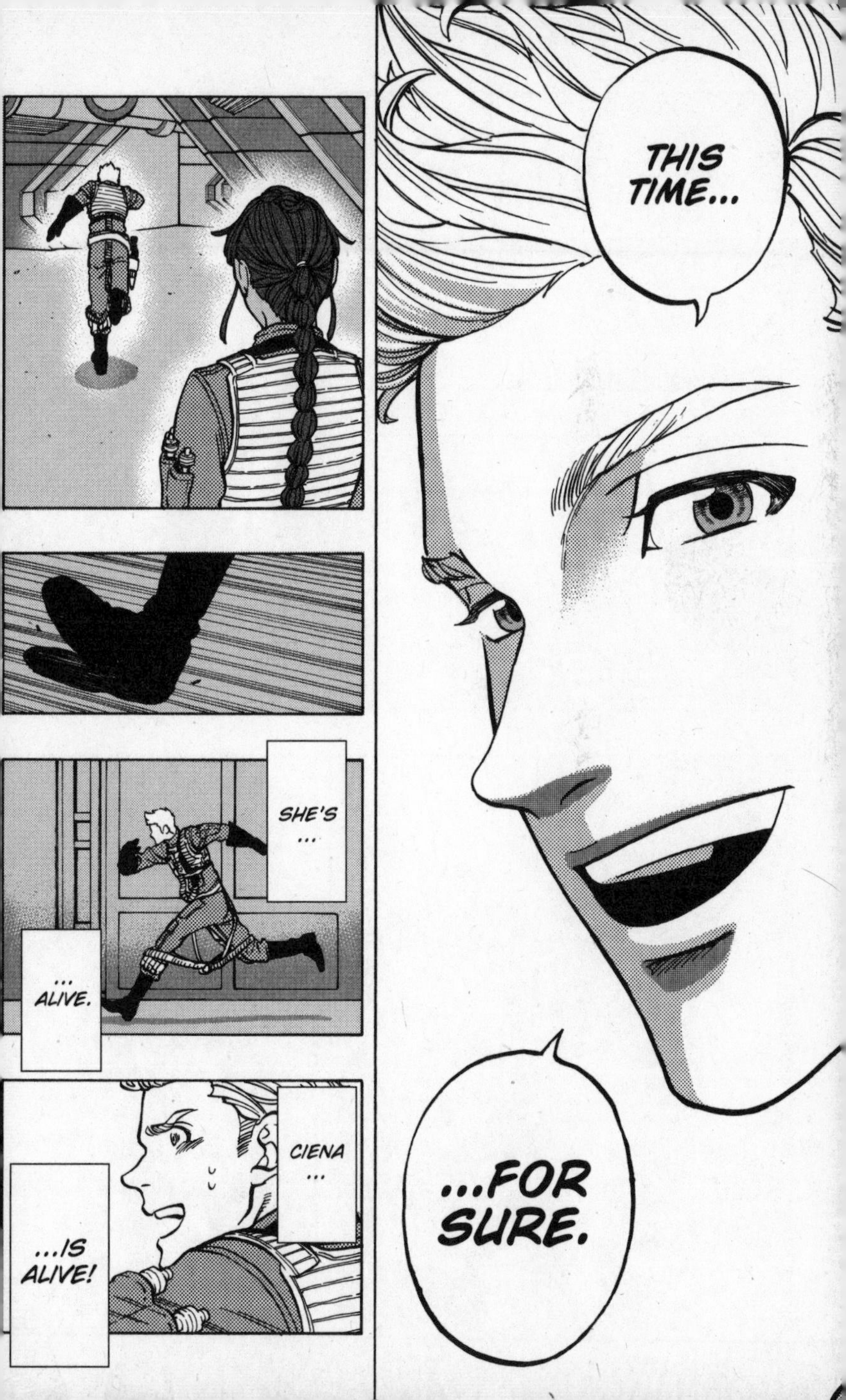
THIS TIME...
...FOR SURE.
SHE'S ...
... ALIVE.
CIENA ...
...IS ALIVE!

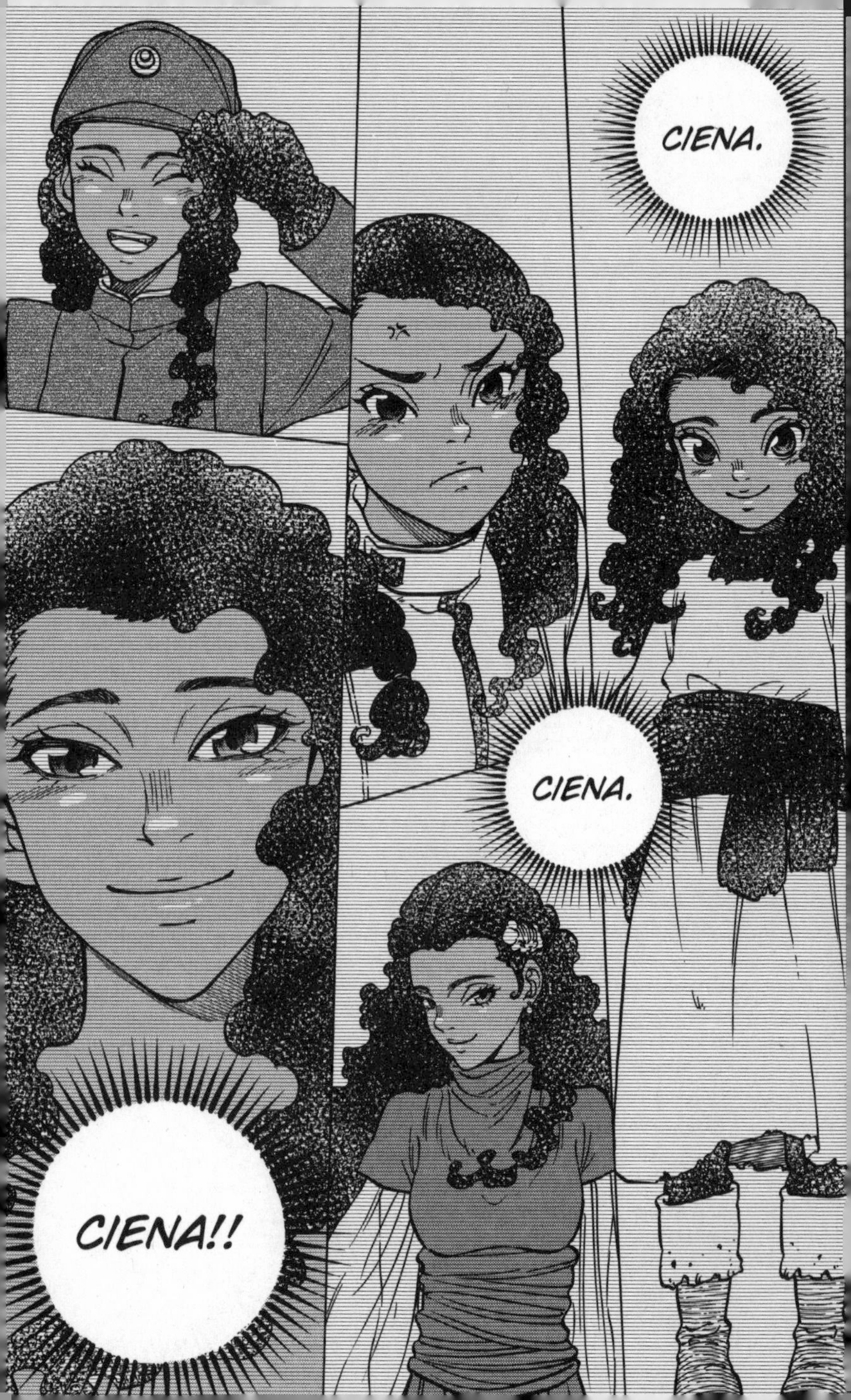
CIENA.
CIENA.
CIENA!!

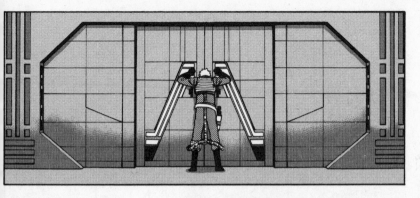

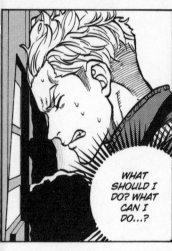

WHAT SHOULD I DO? WHAT CAN I DO...?

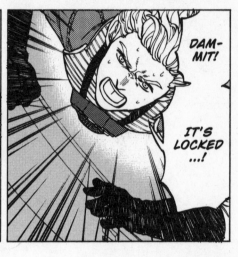

DAMMIT!

IT'S LOCKED...!

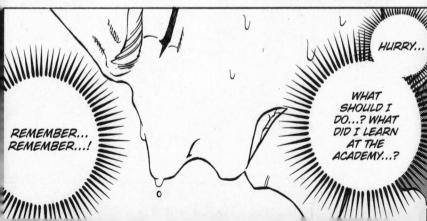

HURRY...

WHAT SHOULD I DO...? WHAT DID I LEARN AT THE ACADEMY...?

REMEMBER... REMEMBER...!

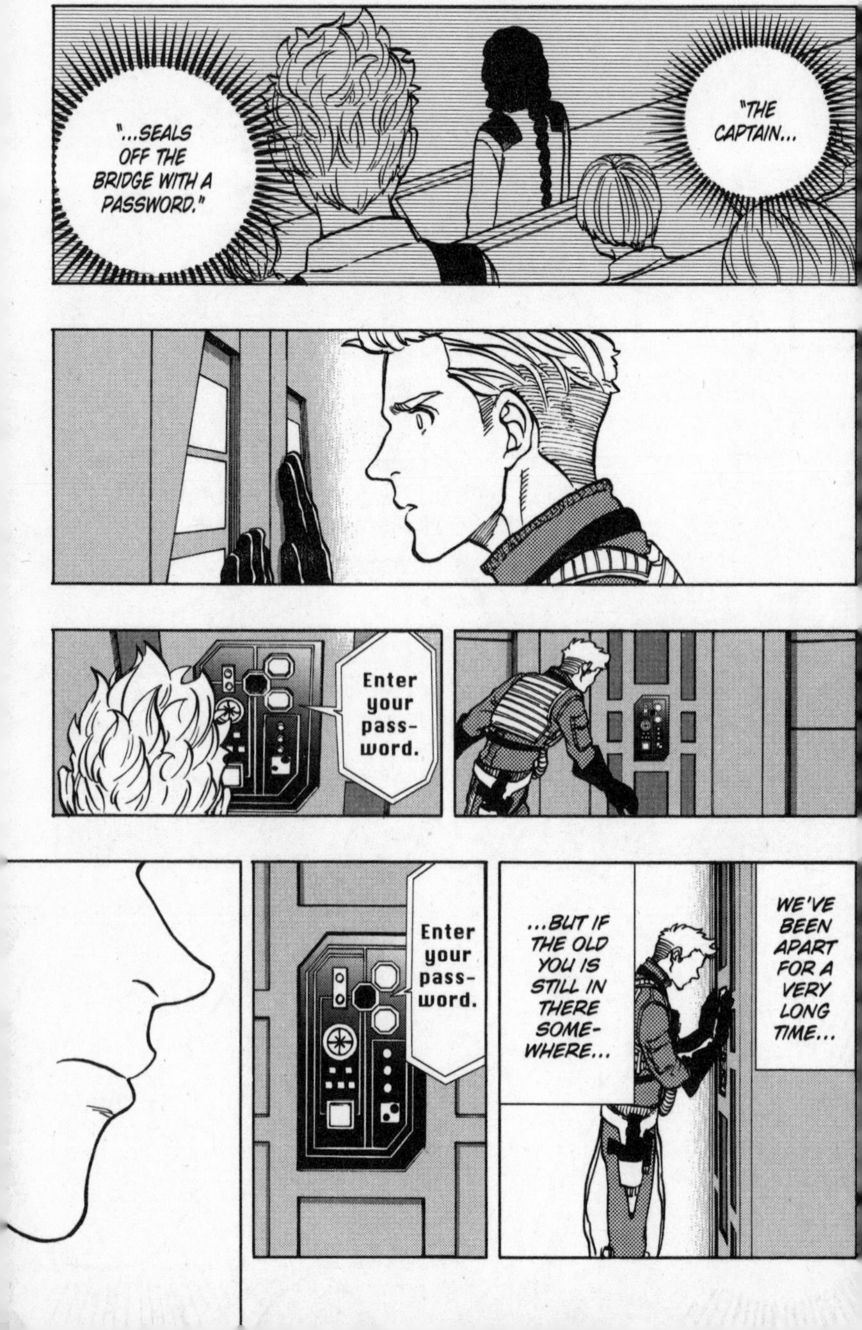
"THE CAPTAIN...
"...SEALS OFF THE BRIDGE WITH A PASSWORD."
Enter your pass-word.
WE'VE BEEN APART FOR A VERY LONG TIME...
...BUT IF THE OLD YOU IS STILL IN THERE SOME-WHERE...
Enter your pass-word.

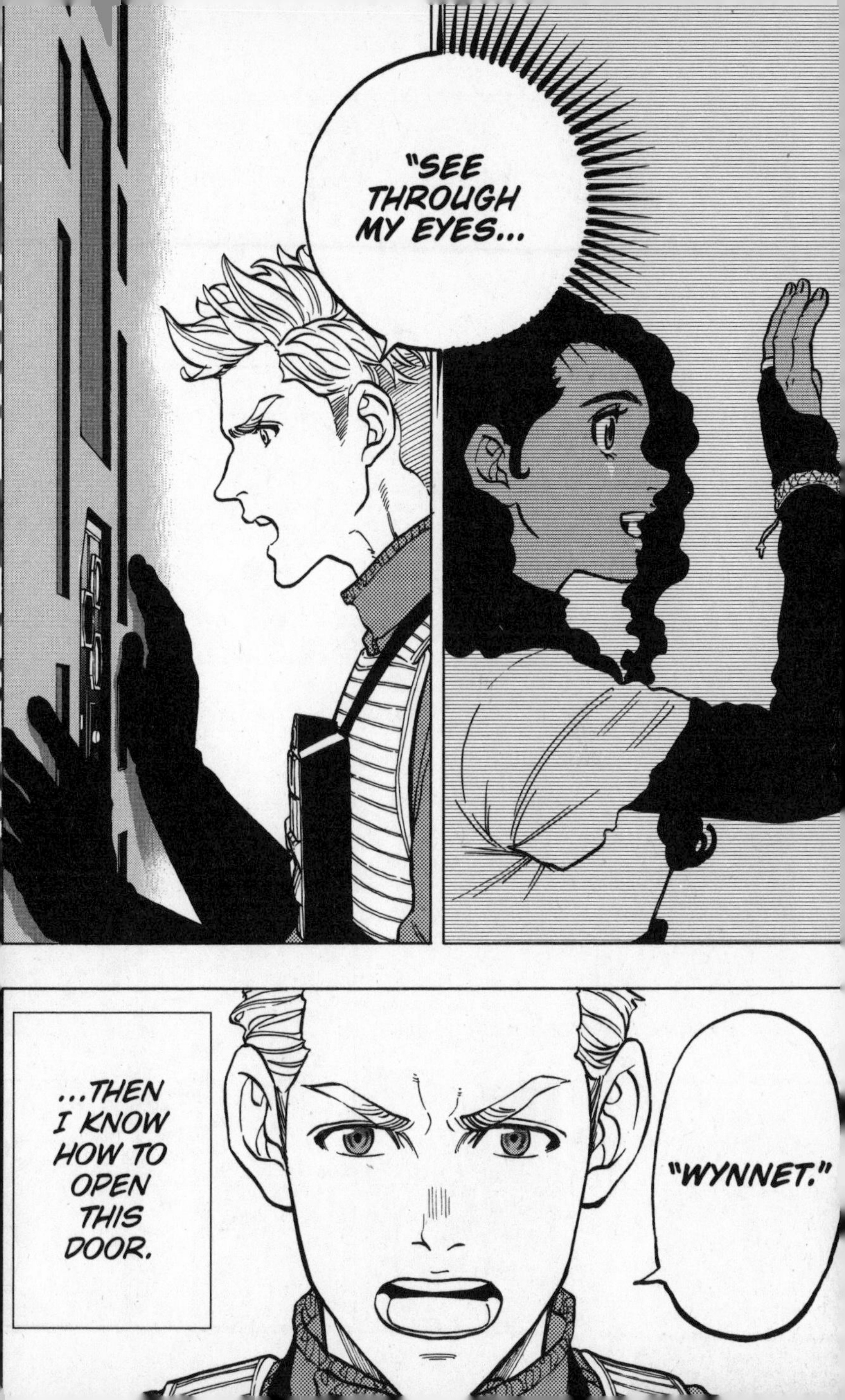
"SEE THROUGH MY EYES...
"WYNNET."
...THEN I KNOW HOW TO OPEN THIS DOOR.

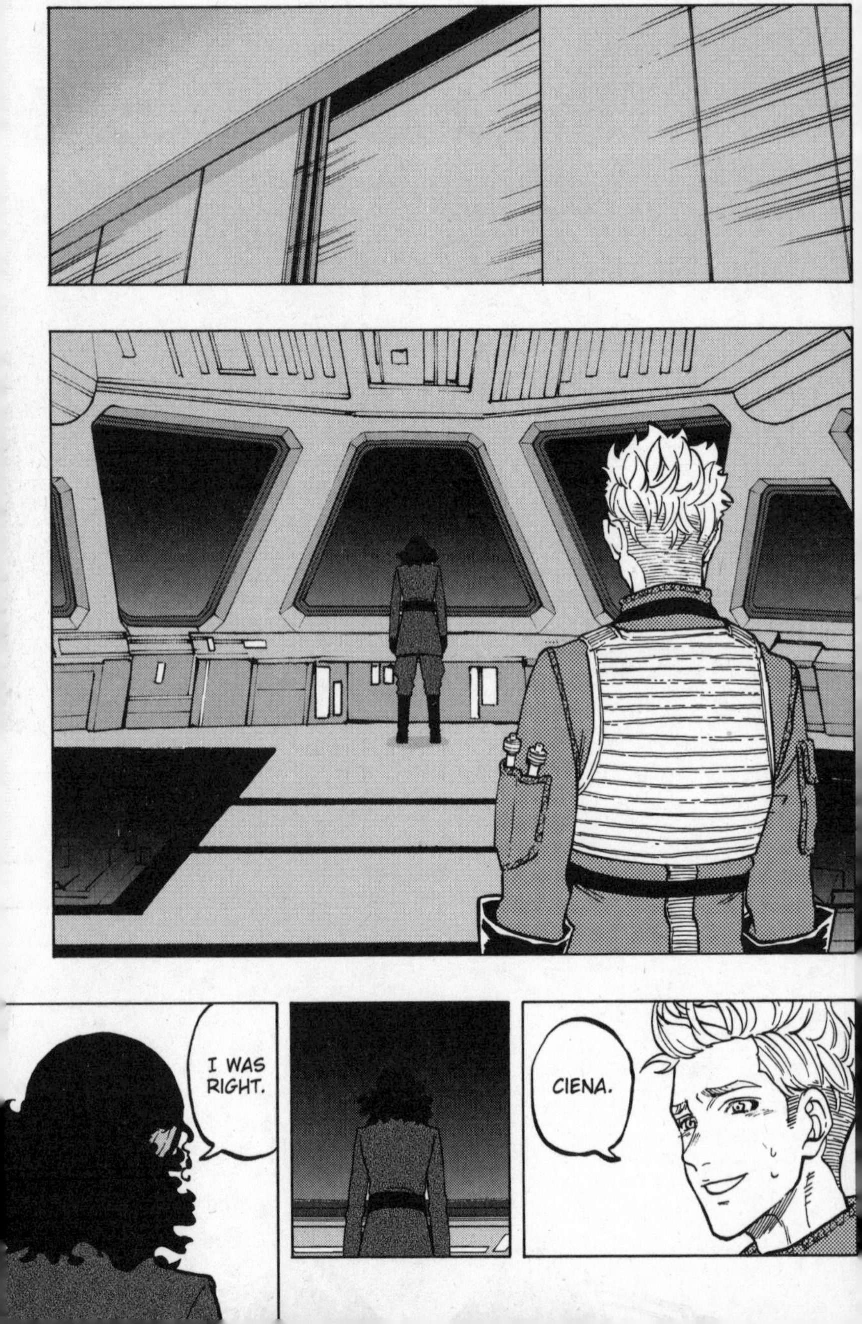
CIENA.
I WAS RIGHT.

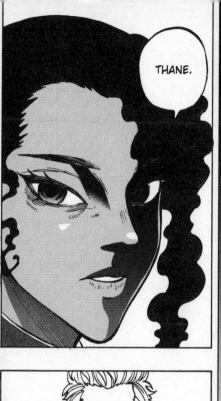

THANE.

YOU WERE ONE OF THE INTRUDERS.

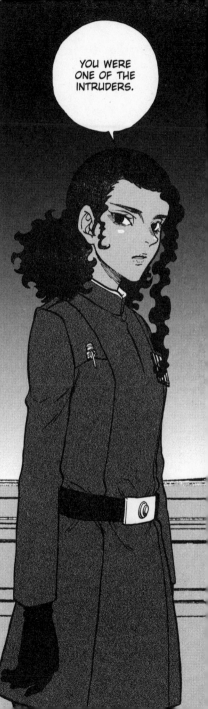

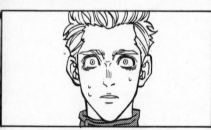

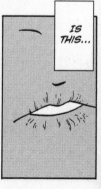

IS THIS...

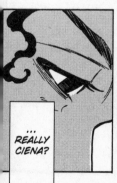

...REALLY CIENA?

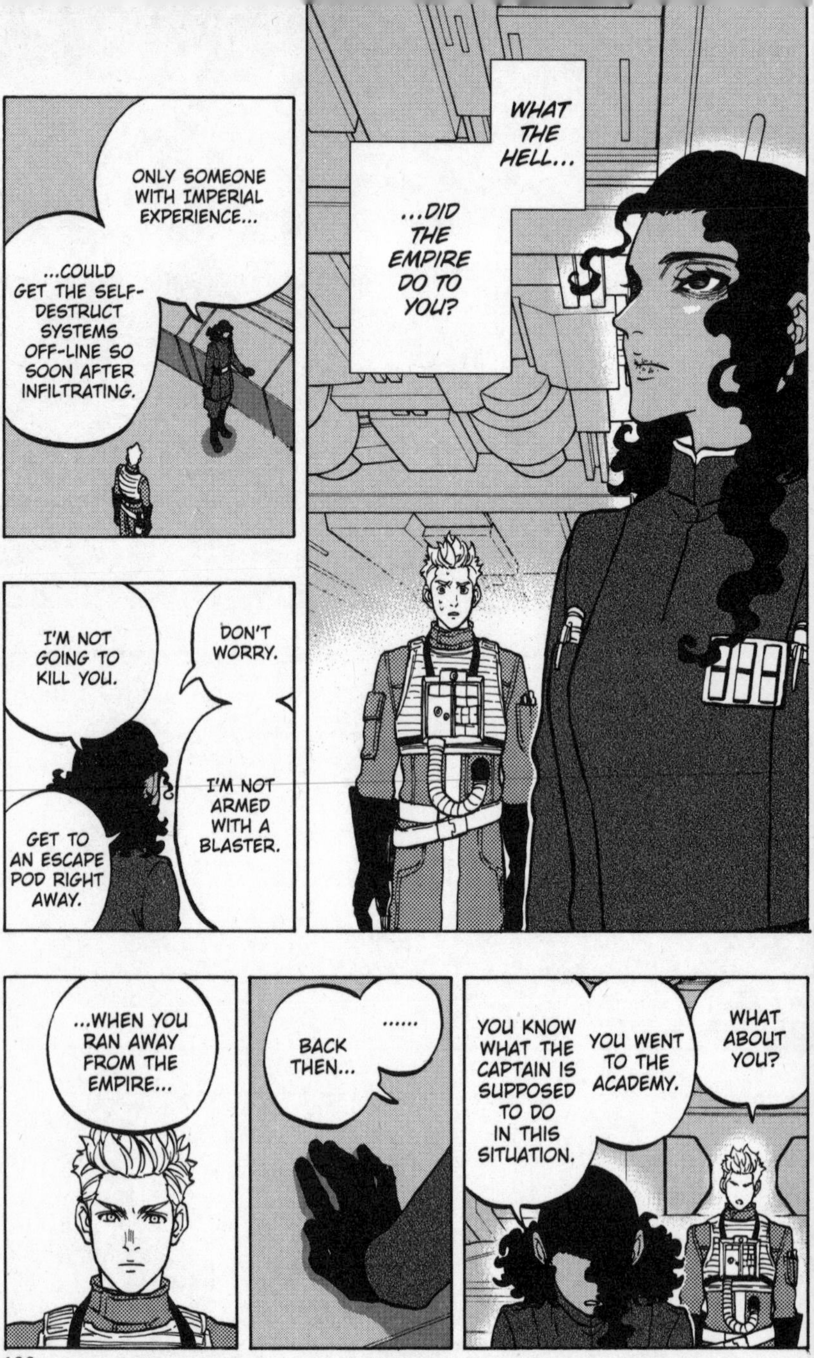
WHAT THE HELL...
...DID THE EMPIRE DO TO YOU?
ONLY SOMEONE WITH IMPERIAL EXPERIENCE...
...COULD GET THE SELF-DESTRUCT SYSTEMS OFF-LINE SO SOON AFTER INFILTRATING.
DON'T WORRY.
I'M NOT GOING TO KILL YOU.
I'M NOT ARMED WITH A BLASTER.
GET TO AN ESCAPE POD RIGHT AWAY.
WHAT ABOUT YOU?
YOU WENT TO THE ACADEMY.
YOU KNOW WHAT THE CAPTAIN IS SUPPOSED TO DO IN THIS SITUATION.
......
BACK THEN...
...WHEN YOU RAN AWAY FROM THE EMPIRE...

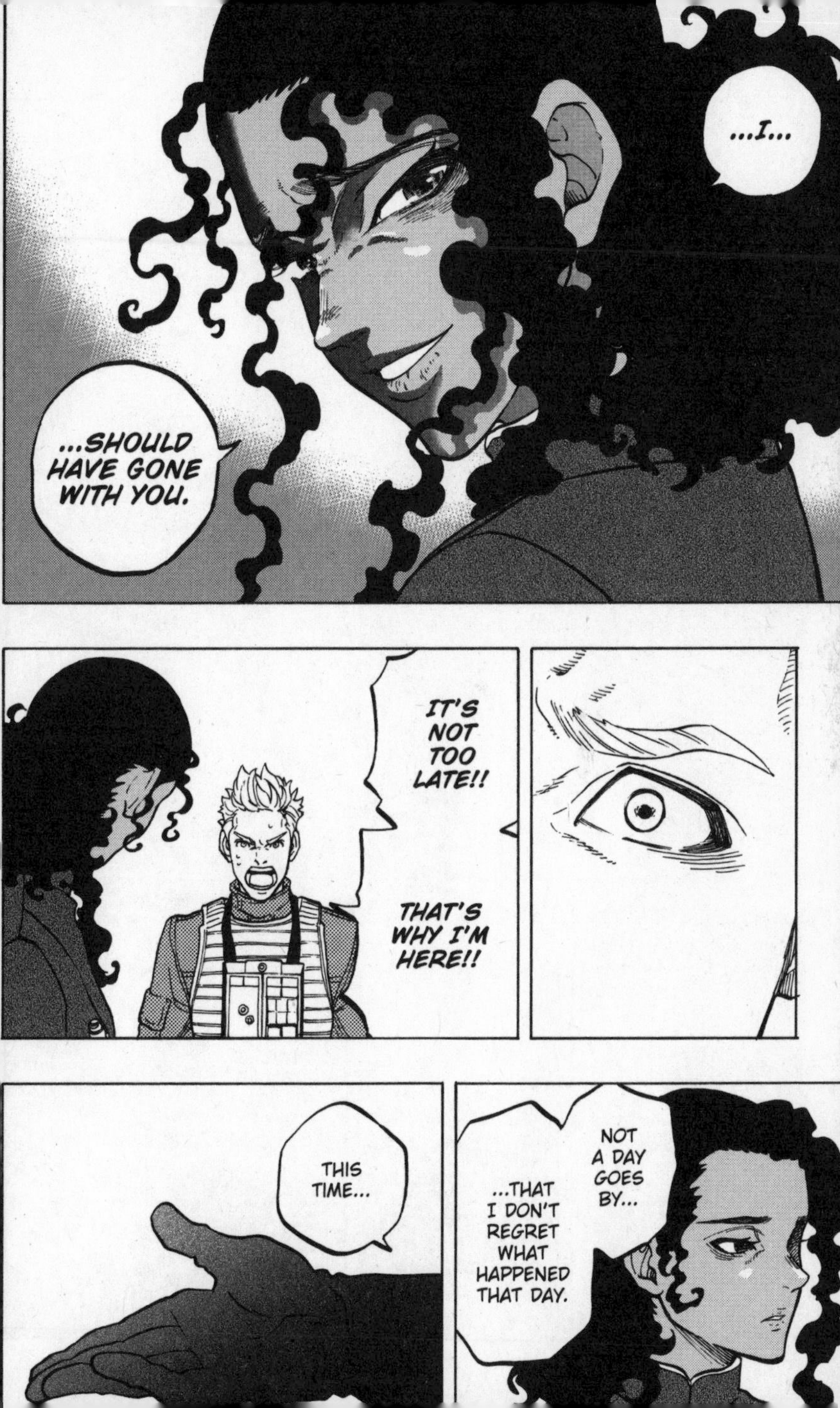
...I...
...SHOULD HAVE GONE WITH YOU.
IT'S NOT TOO LATE!!
THAT'S WHY I'M HERE!!
NOT A DAY GOES BY...
...THAT I DON'T REGRET WHAT HAPPENED THAT DAY.
THIS TIME...

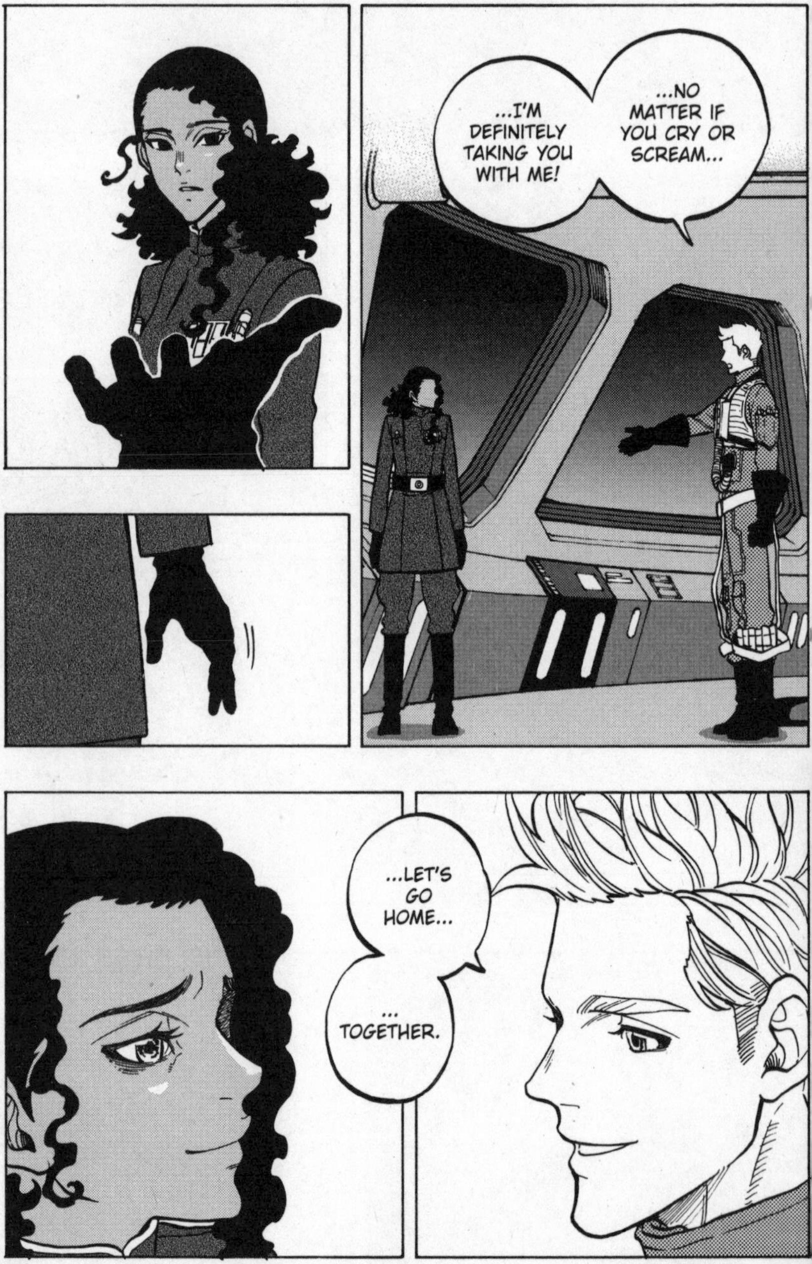
...NO MATTER IF YOU CRY OR SCREAM...
...I'M DEFINITELY TAKING YOU WITH ME!
...LET'S GO HOME...
... TOGETHER.

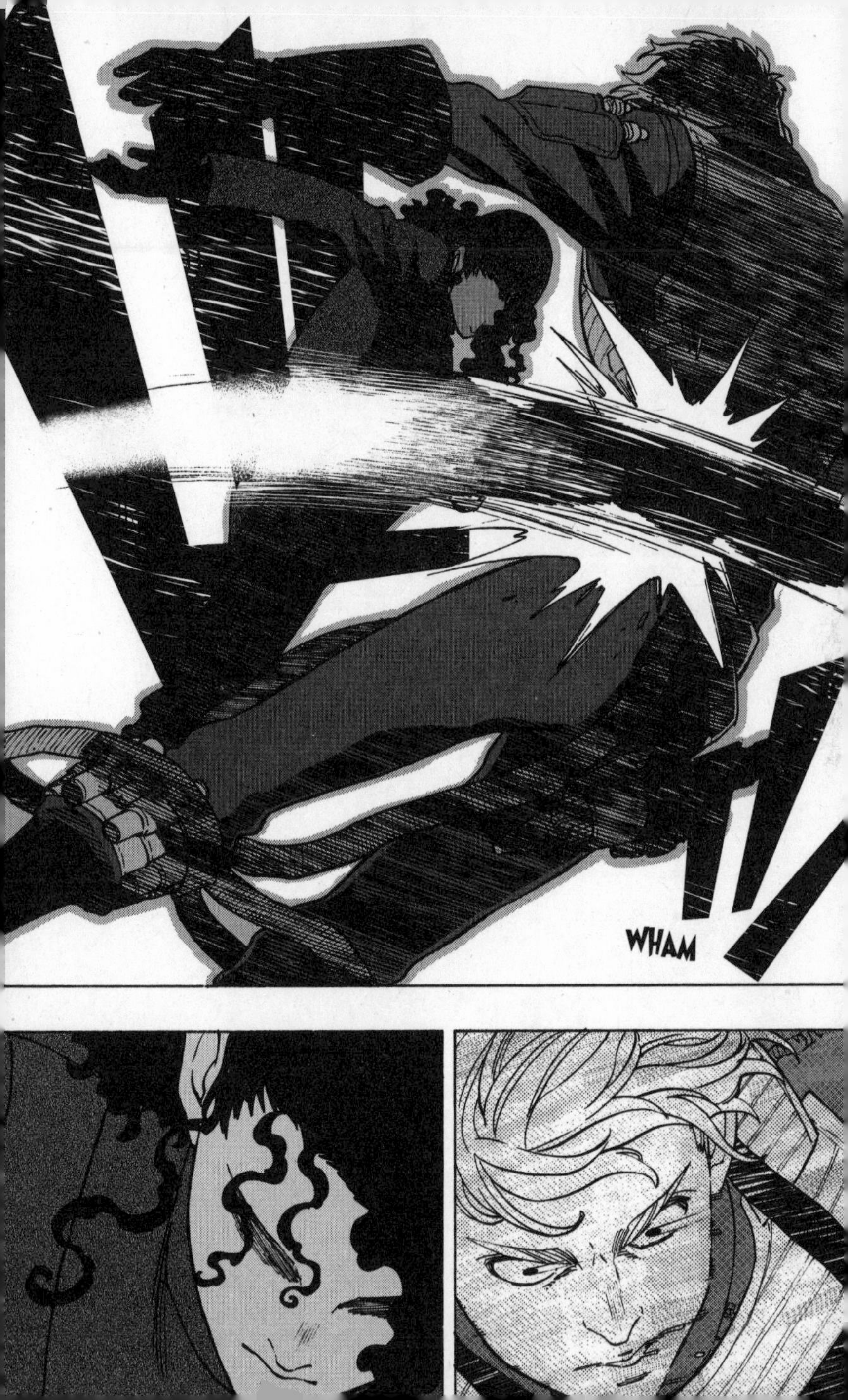
WHAM

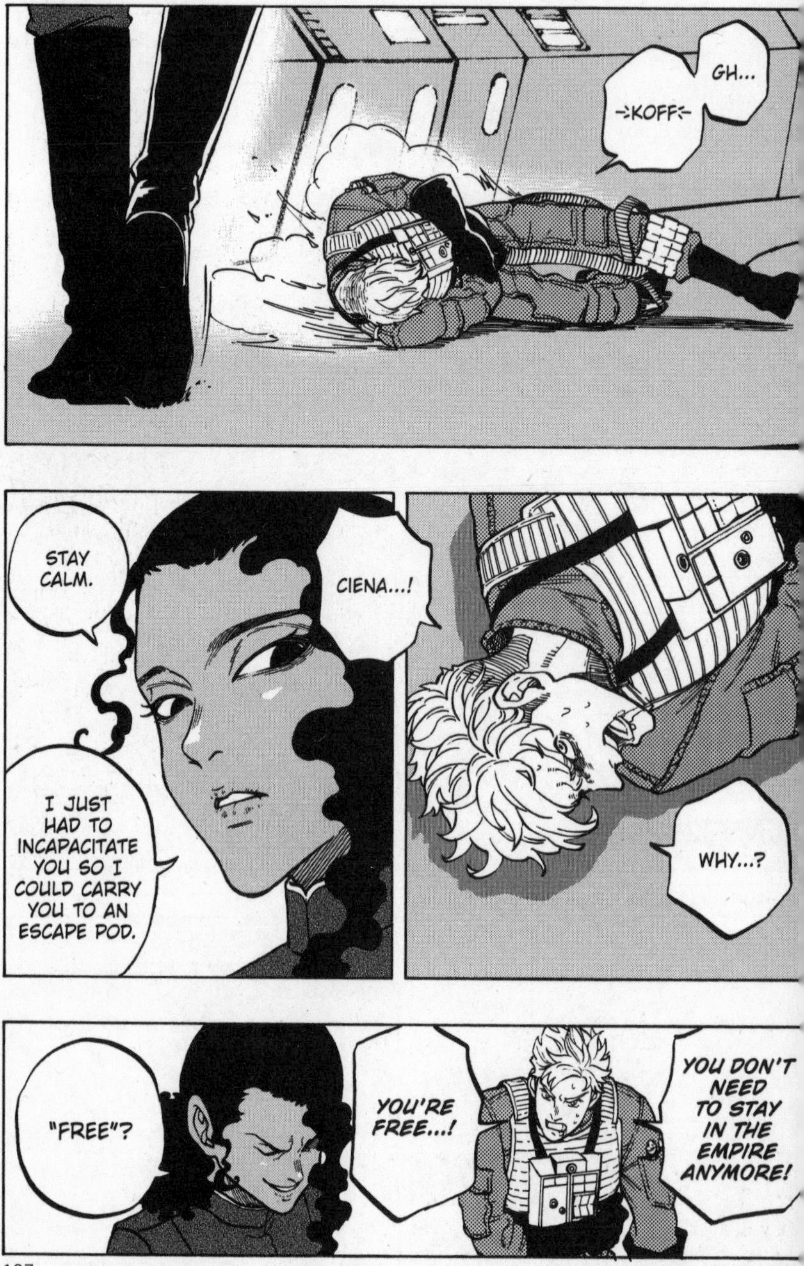
GH...
-KOFF-
WHY...?
CIENA...!
STAY CALM.
I JUST HAD TO INCAPACITATE YOU SO I COULD CARRY YOU TO AN ESCAPE POD.
YOU DON'T NEED TO STAY IN THE EMPIRE ANYMORE!
YOU'RE FREE...!
"FREE"?

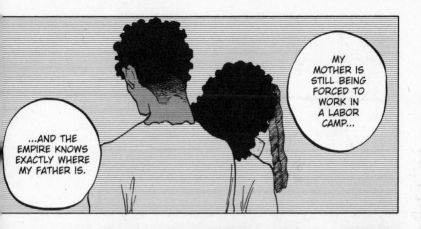

MY MOTHER IS STILL BEING FORCED TO WORK IN A LABOR CAMP...

...AND THE EMPIRE KNOWS EXACTLY WHERE MY FATHER IS.

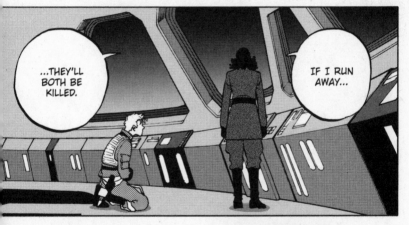

...THEY'LL BOTH BE KILLED.

IF I RUN AWAY...

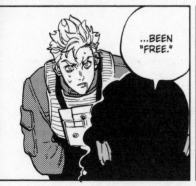

...BEEN "FREE."

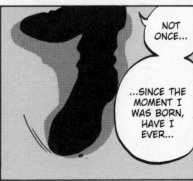

NOT ONCE...

...SINCE THE MOMENT I WAS BORN, HAVE I EVER...

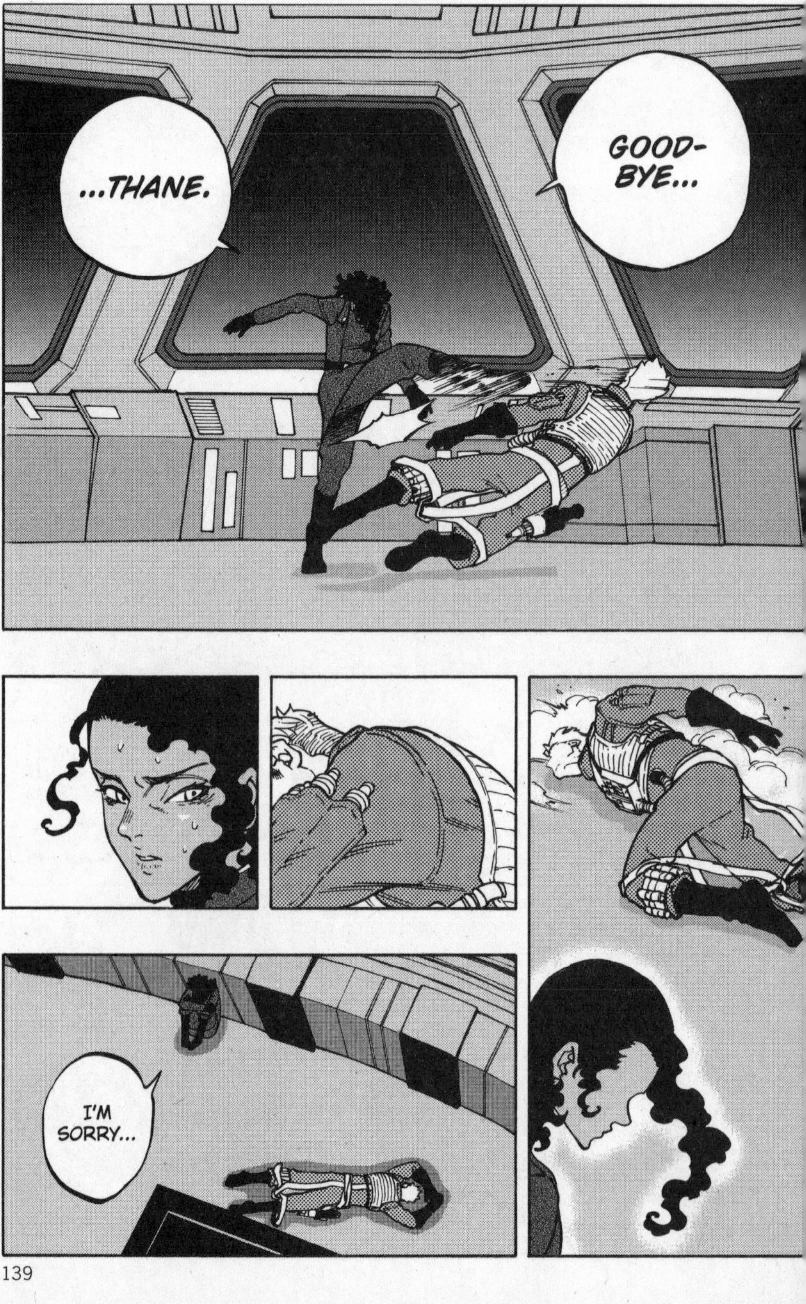
GOOD-BYE...
...THANE.
I'M SORRY...

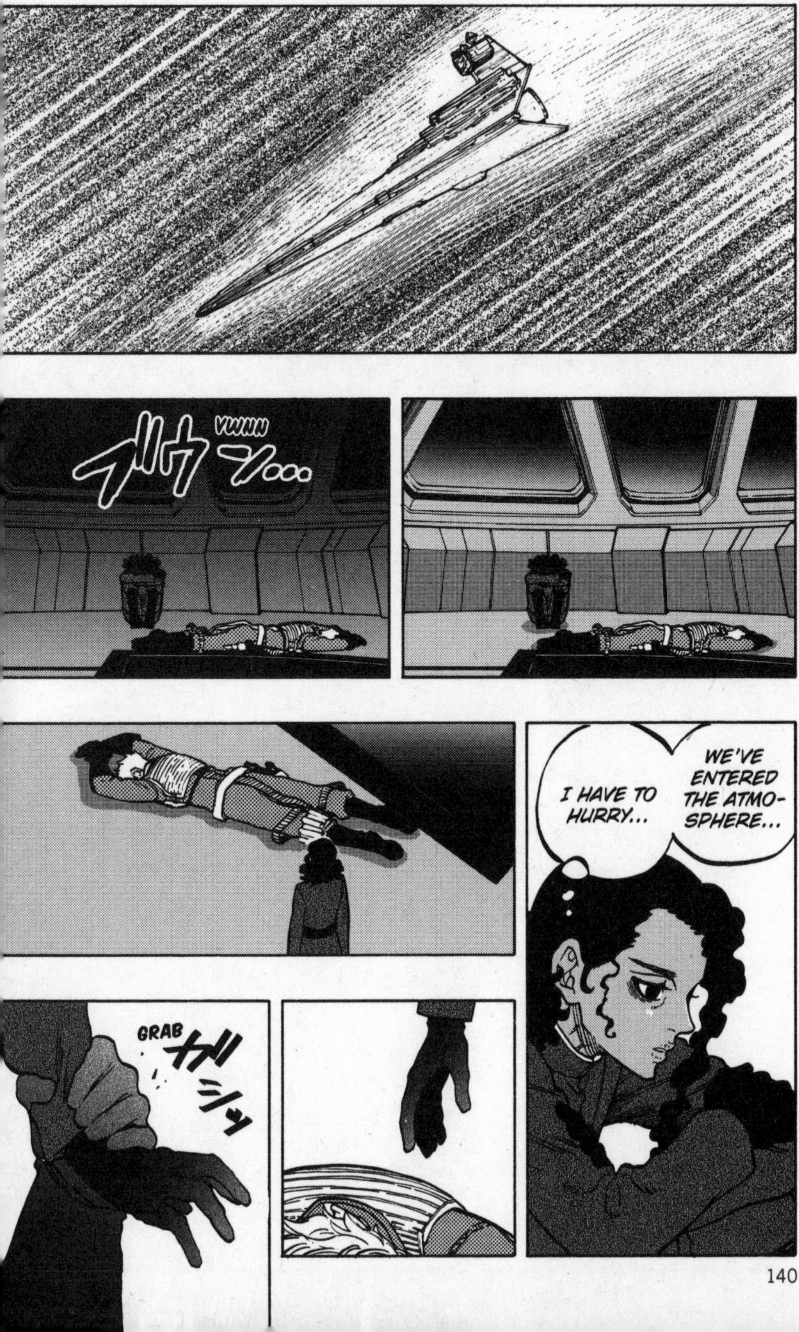
VWNN
WE'VE ENTERED THE ATMO-SPHERE...
I HAVE TO HURRY...
GRAB

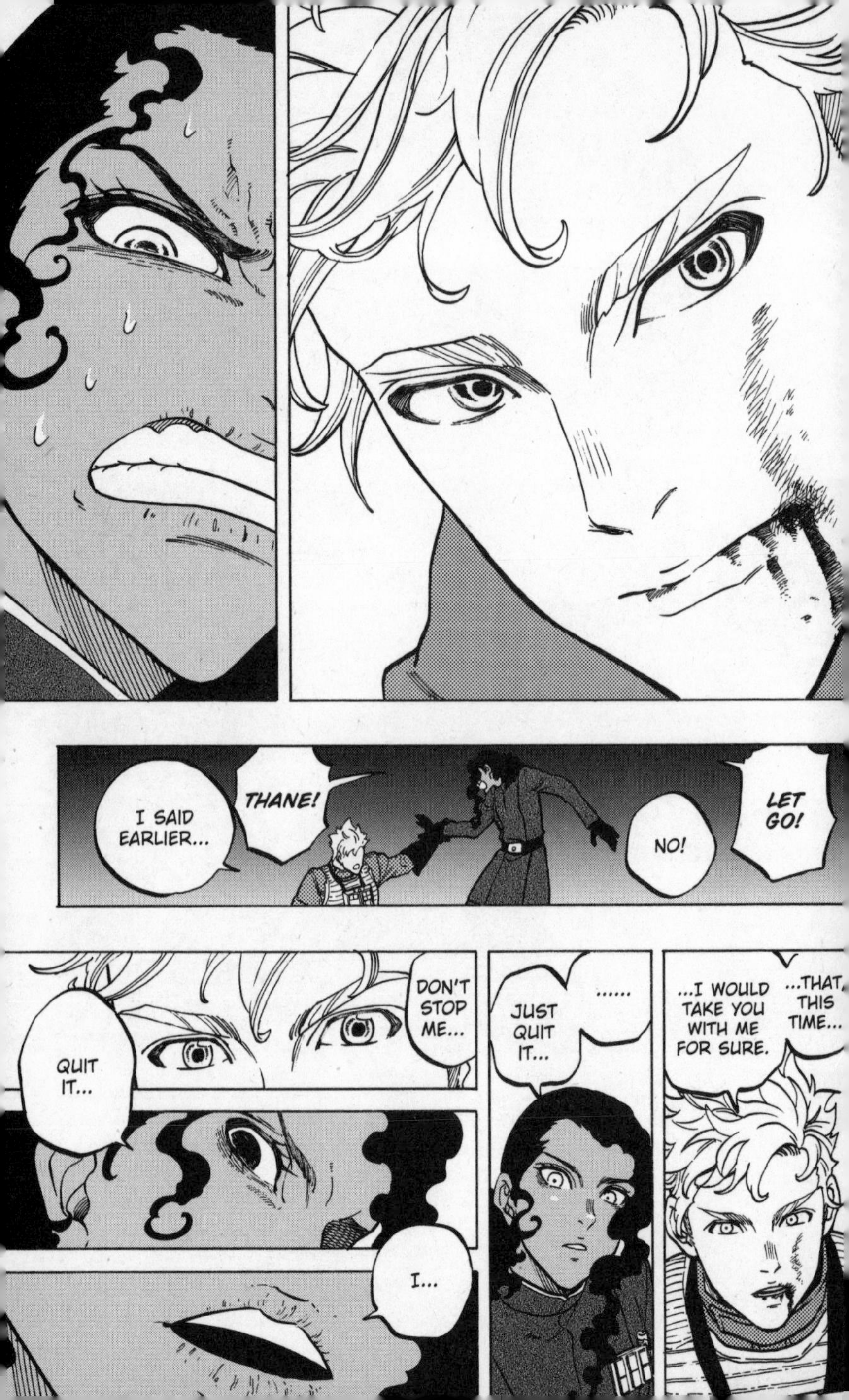
LET GO!
NO!
THANE!
I SAID EARLIER...
...THAT, THIS TIME...
...I WOULD TAKE YOU WITH ME FOR SURE.
......
JUST QUIT IT...
DON'T STOP ME...
QUIT IT...
I...

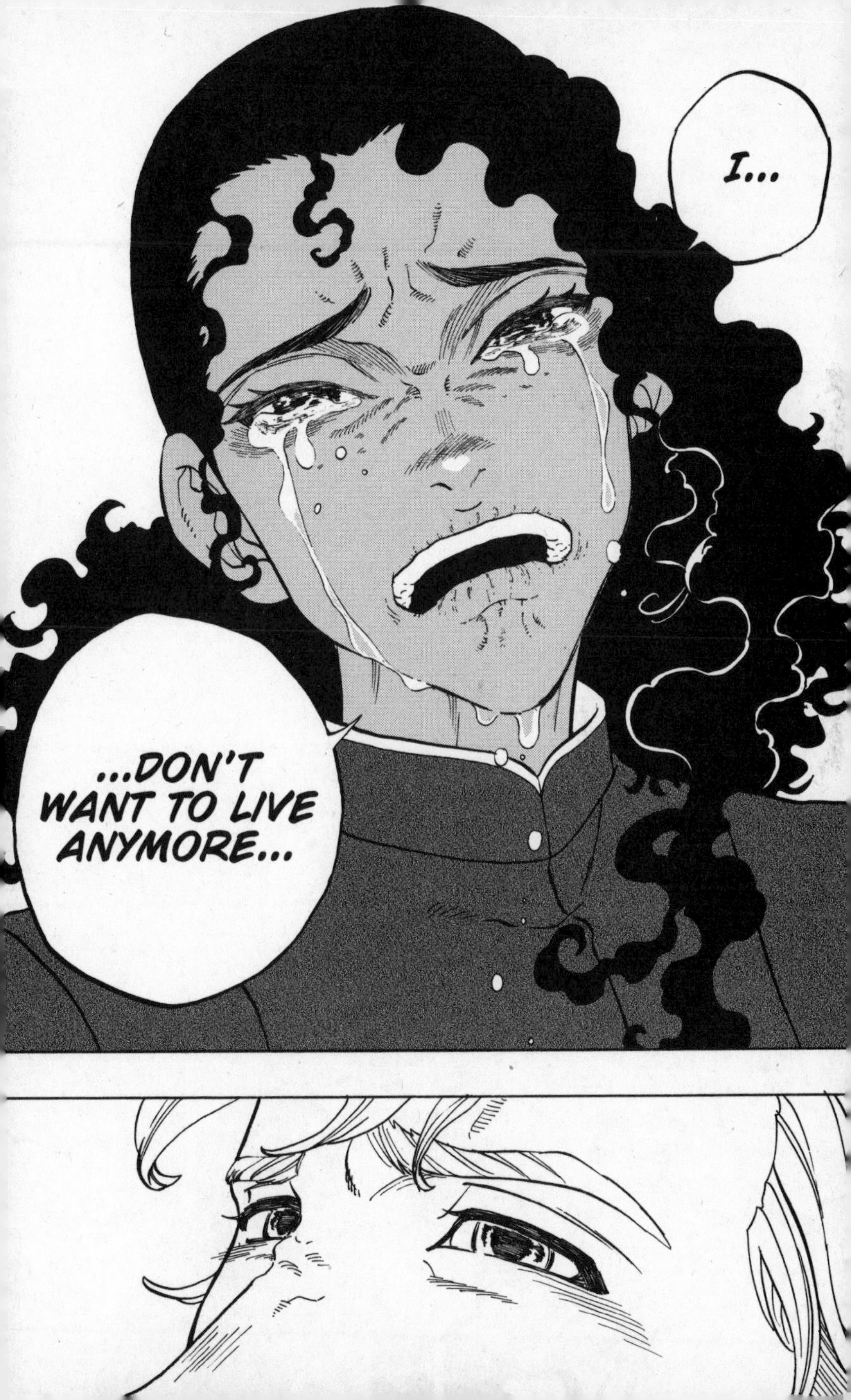
I...
...DON'T WANT TO LIVE ANYMORE...

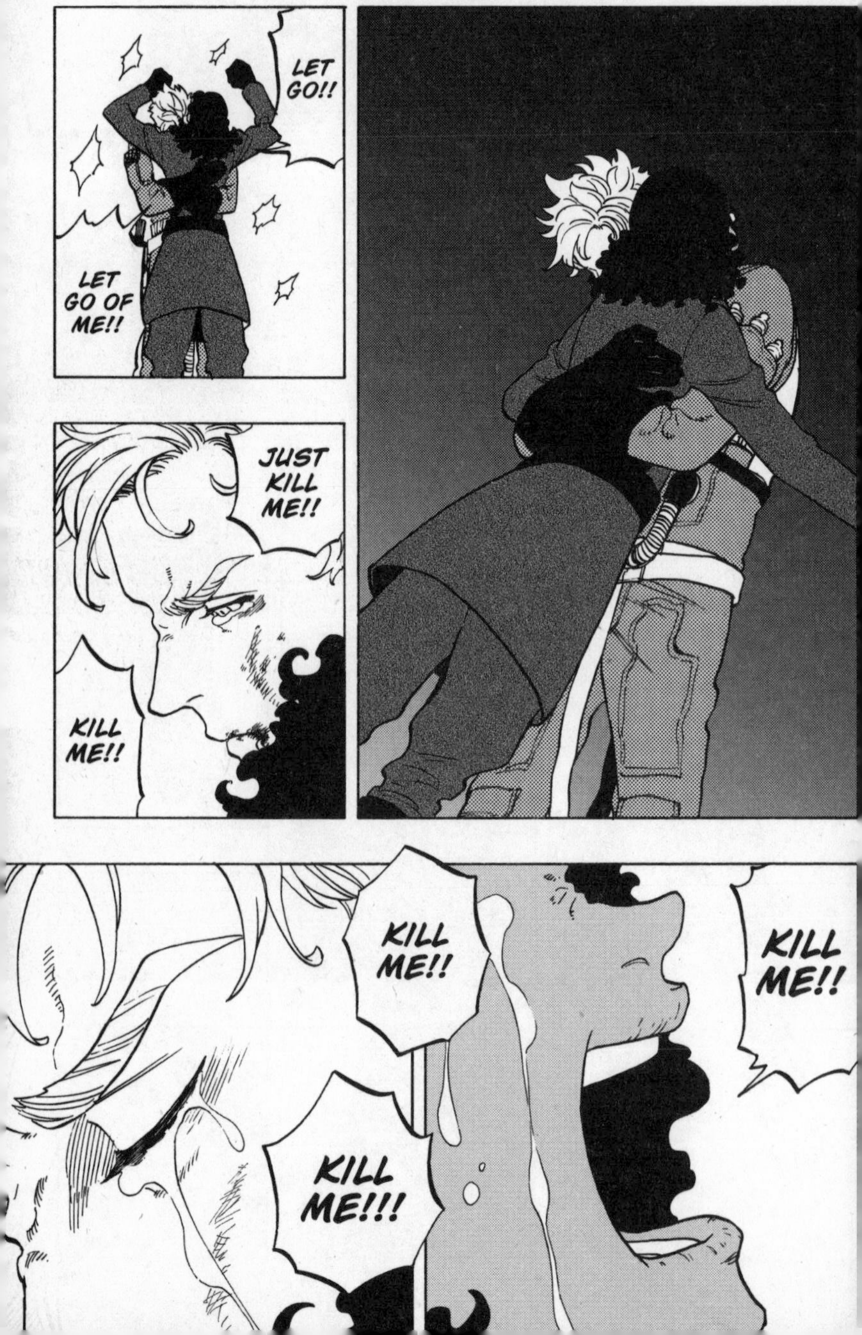
LET GO!!
LET GO OF ME!!
JUST KILL ME!!
KILL ME!!
KILL ME!!
KILL ME!!
KILL ME!!!

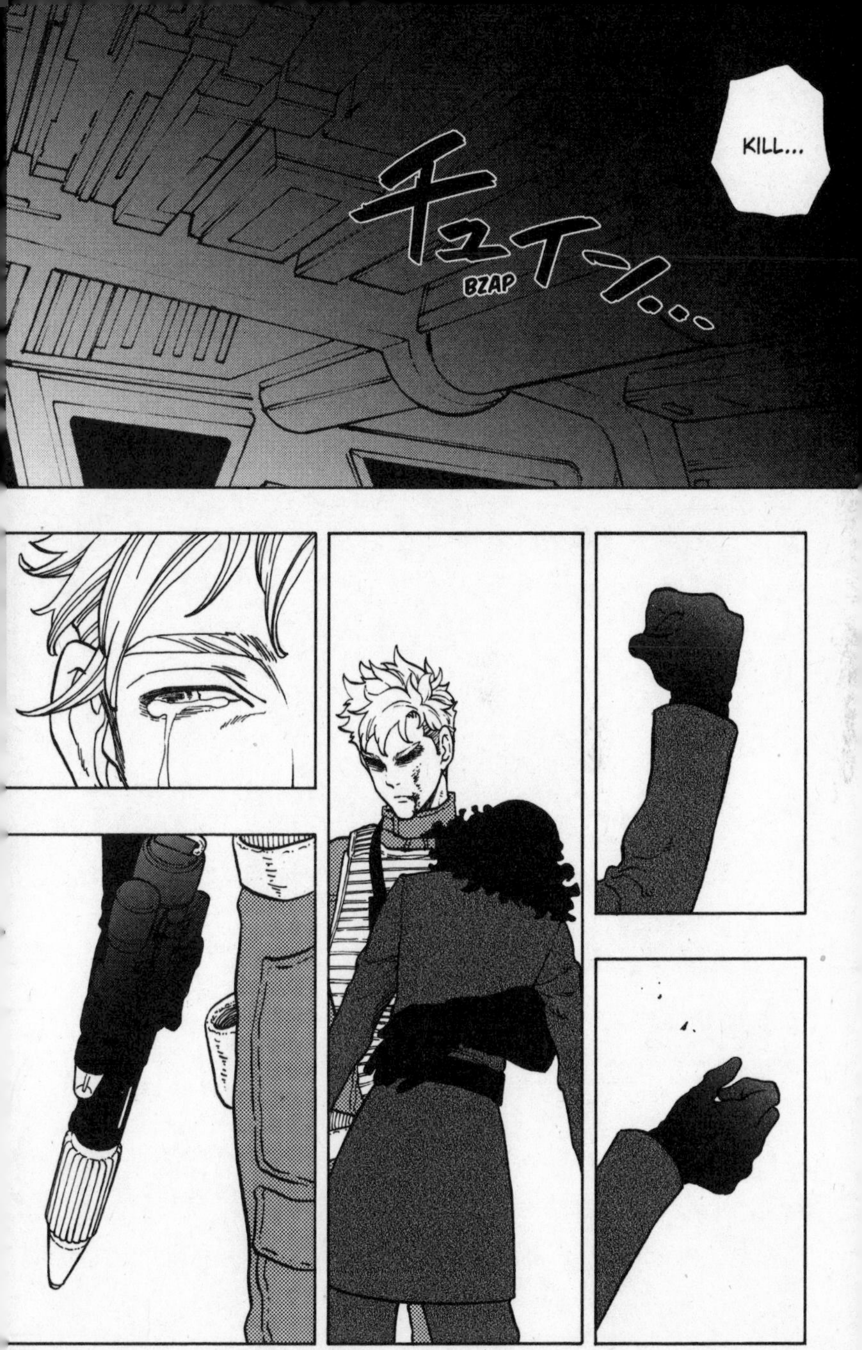
KILL...
チュイーン...
BZAP

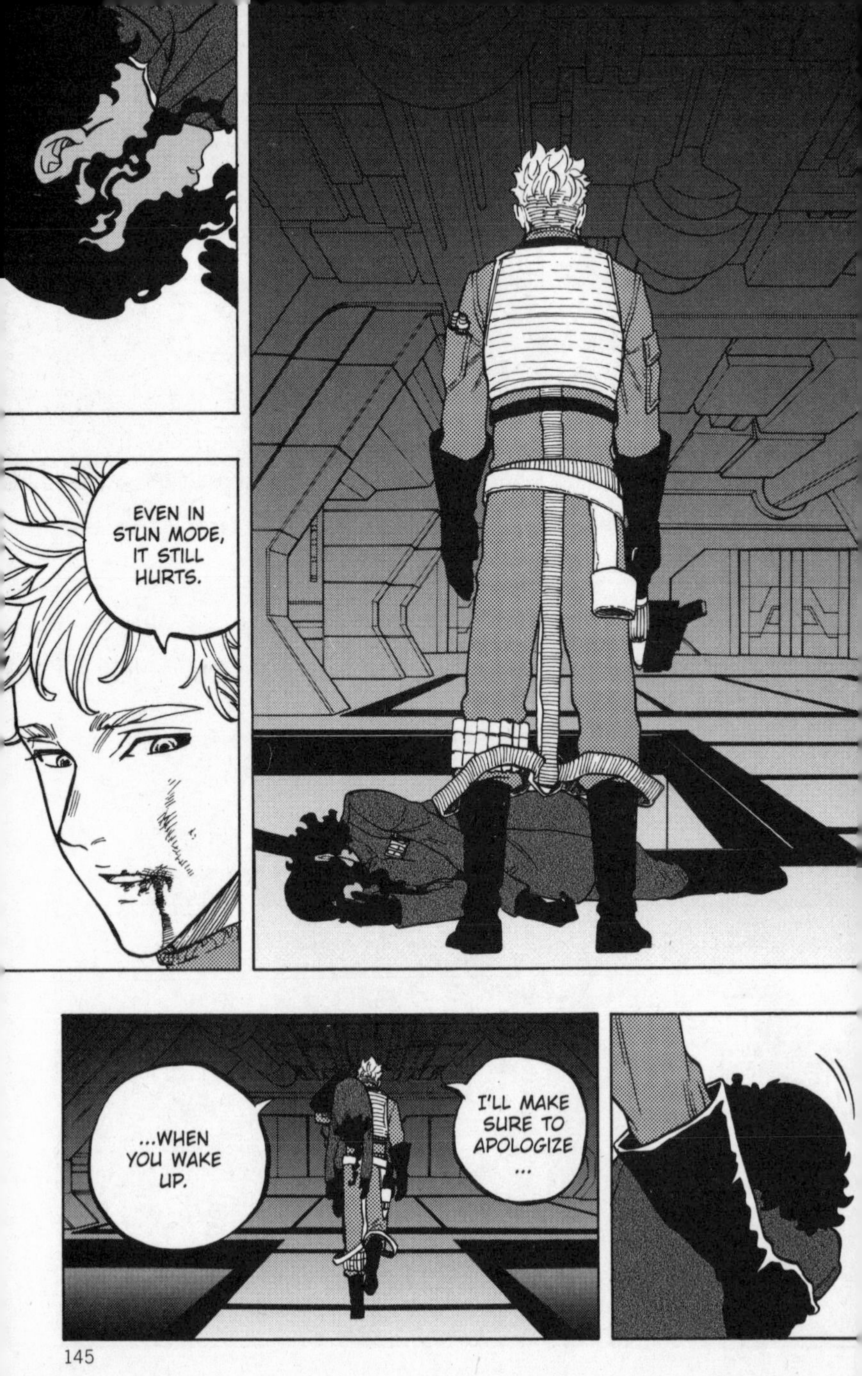
EVEN IN STUN MODE, IT STILL HURTS.
I'LL MAKE SURE TO APOLOGIZE ...
...WHEN YOU WAKE UP.

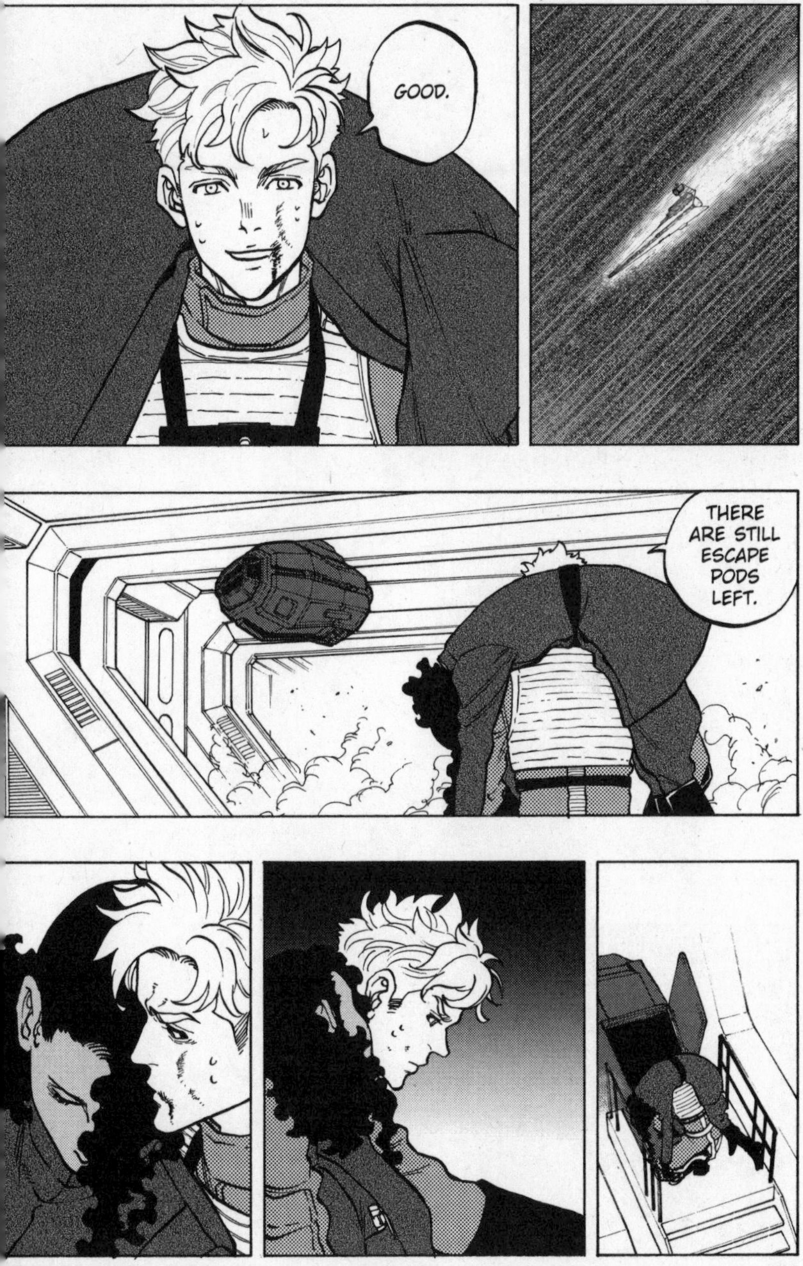
GOOD.
THERE ARE STILL ESCAPE PODS LEFT.

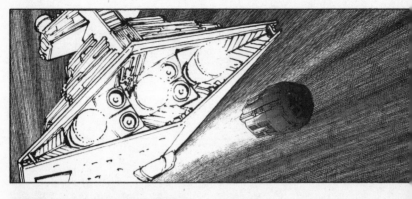

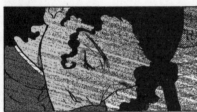
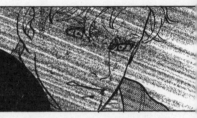

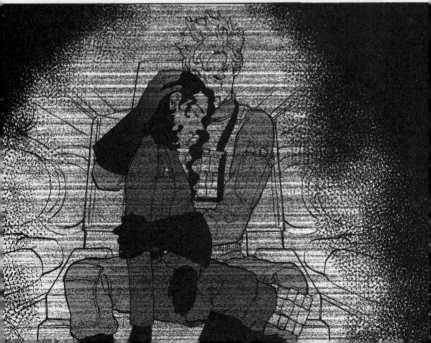

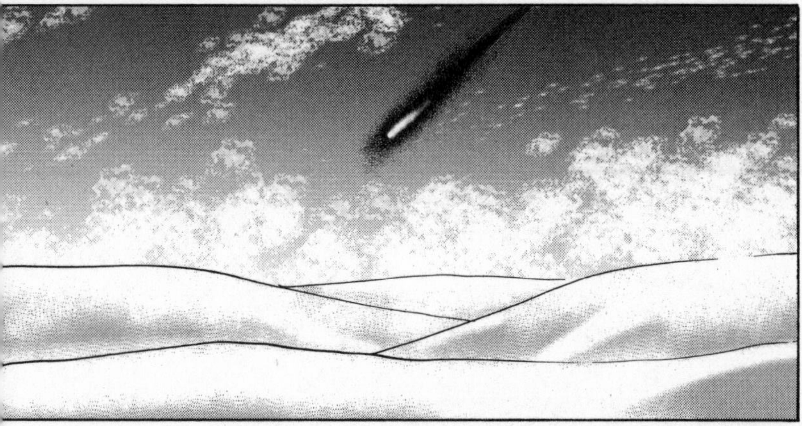

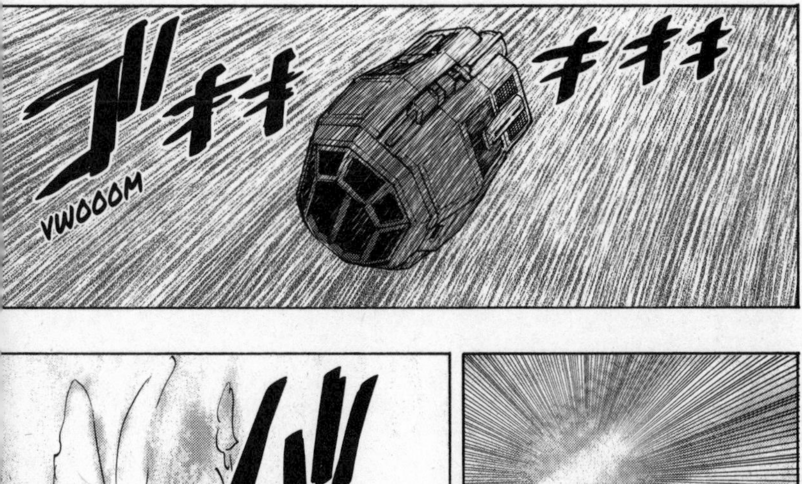
VWOOOM

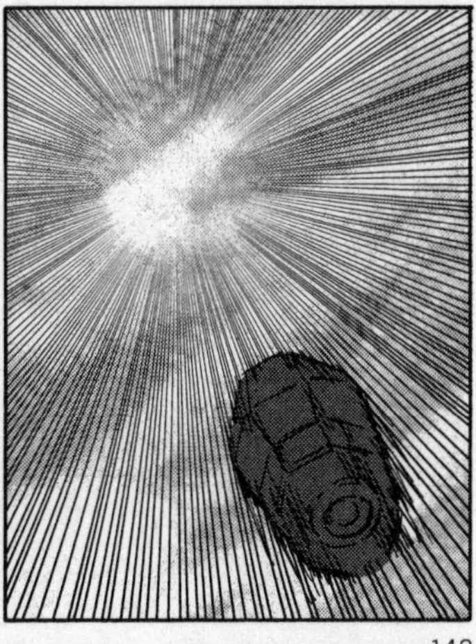

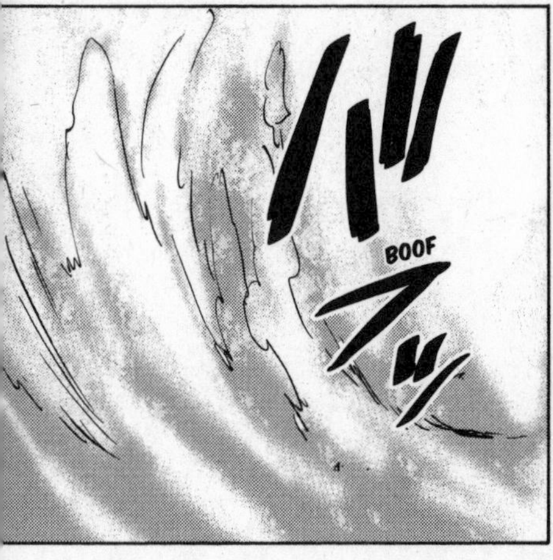
BOOF

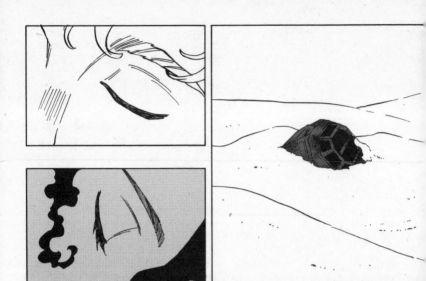

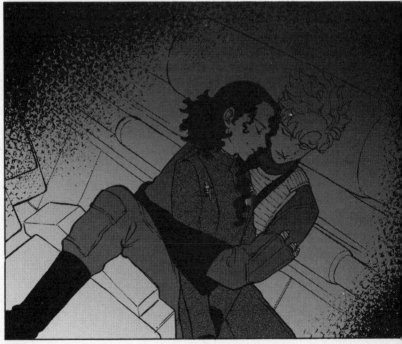

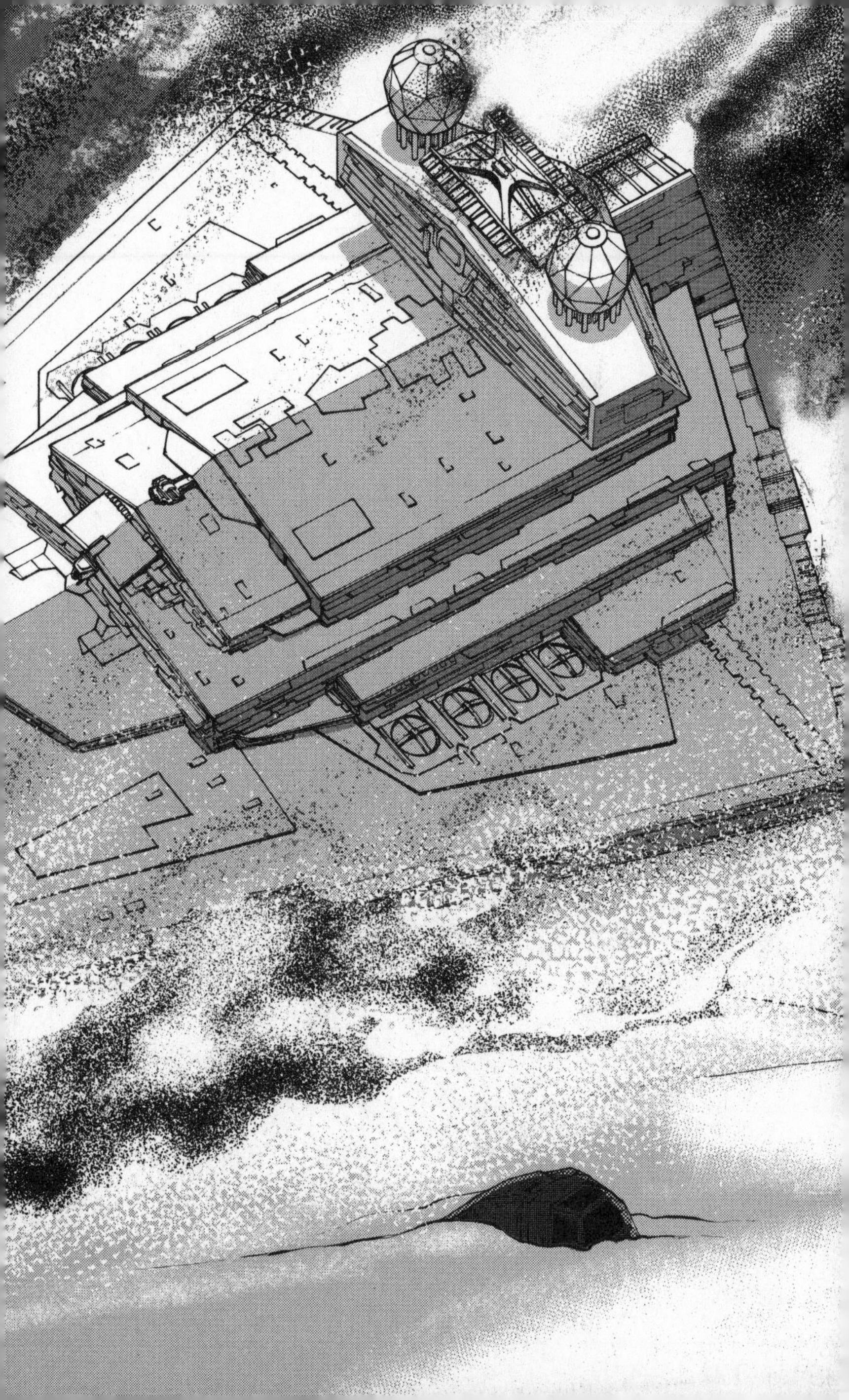

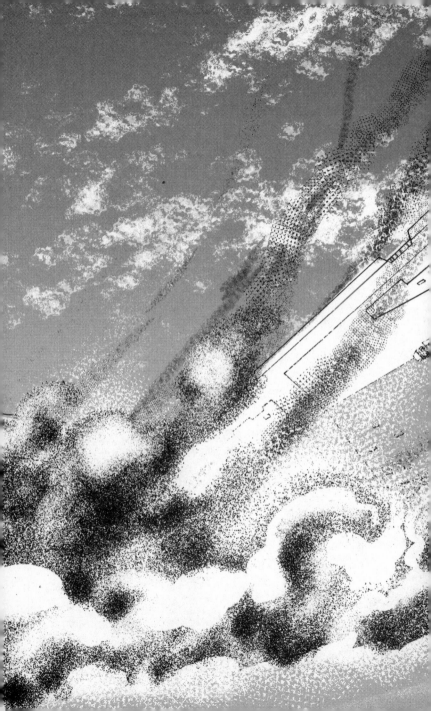

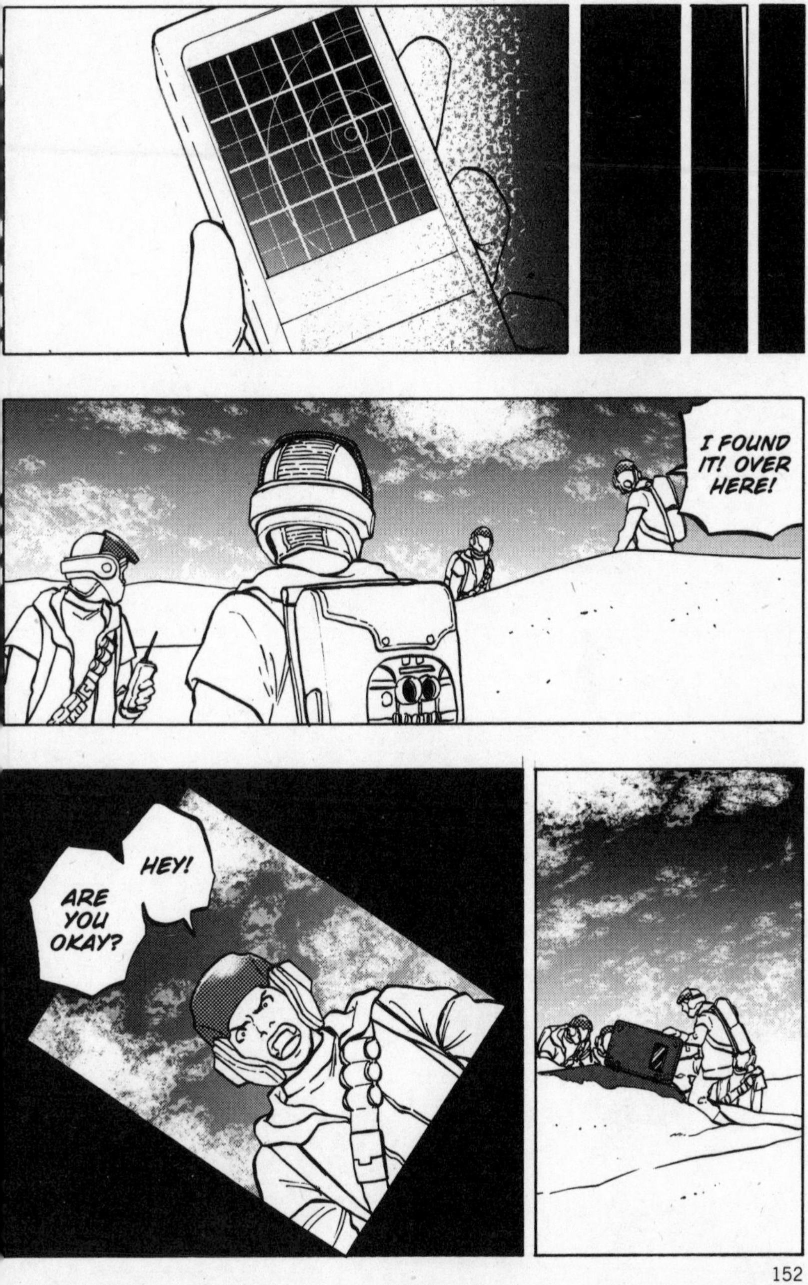
I FOUND IT! OVER HERE!
HEY!
ARE YOU OKAY?

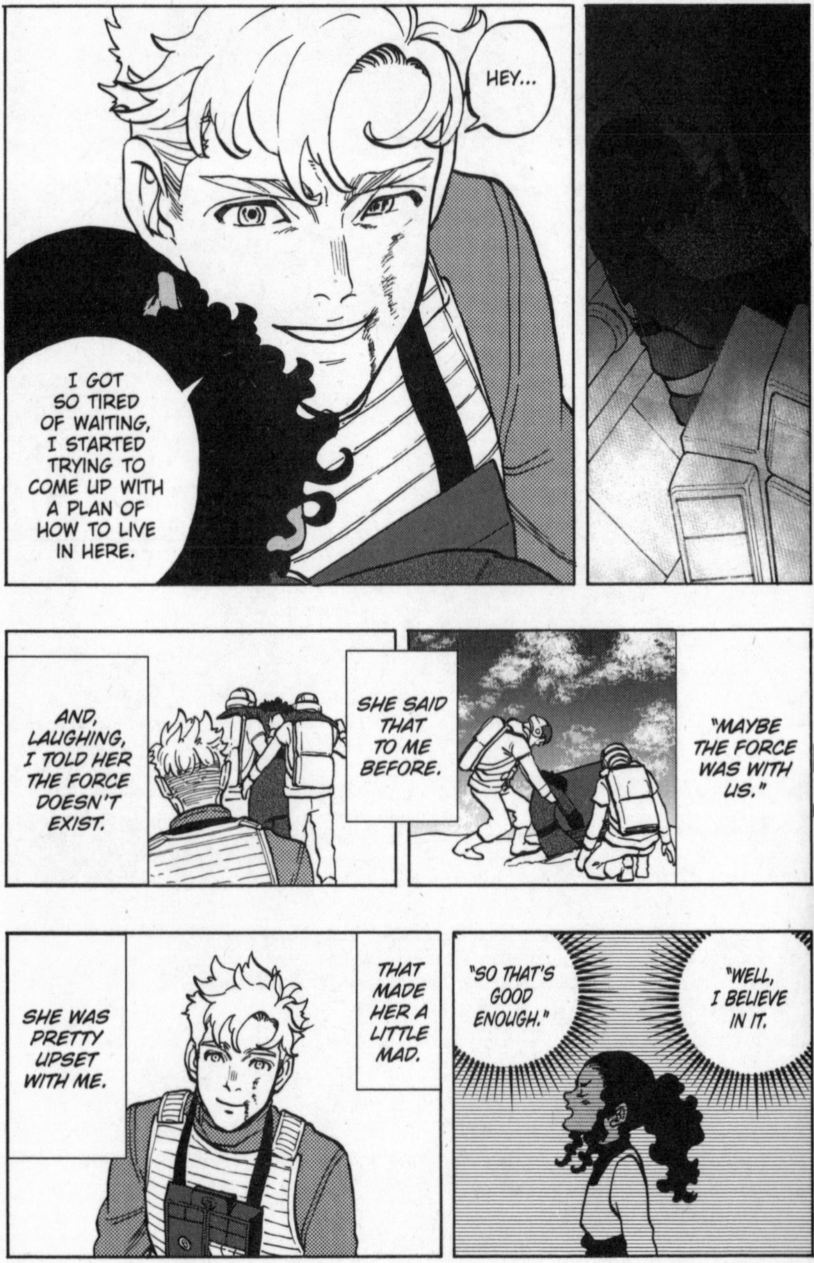
HEY...
I GOT SO TIRED OF WAITING, I STARTED TRYING TO COME UP WITH A PLAN OF HOW TO LIVE IN HERE.
"MAYBE THE FORCE WAS WITH US."
SHE SAID THAT TO ME BEFORE.
AND, LAUGHING, I TOLD HER THE FORCE DOESN'T EXIST.
"WELL, I BELIEVE IN IT.
"SO THAT'S GOOD ENOUGH."
THAT MADE HER A LITTLE MAD.
SHE WAS PRETTY UPSET WITH ME.

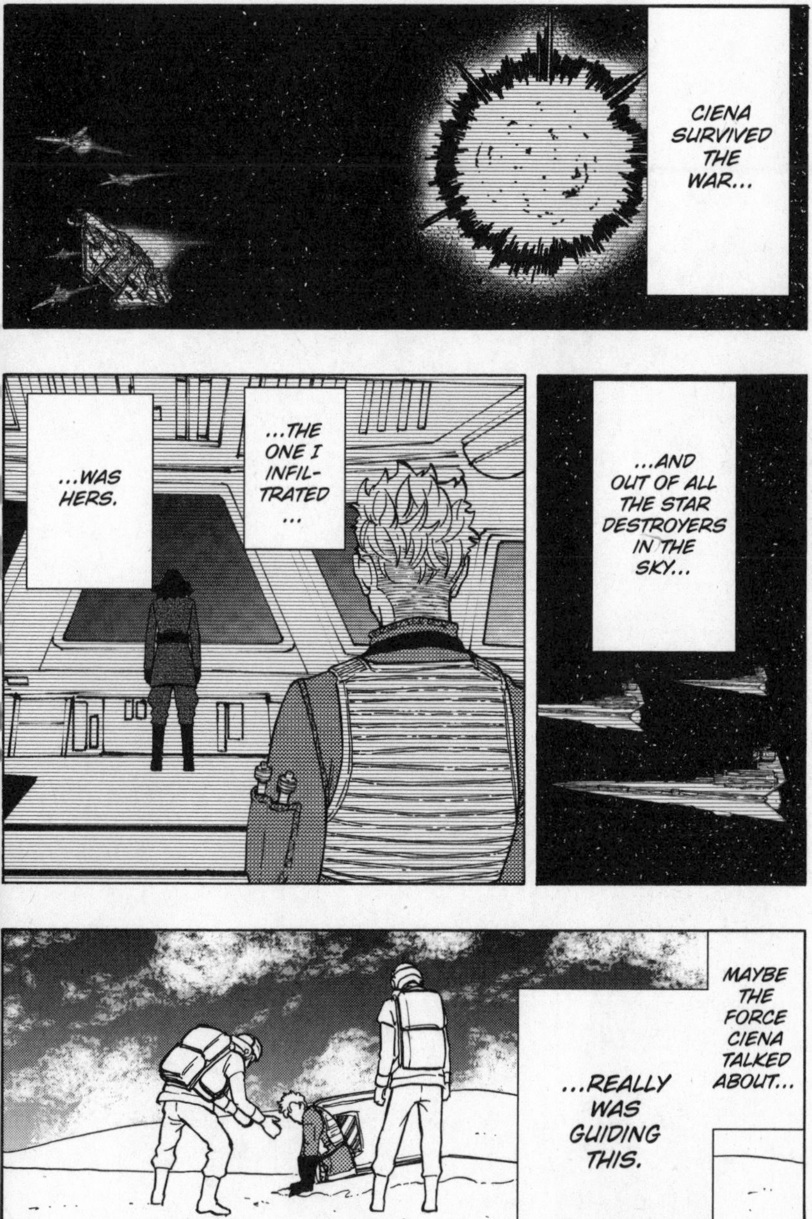
CIENA SURVIVED THE WAR...
...AND OUT OF ALL THE STAR DESTROYERS IN THE SKY...
...THE ONE I INFILTRATED...
...WAS HERS.
MAYBE THE FORCE CIENA TALKED ABOUT...
...REALLY WAS GUIDING THIS.

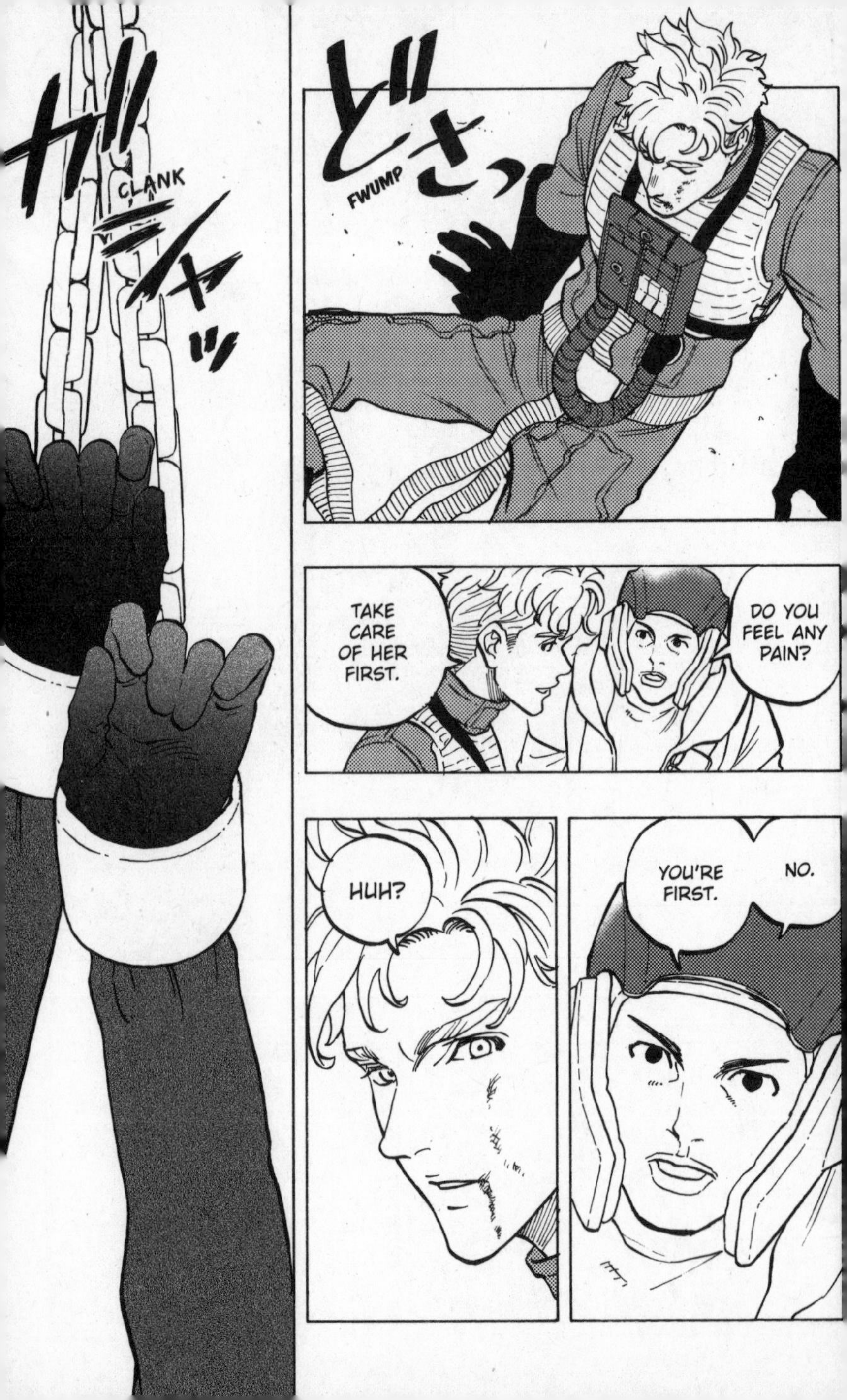
どさっ
FWUMP
DO YOU FEEL ANY PAIN?
TAKE CARE OF HER FIRST.
NO.
YOU'RE FIRST.
HUH?
CLANK

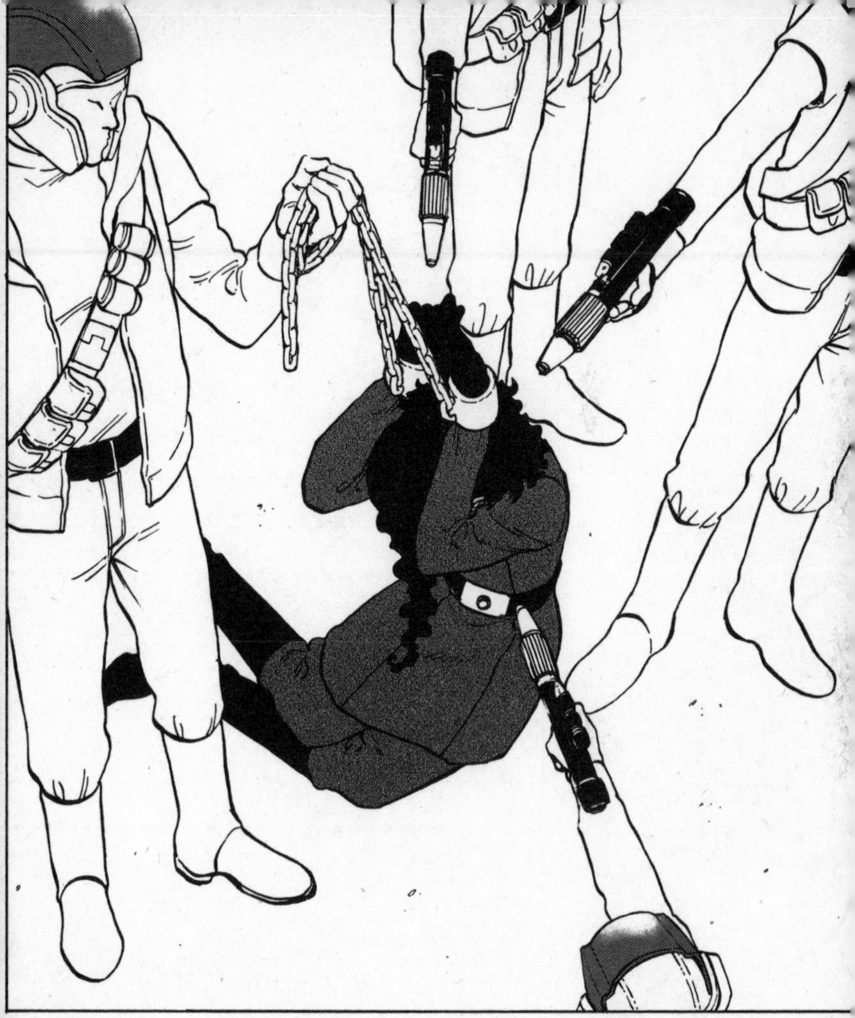

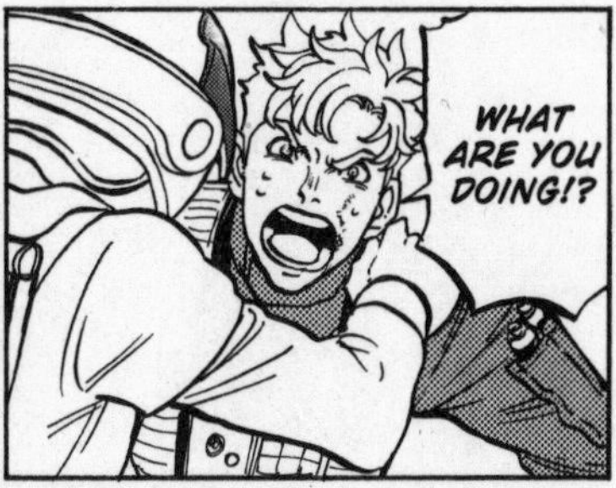
WHAT ARE YOU DOING!?

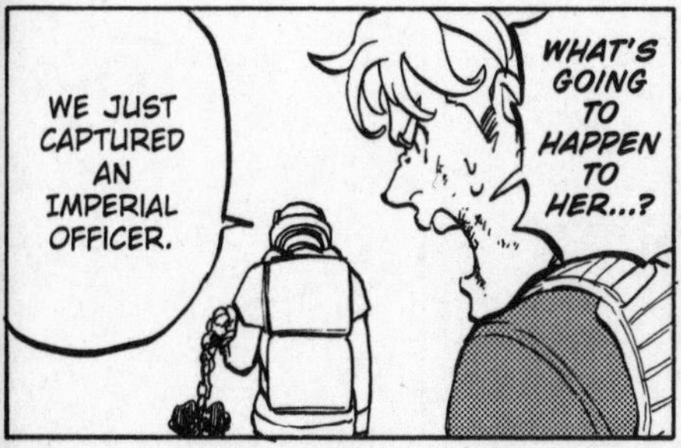
WHAT'S GOING TO HAPPEN TO HER...?
WE JUST CAPTURED AN IMPERIAL OFFICER.

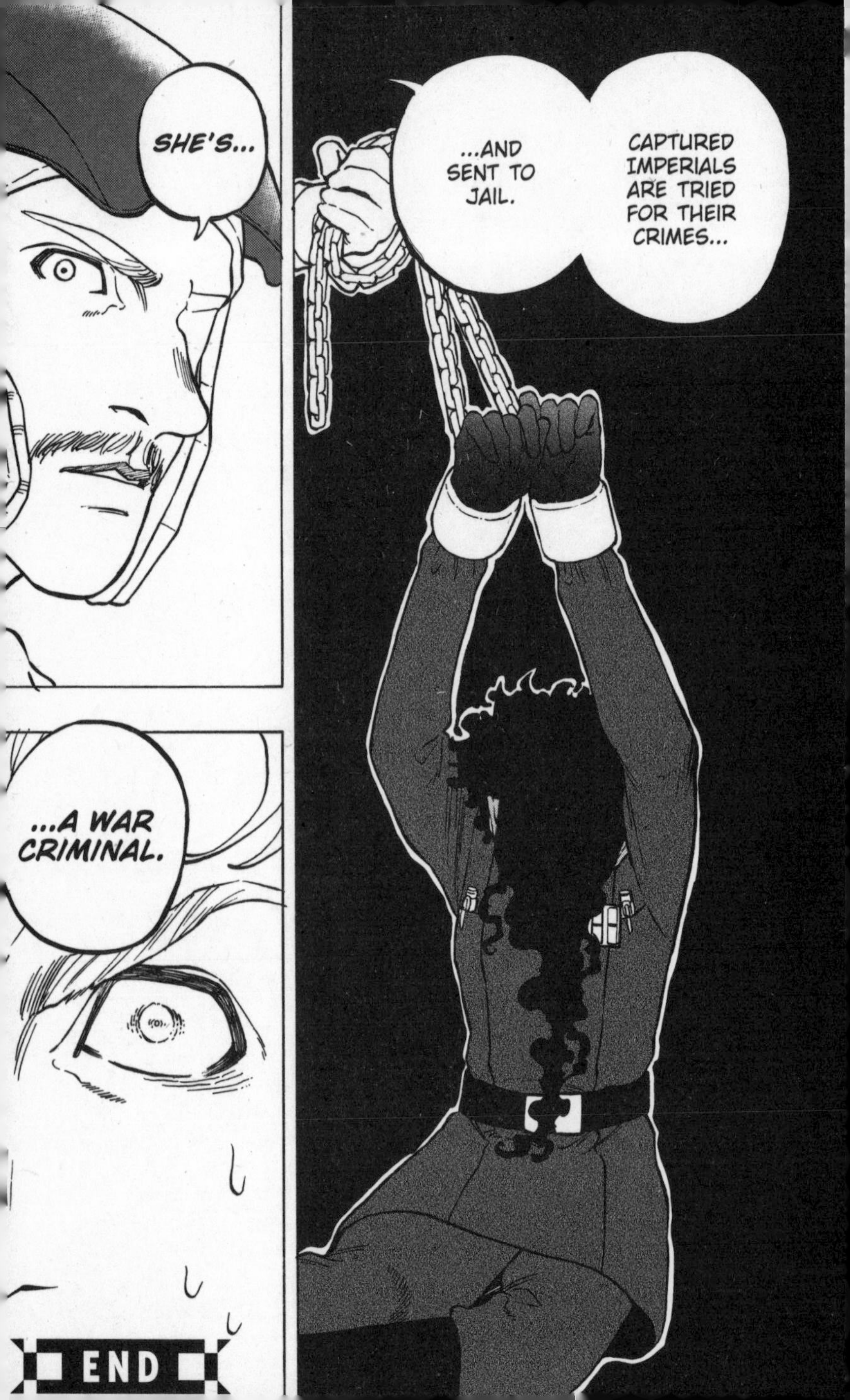
CAPTURED IMPERIALS ARE TRIED FOR THEIR CRIMES...
...AND SENT TO JAIL.
SHE'S...
...A WAR CRIMINAL.
END

STAR WARS
LOST STARS

Chapter. 17

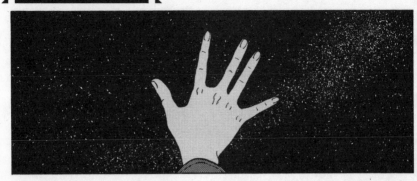

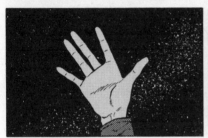

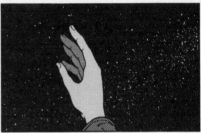

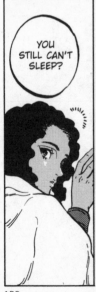

YOU STILL CAN'T SLEEP?

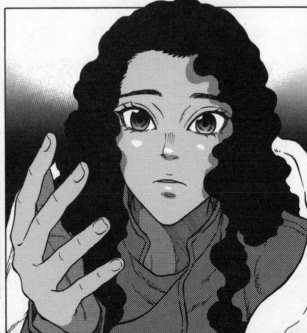

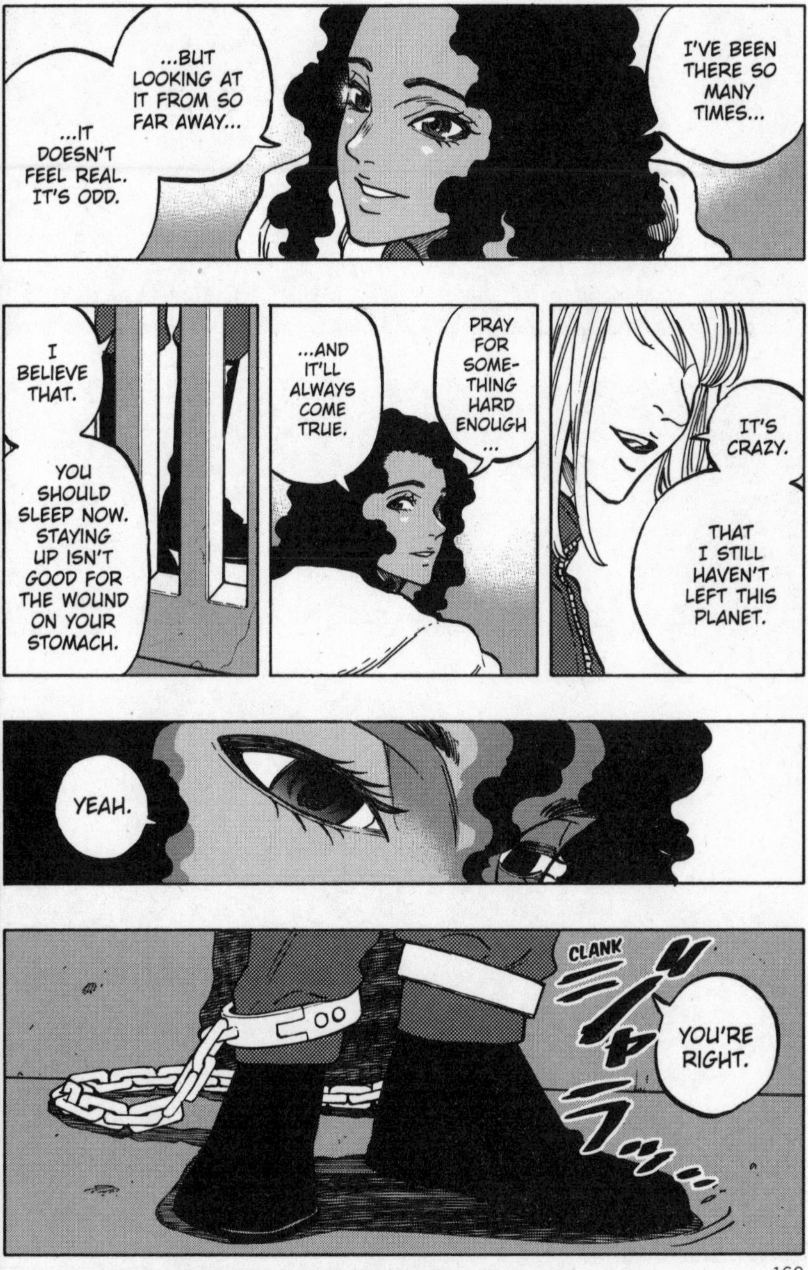
I'VE BEEN THERE SO MANY TIMES...
...BUT LOOKING AT IT FROM SO FAR AWAY...
...IT DOESN'T FEEL REAL. IT'S ODD.
IT'S CRAZY.
THAT I STILL HAVEN'T LEFT THIS PLANET.
PRAY FOR SOME-THING HARD ENOUGH...
...AND IT'LL ALWAYS COME TRUE.
I BELIEVE THAT.
YOU SHOULD SLEEP NOW. STAYING UP ISN'T GOOD FOR THE WOUND ON YOUR STOMACH.
YEAH.
CLANK
YOU'RE RIGHT.

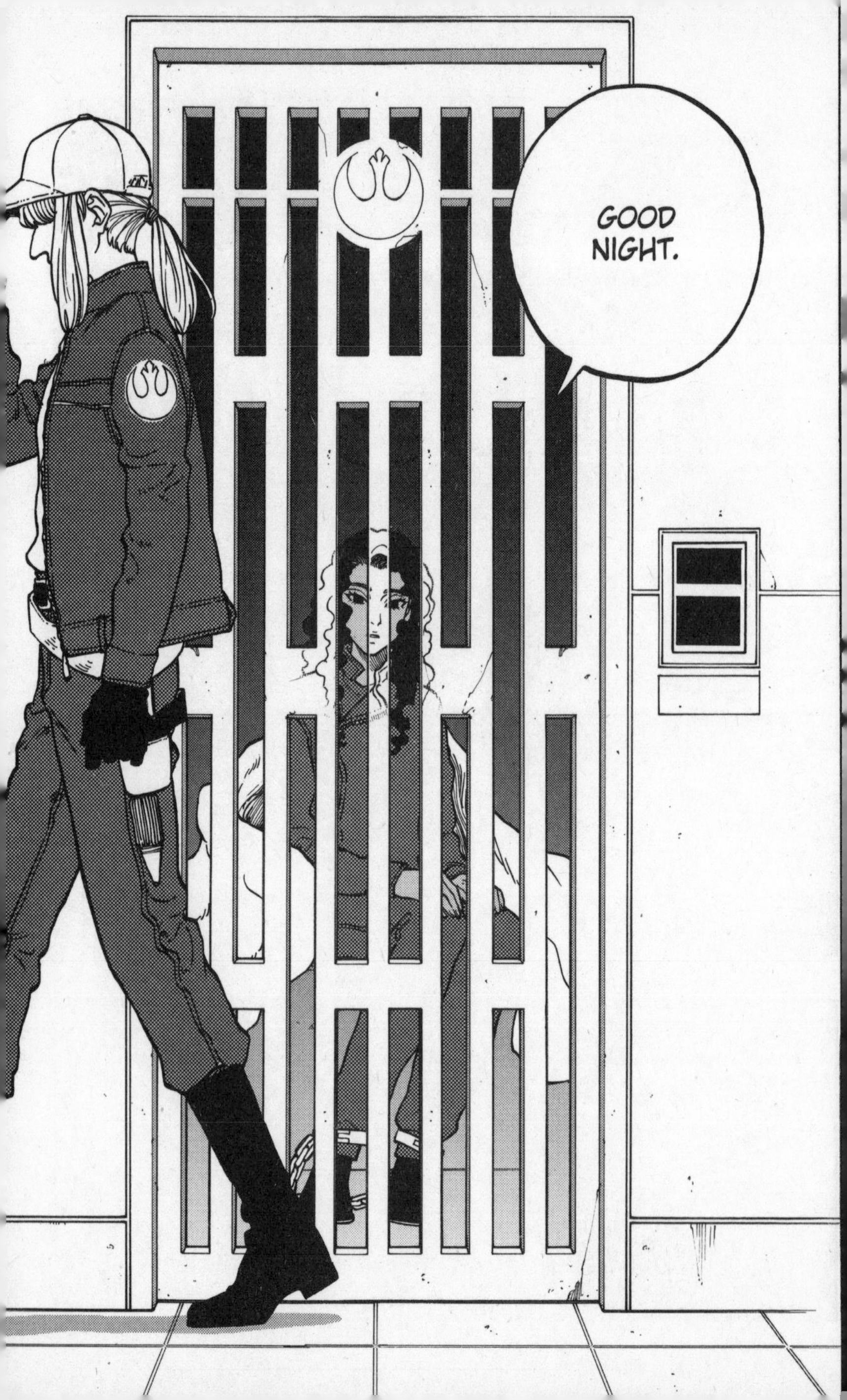
GOOD NIGHT.

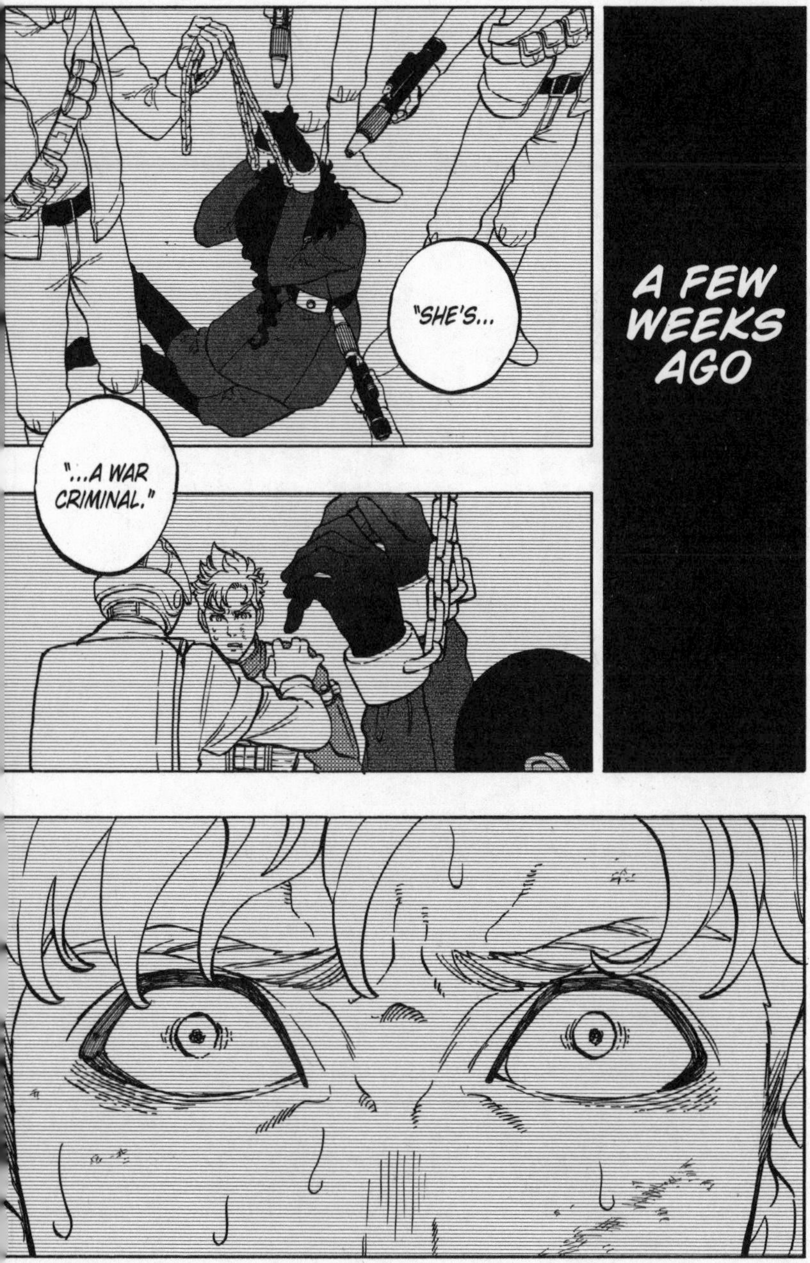
A FEW WEEKS AGO
"SHE'S...
"...A WAR CRIMINAL."

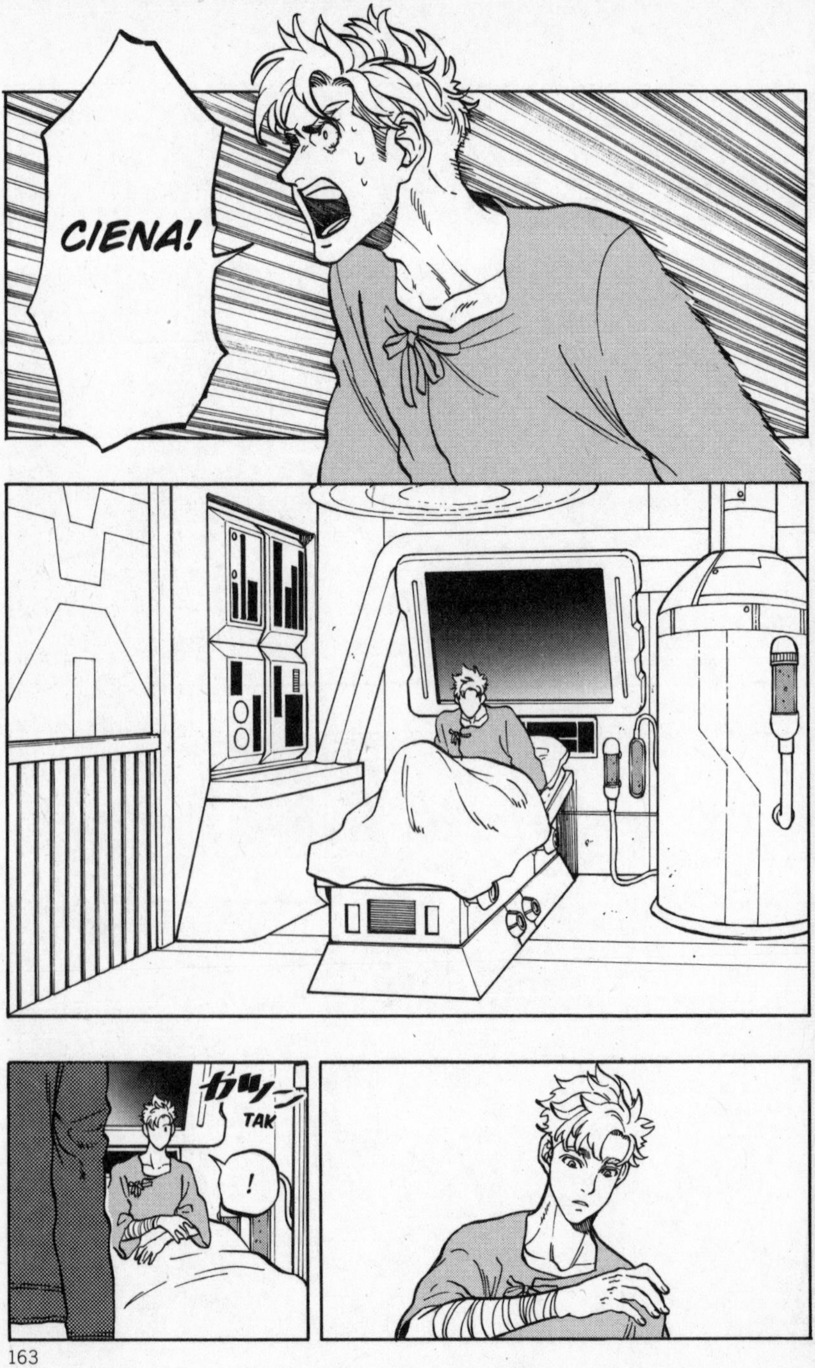
CIENA!
TAK
!

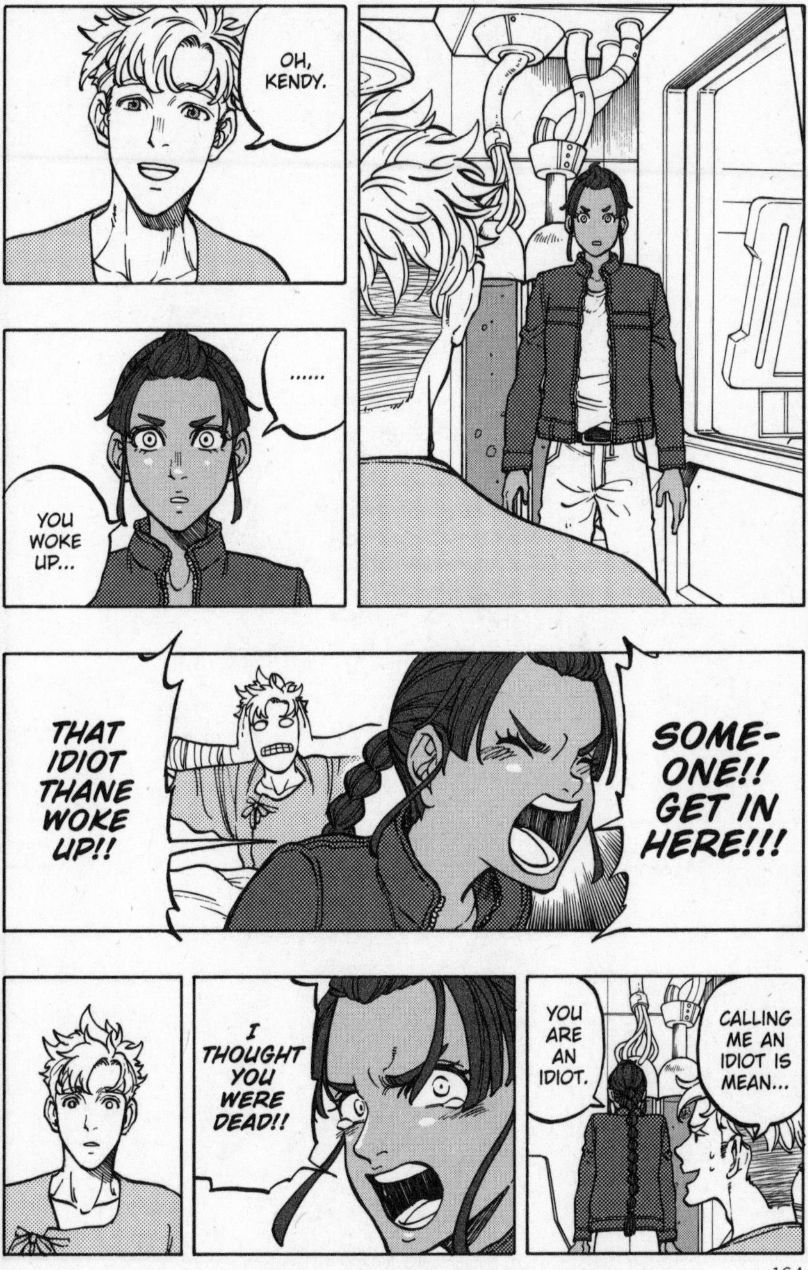
OH, KENDY.
......
YOU WOKE UP...
SOME-ONE!! GET IN HERE!!!
THAT IDIOT THANE WOKE UP!!
CALLING ME AN IDIOT IS MEAN...
YOU ARE AN IDIOT.
I THOUGHT YOU WERE DEAD!!

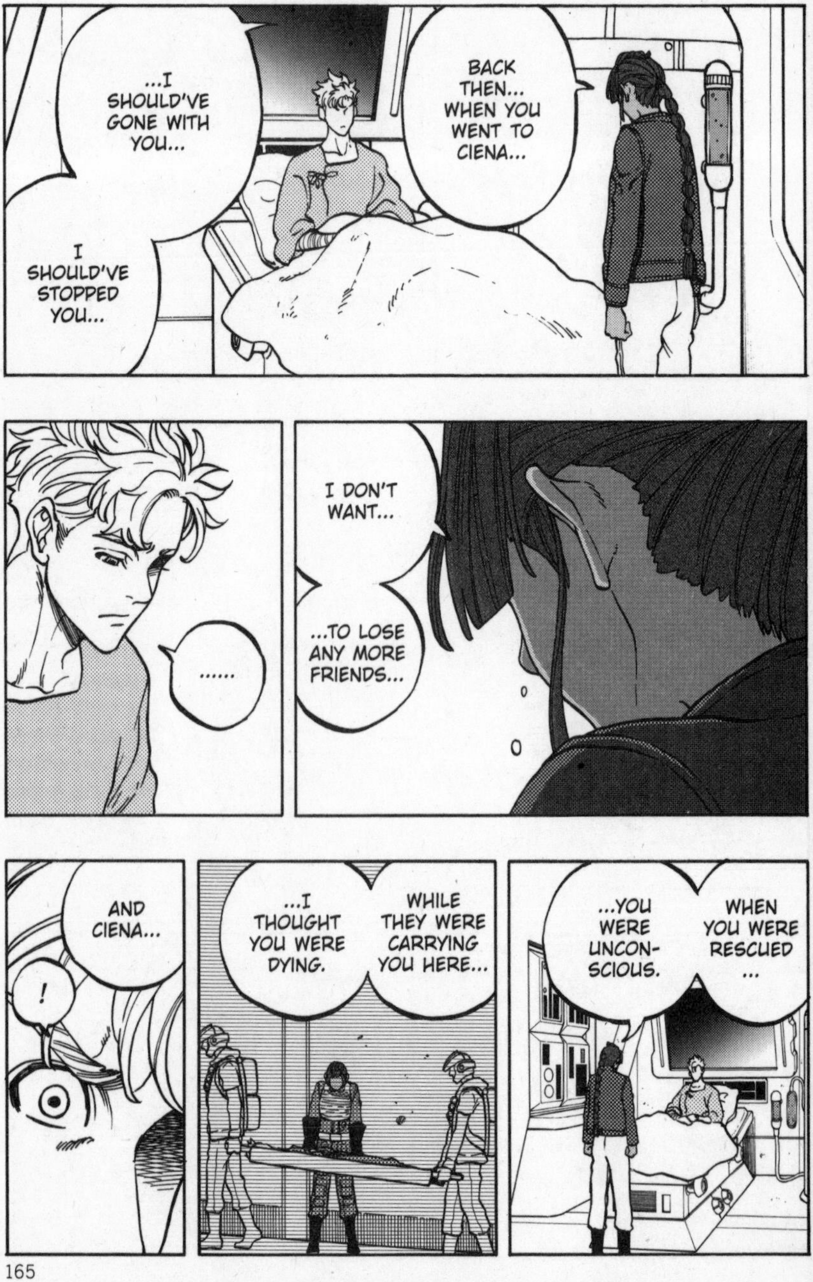
BACK THEN... WHEN YOU WENT TO CIENA...
...I SHOULD'VE GONE WITH YOU...
I SHOULD'VE STOPPED YOU...
I DON'T WANT...
...TO LOSE ANY MORE FRIENDS...
......
WHEN YOU WERE RESCUED ...
...YOU WERE UNCON-SCIOUS.
WHILE THEY WERE CARRYING YOU HERE...
...I THOUGHT YOU WERE DYING.
AND CIENA...
!

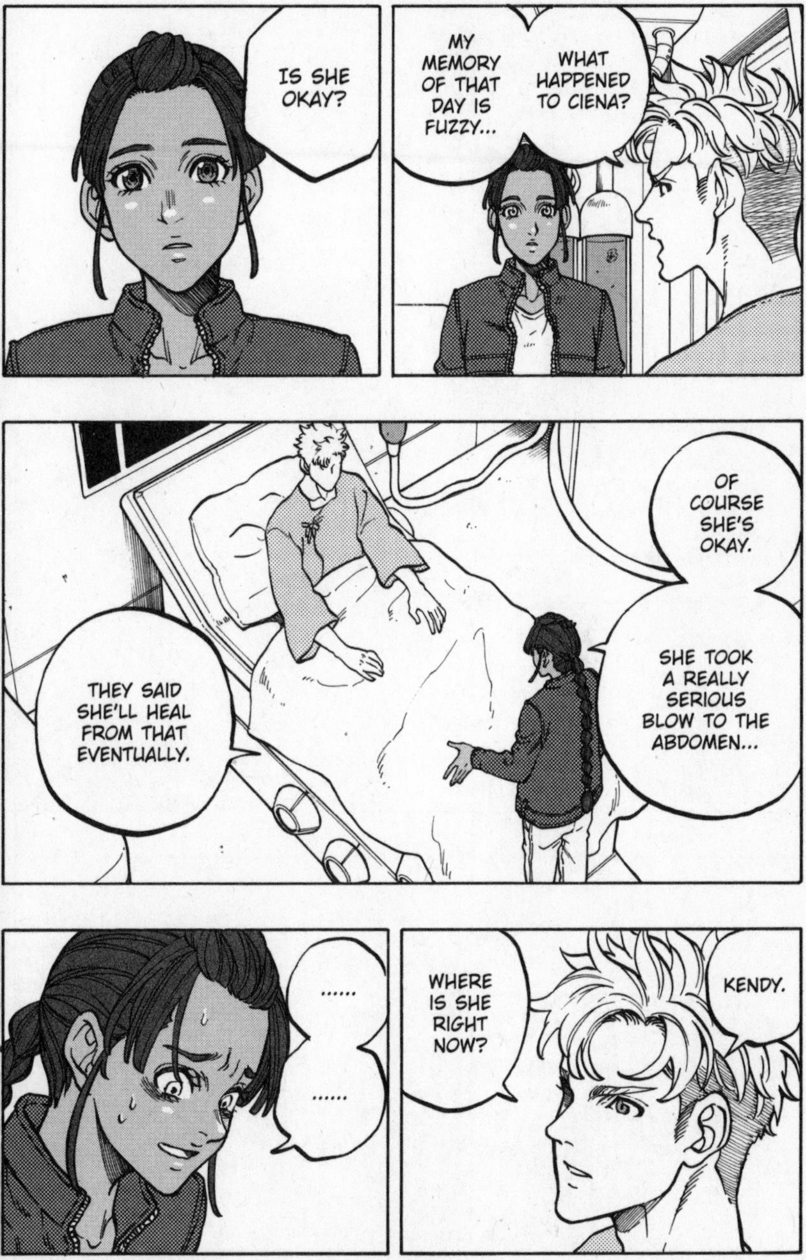
WHAT HAPPENED TO CIENA?
MY MEMORY OF THAT DAY IS FUZZY...
IS SHE OKAY?
OF COURSE SHE'S OKAY.
SHE TOOK A REALLY SERIOUS BLOW TO THE ABDOMEN...
THEY SAID SHE'LL HEAL FROM THAT EVENTUALLY.
KENDY.
WHERE IS SHE RIGHT NOW?
......
......

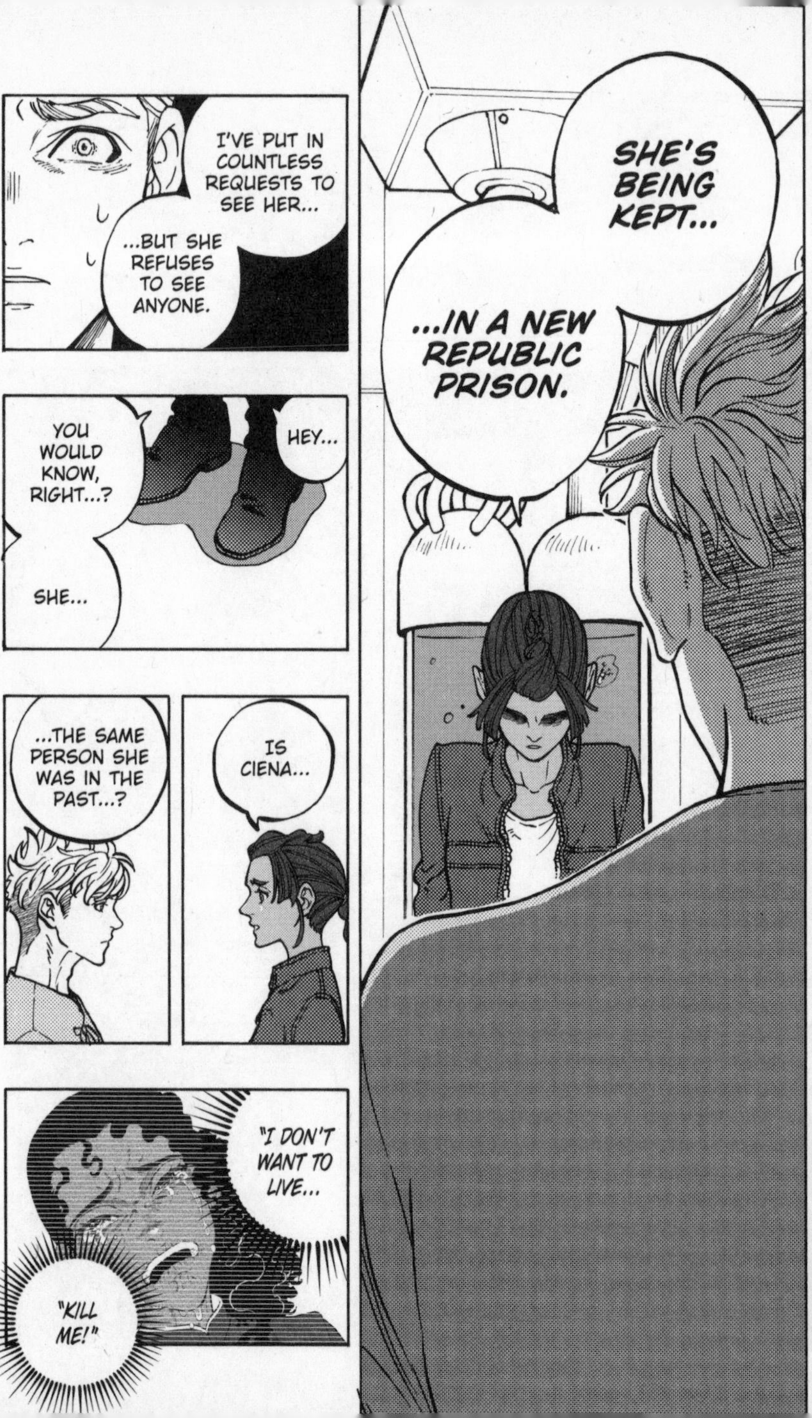
SHE'S BEING KEPT...
...IN A NEW REPUBLIC PRISON.
I'VE PUT IN COUNTLESS REQUESTS TO SEE HER...
...BUT SHE REFUSES TO SEE ANYONE.
HEY...
YOU WOULD KNOW, RIGHT...?
SHE...
IS CIENA...
...THE SAME PERSON SHE WAS IN THE PAST...?
"I DON'T WANT TO LIVE...
"KILL ME!"

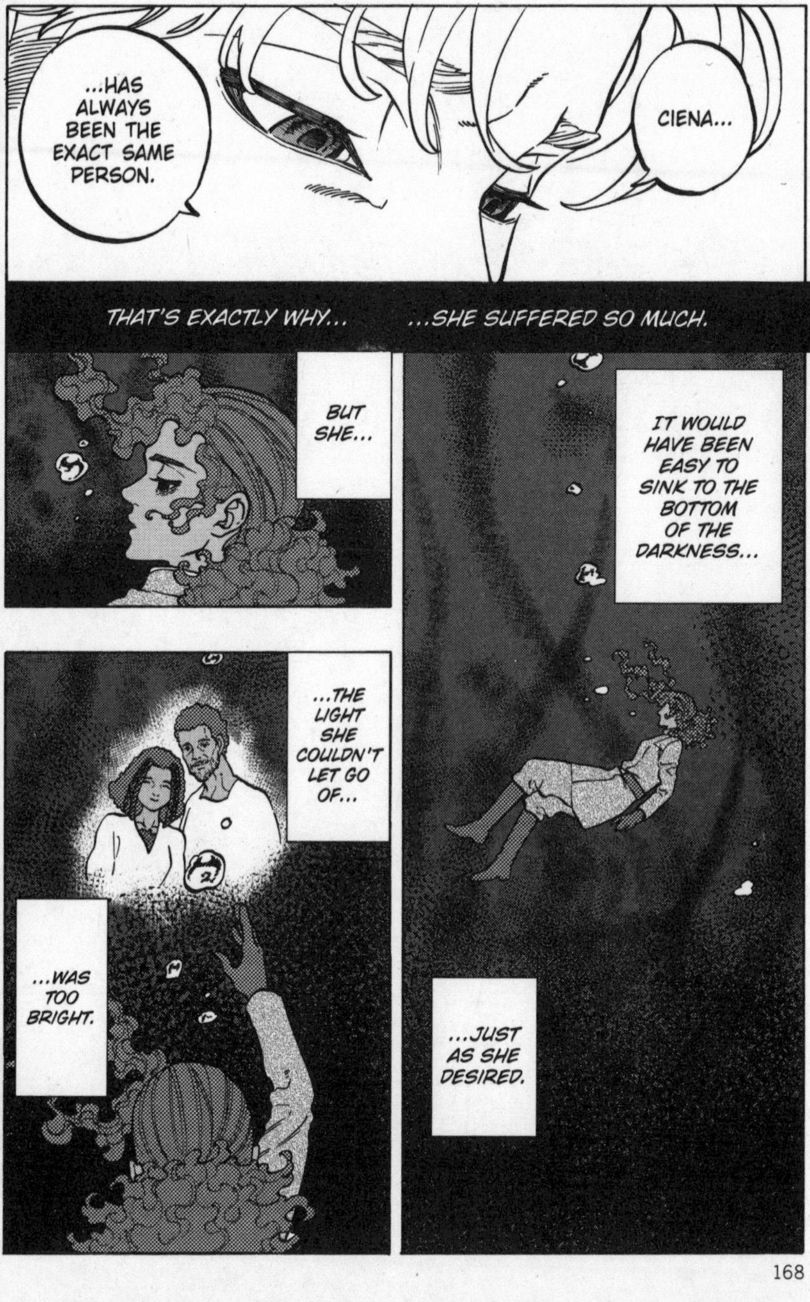

CIENA...
...HAS ALWAYS BEEN THE EXACT SAME PERSON.
THAT'S EXACTLY WHY...
...SHE SUFFERED SO MUCH.
IT WOULD HAVE BEEN EASY TO SINK TO THE BOTTOM OF THE DARKNESS...
...JUST AS SHE DESIRED.
BUT SHE...
...THE LIGHT SHE COULDN'T LET GO OF...
...WAS TOO BRIGHT.

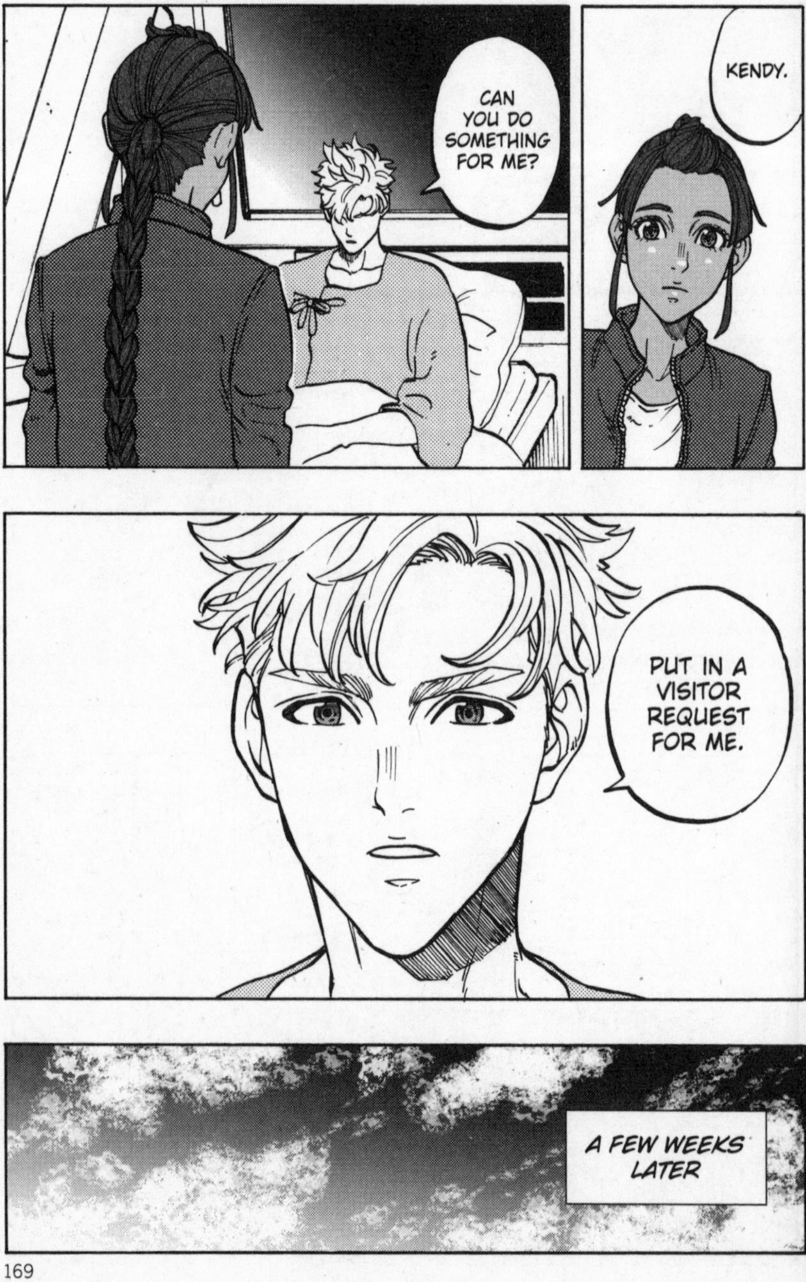
KENDY.
CAN YOU DO SOMETHING FOR ME?
PUT IN A VISITOR REQUEST FOR ME.
A FEW WEEKS LATER

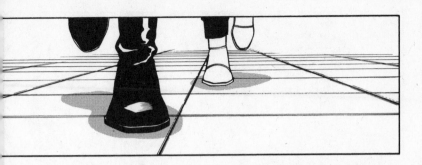

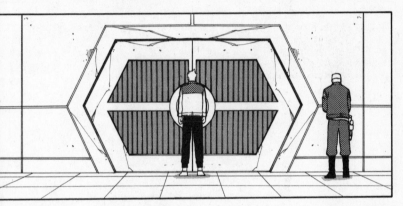

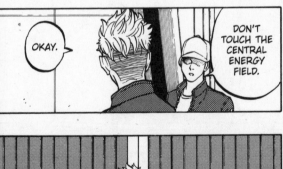

OKAY.

DON'T TOUCH THE CENTRAL ENERGY FIELD.

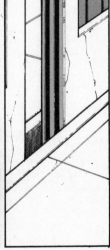

170

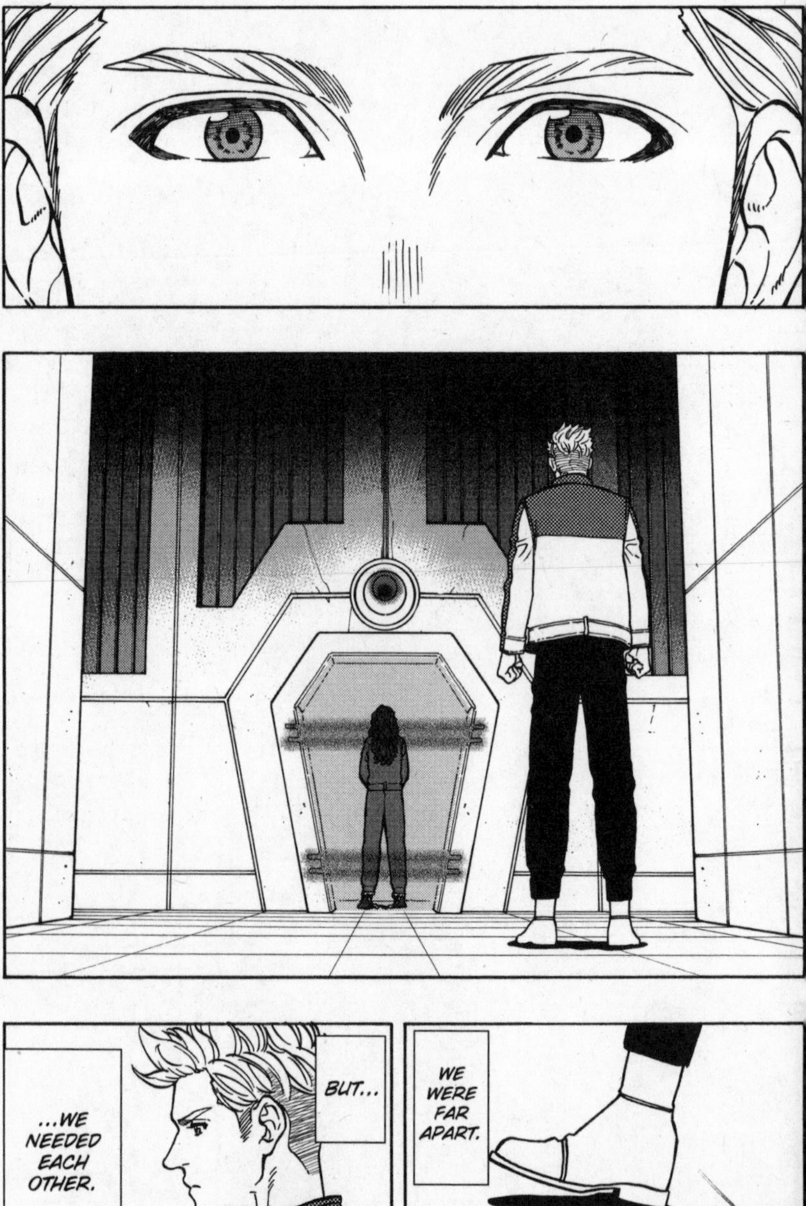
WE WERE FAR APART.
BUT...
...WE NEEDED EACH OTHER.

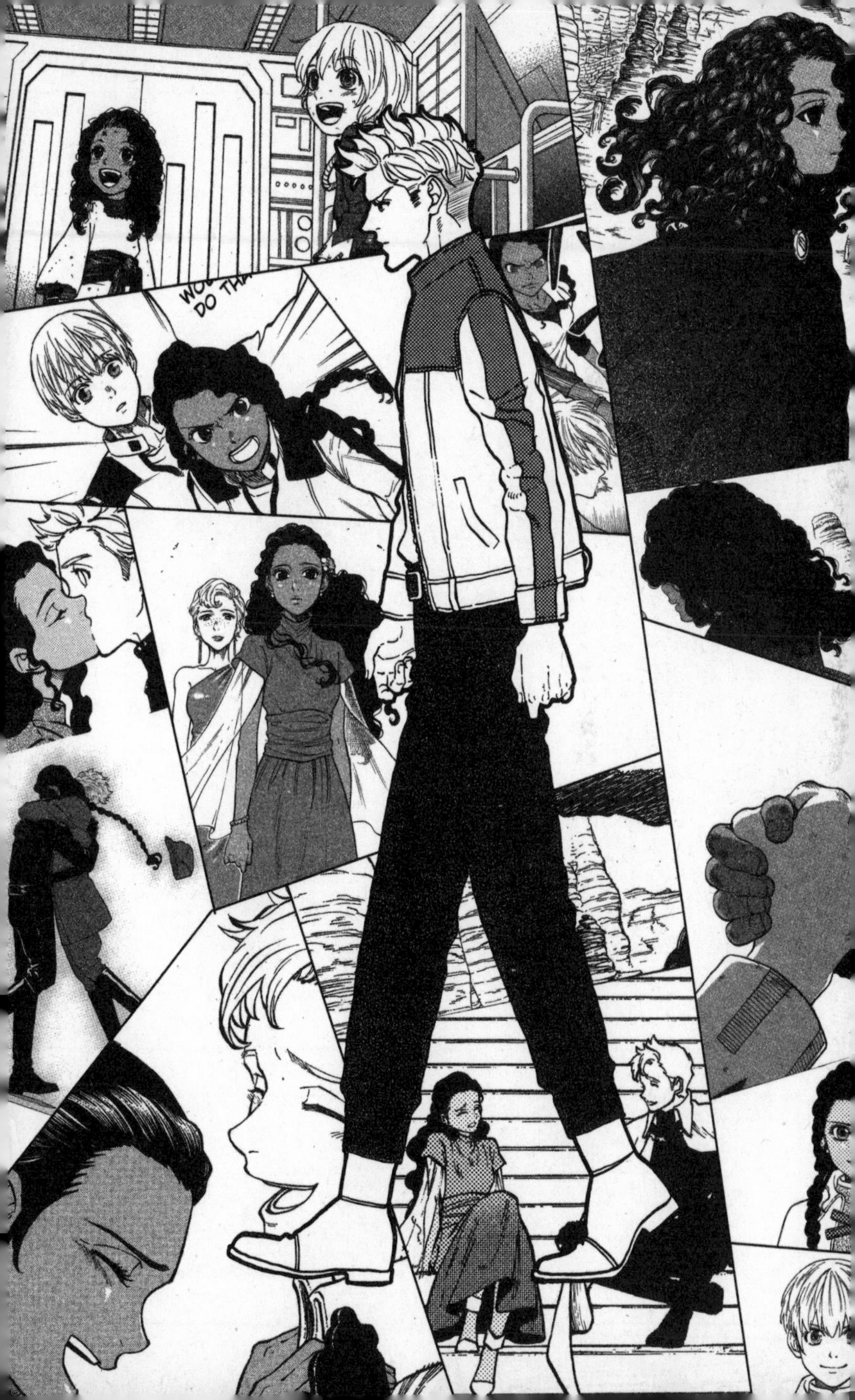
WOU DO THA

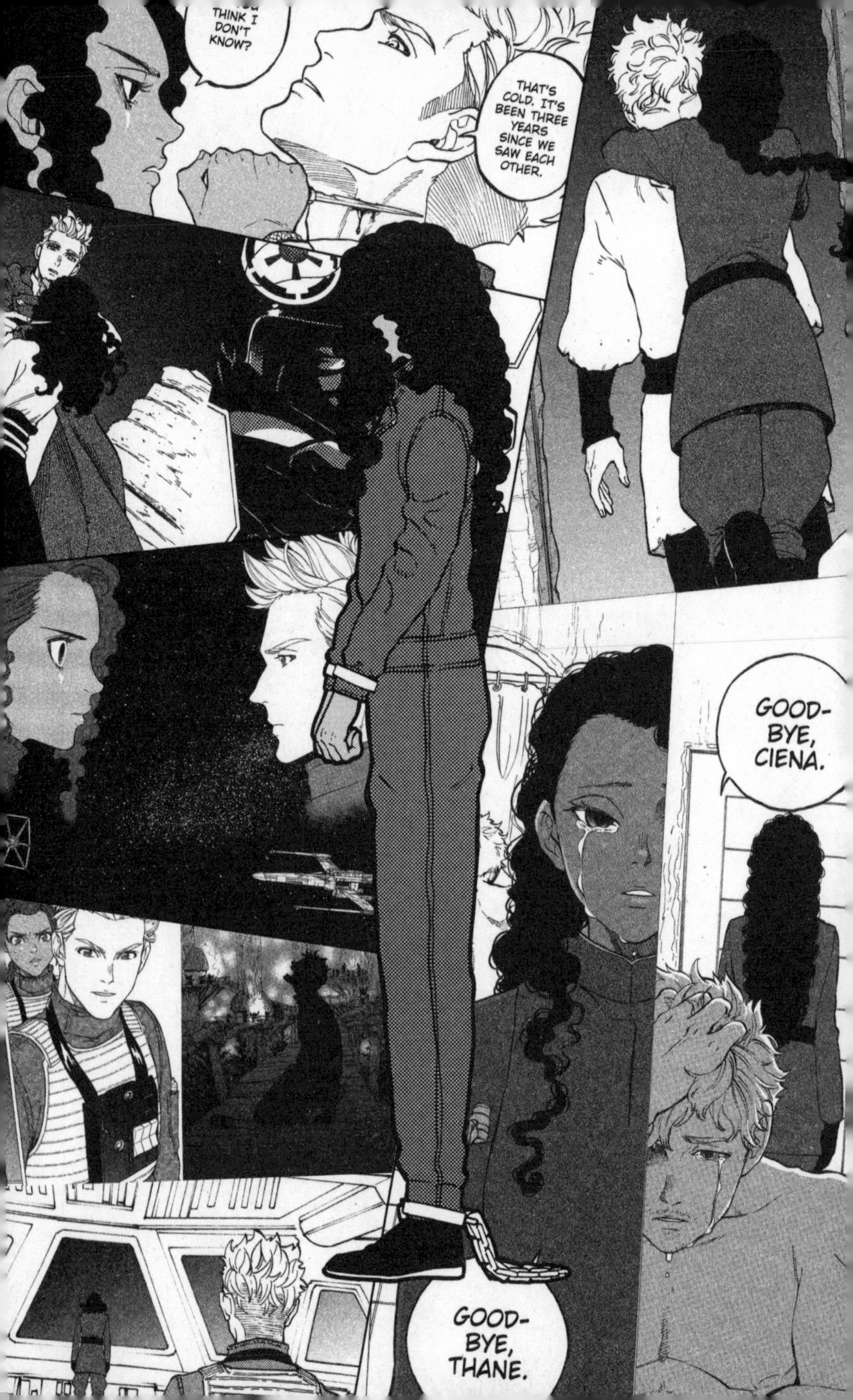
THAT'S COLD. IT'S BEEN THREE YEARS SINCE WE SAW EACH OTHER.
THINK I DON'T KNOW?
GOOD-BYE, CIENA.
GOOD-BYE, THANE.

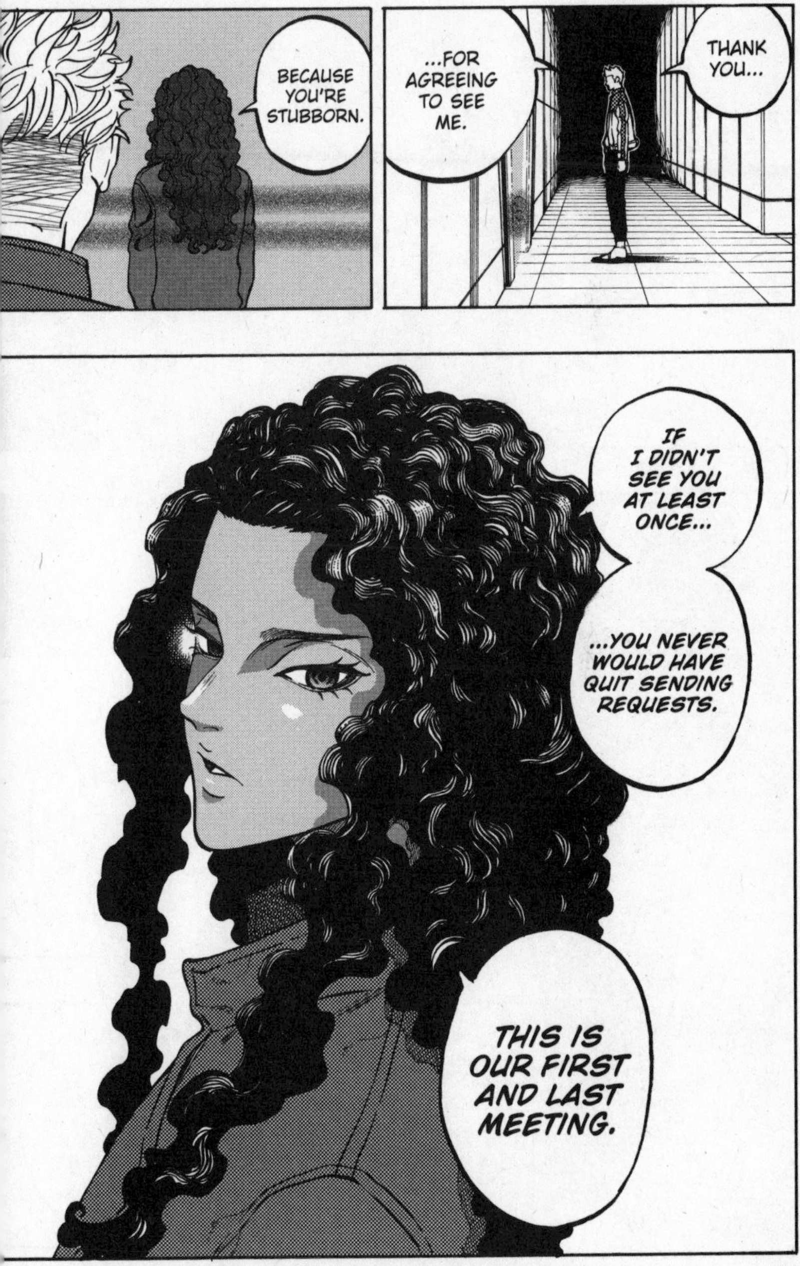
THANK YOU...
...FOR AGREEING TO SEE ME.
BECAUSE YOU'RE STUBBORN.
IF I DIDN'T SEE YOU AT LEAST ONCE...
...YOU NEVER WOULD HAVE QUIT SENDING REQUESTS.
THIS IS OUR FIRST AND LAST MEETING.

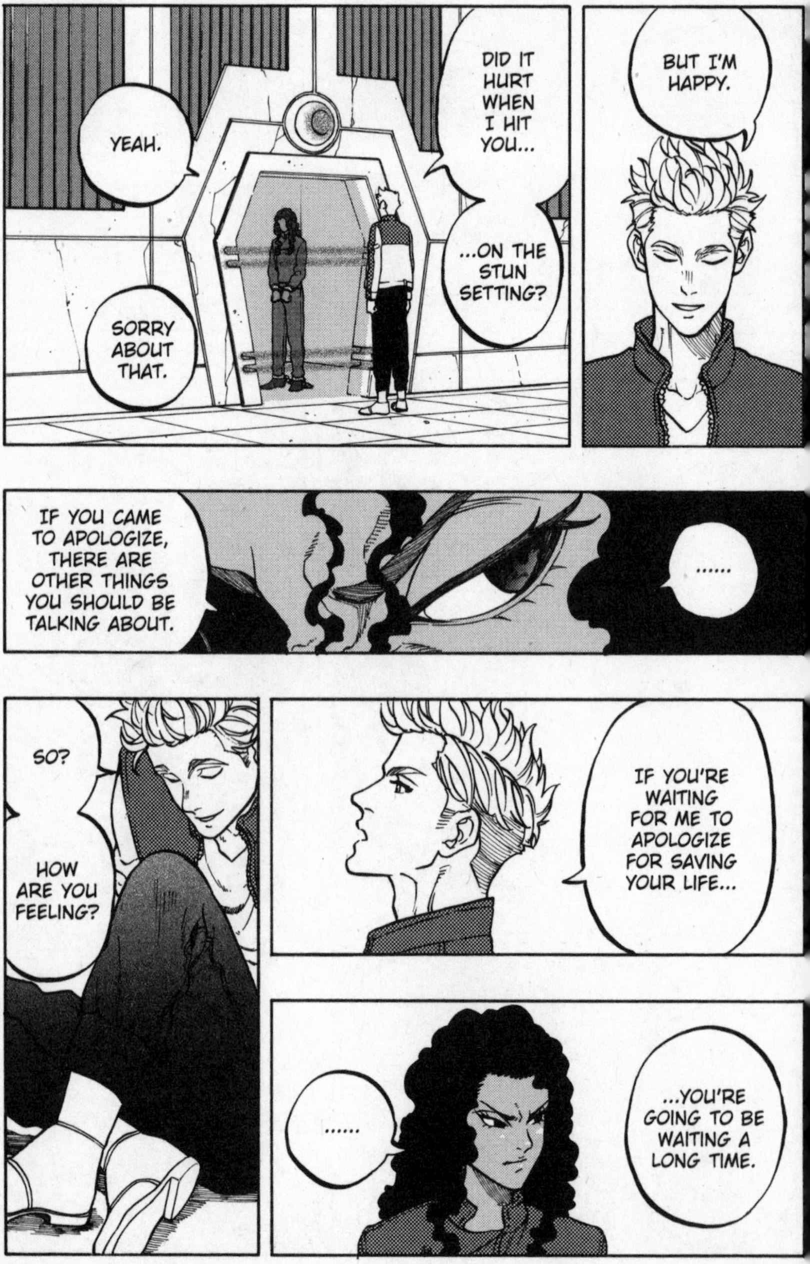
BUT I'M HAPPY.
DID IT HURT WHEN I HIT YOU...
...ON THE STUN SETTING?
YEAH.
SORRY ABOUT THAT.
......
IF YOU CAME TO APOLOGIZE, THERE ARE OTHER THINGS YOU SHOULD BE TALKING ABOUT.
IF YOU'RE WAITING FOR ME TO APOLOGIZE FOR SAVING YOUR LIFE...
...YOU'RE GOING TO BE WAITING A LONG TIME.
......
SO?
HOW ARE YOU FEELING?

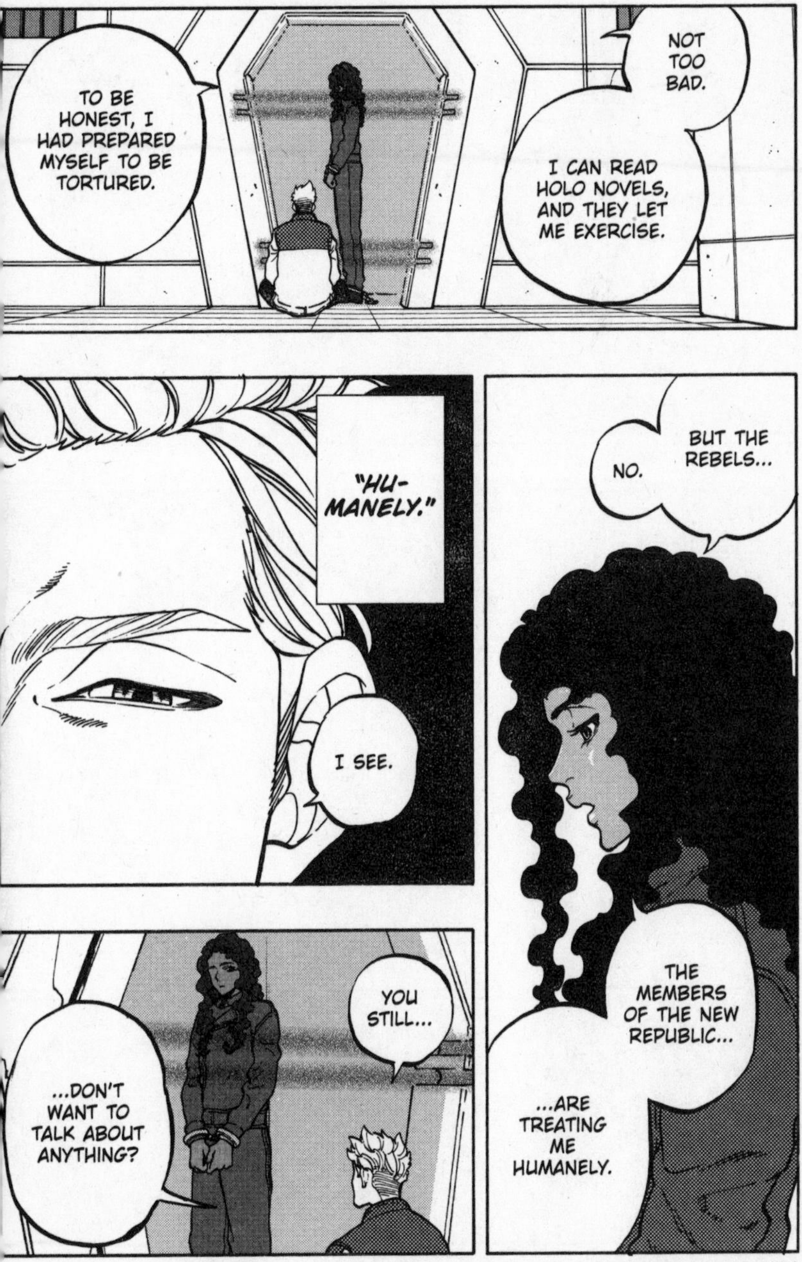
NOT TOO BAD.
I CAN READ HOLO NOVELS, AND THEY LET ME EXERCISE.
TO BE HONEST, I HAD PREPARED MYSELF TO BE TORTURED.
NO. BUT THE REBELS...
THE MEMBERS OF THE NEW REPUBLIC...
...ARE TREATING ME HUMANELY.
"HU-MANELY."
I SEE.
YOU STILL...
...DON'T WANT TO TALK ABOUT ANYTHING?

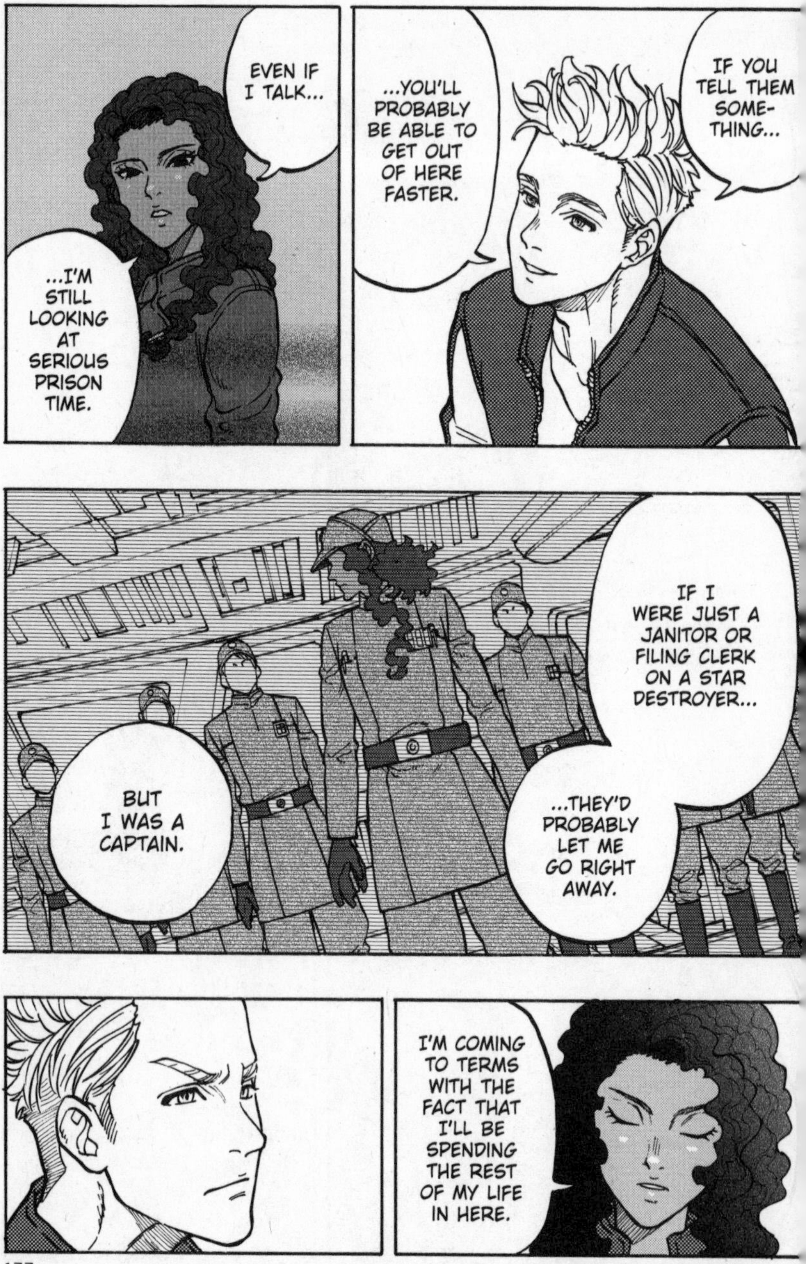
IF YOU TELL THEM SOME-THING...
...YOU'LL PROBABLY BE ABLE TO GET OUT OF HERE FASTER.
EVEN IF I TALK...
...I'M STILL LOOKING AT SERIOUS PRISON TIME.
IF I WERE JUST A JANITOR OR FILING CLERK ON A STAR DESTROYER...
...THEY'D PROBABLY LET ME GO RIGHT AWAY.
BUT I WAS A CAPTAIN.
I'M COMING TO TERMS WITH THE FACT THAT I'LL BE SPENDING THE REST OF MY LIFE IN HERE.

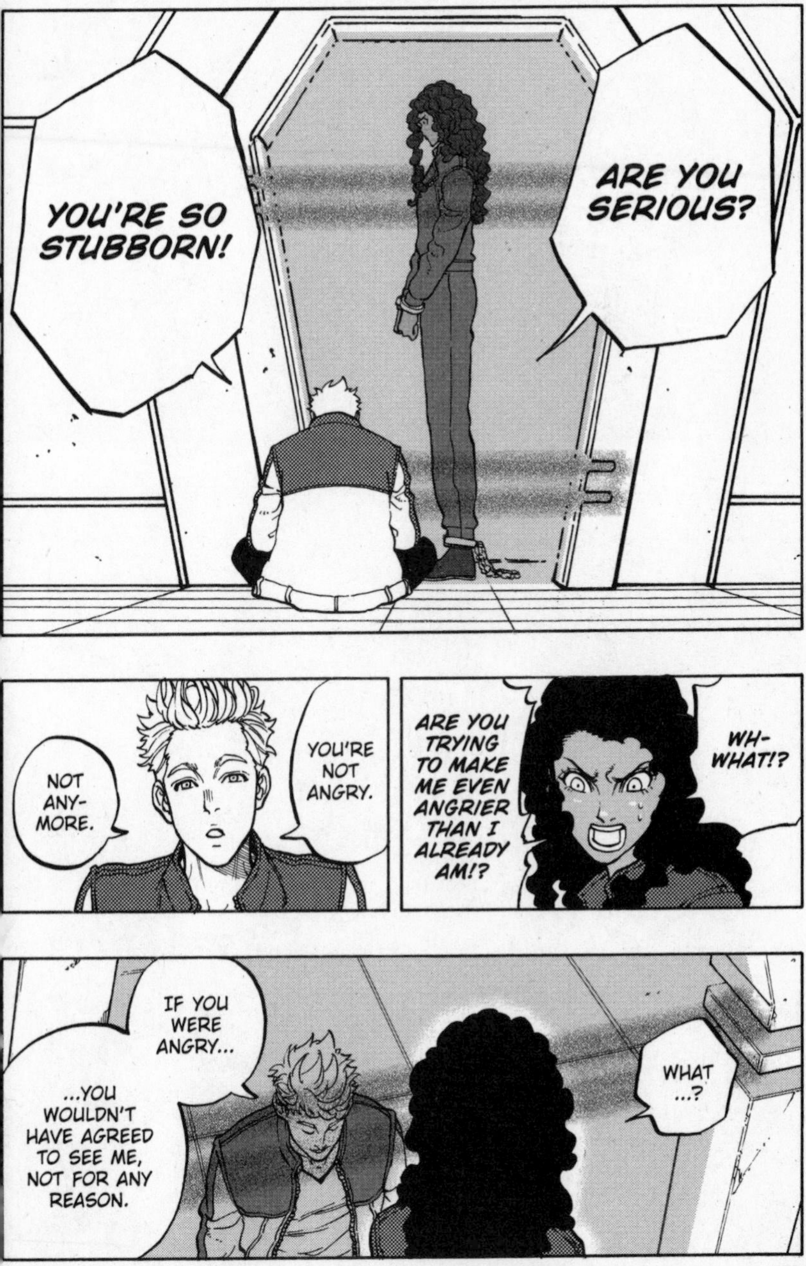
ARE YOU SERIOUS?
YOU'RE SO STUBBORN!
WH-WHAT!?
ARE YOU TRYING TO MAKE ME EVEN ANGRIER THAN I ALREADY AM!?
YOU'RE NOT ANGRY.
NOT ANY-MORE.
WHAT ...?
IF YOU WERE ANGRY...
...YOU WOULDN'T HAVE AGREED TO SEE ME, NOT FOR ANY REASON.

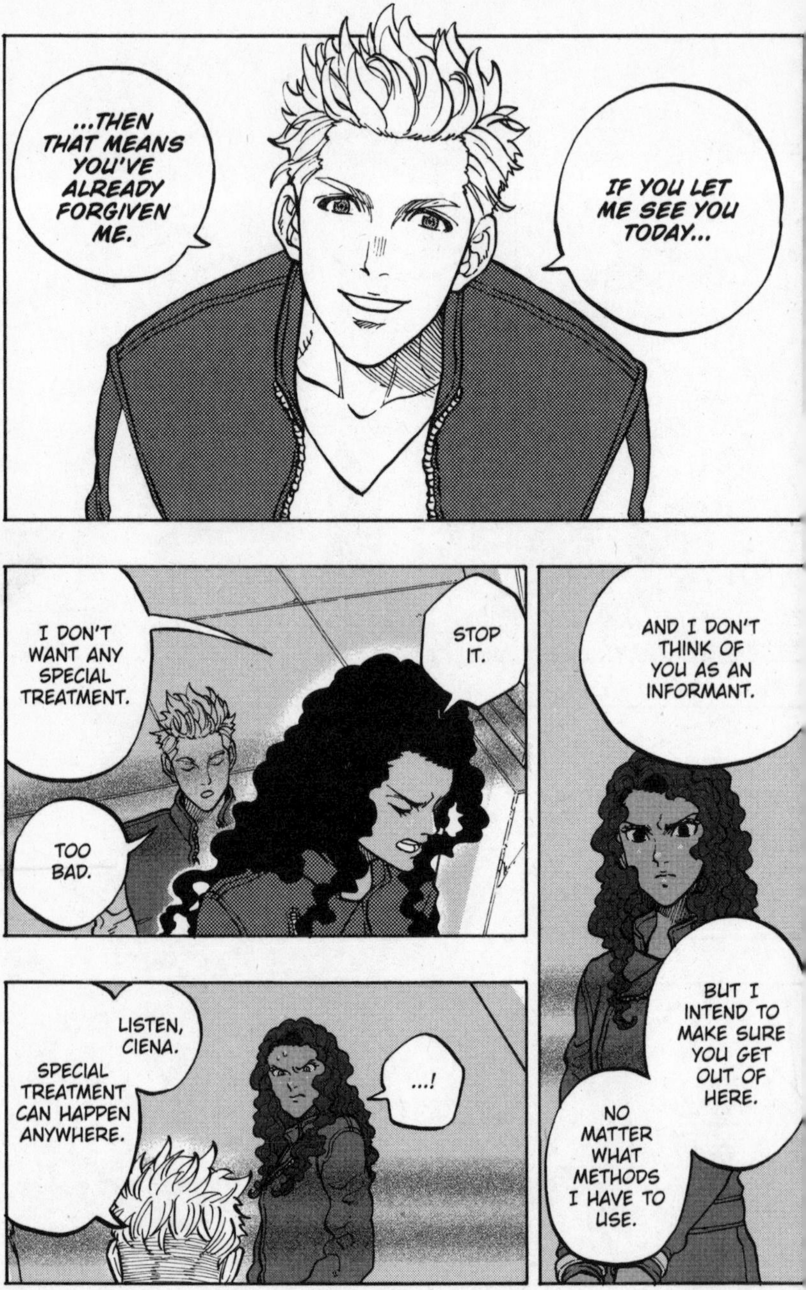
IF YOU LET ME SEE YOU TODAY...
...THEN THAT MEANS YOU'VE ALREADY FORGIVEN ME.
AND I DON'T THINK OF YOU AS AN INFORMANT.
BUT I INTEND TO MAKE SURE YOU GET OUT OF HERE.
NO MATTER WHAT METHODS I HAVE TO USE.
STOP IT.
I DON'T WANT ANY SPECIAL TREATMENT.
TOO BAD.
...!
LISTEN, CIENA.
SPECIAL TREATMENT CAN HAPPEN ANYWHERE.

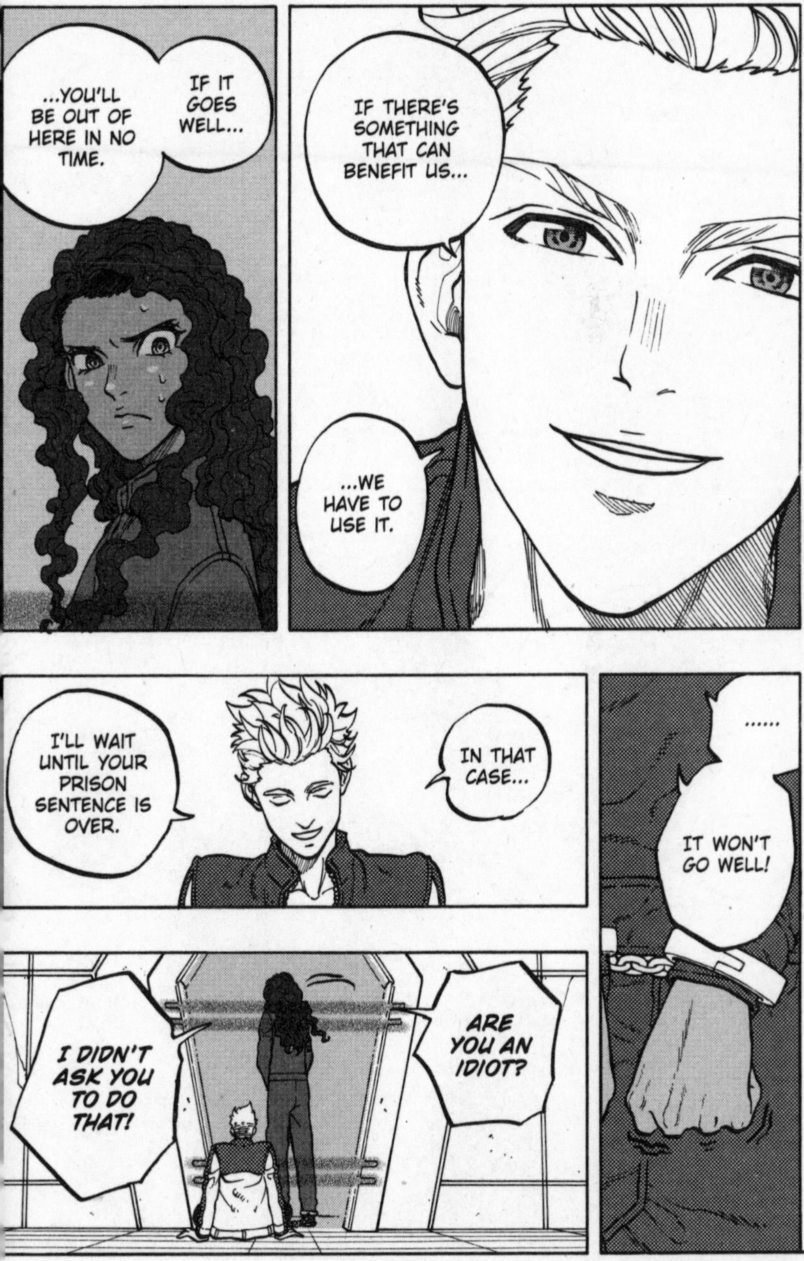
IF THERE'S SOMETHING THAT CAN BENEFIT US...
...WE HAVE TO USE IT.
IF IT GOES WELL...
...YOU'LL BE OUT OF HERE IN NO TIME.
......
IT WON'T GO WELL!
IN THAT CASE...
I'LL WAIT UNTIL YOUR PRISON SENTENCE IS OVER.
ARE YOU AN IDIOT?
I DIDN'T ASK YOU TO DO THAT!

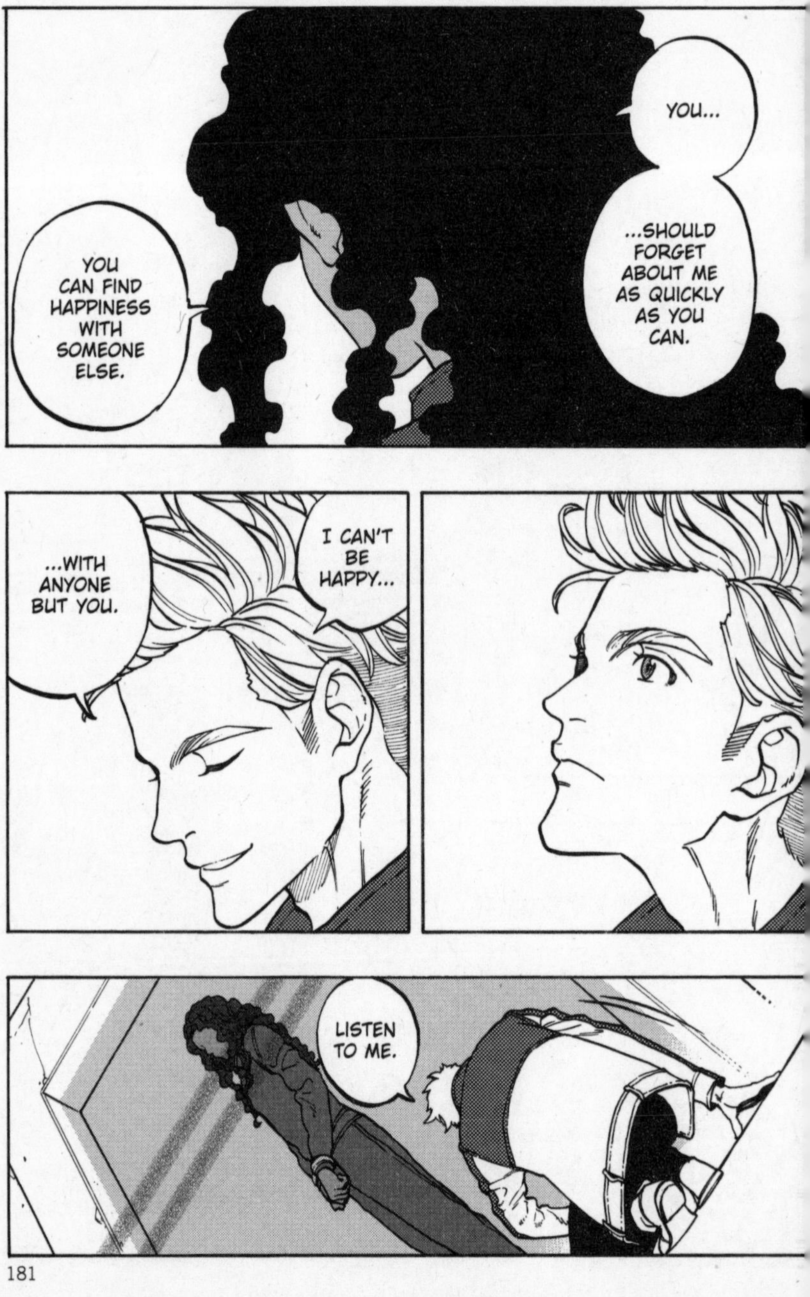
YOU...
...SHOULD FORGET ABOUT ME AS QUICKLY AS YOU CAN.
YOU CAN FIND HAPPINESS WITH SOMEONE ELSE.
I CAN'T BE HAPPY...
...WITH ANYONE BUT YOU.
LISTEN TO ME.

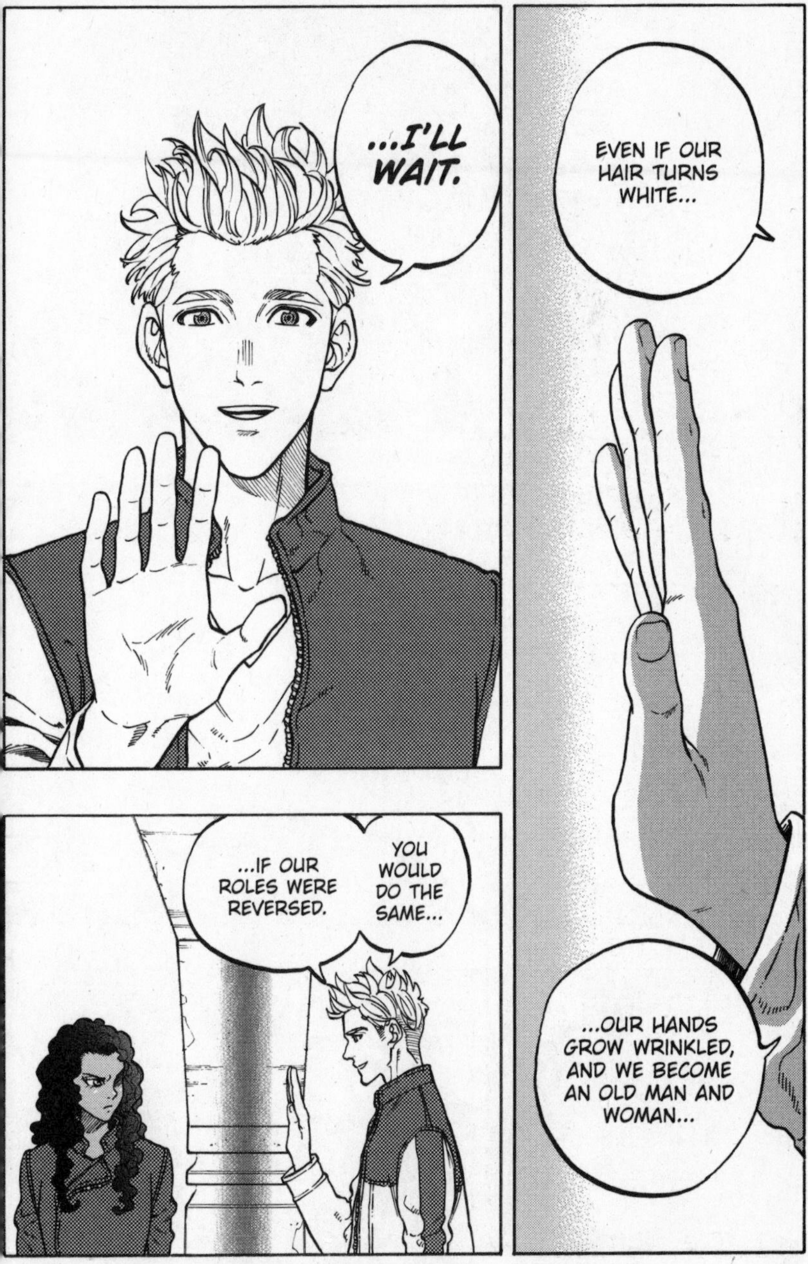
EVEN IF OUR HAIR TURNS WHITE...
...OUR HANDS GROW WRINKLED, AND WE BECOME AN OLD MAN AND WOMAN...
...I'LL WAIT.
YOU WOULD DO THE SAME...
...IF OUR ROLES WERE REVERSED.

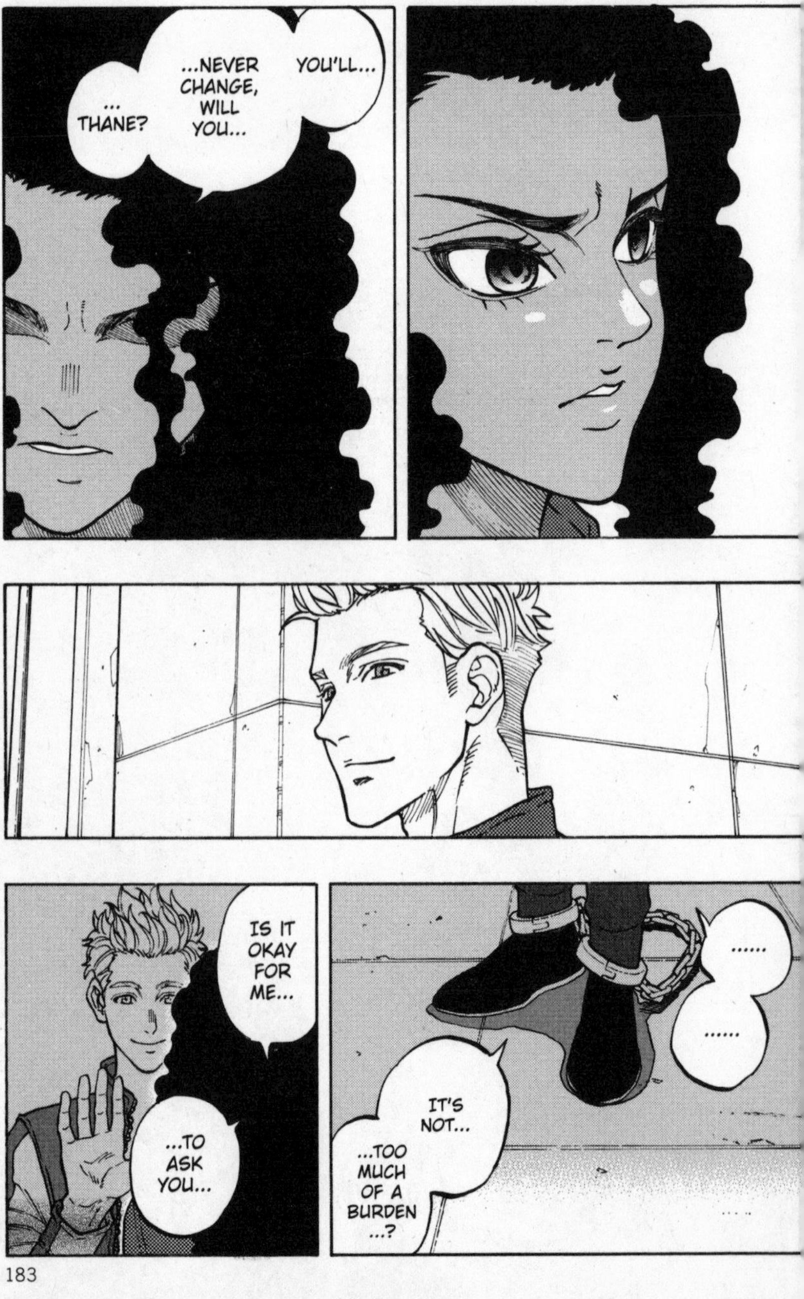
YOU'LL...
...NEVER CHANGE, WILL YOU...
...THANE?
......
......
IT'S NOT...
...TOO MUCH OF A BURDEN ...?
IS IT OKAY FOR ME...
...TO ASK YOU...

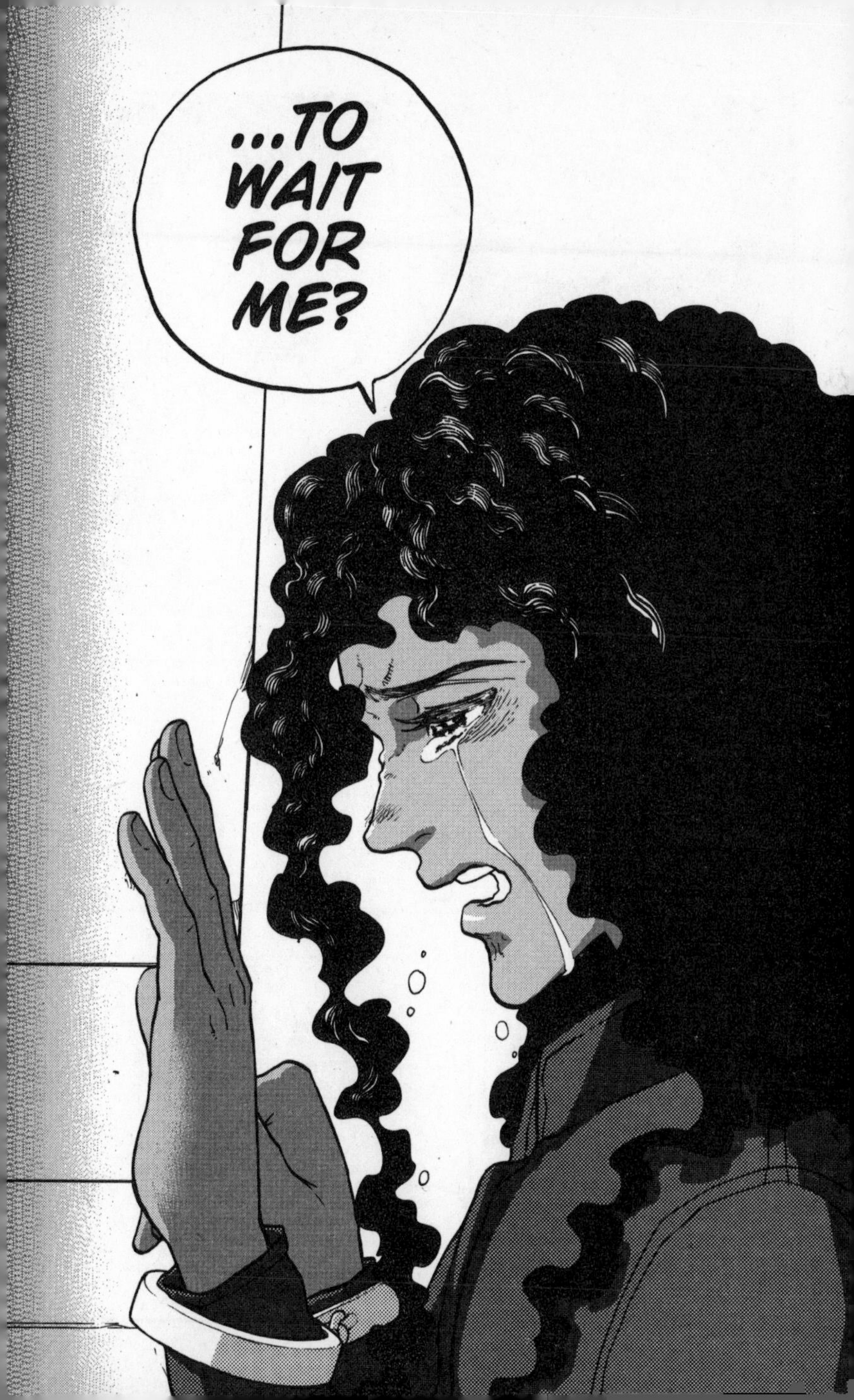
...TO WAIT FOR ME?

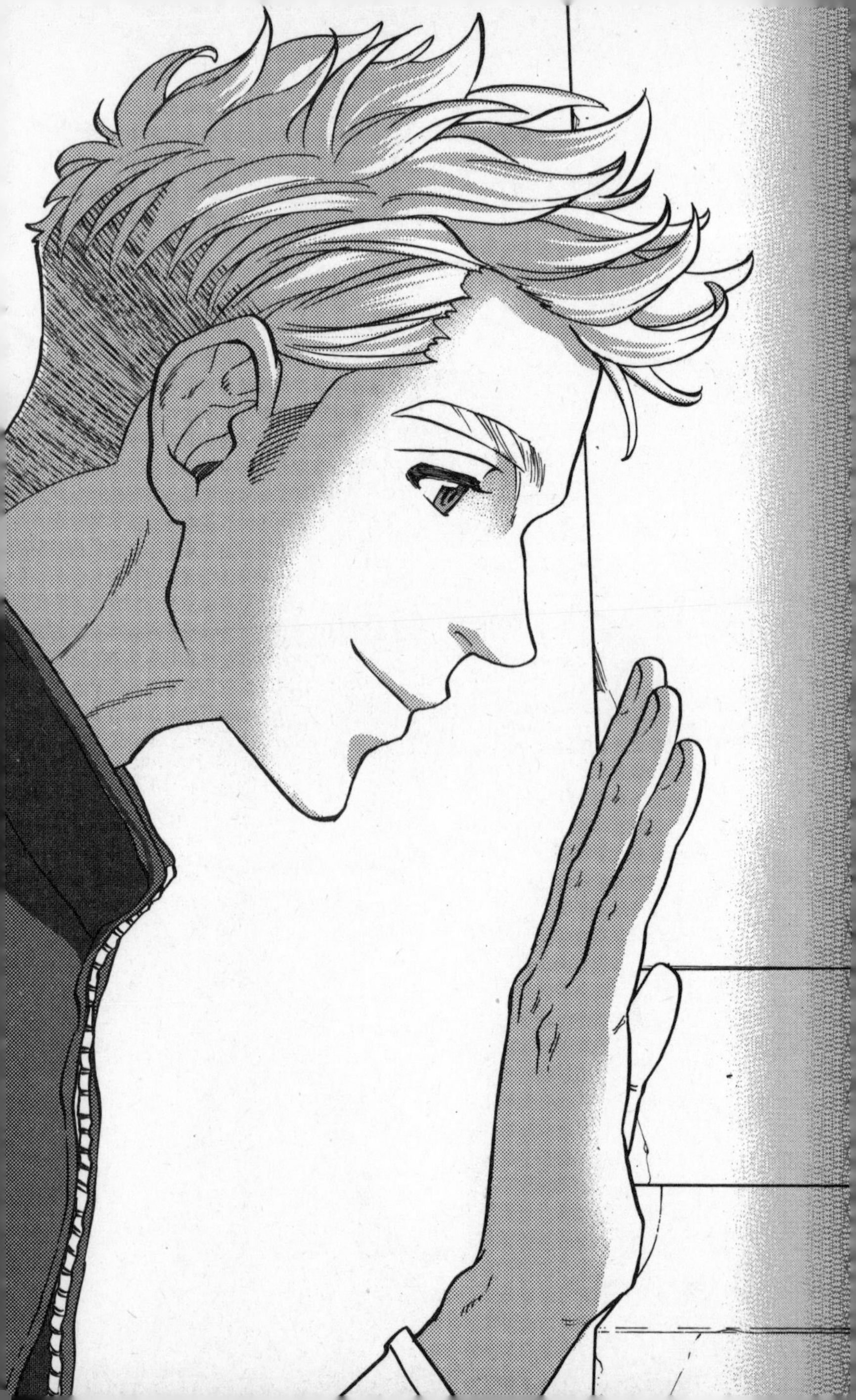

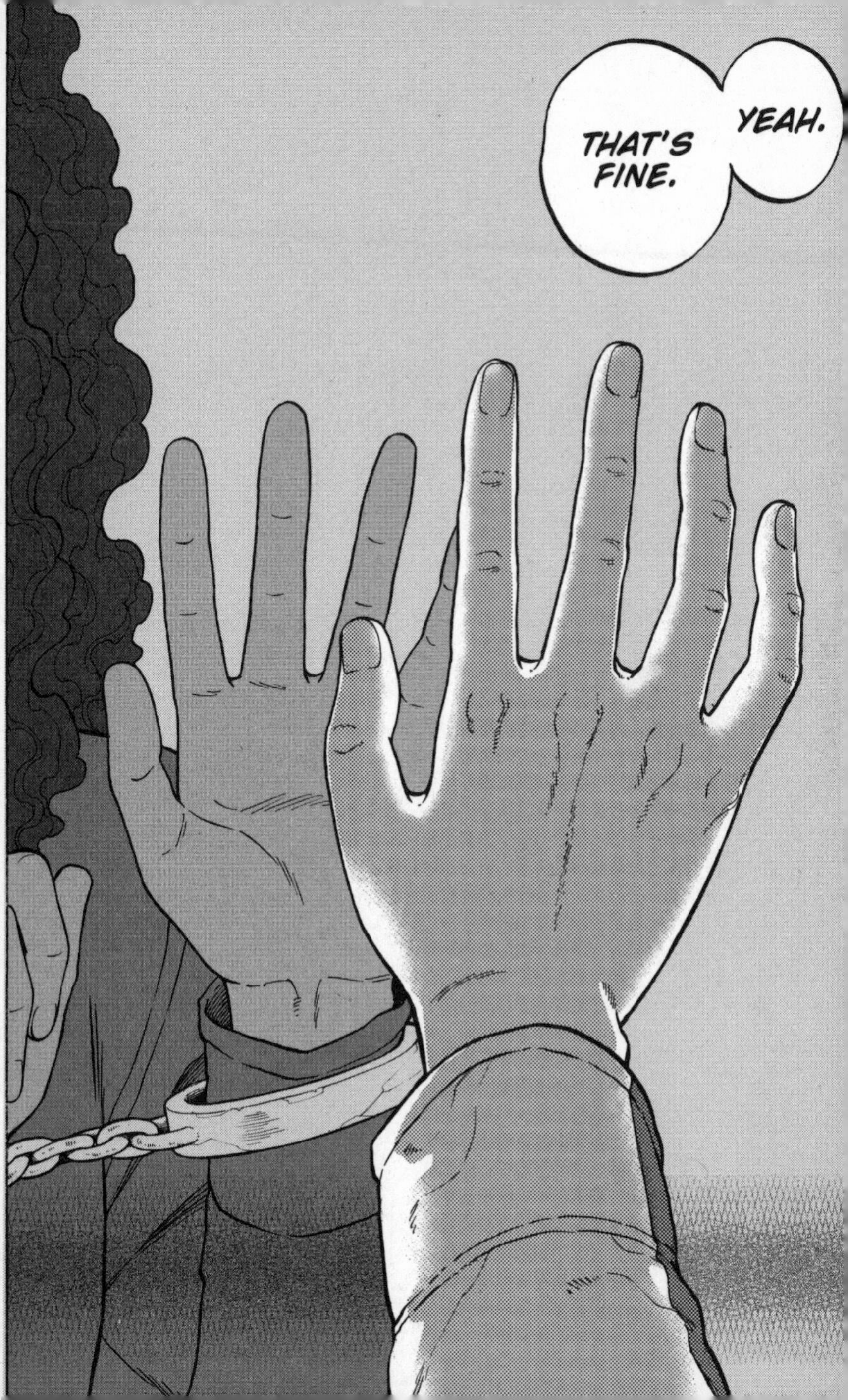
YEAH.
THAT'S FINE.

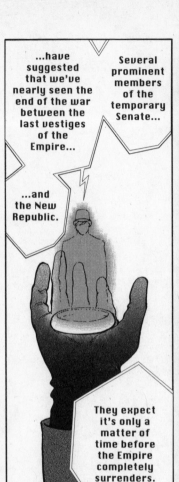

Several prominent members of the temporary Senate...

...have suggested that we've nearly seen the end of the war between the last vestiges of the Empire...

...and the New Republic.

They expect it's only a matter of time before the Empire completely surrenders.

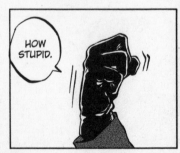

HOW STUPID.

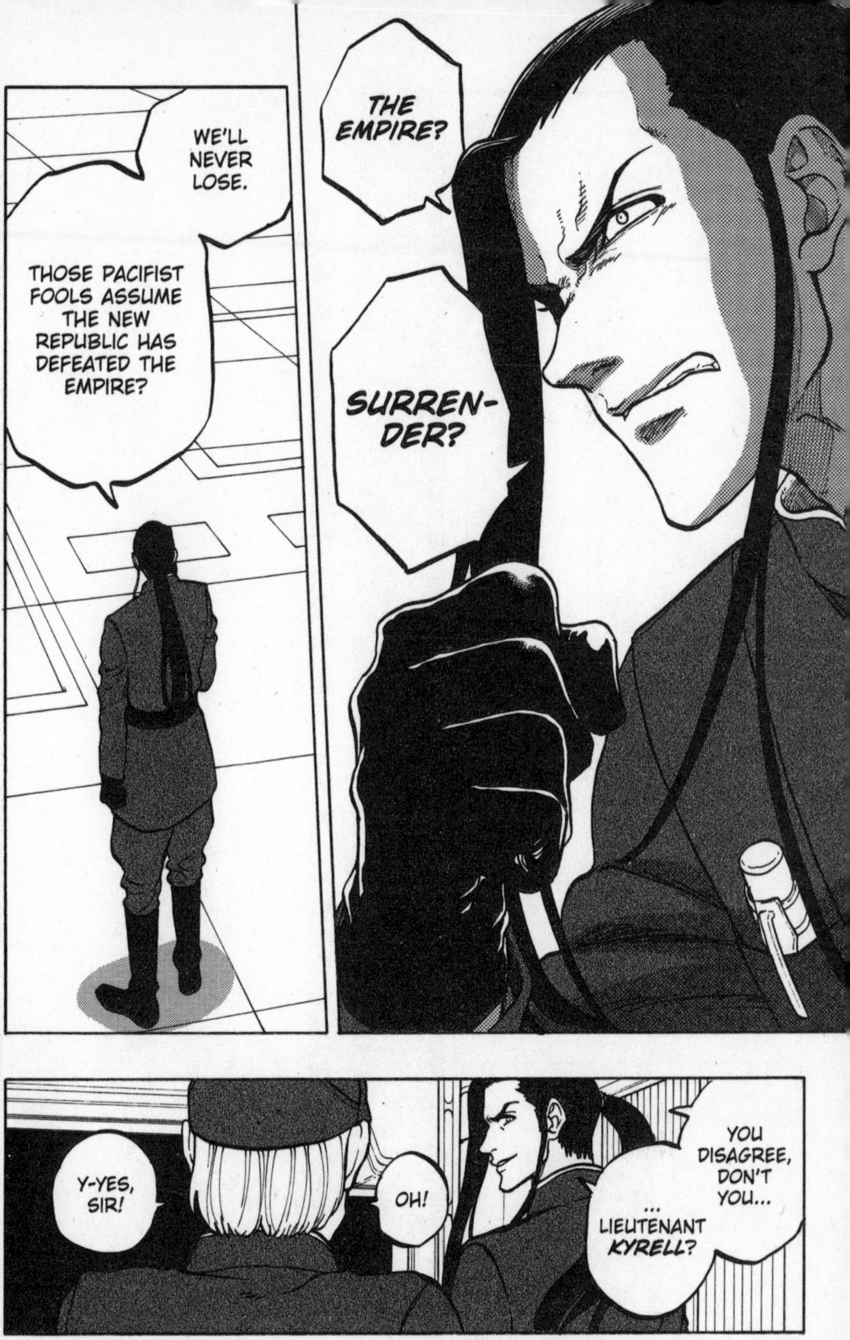
THE EMPIRE?
SURREN-DER?
WE'LL NEVER LOSE.
THOSE PACIFIST FOOLS ASSUME THE NEW REPUBLIC HAS DEFEATED THE EMPIRE?
YOU DISAGREE, DON'T YOU... ...LIEUTENANT KYRELL?
OH!
Y-YES, SIR!

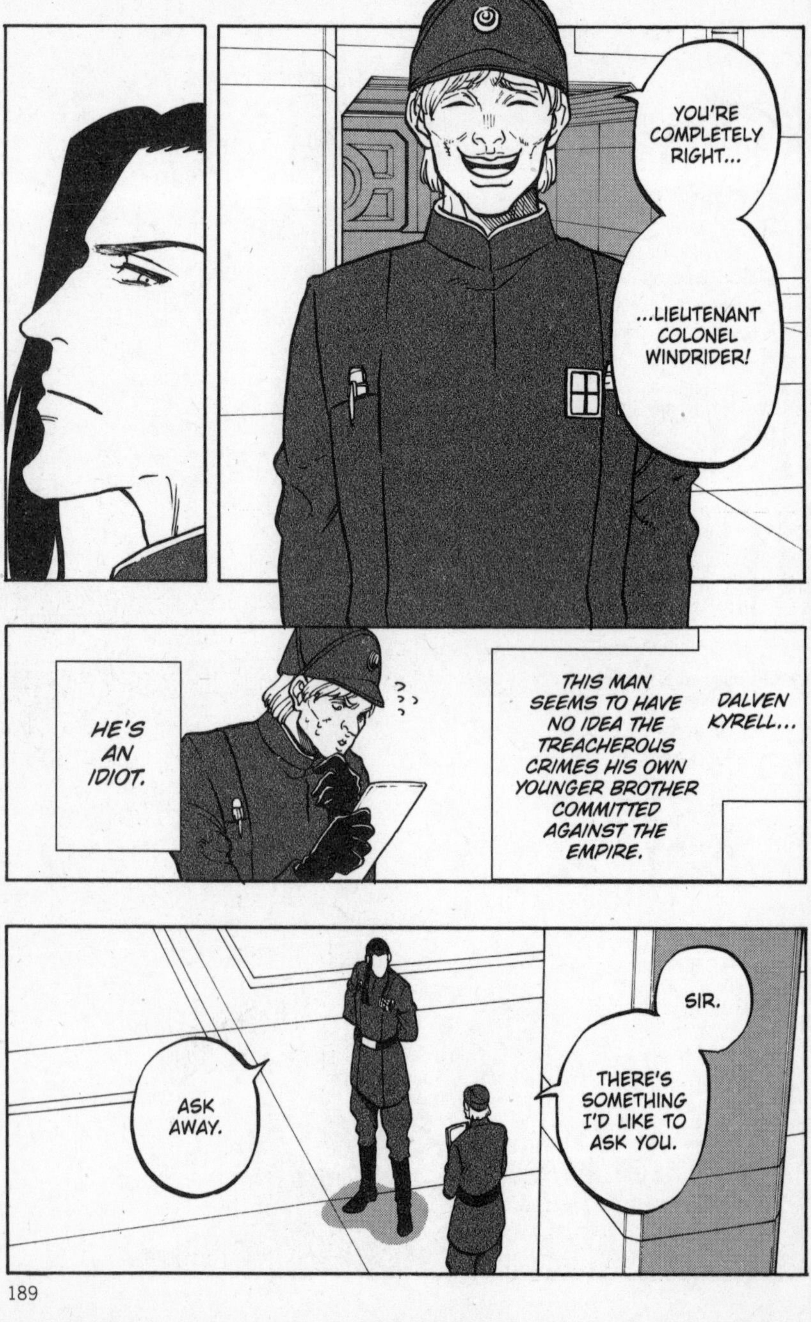
YOU'RE COMPLETELY RIGHT...
...LIEUTENANT COLONEL WINDRIDER!
DALVEN KYRELL...
THIS MAN SEEMS TO HAVE NO IDEA THE TREACHEROUS CRIMES HIS OWN YOUNGER BROTHER COMMITTED AGAINST THE EMPIRE.
HE'S AN IDIOT.
SIR.
THERE'S SOMETHING I'D LIKE TO ASK YOU.
ASK AWAY.

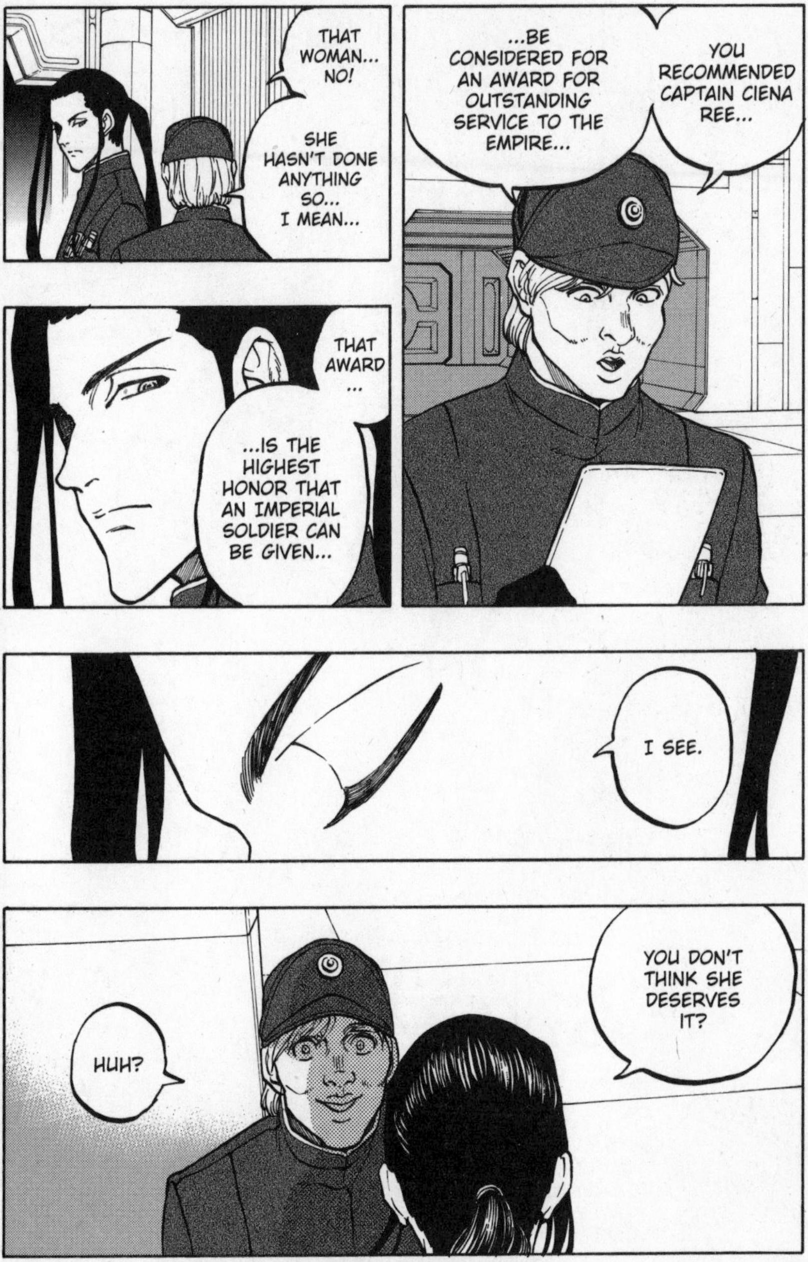

YOU RECOMMENDED CAPTAIN CIENA REE...
...BE CONSIDERED FOR AN AWARD FOR OUTSTANDING SERVICE TO THE EMPIRE...
THAT WOMAN... NO!
SHE HASN'T DONE ANYTHING SO... I MEAN...
THAT AWARD ...
...IS THE HIGHEST HONOR THAT AN IMPERIAL SOLDIER CAN BE GIVEN...
I SEE.
YOU DON'T THINK SHE DESERVES IT?
HUH?

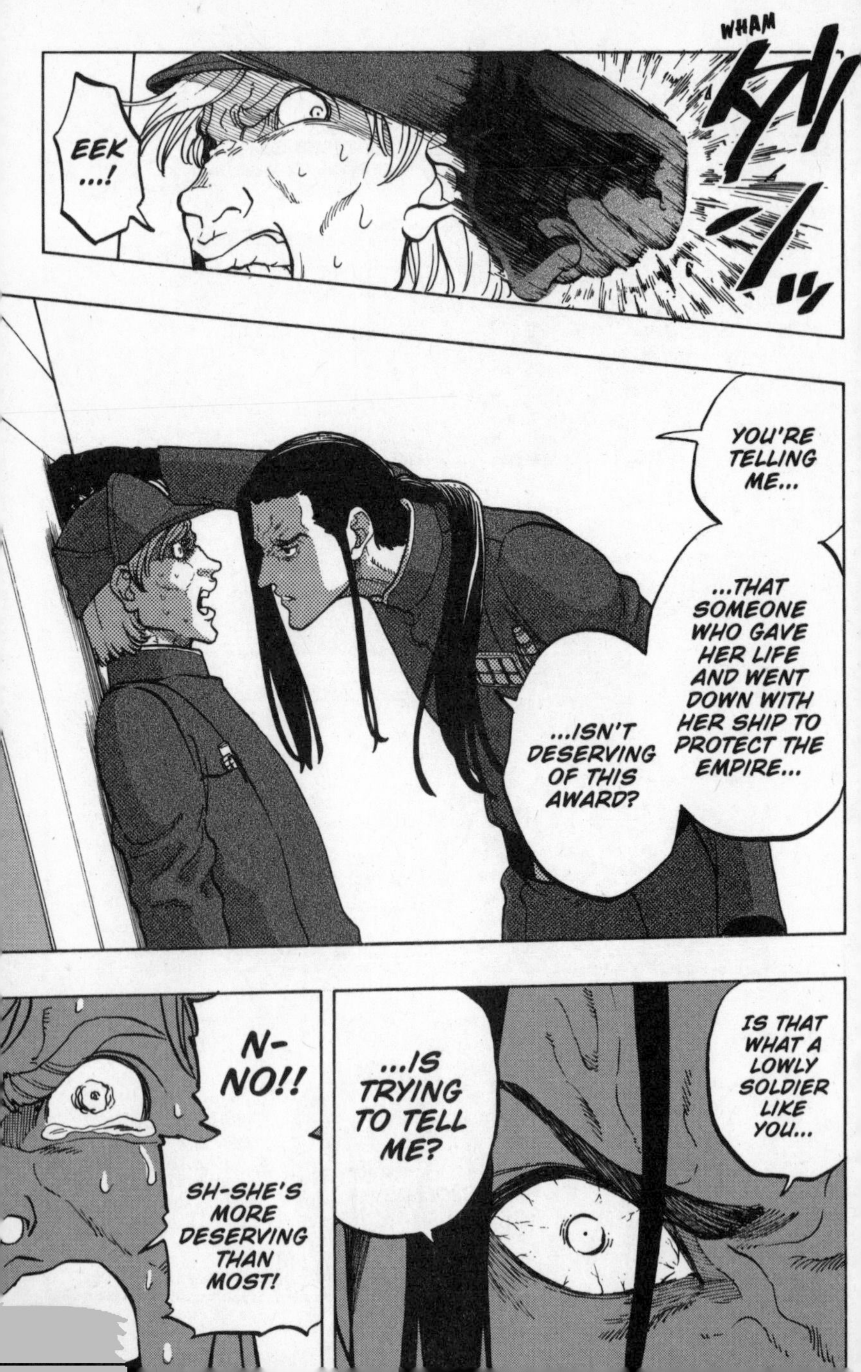
WHAM
EEK ...!
YOU'RE TELLING ME...
...THAT SOMEONE WHO GAVE HER LIFE AND WENT DOWN WITH HER SHIP TO PROTECT THE EMPIRE...
...ISN'T DESERVING OF THIS AWARD?
IS THAT WHAT A LOWLY SOLDIER LIKE YOU...
...IS TRYING TO TELL ME?
N-NO!!
SH-SHE'S MORE DESERVING THAN MOST!

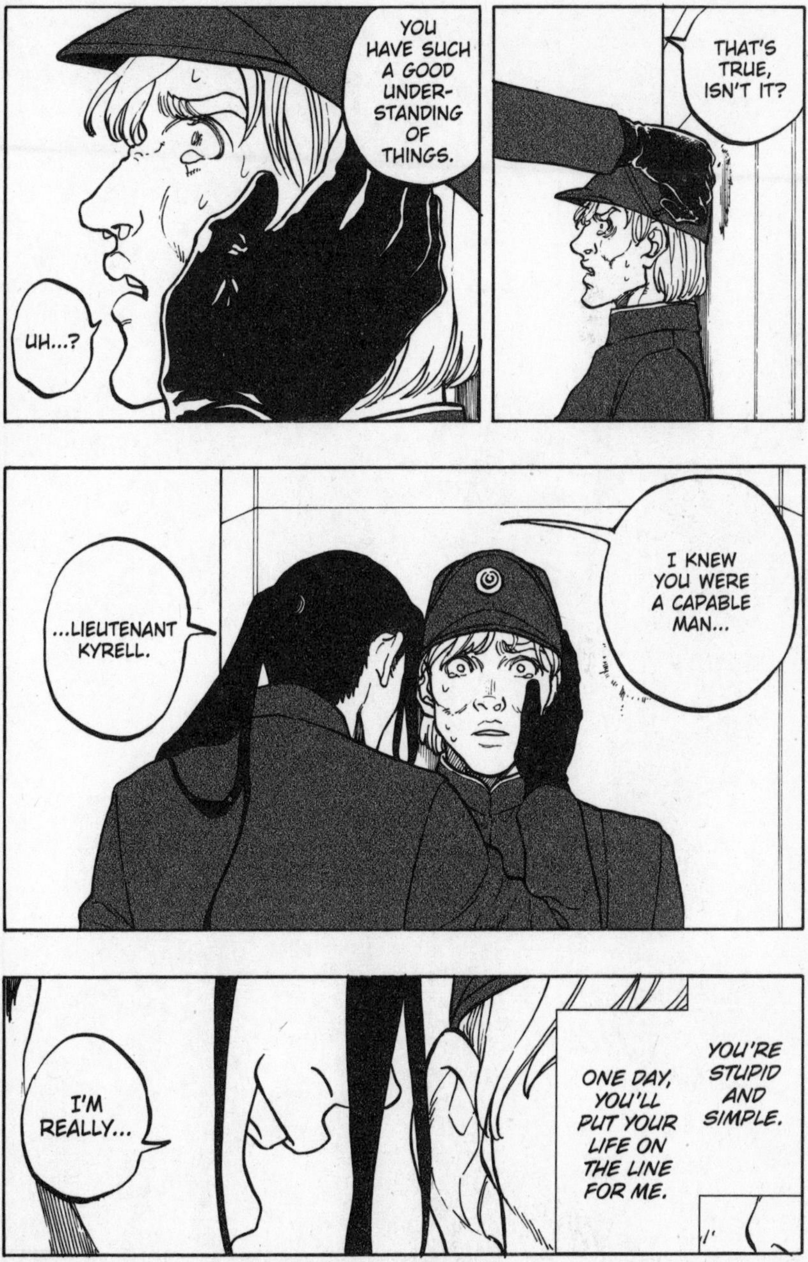
THAT'S TRUE, ISN'T IT?
YOU HAVE SUCH A GOOD UNDER-STANDING OF THINGS.
UH...?
I KNEW YOU WERE A CAPABLE MAN...
...LIEUTENANT KYRELL.
YOU'RE STUPID AND SIMPLE.
ONE DAY, YOU'LL PUT YOUR LIFE ON THE LINE FOR ME.
I'M REALLY...

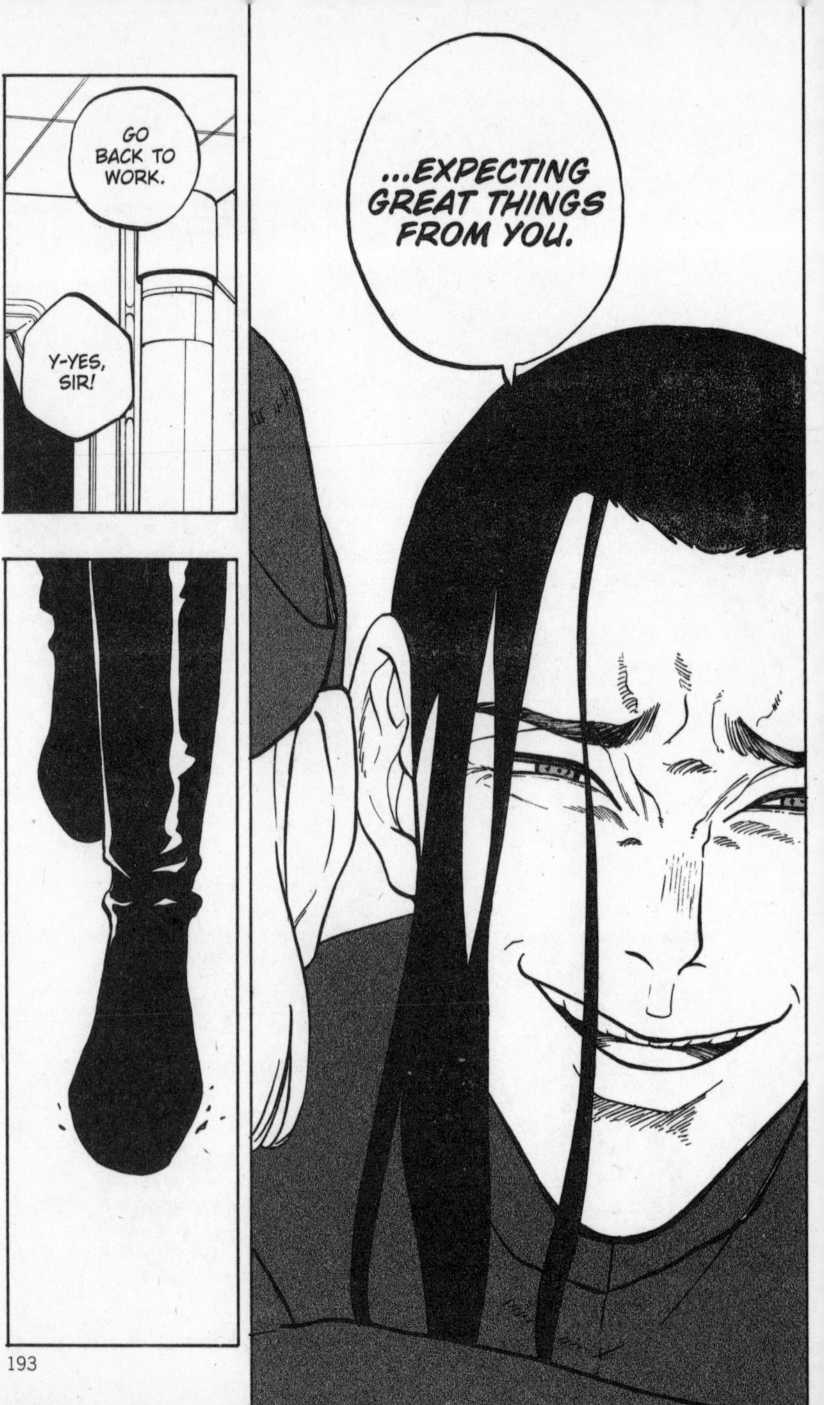
...EXPECTING GREAT THINGS FROM YOU.
GO BACK TO WORK.
Y-YES, SIR!

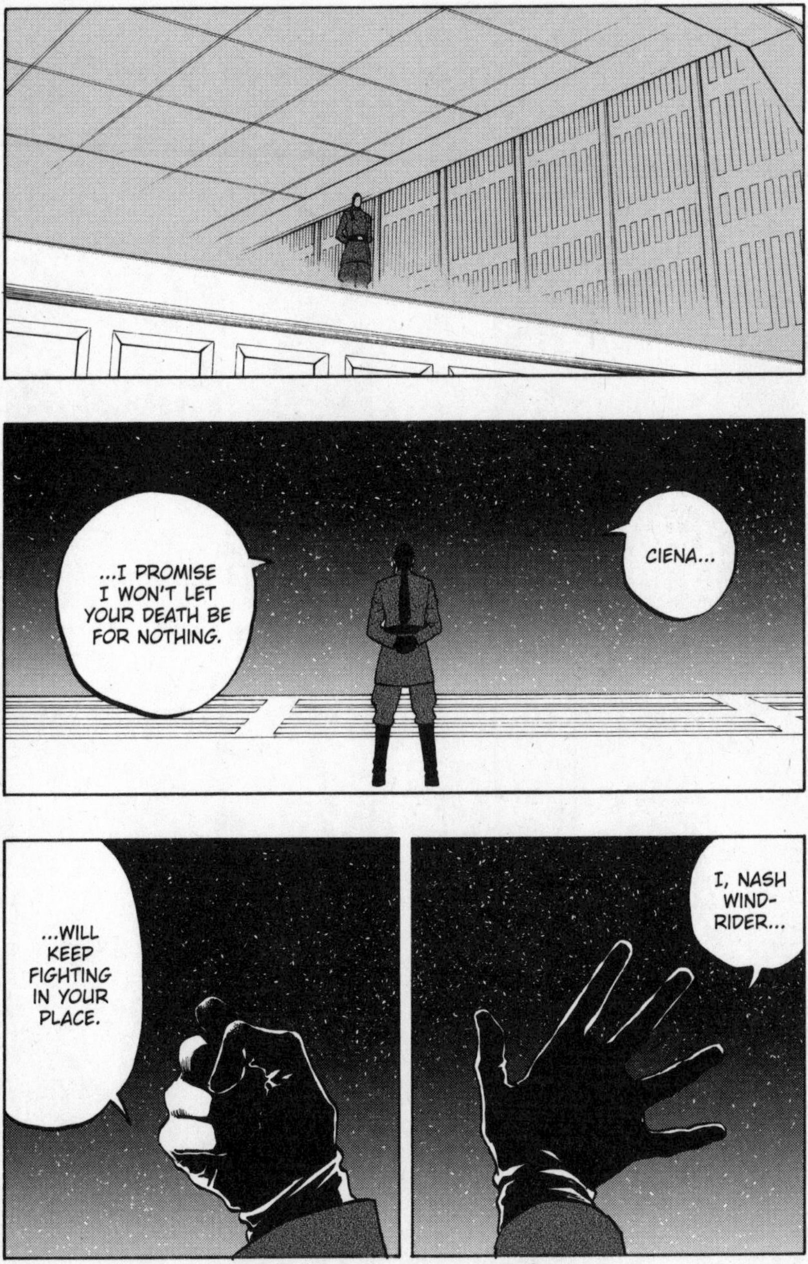
CIENA...
...I PROMISE I WON'T LET YOUR DEATH BE FOR NOTHING.
I, NASH WIND-RIDER...
...WILL KEEP FIGHTING IN YOUR PLACE.

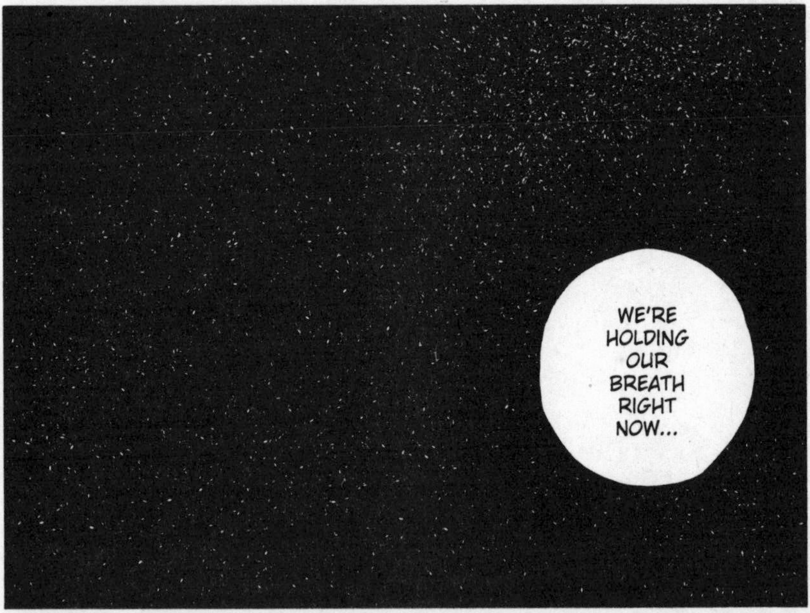
WE'RE HOLDING OUR BREATH RIGHT NOW...

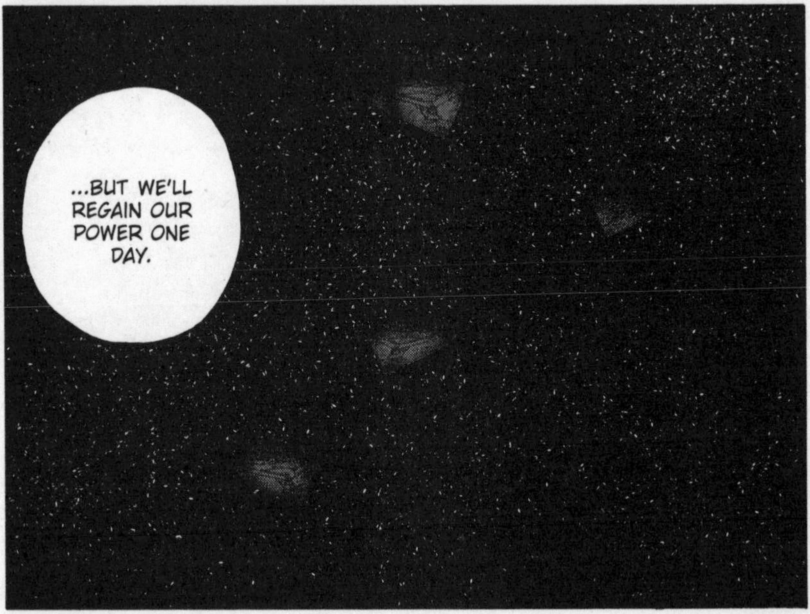
...BUT WE'LL REGAIN OUR POWER ONE DAY.

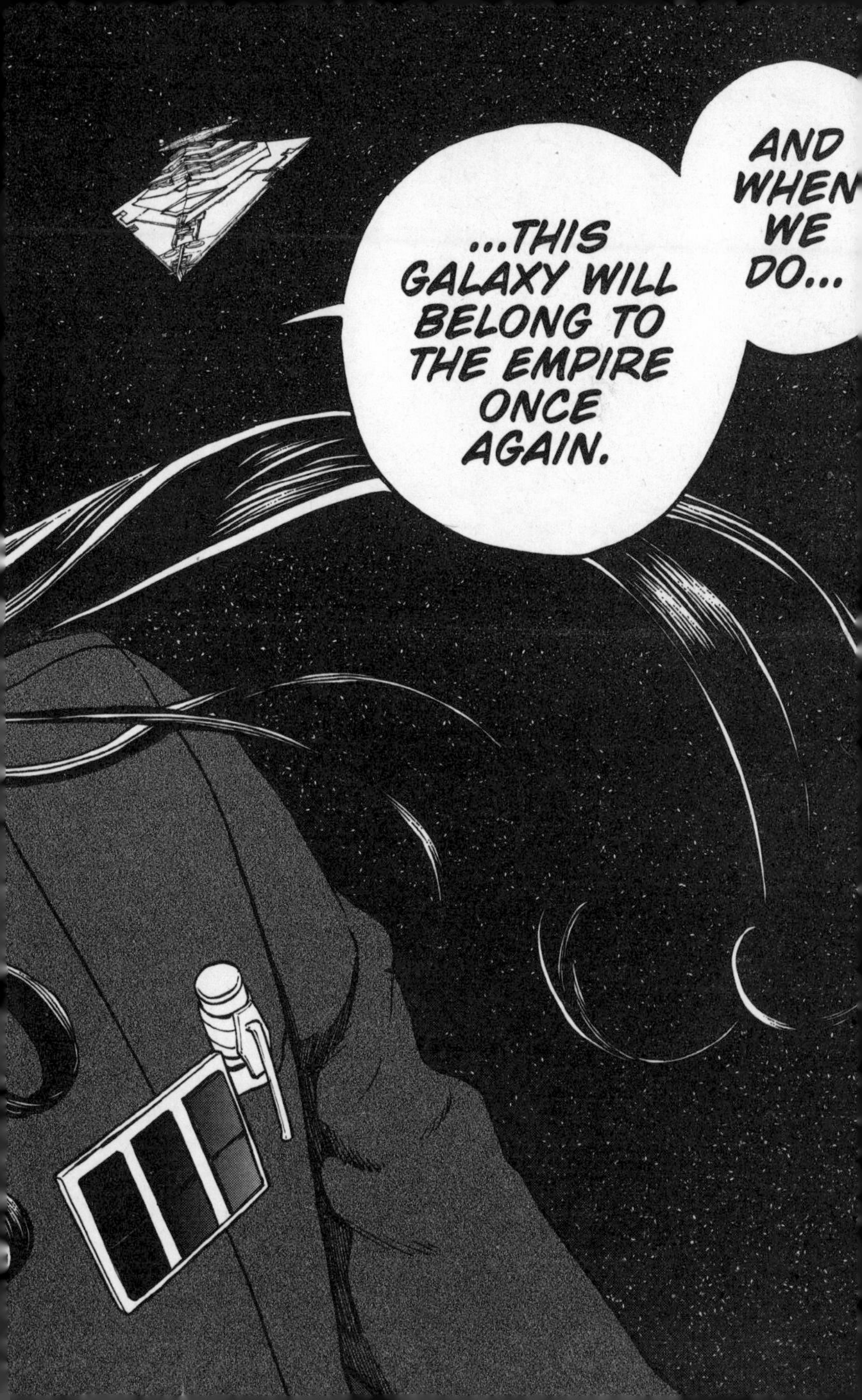
AND WHEN WE DO...
...THIS GALAXY WILL BELONG TO THE EMPIRE ONCE AGAIN.

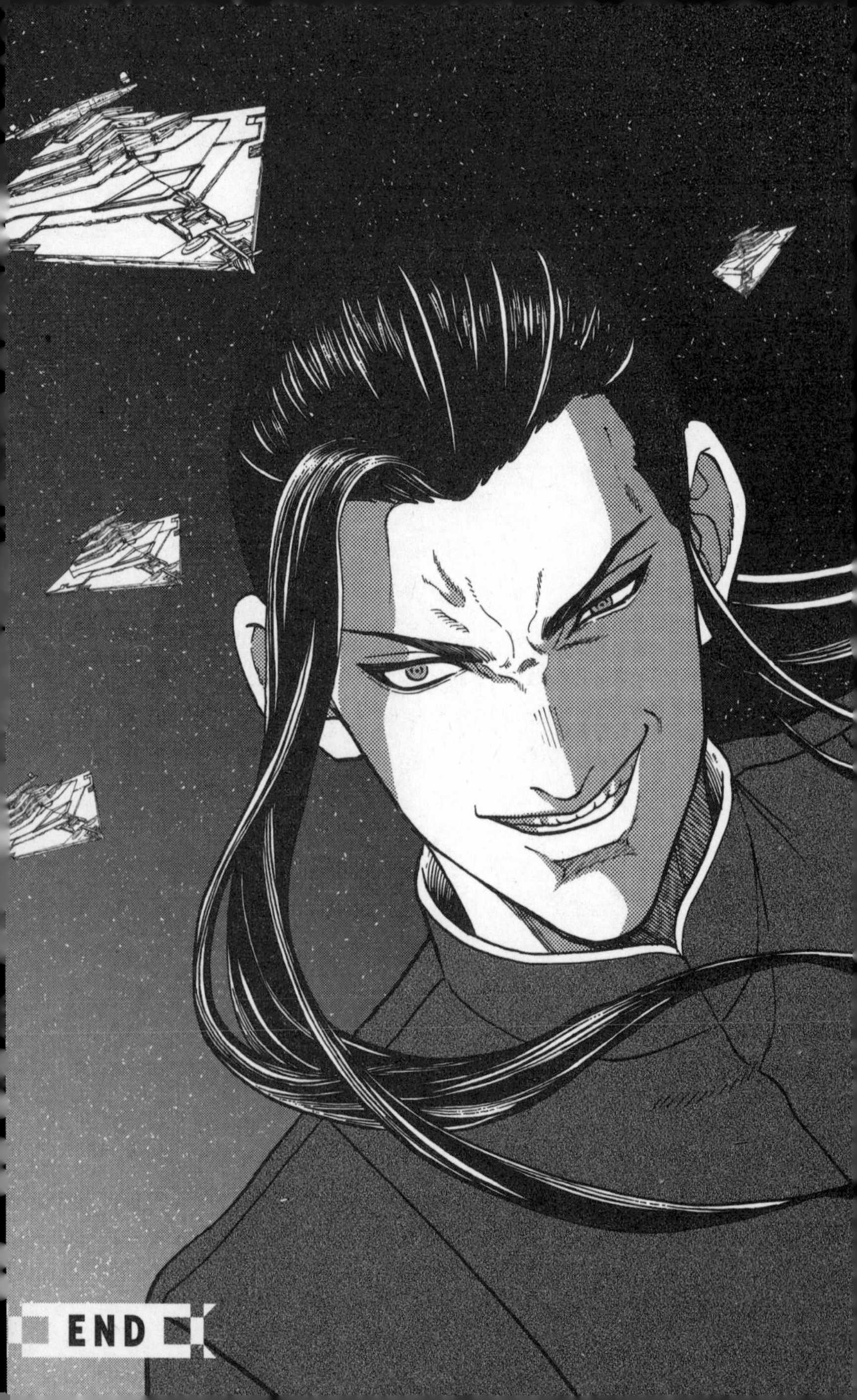
END

STAR
WARS
LOST
STARS

Thank You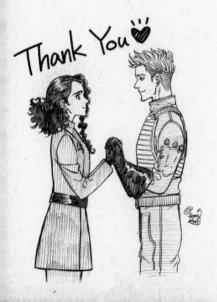

Original Story:
Claudia Gray

Art and Adaptation:
Yusaku Komiyama

Lettering:
Abigail Blackman

STAR WARS

LOST STARS

③

This book is a work of fiction. Names, characters, places, and incidents are the product of the author's imagination or are used fictitiously. Any resemblance to actual events, locales, or persons, living or dead, is coincidental.

STAR WARS LOST STARS, Vol. 3
© & TM 2019 LUCASFILM
First published in Japan in 2019 by LINE Corporation 4-1-6 Shinjuku, Shinjuku-ku, Tokyo, Japan.
Produced by LINE Coporation 4-1-6 Shinjuku, Shinjuku-ku, Tokyo, Japan.

Yen Press
150 West 30th Street, 19th Floor
New York, NY 10001

Visit us at yenpress.com
facebook.com/yenpress
twitter.com/yenpress
yenpress.tumblr.com
instagram.com/yenpress

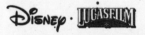

First Yen Press Edition: October 2019

Yen Press is an imprint of Yen Press, LLC.
The Yen Press name and logo are trademarks of Yen Press, LLC.

The publisher is not responsible for websites (or their content) that are not owned by the publisher.

Library of Congress Control Number: 2018932508

ISBNs: 978-1-9753-5867-9 (paperback)
978-1-9753-5868-6 (ebook)

10 9 8 7 6 5 4 3 2 1

WOR

Printed in the United States of America

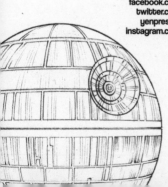